IN THE HEAT OF THE SUMMER

At first the murdered girl is just a good story for Anderson, even after he interviews her family and friends, and sees the pain and fear in their eyes.

But that is before the murderer calls him.

The killer likes Anderson's stories. He wants to tell why he killed the girl—and that he'll kill again.

In the days and weeks that follow, more people die brutally. Each time Anderson gets a call. Each call draws him little by little into the murderer's world, until finally the city, the newspaper, and the reporter himself are trapped by explosive fear and rage—in the most dazzling, gripping, and original thriller to come along in years.

Please turn the page for the smashing reviews of

IN THE HEAT OF THE SUMMER

"A DAZZLING PERFORMANCE
Through the prism of a newspaper covering a mad killer on the rampage, John Katzenbach explores the nerves of our national being."

Joseph Kraft

"A FIRST NOVEL
WHICH IS MANY THINGS:
An exciting story of the hunt for the very bold and clever killer, an insider's view of the way the press can lose its supposed detachment in the pursuit of a story, and an examination of a city under the pressure of heat and fear . . . This novel shows in a way only an insider could have written what can happen when a reporter gets too close to a story."

Boston Herald American

"DESPERATELY SCARY
AND SUSPENSEFUL . . .
I couldn't put this one down, though there were times I wanted to—and the ending would raise goose bumps on a corpse."

Jane Clapperton
Cosmopolitan

"GRIPPING, SUSPENSEFUL,
AND BRILLIANT . . .
Mystery, thriller, suspense fans, this one is a winner."

Houston Chronicle

"A TAUT . . .
SOPHISTICATED THRILLER . . .
The book has any number of qualities to recommend it—its realism, its cleverly twisted plot, its rich use of dramatic metaphor, its sensitive development of the dilemma faced by a reporter in telling a news story of which he has become a part . . . extraordinary . . . mesmerizing . . . Mr. Katzenbach is a writer of subtlety and brutal toughness."

The New York Times

"METICULOUS HONESTY
AND RARE INSIGHT . . .
The story rocks along splendidly . . . Mr. Katzenbach has a precise, compelling style that would probably keep you turning pages as if the house were on fire."

San Francisco Chronicle

In the Heat of the Summer

JOHN KATZENBACH

BALLANTINE BOOKS • NEW YORK

 Published in the United States by Ballantine Books, a division of Random House, Inc., New York, and simultaneously in Canada by Random House of Canada Limited, Toronto.

Library of Congress Catalog Card Number: 81-69158

ISBN 0-345-30857-3

This edition published by arrangement with Atheneum

Printed in Canada

First Ballantine Books Edition: July 1983

FOR MADDY

CHAPTER ONE

A RUNNER found the first victim near the thirteenth green.

He was an ordinary man, middle-aged, worried about his heart and his paunch; a broker whose mind fixed on figures, stocks and options as he pounded out laps around the perimeter of the golf course. It was a private club in the midst of an exclusive section of the county, a place of manicured lawns, high pines and sweeping palms. The morning heat had risen fast and hard, and the runner traveled his route out of instinct and familiarity, not watching where his feet landed. He had circled the golf course three times, thinking more about the Dow and his work and what he would do with this holiday off than of what he was passing. As he cut by the edge of the green his hand came up reflexively to wipe the sweat from his eyes, and in the same quick clearing motion he noticed a streak of color in the ferns, ground palms and brush of the rough, a shape amidst the morning shadows.

The broker kept running, listening to the muffled sound of his feet hitting the fairway. He finished another long pass of the course, wondering what it was that had caught his eye.

And so, as he approached the thirteenth green for the fourth and final swing, he slowed his pace gradually in order to get a longer look. He was aware then, suddenly, of the heat and the sun that seemed suspended over the golf course like a lamp. This time he saw flesh and a glimpse of blond hair. He stopped and sucked in his breath for a moment, then stepped through the scrub brush to the body. "Oh my God," he said out loud, though no one could hear him. He told me later that when he realized what it was that he was looking at, it took all the wind out of him like a hard sprint and that for a moment he had stood dizzily in the sun, locked in place, trying to catch his lost breath. He said he'd never seen a murdered person before; that he'd stared in mingled horror and fascination for a minute, maybe two, and then he'd run as fast as he was able, heart starting to pound so loud he thought he could hear it, for the nearest house and a telephone to call the police.

The victim was a teenage girl.

I did not realize then, at the beginning, that it would become the biggest story of my life. Nor did I have any precognition, any reporter's sixth-sense suspicion, that I would be drawn into the story, my usual detachment shattered and ultimately abandoned. The story took place during that year's hurricane season. It started in July at the time that the first big storms of summer begin to gather thousands of miles away across the Atlantic. It is the mean season in Miami; the tropical sun hits the city streets like a spotlight, eliminating all shadow and shade, leaving the air thick and still with an angry heat.

In its own way the story followed the same pattern as a big storm, gathering momentum as it developed. I remember that there was a big storm forming then, in the Caribbean off the coast of Venezuela. It had blown up in the waters off Africa, then ridden the air currents across the expanse of ocean, a huge, misshapen force of wind and rain. It was the first storm of the season and the National Weather Service had dubbed it Amy, which turned out to be the name of the first victim.

A large weather chart hung in the rear of the newsroom which, during the storm season, was marked with the locations and courses of all the storms. Following the path on the map was a part of all the cityside reporters' lives; daily we would check the progress of the storm, check the assignments, talk about the chances and point at the satellite photos transmitted by the wire services. The photo of that storm, I remember, showed a great diffuse mass of swirling gray clouds, superimposed over the map of the Caribbean. It seemed then that the Florida peninsula was like some large beckoning finger reaching down toward the storm. We would watch the photos for the signs that this storm was going to change, gather shape and consolidate into a hurricane and come raging and screaming across the waters toward the city.

On the wall next to the weather chart was a framed old photograph, yellowed and creased, a reminder for all of us who worked at the *Journal*. It was taken during the 1939 storm, a Force Three blow. It showed a large palm tree bent over so that the trunk was parallel to the ground. In the background I could make out the wave of water some twelve feet high that had swept across Miami Beach and the Bay and finally spent itself on Biscayne Boulevard downtown.

Of course, the story was not about a hurricane, but in their own way, I thought afterwards, the killings seemed much the same; blowing up in some strange distant place, then breaking over the city like a wave, propelled by some great natural force. I remember that on the day of the first murder, the Fourth of July, a year before the Bicentennial, the year after the President resigned, we were all preoccupied with that first big storm off the Venezuelan coast, watching it suck up strength from the warm Caribbean waters. The newsroom was filled with talk about that storm; it seemed it would reach up and become a Force Five storm, the deadliest. The paper bannered speculative stories about the storm's murderous potential. We were long overdue for a major blow, the old hands in the office said, and there was a sense of foreboding that this particular gray mass of wind and rain some two thousand miles away was destined for us.

We were wrong, of course; it never did hit Miami but turned inland instead, rushing ashore in Central America where it killed many people and left many others homeless. That was a few weeks later, however. Then, in early July, it had all our attention, and, at least in my memory, serves as an excuse for why our eyes were elsewhere when the season's true storm broke in our midst.

I went into the office early on the Fourth; it was my first day back at work after my uncle's funeral. I didn't have to work that day, but I returned restless after the trip north, and I wanted something to take the scenes of family out of my head. I find now that my mind tends to run the two together, the teenager's murder and my uncle's suicide, as if they were part of the same play, though they took place a few days and hundreds of miles apart. There weren't many people in the newsroom, it being the holiday and early. I checked my mailbox, which was empty, and glanced over the first edition of the Miami *Post*, which was already out. I sat at my desk and thought of calling Christine to tell her I was home, but she was probably already at the hospital, handing over the sponges, clamps and scalpels in the theater, watching the doctors cut away another cancer. I'd call later, I thought, and we would be together for dinner. I opened the *Post*'s sports pages to check on the baseball scores, but my eyes fastened instead on Nolan, the city editor.

Nolan was a large man, well over six feet, with a sort of constant stoop that made him appear wider, slower than he was; but on a big story, he would straighten suddenly, as if shedding pounds and worries simultaneously, his mind focused on the details. He would lose his joking, playful tone, too, gaining instead a drill sergeant's swiftness and purpose. He was immensely popular in the newsroom, able to joke with reporters one instant, deal with management the next.

Now he was sitting in the center of the newsroom at a bank of desks talking animatedly on the phone. I saw him scribble a few notes, then hang up the phone with a sudden, satisfied motion, turning at the same time to look across the newsroom to see who was in. Our eyes met, and he got up and walked quickly to my desk. He pulled up a chair.

"I didn't expect to see you in," he said. "How'd it go?" He had a shock of dark hair, a child's cowlick that poked down between his eyes so that it bobbed as he spoke, as if underscoring his words.

"Pretty much like you'd think. Tears. A lot of talk about wasted lives. God's will, about going to a better place."

"Sounds grim."

"It was."

"You OK?"

"I'm here, aren't I?" I smiled. "Intact. One model 1970 journalist. High mileage but runs good."

"OK, OK," he said. "Feel like a story, or do you want to take it easy for a couple of days?"

"A story, a story. My kingdom for a story. What there is of it, at least."

"How about a murder?" he said.

"You want me to commit one?"

"Christ," he said. "What turned you into a comedian?"

"I'm sorry," I said. "I'm just trying to put it all behind me."

Nolan's eyebrows rose, fixing me quizzically, cautiously. "OK," he said, "whatever you want. A beer later if you feel like talking it out. . . . A beer later, even if you don't."

I laughed, and he grinned at me.

"But right now, a murder," he said. "Your basic blood and guts, cops and robbers, slow-news-day murder."

"What kind?"

"A teenage girl. Probably from some wealthy family. Her body was discovered just a short time ago over at the Riviera Golf Club."

"Sounds good so far," I said. "What else do you know?"

"Not much. You remember that homicide lieutenant who said he owed me a favor after we held off on the kidnapping story? Well, he just called me. He just dispatched a team out there and he didn't have too much information, only the location and the teenage girl. Could be good. I plan to keep that lieutenant paying off that debt for some time."

"Was she raped?"

"I don't know. Why don't you take the photographer and go out and take a look? Call me on the radio when you get a handle."

"OK," I said. I got up, grabbed a notebook from the pile I kept on my desk and headed back toward the photography department.

"Hey," Nolan called. "Were you close to your uncle?"

"When I was small," I said. "In a small way."

Andrew Porter liked to push the big car around corners, one hand on the wheel, the other gesturing at the early-morning traffic. Most of it seemed to be young people heading out to the beaches. A number of boats were being towed, and traffic was already backing up at the entrance to McArthur Causeway and Key Biscayne. We were hurrying in the opposite direction, moving along fast enough so that I could barely see the faces of the people in the waiting cars. The photographer's voice droned on, a story about another murder assignment, sometime in the past. The sound was low and mingled with the sound of the engine and the air conditioner blasting on high. At one point I watched him load his camera, one hand in his lap winding the film, the other resting loosely on the top of the steering wheel. "Did this once at ninety-plus up on Route Four forty-one. High-speed chase, a couple of kids in a stolen car, a highway trooper and myself all screaming down the highway. Didn't have time to be scared." He was laughing.

I thought how slowly the line of cars had moved from the church to the cemetery. I could see the hearse when it swung around a corner, and the long black Cadillac with my father and his brother's wife, right behind it. It had rained all morning, and the windshield wipers beat a kind of muffled drum dirge. My ears were still filled with the sound of the "Marine Corps Hymn" that had cascaded from the organ through the church; a large, slow sound, the familiar cadence almost unrecognizable when played to celebrate the dead instead of the living. I remember how surprised I'd been when I saw the casket draped with the flag; the vivid colors seemed out of place, incongruous in that gray day and darkened church.

The priest had spoken first. "Hear our prayer, Father, for the soul of Lewis Anderson, and grant him the peace in heaven that he sought here on earth. . . ."

Peace, I had thought. The opposite of war.

My uncle had been a bear of a man, long arms that carried bunched muscles, a chest as broad as a knight's shield. His voice had always been deep and even in his laughter carried a menacing tone, a strained pitch that demanded attention. Then he would fix me a look from his one good eye that would leave me cold and afraid.

He'd lost the right eye on Iwo Jima. Halfway up Suribachi, he said, just before the flag raising; he'd missed that moment, too drugged out on morphine and shock to understand what was taking place around him. He told me once that it was an odd sensation, losing the eye; he thought at first that he was dying, then that it was all happening to someone else.

He could feel the blood, he said, and the pain, like an explosion in his brain. But still, he was convinced, not him. Not then. Someone else entirely.

When I was young, he would give me things. Books about the Corps; a purple heart. A Rising Sun flag, a spoil from Tarawa. For Christmas once, he gave me a long, curved hunting knife in an expensive leather sheath. "That'll come in handy," he said. It stayed on my bureau for years. He told me: "You ever need anything, anything at all, you know where you can get it."

But I never asked.

Then the priest read from Ecclesiastes. The familiar section: to every time, there is a season. I remembered the popular song that had taken the words and set them to music. It sounded different, more sonorous, when read in a church, echoing through the rafters.

He and his wife would show up at holidays: Thanksgiving, Christmas, sometimes on birthdays . . . all the strained times. He had no children of his own, I never knew why.

On those evenings, he would drink too much. I would watch him as he rendered himself pleasantly drunk, pouring and sipping, an endless chain; forgetful of most things, but humming the hymn to himself, his good eye dulled, his fake eye wide open, seeing nothing.

At night, sometimes, I would hear him call out in his sleep.

After the priest finished reading, there was silence, and then my father went up to the altar. The light seemed to reflect the colors of the flag; my father's face caught the light and he was bathed in a multicolored glow. "In 1941 my brother went away to war," he said. I listened closely. "I am not sure that he ever came back. . . ."

I thought: We blame the war. Blame Iwo Jima. Say he left more there than his eye. I put my hand to my forehead, then covered my eyes. I could hear my father's voice rising and falling in the church.

On the telephone he'd been matter-of-fact. "Your uncle has killed himself," he said. "I'm sorry to have to tell you."

"How did it happen?" I asked. The journalist.

"There was nothing specific. In fact, he'd just been offered a new position by a university in the South. Fund raising, overseeing academic programs. The stuff he was good at."

"Had he been drinking?"

"Your aunt says no. She said he was sober, but he'd been looking over his old scrapbooks, from when he was in the Marines. He didn't say anything to her, she said, just went upstairs and took a pistol from his study. A twenty-two, a target gun he kept. Then he went into the bathroom, closed the door and shot himself."

"No note? No message?"

"Nothing."

"I'm sorry for you," I said.

"In a way, it's a relief. He'd been so unhappy for so long."

"Why?"

"Who knows?"

But of course, I thought then, you know. Who else would know?

My father finished speaking, and the organist hit the first few chords of the hymn. From the shores of Montezuma—where? To here. A church, a funeral. There was an honor guard, and they carried the casket out to the hearse. *Semper Fi.* I followed them out. They slipped the casket into the back and stepped away. Their movements were economical, exaggerated. Precise military motion, I thought, it masks everything with pomp. My aunt was crying, but my father's eyes were dry. He seemed to be directing traffic, and we all slipped into the cars for the ride to the cemetery.

The service at the grave had been quicker than I thought it would be. The priest read again, traditional things: ashes to ashes, dust to dust. I didn't listen. I watched the faces of all the people who were there. I looked over at my own brother. If he were dead, I thought, how would I feel? I found myself listening to the rain striking the canopy over the grave. To the side the gravediggers waited next to a backhoe, patiently. I thought one must learn patience by working in a graveyard. And then the service ended. We shook hands and murmured best wishes. I found my father. "I have to go back," I said.

"There's going to be food and drink at your aunt's. I'd like you to come."

"I have to go back," I repeated. "There's a flight this afternoon. I can get a cab."

"All right," he said and turned away.

I thought of the storm off Venezuela. I tried to imagine the center, the winds racing in concentric circles, ever tighter. I had to get back.

"There it is," Porter said excitedly.

I looked ahead and saw a half-dozen police cars, their lights gleaming in the sunlight, parked haphazardly by the side of the road. There was a knot of the curious standing a few feet away, on the lawn of a large, stately mansion. I saw the medical examiner's yellow car and a green and white panel truck that was used by the crime-scene technicians. We pulled in behind the first police cruiser. "Hot damn, we beat everybody else. Not a television camera in sight." Porter had already draped one camera around his neck and was adjusting another. "Let's go," he said, "before they get everything covered up." He bounded from the car and set out across the fairway in a rush. I followed him, a few feet behind, a half-trot, half-walk.

On the thirteenth green a uniformed officer stopped us with a barked "Hold it!" He came up and said, "That's close enough."

"I can't get any shots from here," Porter said. "Just a little closer. Don't worry, I won't shoot anything you don't want shot."

The cop shook his head. I stepped in.

"Who's in charge?"

"Detective Martinez," he said. "Also Detective Wilson. You talk to them when they're finished. You wait here for now." Then he turned his back on us.

"I'm going over there," Porter said, pointing to the rough. "Got to get a better angle." He walked away, trying to keep out of the policeman's sight. I saw one of the detectives look my direction, and I waved. He walked over.

"How you doing, Martinez?" I said. "What have you got?"

"Haven't seen you for a while," he said. "Not since that trial in March." I remembered then that he'd been the chief witness in the trial of a teenage kid accused of murdering a tourist who'd asked for directions. The case had attracted lots of publicity, especially when the defense attorney had argued that the teenager had been rendered insane by daily life in the ghetto. A novel defense; the jury had been out for two hours before rejecting it. Everyone in the newsroom had thought it was pretty funny.

"There's just not enough quality crime, you know what I mean?"

Martinez laughed. "Yeah, just the run-of-the-mill killings, rapes, robberies. None of the good stuff."

"You got it," I said. "But tell me, maybe we've got something here?"

He looked at me. "Bloody," he said. "Teenage girl, probably sixteen or seventeen, judging from her backside. Dr. Smith is here, but he hasn't turned her yet. It appears she was shot in the back of the head with a powerful handgun. A magnum three fifty-seven maybe. Possibly a forty-five or a forty-four special. Something big, though; most of the back of her head is gone."

I had my notebook out and was taking notes. The detective looked at me for a moment, then continued. "Christ, it makes you feel bad, seeing a kid like that get herself killed."

I took down his words verbatim.

"One odd thing, though, but it's not for publication yet."

"What's that?"

"Not for a story yet?" He pushed his question at me.

"OK, OK. What's the story?"

"Her hands were bound behind her. I haven't seen that kind of a shooting since"—he thought for a moment—"that mobster, the gambler we found out in the Glades. You remember?"

"You mean what they call 'execution-style'?"

He laughed. "That's right. Now why would someone want to execute a teenager?"

"Was she raped?"

"Can't tell for certain, but all her clothes seem in place and intact. Can't figure that," he said.

"What's she wearing?"

"Jeans. T-shirt. Sandals. The usual teenager outfit." He paused and looked up. "Oh boy," he said, "here come your brothers and sisters." I looked back and saw that the television people had arrived. They came in squads: a soundman, reporter and cameraman. "Look," Martinez said, "catch me later. Talk to the doctor. Talk to that guy over there, with the shorts. He found the body. Talk to him. One other thing . . ."

"What's that?"

"Get the story from me. Wilson's got a teenage daughter himself. He appears pretty strung out about this already."

"OK," I said. "Hey, any identification on her?"

"Later," the detective said. He hurried back across the green.

With the arrival of the television cameras several of the uniformed officers who had been poking about in the underbrush came over to keep them back. They seemed happy to film from afar as the policemen went through the motions of searching the scene. I walked back to our car and called the city desk on the car radio. A secretary answered, and in a moment I heard Nolan's voice come scratching through the speaker. "So," he said, "what've you got?"

"It's good," I said. "An abduction perhaps. I don't know. It seems like a real weird one. The girl's hands were tied behind her back. She was shot execution-style. That's not for publication yet, but it will be shortly."

"Good art?"

"I think so. Andy Porter's off in the bushes with a long lens. Lots of cops searching the scene."

"Sounds good. Better than the Glorious-Fourth-parade shot that we're planning on running." I could hear him laughing.

"Listen, I need someone to start on something for me."

"What? You name it."

"Have someone call the missing persons bureau and the local desks for the cops. See if anyone called in last night or yesterday from the Gables with a missing kid report. Just a chance."

"Good idea. I'll get somebody to start before the cops think of doing the same thing. See you later."

I hung up the radio and stepped back outside. I could feel the sweat under my arm, sticky, unpleasant. The sky seemed to stretch infinitely high in an expanse of blue. There were no clouds, just the sun, the blue sky and the heat. I walked off to find the man who'd discovered the body.

He was standing by one of the cruisers. I introduced myself, and he told me that he read the *Journal* every day. He was a stocky man, short, with his hair cropped Republican-close.

"This kind of thing has never happened to me before. Even when I was in the Army, back in '54, I never saw anything like that."

"Exactly how was it?" I asked. I took down his words in the notebook. He seemed upset enough and articulate enough to provide a sidebar to the main story.

"I remember looking at her arms. They were thin, a child's arms. They were pulled back, but not tightly, you know; more relaxed, as if the killer didn't want to hurt her. I mean, I would expect them to be pulled back tightly." And he held his arms behind his back to demonstrate, thrusting his shoulder backward. "Like that. But that wasn't the case." I continued taking notes as he talked.

"I could see her face. It was like she was resting, in a way, though I could see that most of the back of her head was gone." He swallowed. "That sounds cold, doesn't it? I don't really know what came over me. I was standing there, looking at her, my mind registering all the clinical perceptions: how she was lying, how her head was resting, the matted mess the blood had made of her hair. Blond hair.

"I went through it all with the detective, you know; simple, to the point, just the details. And then, you know what happened? I got sick, over there." He pointed at some bushes. "I guess you guys see bodies all the time. Murders."

"Enough. Tell me, what do you do for a living?"

I half-listened as he went through his personal history. He told me about the running, and his route and the morning sun and that he must have run by her at least three times. "My own kids are younger."

"Can we get your picture?"

"I'd rather not," he said, after thinking a moment. "Do you have to use my name in the papers?"

"Oh, yes," I said. "No question about it."

"Well, I wish you didn't have to. I don't suppose I'll sleep much until they catch the guy."

"I wouldn't worry about that," I said.

"Why not?"

"Well, it seems to me that some guy who gets off on tying up and killing teenage girls isn't going to want to take on an adult." He nodded. "But I'll tell you one thing," I said. "I would try to steer clear of the television guys; otherwise you'll be all over the air."

"Thanks," he said. "I'll keep that in mind." When I left him I saw him step back further into the shadows alongside the road. I walked over to Porter who was standing by the car, talking on the radio to the photo studio.

"I got a shot of that guy you were talking to," he said. "It's with a long lens, but I think it'll come out all right. You think I can get a close-up?"

"No way. And it might point him out to the television guys."

"OK," he said. "Let's hang around until they bring the body out. The desk always likes that shot, the body bag on the stretcher. Just like in Vietnam, some black bag with a zipper. Isn't technology marvelous?"

"You're a cynic."

"Who isn't?"

We waited in the shade by the roadway, watching the policemen work. After a short while they carried out a stretcher. Porter said, "Here comes my shot." There was a flurry of excitement as the television cameramen ran alongside the rescue-squad men when they brought the body out of the bushes. I watched as they slipped the black bag into the rear of their ambulance. I noticed that Porter had joined the television people and was snapping off pictures rapidly. At one point he looked up at me, smiled and pointed at the body bag. I saw the medical examiner making his way across the fairway, so I walked out into the sun to talk with him. He was lighting a pipe when I stopped him. "What can you tell me?" I asked.

"Won't know too much until I get her cut open. Appears that it was a large-caliber handgun. Probably only one shot, judging from the extent of the damage. Appears to have been fired at close range, maybe a foot, eighteen inches."

"How can you tell?"

"Stippling, the residue of powder around the wound. Really have a better estimate when I get it under a microscope. Just guessing now—but I'm a good guesser."

"Any sign of sexual abuse?"

"Oddly, no. Makes one wonder, doesn't it? I mean, teenage girls aren't ordinarily murdered in that fashion."

"What can you tell me about the way her hands were tied?"

"Not much. The crime-lab boys took the rope."

"Are you sure she was killed here? Not just dumped here afterwards?"

"Oh, yes. I found some matter that was blown away in the explosion on some of the nearby palm fronds."

"Got any theories? Any more good guesses?"

The doctor laughed. "It'll turn out to be either a jealous boyfriend or a sex-crazed stepfather. Either way, it's OK for you people. Still a good story."

I ignored his crack. The doctor puffed hard on his pipe, and I could smell the aroma of the tobacco mixing with the smell of the mown grass. "Any idea who she is?"

"Ask the detectives," he said. "Why don't you call me later, after I've finished with the postmortem? She goes to the top of the list. I'll probably be finished by early afternoon."

"All right," I said. "I'll talk to you then." I saw Martinez and his partner, Wilson, standing by their unmarked car, dealing with a crowd of television reporters. I walked over to the scene to listen. Martinez seemed exasperated. It seemed that someone knew about the hands being tied. So much for it being off the record. Wilson was talking. He was an older man, probably in his mid-forties, on the elderly side for a homicide detective. He had a shock of black hair streaked with gray, a chin that was thrust forward in a constant state of defiance. He was wearing a conservative blue suit with a small American flag in the lapel, and his face was reddened by the sun and by the questions. As I stepped up, I heard him say, "Listen! I'm not giving out any details. It just seems pathetic. I mean"—and he paused, looking out at the cameras—"what's a kid like that ever done? I mean teenagers got the same right to grow up and get old like the rest of us. I just hate it when I see one like that. It really gets to you." He was glaring now, angry. "It really seems a shame," he said. "Lot you guys care."

Martinez cut in. "C'mon, Phil. That's enough. Let's go." He looked across at me, and I saw him raise his eyebrows slightly. I wrote down what Wilson had said, shaking my head.

It's a job for them, I thought, it's a job for us. No difference.

"We'll catch this guy," Wilson was saying. "And I hope he rots away in prison. I wish we had the chair back."

"C'mon, Phil. Enough." Martinez had slipped behind the wheel of the car and started the engine. "Let's go."

Wilson looked down at him. "All right," he said. He looked back at the cameras. "There'll be an official statement later." Then he slid into the seat and slammed the door. The sound was like a shot at the start of a race. There was a quick surge of activity as the camera crews began to wrap up and head out. I found Porter waiting in the car. He had the air conditioner on.

"Hot day for a murder," he said. "Listen, I want to stop and get a parade shot before we go in, OK?"

"No problem." He wheeled the car back onto the roadway, tires complaining.

"The glorious Fourth," he said. "Last year it was Watergate. The year before, the end of the war. Next year, the Bicentennial. A lot of people dressed up to look like George Washington. Transvestites, probably." He laughed. "I mean, who cares?" He paused and thought for a moment. "I guess Boy Scouts care. I remember when I was a kid marching in the parade. It wasn't half bad; made me feel like it was really summer. Gotta say that for it."

I thought of my uncle, in his uniform. My father kept the photo framed in his study. My uncle seemed young and strong. The blue and red dress outfit seemed stark, imposing; a blaze of color that meant more than clothing. When I was young I would look at it with awe and fascination, as if it were possible to put on a uniform and wear bravery and strength and manhood at the same time. In the photo the colors were as vivid as emotions. My mind filled with the music at the funeral, and then I realized the window was rolled down and I could hear the strains of a marching band, the heavy thumping of bass drums and feet, a few blocks away. We parked the car.

"If we try to get much closer, we'll never get out," Porter said. "Come on. It's about three blocks away. Just a small parade down the main street. There's a bigger parade later, but I like to shoot the high school kids. They're fresher than some hotshot college marching band."

I thought for an instant about the girl on the thirteenth green. She probably would have spent the day on the sidewalk watching. Or maybe she would have been a marcher. Blond hair, strutting her youth down the center of the street. I followed Porter toward the growing sound of music and recognized the strains of "Stars and Stripes Forever." What's a parade without Sousa?

The crowd was sparse but appreciative. There were lots of small children with balloons and children in strollers. The band was playing a hit song barely recognizable through the orchestration. The sun glinted off the brass instruments and I heard the sound of feet in cadence. Porter melted through the people and slipped into the street. I had a view of him, ducking and swerving, running in front of the marchers, shooting pictures. As the music swelled and diminished, my eyes fixed on a group of baton twirlers floating down the center of the street their silver sticks flailing in bursts of light around them. The girls wore gold uniforms that reflected the sun, making each, it seemed, gleam especially bright. I watched one girl, on the edge. Her baton seemed to move around her independently, catching the crowd's attention. She stepped back one instant and tossed the baton high into the air. The baton seemed to dance to the band music, twirling against the blue of the sky. Then it fell, tumbling, back toward the girl. Her hand reached out, timing the spin, and she grabbed for the baton.

For a second she seemed to have it, but the same life that she had given it when she tossed it up seemed to infuse it now in her hand, and it broke loose and spun to the ground. The girl broke her rhythm swiftly and swooped down to the baton. In a second it was back in her hand and dancing again, but her face was set, a frown that hid tears. Then she turned and danced out of my view. I thought of the girl on the thirteenth green again. Things were different at that age. A dropped baton brings tears. What else? A broken date, a harsh word, a failed test. No time for death, no tears for the dying.

I listened to the sound of the marching drums until Porter touched my shoulder. "Back to the real world," he said.

CHAPTER *TWO*

IT was afternoon when we returned to the office. Porter went back to the photo studio to begin printing his shots, and I walked slowly toward my desk. I saw Nolan up at the city desk. When he spied me, he turned and came half-dancing across the room, his face open with a grin. "Bingo," he said.

"What bingo is that?"

"It appears that the dispatcher in the Gables logged at least a half-dozen calls last night from a Mr. and Mrs. Jerry Hooks. He's an executive with Eastern Airlines, top executive, big home in the southwest section, just past the Gables border. He's also got a sixteen-year-old daughter named Amy. She went out last night with friends to a party. Didn't come home again. Bingo."

"Are you sure that's the one?"

"My police lieutenant just confirmed it, before you came in. He's already sent the two detectives out to the home. I suggest that you follow them."

I remember thinking that this was the nastiest part of any crime story, especially a murder. Looking at the mangled body was nothing; a cold time of absorbing details. Visiting the victim's family was a different matter, however. I didn't know what to expect. In the past I'd been threatened and embraced, cried on and shouted at. I thought: the dead are so easy to be with, the living so difficult. I collected Porter again—he had just begun his printing process—and we drove back through the city toward the bereaved family.

Martinez and Wilson were standing outside the door when we pulled up. Martinez was wearing reflecting sunglasses so that if you looked into his eyes you saw only yourself. Wilson was wiping his forehead with a white handkerchief. The white of the linen caught the heat somehow; it seemed to glow in his hand. Porter said, "Welcome to reality, folks," and we walked across the lawn.

Wilson spoke first. "Christ, you guys are fast. Just can't wait, can you?"

I stared at him for a moment, then turned to Martinez. "What's the situation inside?"

He looked at me from behind the sunglasses. "They seem in shock. I had to tell them that one of them must make the positive identification at the morgue. We're waiting for the father now."

"How did they take the news?"

"They didn't say anything. It was almost as if they were expecting the worst when the kid didn't come home last night. Apparently she was a regular type, never kept her parents worried, never stayed out late at all."

"Boyfriend? Suspects?"

"Nobody regular. Nobody they knew who carried a grudge. Nobody she just broke up with, I mean."

Wilson interrupted. "She was just a good, straight kid. No drugs. No sex. She was a cheerleader over at Sunset High. Good grades, all A's and B's. Wanted to be a veterinarian, to go to college. Christ, it makes me sick just thinking about it." He looked at me, still wiping his forehead with the handkerchief. "How you going to write this? Let me tell you, you cause this family any more grief and . . ."

"And what?" I said. "What do you think we are? Christ." I turned back to Martinez. "So where do you go from here?"

"Well, we check out the party she went to. But from what the parents say, I doubt it'll be much. Just high school kids. Wait for the autopsy report. Start checking the sex offender file, but that seems like a dead end, too. I mean, this doesn't seem like a sex crime."

I looked at Wilson. "What do you think?" He paused, and I finished taking notes on Martinez, scribbling rapidly across the page of my small notebook.

"I think it's some kind of psycho. Who else? We just haven't got a handle yet. We will, though, I promise." I saw Martinez turn away, as if in frustration over his partner's pledge.

"You know," the younger detective said, "most of the time when we get to a murder scene we already know who did it. Then you have the victim on the ground and the guy who killed him standing there with a smoking gun in his hand, crying. Or the wife gets tired of her old man punching her out after a tough day at work and so she blows him away. Or the father forgets to lock up the gun he keeps in the house to protect the family and then sees his five-year-old shoot himself with it. Then there's a smaller percentage, the guy who gets wasted behind the register of his fast-food store in the ghetto. But we usually get them, too, because sooner or later somebody opens their big mouth and we shut it for them. Or drugs. People shoot up, people get shot. Like peanut butter and jelly, that's the way things work. Organized crime is tough. You know, professional killers cover their tracks. But at least we have some idea who did it, and who cares anyway, huh?

"But the smallest percentage are the random killings. Sex crimes fit into that category. The victim and the killer don't know each other. They may just meet that once. Just two lives that touch one instant. No clues, no witnesses, no leads. Real trouble for us. I think that's the kind of crime we've got here. Except for the sex angle; can't figure it."

"What about the tied hands?" I asked.

"Who knows?" Martinez shrugged.

I looked at the two of them. "You're holding back something," I said. "You give me this big 'We got no leads' speech and you're going to make an arrest in the morning, right? On

Post time. You're holding back. Listen, you don't have to tell me what it is you've got, but let me know what to expect."

Martinez looked angry and Wilson turned away. "I'll tell you nothing!" he said. "A body, hands tied, in the bushes. That's it. Nothing magical. The killer didn't leave his prints on a nice white card with his name and address at the scene! You want an arrest fast? Well, you go make one. Christ."

I didn't have time to reply because the front door of the house opened. The two detectives stepped back, leaving me a lane to the front. I tried to wipe the anger from my face, and I adopted my most solemn voice. It was a practiced tone I had for dealing with any bereaved family, whether victimized by crime, accident or act of God. I wanted to convey that I felt their tragedy but that at the same time I was insistent on getting my story. I introduced myself first to the man who emerged from the door, then to his wife, a half-step behind him. I could see that their eyes were red with tears.

"I realize that this is a difficult time," I said. "But it would be very helpful for me if one of you could take the time to tell me about your daughter, her hopes and dreams."

The father nodded. He seemed in shock, my words barely registering. He looked toward the two detectives, who remained impassive. "She's a lovely girl," he said, his voice in the active tense. "I mean, nearly perfect. Everyone loves her very much. We're very worried."

Martinez took him by the arm. "This will be difficult," the detective said. "It's better to get it over with now." The man nodded, and Wilson and Martinez led him away from the porch to their car. I watched the three of them cross the lawn, the light seeming to accentuate each difficult step. I could hear the clicking and whirring of the camera behind me. I turned to the mother. "Perhaps we could sit down and talk," I said. "They're likely to be some time." She nodded, and I snaked into the house behind her, leaving the door open so that Porter could slip inside with me.

I watched the mother walk slowly through a vestibule into a large living room. My eyes searched the room carefully, taking down details as accurately as in my notebook. I quickly asked, "Do you think I could have a glass of water? It's terribly hot outside."

She looked confused for a moment, then replied, "Of course. Let me get you one." Then she walked through a doorway into what I took to be the kitchen. I used the time to get my bearings, organize my thoughts. I examined one wall of the room which was filled with pictures of the family. I noted the careful placing of the furniture, modern, low-slung. Expensive, I thought. In one corner of the room there was a piano. I registered a question about that. There was a large stereo console and I noted the titles of records that were out; several rock, several classical. There was no television in the living room. I walked to the back of the room and looked out through sliding glass doors onto a rear patio. I could see a swimming pool, some trees and a lawn that appeared lush. In Florida, a green lawn tells you something about the dedication of the homeowners, to fight that battle against the sun. I heard the mother enter and turned to face her. "I was just admiring your lawn. It reminds me of the North."

She managed a short smile, as she handed me the glass with ice and water, and glanced at Porter, who was standing in the background, trying to take shots inconspicuously. She seemed almost resigned, gave a small shrug and slipped into a chair. For a moment she rested her head in her hands, and then she looked at me.

"You can't imagine the worry. How scared I am." Her voice was even, but her eyes were filling with tears. She showed remarkable restraint. "I didn't sleep last night. Neither did Jerry. Once he went out and just drove around the neighborhood. He said he knew he wouldn't see her but that he felt he had to be doing something. You see, she's never done this before, stayed out all night. None of our kids did." (The present tense, too, like her husband. It hadn't hit her yet.)

"How many children do you have?" I asked. I was scribbling in my pad as fast as I could. Just keep her talking, I thought. The story will write itself.

"Three," she said. "Amy is the youngest. Jerry Junior is a sophomore at Stanford, and his older brother Stephen is in medical school in Boston."

"Harvard?"

She smiled. "I suppose he wishes it was. No, at Tufts."

"Still," I said, "that's quite an accomplishment."

She nodded. "He was in the war, you see. As a medic with the Americal Division. I can't remember which number. But he saw a lot of action, and I guess it was there that he made up his mind. He came back and took summer-school courses in chemistry and I don't know what else and got accepted. He's in his second year now."

"Tell me about your daughter," I asked.

She caught her breath, as if surprised. "They were all good children. I never had any real trouble. Stephen went to war over our objections, because, he said, he'd graduated from school and thought it was his duty to go. He'd taken all the deferments and everything. Jerry Junior, well, he gave us some worries during high school, with marches and long hair and all that. But it seemed to have less passion for him. We worried mostly about drugs because it seemed everyone at his school was turning on, as they say. But he's done very well at school. He always did well at school, like his brother. I worry sometimes that Amy has had to live up to a great deal. Her brothers are very important to her; she always tried to do what they did, act like they did. I think sometimes it was confusing for her to be a girl and different. She was an outdoors type, and I guess that running and horsing around was more of her upbringing than dolls and—oh, what other things do little girls do? When we moved here—Jerry used to be with Northwest, and for years we lived in Minneapolis. We just came here—oh, two years ago, this October—I was glad because she could still be outside and enjoy herself. It wasn't as if we'd moved to New York City or anything. You know, where you have to worry all the time. And she's such a sensible girl."

"A cheerleader?"

"That's right." The mother laughed briefly, a short abrupt sound in the stillness of the living room. "And vice-president of her class. She's going to be a senior at Sunset. She wants to go and become a veterinarian. I guess that's just a non-threatening approach to her older brother. I think she'll go to medical school, too. . . ." And then she caught herself suddenly, like a diver stopped in mid-fall, suspended over the depth of waters. "That is, of course . . . I don't know. Oh, my God, what's happened?" And the tears that had been held back burst forth unchecked. The mother gave a low moan and seemed to slump in the chair. It was a moment of defeat, and she seemed to be lost and confused. It was a look I'd seen before. The room was silent except for the whirring of the camera. The mother put her face in her hands and leaned back and forth as if she were physically hurt. "My God," she said. "My child."

"Please, ma'am," I said. "Just another minute or two. Do you have a photo of Amy that we can take along? We'll be happy to send it back. Something recent?"

The mother took her hands away from her face and stared at me. "A picture?"

"That's right. Yearbook, perhaps, or maybe a family shot?"

"I'll get you one." She turned to Porter. "Do you care for a glass of water also?"

Even I was impressed. I thought of fighters I'd seen, the type who could take a solid punch and then keep their wits about them. She stood as Porter nodded, and I watched her move. She was a tall woman, dressed in a simple, colorful dress, stylish, her light brown hair pulled back from her face. I noticed she wore little makeup. It would have run wet from the tears. She moved easily, gracefully. I looked over to Porter as the mother left the room, but he was looking at the photos on the wall. "These are good," he said. "Somebody knows their way around a camera. Or they're professional. Good composition, lighting, the works."

The mother walked in with a photo in one hand and a glass in the other. "Jerry Junior took most of them," she said. She'd overheard his comments and reacted like any proud mother.

"He may try your profession when he finishes school."

Porter said, "Well, if you get a chance, tell him that I thought they were very good."

She smiled. "Thank you. It will mean a lot to him."

She handed me the photo. "Is that all right?" I looked at it closely. It was of a pretty blond teenager; wide smile, open face. She was wearing jeans and standing by the pool. There was a collie at her feet. "That's Lady. I'm afraid we had to put her to sleep a few months ago. Amy was heartbroken. I think that's when she decided to become a vet. Jerry Junior took the photo."

"It's perfect," I said. It will break the readers' hearts, I thought. "I'll send it back when we've finished."

"That would be fine." For a moment the three of us stood in the room. "Do you suppose there's any chance, I mean, a possibility, that the police are wrong?" I could see the tears beginning to form again. "They've been wrong before about these things, I believe. Did you, uh, see the . . ." She couldn't get out the next word.

I decided to lie. "There are often mistakes. You should wait until you get word that's definite. I saw the remains, but"—I motioned to the picture—"there's really no way of telling."

"She was wearing blue jeans and a red-and-blue-striped shirt when she went out last night."

I looked at Porter. The same mental image must have passed through his mind at the same instant. He looked away. "I'm sorry I didn't get that close."

But I had.

The mother sat back down. "It all seems so unreal. It's like I don't know what's happening, but I know it's important. It's like it's happening to someone else. Not me. Like you're here for someone else. It's all a big mistake. Is this real? Oh, my God! I don't know what to feel, what to think." She looked up at me. "How can I make sense when the whole world seems suddenly out of whack?" I didn't know what to say.

And then the telephone rang. It was an angry, frightening sound.

The mother walked across the room and picked up the receiver. I listened. I knew what it was, although I could only hear her responses.

"Yes, dear," she said. "I'm OK."

Her face seemed to pinch in suddenly, and her eyes went wide.

"Tell me!" she shouted. "Tell me!"

I saw her close her eyes and grit her teeth. She sat down on a chair, her back rigid, her face thrust forward.

"I am sitting down! Tell me! Tell me! Tell me!"

And then her hand came up abruptly to her mouth, a single movement of horror.

"Oh, my God," she said. "My baby."

She placed the receiver down carefully, gently, I thought, as if trying not to disturb anything. She looked at me.

"It's her," she said. Her voice was flat. "My child. My baby girl."

"Ma'am," I said. "Is there someone we can get? A neighbor, perhaps?"

She didn't seem to hear me. "My baby," she repeated. Porter jerked his head toward the door. I nodded.

"We're going now, ma'am," I said. "We're sorry."

Her voice remained cold and monotonal, "Who could do this?" she said. "What animal would do this? Oh, my God, what has happened? Who would want to kill my baby? Oh, my baby." Finally the words seemed to break, as if they were crystalline, and she began to moan, rocking back and forth, holding her stomach. The telephone began to ring again, over and over, but she made no move toward it. After a second I stepped over and picked it up. It was her husband.

"Hello, hello, dear?" he was shouting.

"No," I said. "This is the reporter from the *Journal*. Listen, I think she needs someone to be with her. A neighbor, maybe?"

The husband seemed confused. There was a silence. Then he said, "Yes. Next door. The Allens. To the right. I have to give a statement to the police. Tell her I'll be home as soon as possible. Thank you, uh, for helping."

"We'll get the neighbors," I said, and I hung up. Porter had handed her the remains of his glass of water and she was gulping it down. "We're leaving now, ma'am. You'll be OK." But she didn't seem to hear anything. She continued to moan.

When we stepped outside it seemed, if possible, that it was even hotter. "Next door," I said, "the Allens."

Porter nodded and ran across the yard. I saw him step inside for a moment and then reappear, leading a man and a woman across the lawn. He let them into the house and then joined me.

"Did you warn them about the television people? They're sure to be here any minute."

"I mentioned it," he said. "But I don't know if it registered. They'll figure it out, though, soon enough."

"Let's go, then. Maybe we can catch the father at Police Headquarters. And we're beginning to run tight on time."

Porter said little, then, and pulled away from the curb slowly. It must be getting to him, I thought, just a little bit, and I smiled. He grabbed the radio and called the photo department to let them know where we were heading. Nolan must have been listening in, because he came on the box next, asking to speak to me. "So," I heard him say, "what's it look like?"

"Nolan," I said. My voice was full and confident. "Let me tell you this: I've got a hell of a story."

The sun seemed to reflect off the road, washing the windshield with a blast of bright light. In silence but for the humming of the air conditioner and the tires on the road, we headed to the center of the city.

I saw the two detectives accompanying the father as they exited the Police Headquarters' side entrance. We were just pulling into the parking lot and I slid from the car before it had fully stopped. I managed to intercept the group a few feet before the police cruiser and placed myself between them and the car. I could hear Porter's steps behind me. "Mr. Hooks," I said, "can I speak with you a moment?" The policemen looked annoyed and hesitated. I could see that the father didn't really place me. "From the *Journal*," I said. "We talked on the phone just a little while ago. The neighbors are with your wife now."

I could see recognition hit his face. He was reluctant. "I really don't know what to say. I want to thank you for helping my wife, but I really don't have anything I want to say right now. I just hope they catch the person. I don't see how anyone could do that . . . but I really don't have anything to say. You understand?"

"Of course," I said. But I didn't move from my position, blocking them from the car. "Did you suspect anything like this last night?"

"How could I? How could anyone imagine this? Oh, I suppose I was worried. Who wouldn't be? I called all the emergency rooms in the city, to see if she'd been brought in. I thought she'd been in a car accident. That's what really scared me. A car accident. But I don't really want to say anything, all right?"

I continued taking down his words in my notebook. "Would you like to see the man who killed your daughter punished?"

"God! Yes! I want him to suffer," the father said, and I looked up because his voice was cracking, like thin ice beneath a skater's feet. "I'd like him to feel what I'm going through now! I hope he can get just a taste of it." And then the father stopped and looked at me. "But I really can't say anything now," he said.

"Of course," I replied. "I understand." And then I stepped out of the way. Wilson glared at me as he got behind the wheel of the cruiser. I saw the father cover his eyes with his hands as the car pulled out of the lot. It was much the same motion the mother had used, as if they were trying to prevent their eyes from seeing some inner vision, some imprint on their imagination. I turned to Porter. "Good stuff?"

"Yes," he said. "Top-notch."

"Front page?"

"Can't miss."

"Can't miss," I agreed. The afternoon was late now, and I noted that the heat was beginning to diminish, as if hiding for the night. We turned and headed back to the newsroom.

Nolan was emerging from the last afternoon news conference when I walked in. He motioned to me and I walked up grinning. "Good story?" he asked.

"I think so," I said coyly.

"Fill me in while I get a cup of coffee." He walked to a machine in the corner of the newsroom. I told him quickly, running down the main highlights of the story, skipping over some of the detail. I told him about the body next to the green and the runner who'd picked out the color in the rough. I told him about the mother and the photos on the wall and the telephone call and how she'd cracked then under the strain. Then I described the father and the detectives and read him a few of the quotes. Finally I paused, and he sipped on the coffee and thought for a moment. "OK," he said. "I argued for the front page and got it. They knocked a feature back. Listen, here's what I want: about thirty inches for the mainbar and about fifteen for the sidebar. Incorporate the jogger into the main, using his quotes and color. Write a separate on the mother and the father. But save a quote or two from each for the main story. Lead with the body and the status of the police investigation, but work the color and the parents' reaction in very near the top. OK?"

"Sounds good, but I really would like to do a sidebar on the guy who discovered the body. And can I run long?"

"Tell you what," he said, smiling. "You run long, but only with color. I mean, I want people to really feel that girl. And just the one sidebar. On the parents. In a couple of days you can go back and talk with the guy who found the body and see if he's still running the same route. It'll make an interesting follow."

I nodded. "But I'm still going to work his stuff into the main."

"Of course," Nolan said. "Don't hold anything out. This'll be the best-read story in the paper tomorrow by a long shot. And what about the art? Is it good?"

I handed him the photo the mother had given me. He stared at it for a second. "Christ," he said, "she was pretty cute. This is really good. I'm going to go start negotiating for space with the newsdesk. You start writing now; I want to move all this stuff myself."

"OK," I said. "Don't lose the photo. I promised I'd send it back."

"Who took it?" Nolan asked.

"The brother. Jerry Hooks, Junior."

"We'll give him a credit line then," Nolan said. "All right?"

"Good idea."

I called Christine then, catching her as she was leaving the hospital. "Are you OK?" she asked. "How did the funeral go?"

"I survived," I replied. "Everyone survived."

"When will I see you?"

"Not too early. I have a big story I have to finish."

"You went to work?" She sounded surprised.

"I wanted to. Why sit around brooding? Work takes my mind off things, puts it somewhere else. It's a marvelous release."

"You love it." It was a small accusation.

"I must." I laughed, and after a moment she joined me.

"Shall I get us something to eat?"

"How about a steak?"

"See you later," she said. "Sounds like you want to celebrate."

"Just a good story," I said. I hung up the phone and turned to the typewriter. Around me worked other reporters, and the sound of their voices on the telephones mingled with the staccato noise from the electric typewriters. The room seemed filled with the soft light of late afternoon; large windows on one side covered the whole wall. I could look out over downtown from where I sat. The buildings seemed to reach out and catch the evening shadows. I turned away and looked across the room at the old photo of the palm tree blowing in the storm. I could see that the big storm had moved slightly in its course, heading north by northeast, on a path with Miami. I closed my eyes for a moment and began to summon up images, like a conjuror with facts. I could see the body, and the sunlight reflecting off her blond hair. I pictured the mother, then the father, each in their own state of panic. I slipped a sheet into the typewriter and began to punch out letters, forming words, shaping sentences and paragraphs. It was as if I were connected to the machine then; it was an instrument and I a musician.

I wrote:

A sixteen-year-old Sunset High School cheerleader...
Discovered by an early-morning jogger...
Her hands were bound and she had been shot "execution-style"...
Her mother's face was drawn and frightened...
Her father's words were twisted and angry...
Police are still seeking clues but have no suspects...

The pages slid through the machine swiftly, and slowly the other sounds in the newsroom slipped away from me; I was aware only that I was in my element, working with the thoughts and impressions of the day. I finished the main story and continued on with the sidebar on the parents. I hardly noticed when an assistant city editor picked the sheets off my desk and took them to the computer scanner to be fed into the newsroom system. I finished some fifteen minutes before deadline, with a quote from the mother: "Who would want to do such a thing?"

I looked at it for a moment, and my mind filled with images of my uncle. I pictured him, highball in one hand, album in the other, poring over the moments of his past. I could see his face in my mind, his lips quivering with remembrances, his one good eye filling with tears. And I saw the abrupt, military movement of his hand as he snapped the album closed, closing his life at the same moment. His steps must have been measured, slow, like the pace of a funeral caisson. I could see him mount the stairs to his bathroom, his pistol, carefully cleaned and polished, in his hand. The crack of the gun must have seemed to him more like taps.

Nolan leaned over me. "It's good," he said. "Are you finished?"

I handed him the final page. I followed his eyes as they scanned the words. "OK," he said. "Come on up. I'll show you what changes I've made." He dropped the last sheet with the computer clerk and then went to his desk. Next to it was a small television screen with a keyboard: the video display terminal. He punched a series of keys and my story appeared on the screen. "Read it over." There were a few minor changes, a few words slipped into different spots; a few paragraphs had changed location. Nothing major. Then he punched up the sidebar, and together we read through it. "Not bad at all," he said, smiling. "Don't want to forget this." And in quick succession he typed:

BY MALCOLM ANDERSON
Journal Staff Writer

at the top of each story.

He rolled through the two stories again and finally got to the mother's last quote. "It's a really good quote to end on," I said.

He agreed. "Kinda says it all, doesn't it? Sums it right up."

I nodded.

But, of course, we were both completely wrong.

CHAPTER *THREE*

THE next morning, I didn't look at the front page right away. Christine rose first and retrieved the paper from the front doorstep. She made coffee and breakfast while I showered, and I heard her call through the bathroom door the same question as the mother: "Jesus. Who would do such a thing?" I called back that it would probably turn out to be someone usual, an estranged boyfriend probably, someone that the parents didn't know about. Then I heard her shout, "But that still wouldn't explain it." I made no reply but continued rinsing the soap from my body, feeling the lukewarm water rush through my hair and onto my face. The bathroom window was open, and I could already feel the day's heat starting up, like an engine.

"It makes me sick," she said, when I came out.

"What does?"

"That kind of crime. You know, your mind can envision a dozen explanations for the crime—passion, perversion, robbery, I don't know what else—but none of them really provide sufficient reason to rob that poor kid of her life. It makes me ill just to think about it. Didn't it bother you?"

"I don't think of it that way."

"Well, then," Christine asked, "how do you think of it?"

She was spreading an English muffin with butter and marmalade. I saw the sunlight slip through the kitchen windows and glint off the knife handle as she put it down on the table. She had reddish-brown hair that was cut to frame her face and fell to her shoulders. The sunlight in the room brought out the red, and she seemed suddenly to be surrounded by color. "Well?" she said.

"It's just a story," I said. "It's what I do. Look, the newspaper is mostly a chronicle of tragedy, OK? Yesterday was my turn to delve into a particular tragedy and then express it for all the other tragic people in the world, or at least in our circulation area, to shake their heads over. Your reaction was probably the breakfasttime norm for the Greater Miami area. But everyone who reads the story at least gets to say, 'At least it didn't happen to me,' and that's part of why it's there. Listen, it's probably the same in your business; when you perform surgery don't you feel a kind of divorce from the proceedings? As if you're glad to be unaffected?"

"No," she said. "Not exactly."

I drank orange juice and picked up the sports section. The Yankees were widening their lead in the East, burying Baltimore and the Red Sox. The National League seemed to be all Cincinnati. I saw that Tom Seaver had pitched for the Mets. I liked to watch Seaver pitch; his body always seemed in complete commitment to the act of throwing the ball. He would rock back ever so slightly, then explode his arm and body toward the batter. His knee would dip down, scraping the mound, and his arm, like a shot, would race past his ear, releasing the ball at the proper moment. It seemed that there was no time at all between the release from his fingers and the appearance of the ball over the plate, as if Seaver were some wizard who made the ball's flight invisible. I liked to see him throw the hard stuff at ninety, ninety-five, so that when it detonated over the plate it was dipping and swerving, the ball no longer inanimate but infused with a life of its own.

When I walked into the newsroom I could see that most of the other reporters were standing around, drinking coffee and looking over the paper. There was always a stack of the day's papers by the entranceway; I picked one up, glancing at the front but not taking it in; I wanted to sit at my desk and savor the story. I also picked up the first edition of the afternoon *Post* to see how they had played the story. I couldn't remember seeing any *Post* reporters during the day, but that did not mean that they weren't there. As I walked to my desk a few of the other reporters called to me. One said, "Good story," and another joked, "Encore, encore!" It was pretty much the same anytime anyone had a big assignment, a story that had jumped from the routine to the front page. I nodded my head in mock appreciation and settled into my desk.

The story had been played above the fold, skylined on top of the national lead for the day. TEENAGER FOUND MURDERED; POLICE SEEK 'EXECUTION' KILLER, the headline read. It was spread across all six columns, and I looked at the picture of the girl. Even in the fuzzy black and white reproduction of the paper she still seemed pristine, beautiful. The sidebar started on the front page also, indented in the major story. The headline there was smaller type: A PHONE CALL . . . AND TRAGEDY STRIKES, it read. I thought that it was perhaps a little overdone, but then, I considered, the newspaper is not in the business of subtlety. I scanned over the words of both stories with an inner satisfaction, a familiarity. It was as if the memories of the day before had slipped away and were replaced by the words of the newsprint, the real people replaced by the descriptions in the story. As I read, the telephone rang on my desk. It was Christine.

"I didn't want to have an argument," she said.

"Did we?" I asked and laughed.

"No," she said. "I didn't want to accuse you of being cold."

"I am. It goes, as they say, with the territory."

"Well . . . you're not like that really."

"But I am." I laughed again.

"I don't believe so." Her voice was exasperated.

"Where are you?"

"I'm at the hospital. I only have a few minutes. The doctors will be down to scrub in a moment and I have to check on things. I just wanted to call because, I don't know, you seem so unconcerned."

"I am unconcerned. I'd go crazy if I let it all bother me. Anyone would. It's just my defense to the whole crazy show."

"Well," she said, "I think you shouldn't be."

"Look," I replied, "tell me this: who are you cutting into today?"

"A businessman. Or a lawyer, I forget right now. Middle-aged."

"Family?"

"Of course."

"Chances of survival?"

"I don't know. It's an exploratory, into the stomach. I don't really think they know what they'll find, but it won't be good, no matter what it is."

"Have you talked with him, seen him with his family?"

"A little. I saw him yesterday, with a woman and a teenage son. They all looked so ill, especially the two who weren't."

"And tell me, what went through your mind?"

"I don't know. Sadness. A kind of hopelessness. I wanted to walk up to them and tell them that they had nothing to worry about, that the surgeons were perfect and the disease in retreat. That they could relax and enjoy their time together because they had a future."

"So why didn't you?"

"It would have been a lie." There was a pause. I could hear voices in the background. "I have to go," she said.

"Well," I said, "in a way that's my point. I just can't stand thinking I'm lying."

"Is it that simple for you?"

"Yes. I just watch and record. Sometimes I think of myself as a camera. My eyes are the shutter, the words are the print. Does that make any sense to you?"

"I have to go."

"I'll see you tonight," I said.

"Tonight."

When I hung up the phone I had a picture of her in my mind, dressed in the baggy pale blue or green surgical outfit, her hair pulled back severely and hidden beneath the sanitary helmet, the mask she would wear dangling around her neck like jewelry. She was a slender woman; she could wear the loose shirt and slacks of the operating theater and still appear thin. With the mask pulled up all one could see would be her eyes.

I didn't think she was an overly pretty woman, but her eyes were exceptional; they jumped and shone and showed off her emotions. Her eyes sometimes seemed to speak before the words were out of her mouth. Often I watched them closely, to anticipate the swings of her mood. We had been together some time now, in essence living together, though she kept a one-room studio apartment near the hospital. She stayed there when I went out of town, on assignment or, as the day before, to my uncle's funeral.

She had questioned me about it when I saw her. I'd wanted to talk of the story instead, but she'd persisted in getting me to describe my family's responses.

"My father was the only interesting person," I said.

"Why?"

"Because he was the one who was suffering the most and showing it the least."

"How so? Was he close to his brother?"

"All brothers are close," I said, "regardless of the differences in their lives. Even if they hate each other, they have a kind of close hatred. One never equivocates on the subject of one's brother."

She had nodded then and asked no more questions.

Christine and I had met a year earlier. I'd been filling in on the night cop beat while the regular was on vacation, and I had picked up the garbled transmission of a high-speed chase up on Route 95 that cut through the center of Miami. There wasn't much else doing, so I went out to see what happened when they caught up with the speeder.

It turned out to be the eighteen-year-old son of a county commissioner. And before he finished leading a dozen patrol cars through the city, he managed to run two other drivers off the road, wreck several of the cruisers pursuing him and finally wrap himself around a telephone pole. I latched onto the parade of angry and wounded at the downtown medical complex. I saw one uniformed officer, holding a bloody compress to his forehead, watch as the kid was carried in on a stretcher. "I hope this little sucker buys it," the cop said. I got his words down, thinking. "There's my second graf," when I was shoved out of the way by a nurse.

"Please," she said, "don't get in the way."

"It's my job," I said.

She looked at me oddly, then tried a small laugh. "I guess it is."

I measured her trim figure, the smooth manner she handled herself amidst all the broken and frightened people crowding into the emergency room. My eyes tracked her as she swept quickly from litter to bed, pausing to take vital signs, then moving on. I admired her efficiency at first, then her calm. She seemed such an island in a storm, I thought, then smiled at the cliché. She caught my look and smiled back. "Humor?" she asked. "Please share it." It wasn't a reproach.

"I was watching you," I said.

"Ah," she said and smiled again. I remember how out of place the smile was in the room; it seemed to rise above all the sounds of hurt. "It helps to keep one's sense of humor."

"It does," I agreed.

Then she turned away, back to one of the patients. I was closing in on a deadline; I needed to get to a phone, then a typewriter. But as I left, I stopped at the nurses' station and found her name written on a log. There was a home phone number. I took that down.

The next afternoon I called her.

My eyes turned back to the paper on my desk. I opened it to the jump on the inside page and saw that it had been laid out with photos of the man who'd discovered the girl's body, and of the parents, different poses. The father was captured slipping into the patrol car at police headquarters. His face was set and grim. The mother was pictured hanging up the telephone, a blank look on her face, caught in the moment of dissolution turning to distress. They were powerful photographs. I picked up the telephone on my desk and dialed the photo-studio number. I asked for Porter, and in a moment he came on the line. "Really good shots," I said.

"Thanks. I had a lot of good stuff. They never did use the photo of the body in the bag like I said they would. They came close, though. They were going to use it until they saw the photo of the girl that the mother gave us. Still, all in all, they were good subjects for the camera. And for the typewriter."

"True."

"So," he said, "what's for an encore? Have you got some kind of follow?"

"I don't know yet. I'm going to talk with Nolan now."

"Well, if you need photos, call me. I'd like to stick with this one, if possible."

"I'll let you know," I said and hung up.

I checked the *Post*'s coverage. They'd also played the story on the front page but didn't have many of the details that I had. They'd found one of the neighboring teenagers who'd seen the girl that evening. The kid had said he'd seen the girl walking alone through the neighborhood. It didn't really mean much, but the way they had written it implied that no one else had seen the girl later and that she'd been snatched during that evening walk. It was a skillful writing job, to create an illusion of knowledge where none really existed. I noticed also that they did not have a photo of the girl; they'd relied on the shot of the rescue personnel carrying her body off the thirteenth green in the body bag. They'd also been forced to interview the Allens, the neighbors we had summoned. I smiled and shut the paper, a sense of satisfaction running through my head. There is a kind of glow, a mixture of aggressiveness and pride that comes when one beats the competition in the newspaper business. Results are so immediate, so clear.

I picked up the phone again and started to work. It would be worthwhile to check with the detectives before I spoke with Nolan to give us at least some idea of what to do next. A voice answered, "Homicide."

"Martinez," I said. "This is Anderson at the *Journal*."

I heard the clicking sounds of the call being transferred and then Martinez' voice. "Big day in the news business," he said. "I can see the headline now: *Journal* reporter hits big time, gets job at *New York Times*." He laughed.

"I'd never leave you guys," I said. "How would I get any stories if it weren't for you?"

"You'd make them up. You already do." He laughed again.

"Touché."

"So what can I do for you? Listen, I think you did OK. Even Wilson does, but he won't admit it. He's still pretty angry about the whole thing."

"What's new?" I asked. "I need a follow-up."

"Well," Martinez answered, "we're going to get the autopsy report this morning, and ballistics says they can have a preliminary idea pretty soon, too. Other than that, all we've got planned is to canvas the neighborhood. Pretty routine stuff. Did anybody see her maybe get into a car or see anyone suspicious in the neighborhood? Talk to some of her friends. Drudgery. Not the exciting stuff your readers are waiting for."

"How long are you going to be at it?"

"Probably all day. There's going to be a lot of pressure on Wilson and me to get this guy, but I doubt we will. That's not for publication, of course. We've got a few ideas, mostly that he's whacko. I don't want to talk too much about that."

"All right," I said. "It's pretty early for me. I'll talk to you again this afternoon. OK?"

"Fine. The medical examiner will talk about the autopsy. I don't suspect there will be anything in it that needs to be confidential. He'll know, anyway."

I hung up the telephone and looked down at the notes I'd taken of the conversation. Whacko, I thought. Maybe that's something we can follow up on. I picked up the sheaf of papers and walked over to the city desk. Nolan was on the telephone with another reporter, the courthouse man, arguing about the coverage of a trial. After a few minutes he turned to me. "The bastard doesn't think that murder trial is worth much of a story. The irritating thing is he's probably right, because he knows an awful lot more about it than I do. So, good job yesterday, but that's water under the bridge. As they say, what have you done for me today?"

I smiled. "We'll get the autopsy report and ballistics today. Martinez says he's going to be out canvassing the neighborhood. He doesn't expect too much."

"Maybe we should do some of the same?"

I groaned. "It's hot. If my mother wanted me to be a door-to-door salesman she'd have given me an encyclopedia."

Nolan laughed. "I took cruelty pills this morning. Along with my usual dosage of sadism and an injection of bilious bad temper. Before I do something rash, like send you out there, suggest something better."

"Well," I said, "Martinez suggested that the killer might be some sort of crazy. A sex criminal, I suppose. I could interview some of the forensic psychiatrists over at the courthouse, see what they think."

"A good idea, but I don't think we have enough information yet for them to go on. You might try calling a few and see if you can set up an appointment later in the week or tomorrow. We'll know a little more and things will be a little slower. Then head out into the neighborhood and knock on some doors. Get the people's reactions. See if they're buying attack dogs, that sort of thing."

"Fear stalks," I said.

Nolan laughed. "That's right. Fear stalks quiet neighborhood in wake of teenager's murder. I realize it's standard newspaper fare, but it's still a good story, regardless of how often it's written. And it will keep the story on the front page for another day. Take a photographer."

I waited outside for Porter to bring the car around. The *Journal* building was right on the bay, and I stood to the side, feeling the warm breeze that was lifting the slight chop on the waters. The bay seemed the same color as the sky, a pale blue, and for a moment I felt suspended between the two, the heat seeming to slip over me like fog. I heard the sound of a car horn, turned and saw the photographer. "Back into the fray," he said. I grunted as I slid into the seat, the sweat already slick on my forehead.

We drove by the murdered girl's home. It was closed, the window curtains drawn and the door pulled shut. I couldn't see any activity, but I noticed there were several cars in the driveway; friends, perhaps the girl's brothers, I thought, the gathering of death. We parked up the block. I saw a pair of teenage girls walking down the sidewalk and we rushed up to them.

"Are you a real reporter?" one asked. I smiled and showed her my police identification card. She looked at it and then at me. "It's not a good picture," she said. Her friend leaned over and looked at it wordlessly.

"Did you know the victim?" I asked.

"Oh, sure," the first girl said as her friend nodded her head. "Everyone in the neighborhood knew her. She was real popular."

"Was she a classmate?"

"No, she was a grade ahead of us." The second girl finally spoke. "But we saw her all the time."

"Tell me, are you scared? I mean, here you are walking around as if nothing happened. What do you think?"

The two girls looked at each other. They seemed to be twins in their cut-off blue jeans and T-shirts. They both had the same shoulder-length hair, too, and it seemed they could not speak without moving their hands or pouting or grinning, somehow punctuating their words with some motion or expression. "My dad," the first girl said, "says I can't go out at night until the murderer is caught."

"And you?" I asked the second girl.

"My mom gave me a lecture," she said. "My mom said I can't go anywhere, not even to the swim club, unless I walk with a friend. And I have to tell them where I'm gonna go at night. I don't think they'll let me go out, anyway."

"When did they talk with you?"

"This morning. Right after the story came out in the papers. But we knew about it last night. Everyone was talking, everywhere. I still can't believe it." It was the first girl speaking.

Her friend joined in. "I mean, I never thought about anything like that before. And I wonder who's going to take her place as a cheerleader?"

Perfect, I thought. The teenage mind at work. "Do you think everyone is scared?" I asked.

"Oh, yes," both girls said quickly. "All the grown-ups," the second girl added.

"You're not scared?"

"Oh," she said, "maybe a little. It's daytime, and it's hard to be scared. Maybe tonight I'll be scared."

I took down their words as they spoke, trying to add details of their expression. I noticed that a few other children, mostly between what I estimated to be the ages of nine and fourteen, had gathered to watch. It's the camera that does it, that always adds the element of fascination to the proceedings. I motioned some of the children over, and in a moment I was surrounded by perhaps ten of the neighborhood kids. I started to ask my questions as Porter swooped around the periphery, snapping shots of the children.

"I'm scared. I don't want it to happen to me," said one boy.

"I think I'd punch the killer right where it hurts," said one teenage girl, a child on the verge of adulthood. Her response gained a ripple of embarrassed laughter from the group.

"I don't think the killer will come back," said one small boy, perhaps nine, obviously upset by the situation. "They never return to the scene of the crime. I read that."

As they talked I wrote down their words, their names and their addresses. My notebook was filling with scribbling, hieroglyphics interpretable only by myself. Their voices came at me quickly, excitedly, their opinions probably reaching words for the first time. I thought of the discrepancy in time and place; in the sun, with the reporter and the photographer, the experience was novel. Alone in their rooms tonight, most of them will turn sleepless with dread. A child's imagination, I thought. Remarkable.

They grew quiet, and I looked up to see a woman standing a few feet away in the center of her front yard. We all looked at her. "Who are you?"

"Anderson, *Journal*," I said. "Just asking the kids some questions."

"Joey," she said. "Come here."

The nine-year-old, the scared one, peeled away from the group. "Go inside and play." He marched across the lawn. "I hope you know what you're doing," the woman said to me.

"Ma'am?"

"You're probably scaring the daylights out of these children." It was then that I first noticed the edge in her voice, the quaver of emotions.

"I don't think I follow, ma'am," I said, walking over to her.

"This murder," she said; "you'll just scare everyone more by coming around here. Oh, my goodness, are you planning to run their names?"

"Probably just their first names, ma'am," I lied. "No one could figure anything out."

She was shaking her head back and forth, as if trying to

shake loose from some fearful thought. "I can't believe what has happened. We're not freaks, you know. What gives you the right to poke around here, trespassing?"

"Take it easy," I said.

"How can I?" Her voice was raised now and had the stretched quality of fear. "How can anyone after what happened? I could hardly sleep last night after I heard. And then the papers, this morning. There's a fiend loose, I say, a madman. I just don't want him to come back again." Then she turned and looked toward her house and yelled, "Joey! I told you to stay inside!"

I remained busy scribbling in the notebook.

"I'm sorry," the woman said suddenly, her voice gaining a more even tone. "Everyone here is very upset over the Hooks child. Some of the parents were on the phone this morning, trying to organize people to patrol the streets. Nothing came of it, but people are upset. I'm upset."

And then the woman paused. She looked at me and our eyes met. She seemed to be looking for some sort of answer.

I said, "This is probably just a once-in-a-million-type thing, don't you think?"

"Oh," she said. "I know you're probably right. That's what my husband said, too. But I can't help but feel that it shows that we're all, I don't know, open to attack, vulnerable. And that's why I'm afraid. It's like an invasion of invisible enemies. You know that they're out there, but you can't see them to fight them, and that's what makes me so scared. I shouldn't yell at Joey, I know, because he's scared enough and it makes it worse for him to see me and his father so nervous, but how can you fight the feelings you have? And why should you? I'd rather have him safe indoors, if just until this blows over. I mean, this is the suburbs. We don't have this sort of inner-city crime here. Burglaries and robberies, but not this . . ." Her voice trailed off. Then she thought to ask me a question. "You tell me," she said, "you're the professional. You've seen this type of thing before, I bet. What's going to happen; when will the police catch the guy?"

I thought for an instant, torn between reassuring the woman and frightening her more. It was as if I were considering the value of two responses, placed within the context of the story I was going to write.

"I think you're right to be concerned," I said. "But no one can really predict what this type of criminal will do. It's wrong to speculate." I watched as her face grew unsettled.

"You think he might come back." It was only a half-question. Her voice had grown flat with a fear I did not really grasp, that seemed half-acceptance.

I shrugged.

"I guess no one's safe. Really safe, anymore. Oh my God," she said, "that's a terrible, horrible thing."

I nodded my head. I could feel the hot wind pushing on my back, sticking my shirt to my skin.

"Oh, God," she said. "What are we in for?"

Later, in the car, Porter said, "That woman was perfect, wasn't she? The right mixture of pathos and fear, the rational and the irrational. She didn't know if it was more reasonable to panic or keep her head."

"Yes," I said. We discussed her as we drove, both young men slipping easily from what we saw. The car was shut tight, the heat and noise of the streets locked out by the droning air conditioner and the scratch and whine from the radios.

Back in the office, I settled into my desk and dialed the homicide number. After a moment Martinez came to the phone. I heard another extension being picked up and assumed that Wilson had joined in on the conversation. "So," I said, "fill me in. What about the autopsy?"

"Call the medical examiner," the detective said. "It's weird. But this much I can tell you: she was killed with a single shot from a forty-five-caliber automatic, and she wasn't sexually molested. That's pretty much what we expected."

"Well, what's so unusual?"

Martinez hesitated. "Well, hell, I don't see why you can't know. The doctor says she wasn't killed until the early A.M. Probably around four-thirty or five in the morning. He figures it out by the rate of body-temperature loss. It's kind of interesting."

"So why is that important?" I asked.

"Because," Wilson cut in impatiently, "she must have been snatched around ten the night before. Where was she all that time, and if this was an abduction, why not sex? Or a kidnapping that went wrong? She must have been somewhere, and it's going to be a bitch to find out."

"Where was she killed?"

"You already know that," Martinez said. "Right where they found her. It was in your story."

"Christ," said Wilson, "you ought to read what you write."

I'd forgotten. Sometimes I asked questions to which I already knew the answers in order to get time to think up other questions. This wasn't one of those occasions. "What about the murder weapon? I thought a forty-five would blow her head off at that range."

"The bullet was fired at an angle," Martinez said.

"Let me tell you something," Wilson interjected again. "This bastard really knows weapons. You can just sense it."

"Maybe a professional, a kidnapping?" I asked.

"Let's just say we're trying to look at everything." There was silence for a moment. "Listen," Martinez continued, "we're trying to be helpful on this. We expect the same with you. You use your judgment writing this up. But let me tell you, we're going to look under every rock out there. We've got divers working the water hazard at the golf course, looking for the gun, and all the nearby waterways. It's just that we aren't sure yet what kind of crime it was. But something will shake loose, I promise you. It always does. We may not get anywhere, but something will happen."

"Yeah," said Wilson. "Something."

I was unable to reach the medical examiner and left a message for him to call me. I talked briefly with Nolan about the follow-up story; he wanted me to blend the scene on the street with the status of the police investigation. I sat at the desk for a moment, staring at the paper in the typewriter. I always tried to pause before writing, even on the closest deadline, to construct the images in my mind. In quick order I pictured the house shut to the world, the children on the street. I heard their voices and saw their faces as they twisted with questions. Then I envisioned the mother who'd stepped out and added to the sensation of panic, an element of fear and confusion in her voice. I wrote:

The house on Southwest 62nd Street is closed, curtains

> drawn, shutting out the curious; mute testimony to the tragedy that has struck the occupants.
>
> But outside on the sunlit streets of this exclusive residential area there is a new sense, a new mood. In a neighborhood usually filled with the suburban sounds of children playing, there is quiet.
>
> People are afraid.
>
> It is an atmosphere created by the murder early Tuesday of their 16-year-old neighbor, Amy Hooks. As police continue searching for clues in the still undefined crime, this neighborhood has drawn together in fear. . . .

Nolan came over to my typewriter and watched the words as they appeared on the page. I stopped for a moment and he read silently. Then he nodded. "Good, fine. Now work in a few quotes and then the police and the autopsy. Give the people some news, and then return to the scene on the street." He walked away to talk with some of the other reporters working on stories, but I called after him.

"Hey, Nolan! Don't you live out there?"

"No," he said, "I live further out, towards the south in Kendall. Fear doesn't stalk my streets." He laughed. "At least, not yet."

I returned to the story, thought of what Martinez said and looked down at my notes. I thought I would downplay the police inability to get a handle on the crime and emphasize instead that they were looking at several possibilities. I would work in a little speculation about the difficulty in solving the crime; the detectives would like that. It could make the killer relax, which was good, and take a little heat off them with the public. And, I thought, if they do catch the guy, it will make them look just that much better. I pictured the woman outside her house again, the look behind her eyes, the tone of her voice, the combination of fear and abandonment. I wondered how many others there were like her.

I looked back down at the page and my fingers hovered over the keyboard. The descriptions started to flow again, and within seconds I was back in the rhythm of the words and the story.

* * *

Nolan wanted to go out for a drink that evening. I called Christine to tell her I would be late. She was used to this particular type of delay and said little. "I'll be here. I've got a book to read."

"What's that?" I asked.

"Camus. *The Plague*. Some of the doctors were talking today, after the surgery, very upset. One of them started to complain that for all our knowledge and technology we were still as helpless sometimes as back in the fourteenth century, when the plague hit the cities. He said maybe we should go back to folk medicines. . . . Then when I got here I happened to be looking over the bookshelf, and my eyes fell on the book, from school or whenever. . . . You remember the opening? The doctor notices a dead rat on the landing of his apartment building, and then everyone starts to complain about the dead rats, coming out of every hole in the earth and the darkness to die in the sunshine. The city reminds me, the descriptions do, of Miami. And then the people start to die. . . ."

"Why were the doctors so angry?"

"Because when we opened that businessman up, the one I told you about this morning, in the exploratory, it was no good. His whole stomach was falling apart. They kept trying to cut the cancer away, but it was everywhere. It looks black and red and ugly; unmistakable." Her voice began to thicken.

"So," I interrupted. "What happened?"

"He died."

"Oh," I said. "I'm sorry."

"It's OK," she replied. "I cried earlier, after they told the family. I don't know why. Just sometimes it affects me and I want to be alone, so I went into one of the storage rooms and I wept a bit. I'm all right now."

When I hung up the phone I felt a moment of guilt, a kind of relief that I didn't have to comfort her. Sometimes, I thought, she allows herself to feel too much. But then I shouldn't criticize her for her feelings, they were probably what made her a good nurse; that, plus efficiency. I looked up and saw Nolan by the door, waving his arm and pantomiming drinking motions. I grabbed my jacket and hurried to join him.

The bar was on Biscayne Boulevard, a place frequented both by reporters and by pressmen, who occupied different sides of the bar in an uneasy truce. The pressmen were union, the reporters were not. It seemed that conversation ended there. In the darkness inside the bar, we all seemed to melt into the atmosphere.

Nolan and I took our drinks to a booth and sat on red vinyl-covered seats. In a moment Porter joined us. "So what do you two think?" Nolan asked. "Where does all this go from here? What other stories can you guys work up?"

Porter shrugged. "Maybe they'll make an arrest."

"I managed to get the scene piece and the photos out front again today," Nolan said. "But after tomorrow's paper, unless we come up with something, the story will go back to the local pages. Then inside, and finally out of the paper altogether. What do you think?"

I considered for an instant. "Maybe that's best," I said. I looked at Porter, but he was drinking beer. "I know that this has people bent out of shape, but then, so do most crimes, especially when they hit close to home. Maybe this is one of those that's bound to fade, unless they make an arrest."

"Maybe," Nolan said. "I'm reluctant just to drop it. Why don't you try tomorrow to talk with some doctors, see if we can't come up with some kind of seat-of-the-pants profile of the killer?"

"I don't know. The cops seemed to be backing off on the psycho angle today. You know, that family has to be pretty well off. Maybe this is some botched kidnapping."

"I don't buy that," Porter said. "I could be wrong, but it just doesn't ring true for me. If that were the case, the kidnappers could just have easily dumped her out in the Everglades, and it would be weeks before she was ever found. Maybe even never, and then she would be considered another teenage runaway. Gone but not forgotten. And they probably would still try to extort the money from the family, especially if they'd already killed the girl. They would have nothing to lose."

"That's a good point," Nolan said. "Let's go back to the psycho angle. It'll keep the story moving for another day, even if it lands off the front pages. Really push Martinez and Wilson for information. I know those guys. They're bound to be holding something back."

Porter got up to get three more beers. I turned and watched him maneuver in the darkness, my ears filled with the soft sounds of people drinking; the cash register ringing. I heard laughter break out from one part of the bar.

"How are things?" Nolan asked.

"OK," I replied. "Oh, Christine said hello."

"Say hello for me to her. I mean, what with the funeral and all, your family—that whole bit." Nolan was leaning over the table, his eyes fixed on my own, as if he could somehow read behind them.

"It's good of you to be concerned," I said. "But there's really nothing to say."

"All right," he said. "I'll drop it. I just wanted to be sure. You seemed distracted when you came back, and I didn't expect to see you in so soon."

"I got a good story, didn't I?"

"That's right, a good story. A good story can go a long way to solving external ills and bumps." He laughed. "There are a lot of things that a good story can help cure."

"A lot of pains," I said. I lifted my glass.

Porter had returned and was settling into his seat. "To pains," he said.

"To all the ills in the world which keep us in business," I said.

"To the good story," Nolan added.

And then we all drank and laughed.

Late that night in bed, Christine said, "I forgot to tell you, your father called. He said he'd call again tomorrow, maybe at your office. I told him you had a big story, but to go ahead and try." We were naked in the darkness. I had the windows open and I could hear the night bugs humming. In the distance a siren wailed; it seemed far away, unconnected with the immediate night that covered us. Christine had shed the blanket, and in the faint moonlight I could see her breasts and her pubic hair. I reached over and stroked her and she turned toward me. "I never know what to say when he calls," she said. "He seems pleasant enough, but intimidating." I felt her hand on my shoulder and her breath as she spoke.

"That's just his lawyer's mannerisms," I said. "I sometimes

think he stepped full-grown, like Athena, from his own father's forehead. Spouting dicta and legalisms, precedents and torts, all the stuff of his life." She laughed. "He's always been a lawyer, sounded like one, acted like one. That's just the way it is in our house. There is the Law, and then there is the law. He defines both." I pictured my father, tall, thickly built, working Sundays in his study, yellow legal pads filled with his scrawled notes, books split open around him like so many bodies on a battlefield. I could picture him that way, unchanged, for years, as if I were looking at him through a child's eyes, an adolescent's eyes and finally an adult's eyes.

"Why didn't you go to law school?" she asked.

"That was for my brother. We never talked about it, of course, but he was the eldest and it was just assumed. He did very well, too."

"What did he want you to become?"

"Nothing."

"I don't understand."

"There is only the law," I replied. "After that, there is nothing. I wasn't a lawyer, my brother was. So there was nothing left, of any importance. Oh, I don't mean to say that he doesn't have a great deal of respect for the profession of journalism. It's just not the law."

"It must be sad for you." Her hand was kneading the muscles on my shoulder, and I turned toward her.

"I don't think about it anymore," I lied.

And then she pulled me toward her, running her fingers down my back, scratching. I made a noise and she said: "See how much nurses know about the body?"

Christine was gone in the morning. An early call, she wrote on the bathroom mirror in lipstick. I took my time, making coffee, some toast and bacon, reading the paper. The Red Sox had taken a twin bill from the Yankees the night before; Luis Tiant pitching a complete game, twisting and spinning and kicking in his own style, finally delivering to the plate unexpectedly sharp curves and dipping fastballs. I thought how much I liked to watch the pitchers, how the game revolved around the rhythm they created.

In my typewriter at the office were messages that the

medical examiner had tried to reach me and that my father had called. I shuffled both aside for the moment. I picked up the phone and called the psychiatrist. He was an eminent man, a transplanted New Yorker who spent much of his time working with the criminal courts. He had served as an expert for me on other stories, and I thought he would enjoy the chance to speculate about this crime. He was with a patient, though, so I left a message with his service; then I sat back and read the *Post* before settling into the day's routine of calls and collecting information. They had already knocked the story back to an inside page, I noticed, and they had little new information. After being beaten initially, it looked as if they were throwing in the towel on the story. All the better, I thought.

As I was reading, the telephone on my desk rang.

I remember that I did not reach out and pick it right up, as I ordinarily did. I suppose I thought it was my father calling. Instead, I looked up first at the clock and noted that it was ten in the morning; then my eyes fastened on the hurricane map in the rear of the room. I could just make out how the storm's path had changed—it was heading now for Central America—and I could see the photo of the tree bent over in the wind. I picked up the ringing phone: "Anderson. *Journal*."

"Hello," said a voice on the other end. "I just wanted to say that I've been reading your stories about the murder. I've really enjoyed them."

"Thank you," I replied. The caller sounded young, unhurried. I fixed a mental picture of someone under thirty—close to my own age.

"I mean," he continued, "they seem very accurate. And descriptive."

"Well, thanks again," I said. Time to cut it off. "Listen, I appreciate what you're saying, but I'm kind of busy right now . . ."

He interrupted my exit line, breaking in on the final words. His voice remained very even, calm, to the point.

"You see," he said, "I have a special interest in your stories." The tone was friendly, unafraid. Usually, congratulatory calls are either angry or somewhat embarrassed. This caller seemed persistent, yet relaxed.

"What's that?" I asked. "Why is this so special to you?"

There was a single second's hesitation.

"Because," the caller said, "I'm the guy who killed her."

CHAPTER FOUR

I FELT hot suddenly, as if the growing heat outside had abruptly burst through the walls of the building. My right hand shot out, reaching for paper and pencil to take notes, a reflex action.

Silence filled the line between us.

I used the moments to gather my confusion and scrawl across a sheet of gray notepaper the words: *I have a special interest in the stories because I'm the guy who killed her.*

I looked down at the words on the page, aware all the time of the quiet that dominated the telephone line. For a moment I was not sure that the voice was still there, almost as if it had never been there. I tried to force myself to think of questions to ask; thinking back, it seems odd that in those moments when my mind was racing with possibilities, the essentials of my profession seemed to slip away. It took me seconds before I could muster the simplest, most obvious questions, and it was moments more before my skepticism returned. Throughout the long pause he waited patiently.

"Who is this?" I finally asked.

He laughed, a short burst. "You don't really expect me to answer that question, do you?"

"No," I said. "But you can give me some idea who I'm talking with."

"All right," he said. "That seems fair." Then he hesitated for an instant, as if ordering his response. "I am an ordinary man. I come from ordinary people, heartland stock. I can blend in anywhere, everywhere; I am comfortable with anyone. I fit into the surroundings like a chameleon on a leaf of grass. I am your average American."

"Average Americans," I said, "don't kill teenage girls."

"Don't they?" he replied.

And then we were silent again for a few moments.

"Tell me why you did it?" I asked.

"That's a difficult question to answer." He paused again, as if reviewing his thoughts before speaking. This was a cautious man. The voice was deep, yet clear. I imagined him in a room staring up at blank walls, doors shut tightly, windows closed against the heat, an air conditioner pushing and straining to keep the room cool. The caller had an unhurried style of talking, precise, literate. It was a voice that seemed unresponsive to stress, to emotion, as if the call and the thoughts that went behind it were among the normal, rather than the abnormal. I had my first feeling that I was dealing with an exceptional malevolence.

"I anticipated the question before calling you," he resumed. "I have spent some time speculating how I would respond. I could tell you that I did the murder for kicks, for thrills, and that would have an element of truth in it. I could say that it was the first act in an experiment in terror, a modern Leopold and Loeb, and that too would be truthful in part. I could tell you that she was randomly picked and randomly executed, and again I would be speaking the truth, but you will still lack the totality, the whole picture. I could go on to say that she was a victim of revenge, a personal vendetta, and other elements of the picture would fall into focus.

"It would be true, too, but you would be confused by the

fact that I did not know her before that night, that I do not know her family and that I have nothing against them. Indeed, I was touched by your portrayal of their grief and my heart goes out to them; I have nothing but compassion for all victims. So you might think that she was killed as a symbol, and I might confirm that, and again we would have disclosed another fact that was accurate.

"Look at it this way: I could say any of these things, and they would all be signposts along the road to the truth. But you won't understand until you follow the whole path. And if I were to tell you now, here at the beginning, all of what I have in mind, then the excitement of discovery would disappear. You might doubt my sincerity also; after all, we hardly know each other, and I thought that the purpose of this phone call would be to find out something about you as much as it would be to let you know that I exist, and that I'm out here, and that this has all just begun."

I got down snatches of his speech. He sounded like a man detached from the reality of what he'd done. It was as if he were discussing a book or politics, not a murder. I became skeptical then.

"Why should I believe you?" I said. "Can you prove that you're really the killer?"

"Proof?"

"Yes," I said. "And I don't understand why you've called me. Or why you killed her, if indeed you did."

"Ah." Again the short bursting laugh, a cold sound without humor. "The reporter as skeptic. I expected as much."

"Right," I said. "Proof. How do I know that you're not some whacked-out crank? It happens all the time. People confess to crimes they didn't commit every day. Misguided guilt. Madness."

He interrupted. "I am not mad. Let's get that straight from the very beginning." For the first time a real edge of anger had slipped into his voice. The words seemed more sharply cut off. "Got that?"

I taunted him. "Let's say I'm keeping an open mind for a while." Again there was a silence.

"All right," he said. His tone had changed abruptly. Now the anger was gone and in its place was the sound of resignation.

"I anticipated this response also. Let's say for the moment that I provided a means for you to know that I am who I am, who I say I am. We'll get to that in a moment. But as for my reasons for calling you and my reasons for the execution, they will become apparent shortly. You've already been given some of the reasons, but in abstract form. You'll just have to start to piece it all together. After all, that's what the *Journal* pays you for, to piece things together."

"How do I know you're telling the truth?" I asked. I was impatient; I didn't want to waste my time with a freak, no matter how well spoken he was. If he was who he said he was, then I would be onto a huge story, a terrific story. If he wasn't, well, I had wasted time before; this would be nothing new.

"All right," he said. "I assume your connections to the police investigators are pretty good. This clue is really simple. Ask them what she had in her right rear pocket. Got it?"

"Right rear pocket. What is it, some kind of note?"

"Just ask them. I'll call you back in thirty minutes, and then we can talk some more. You be at your phone. Someone else picks it up, and I'm gone."

"Right rear pocket," I repeated.

"Just be at your phone. Thirty minutes."

"All right."

"Good," he replied, "now we're getting somewhere."

And then the line went dead. I heard a small click as he hung up the receiver, and for a moment I kept the phone to my ear, listening to the absence of sound. I replaced the receiver in slow motion, thinking of the girl's right rear pocket. I had a flash of memory, picturing in my mind's eye the sun and the green of the underbrush. I could see all the men circled around the body in the bushes. I could see the girl as she lay, and I focused, like a camera lens, on her legs and back. I remembered the jeans, faded to a light blue, and I tried in my mind to see the back pockets. I looked up then and stared across the newsroom. There were reporters working everywhere, and I became aware of the noise of typewriters and telephones, of voices moving loudly across the room. I looked at Nolan, working at the city desk amid papers and the gray lights of the video screens. I thought for a moment of telling him about the conversation, then as quickly discarded the idea. I knew I could answer the most important question by calling Martinez and Wilson. I picked up my phone again, thinking that I was somehow attached to the telephone, that it was an umbilical linking me to the world. I dialed the homicide number quickly from memory and waited for the detectives to get on the line. I heard Martinez' voice first, and I knew that Wilson was listening in also.

"Nothing new to report," Martinez said, anticipating my first question. "Wish we had something to tell you, like that we had the guy now and we were getting a signed statement. But no such luck. I think it's going to take us some time. Maybe you should go to work on another story." He laughed. I decided to dispense with the preliminaries.

"You've been holding out on me," I said.

"What the hell does that mean?" Wilson responded, voice rising.

"What have we been holding back?" It was Martinez, laughter gone.

"Right rear pocket," I said.

They were quiet. I could picture them looking across the desk at each other. Again Martinez spoke first. I could hear the sudden injection of control into his voice, the studied calm that was part of his armor and his weaponry: "What about the right rear pocket?"

"You tell me," I said, my voice rising, too.

"Who told you about that?" It was Wilson, straining harder to control his tone. He was stretched tighter, more urgent.

"I'll answer your questions after you guys answer mine. Now, tell me about the pocket."

"Shit," Martinez said.

"Who told you?" Wilson went on. "Listen, dammit, we're talking about a murder. First-fucking-degree murder and you're jacking us around. Now! Who told you about it!"

"What was in the pocket?" I persisted. I tried to keep my voice even, hard.

"Shit," Martinez said again. "Listen, Anderson, this isn't some game; we're not just screwing around over here. You talk to us, we'll talk to you. Always been that way, you know it. . . ."

Wilson interrupted again, shouting. "Who told you? How do you know?"

"Tell me what was in it first," I said. "That's the deal."

"Wait a second," Martinez said. The line went silent, and I guessed that he had clapped his hand over the mouthpiece while he was talking to Wilson. In a moment their voices returned. "All right," he said, "we'll trade some information. But not for publication, OK?"

"I can't say that until I know what it is."

"Shit," Wilson said, "what's the matter with you? You want to cause a panic? What's the matter? Christ!"

I said nothing in response. I could feel nervous sweat running down from my armpits underneath my shirt. I hugged my arms close to my body while the line went silent again and the two detectives talked together. When they came back on, I could hear Wilson's breathing in the background, short angry gasps for breath.

"All right," Martinez began. "As you know, it's routine to search the area where any body was found and the body itself. That means the clothing and any orifices. Usually, that happens during the autopsy, back at the morgue. You want controlled circumstances, you know, with a photographer, so that any evidence can be preserved for trial. When we got the kid's body back the other day, we started to do just that. While the doc was starting to cut into her, we began going through the clothing. We found in her right rear pocket what we suspect is a message, although the meaning isn't clear."

"What kind of message?" I was excited now, my nervousness dissipated. I was already beginning to think of the killer's return call.

"It was simple," Martinez said. He hesitated. "We're not really sure what it means, although on the surface it looks bad."

"What is it?" My voice could hardly contain my excitement.

"It was written on a small white sheet of paper," Martinez continued irritatingly. "The type you can buy in any five-and-dime store. It was folded several times into a small square. There were two words written on the center of the paper in pencil. The words were written in block handwriting, with each character penciled in thickly several times. Makes any kind of comparison sample in the future virtually useless."

"Jesus, Martinez, what did it say?"

He hesitated again. I could tell he was thinking like a cop, precise, detailed, his mind probably picturing the note, the moment that they first felt the wad in the girl's back pocket, the careful extraction with tweezers and the gentle way they pried it open, all under the harsh fluorescent lights of the morgue.

"It said *Number One*. That's all."

"It was written out?"

"Right. Now, for Christ's sake don't go jumping to any conclusions. Especially the most obvious one."

"Jesus," I said. What a story.

"Listen," Martinez continued. I could picture him, his tall frame bent over a desk, telephone stuck to his ear. The lights in the homicide office were bright, outlining the bleak rows of desks and file cabinets, casting shadows across the faces in the photographs pinned to the wall. He, like his partner and so many of the detectives, was a dapper man. I wondered if he was sweating, too. "Look," he went on, "in a murder like this, that message could mean almost anything, if indeed it is a message at all. The lab still has the paper and is running it through tests, and it doesn't mean that there's necessarily going to be a number two or anything else. I mean, it could just as easily have been placed there to distract us as warn us. Got that?"

"Did you show it to the family? I mean . . ."

"You think we're stupid?" It was Wilson, interrupting. "Of course we did. And of course they didn't recognize it or have any idea where she could have picked it up. Neither do her friends, for that matter. So it seems that it could have come from only one person, the killer. And we sure as hell didn't tell anyone about it, so now, dammit, how come you know about it!"

I thought then of lying, though I knew that the detectives would guess soon enough where I'd found out. And I knew that a lie like that would cost me Martinez and Wilson's co-operation. I added the equation swiftly in my mind, thinking all the time that I had to keep the detectives on my side, while at the same time not let on too much. If this story was going to be as big as I thought, I would need them. "I got a call," I said.

"What kind of call?" Wilson asked.

"On the telephone. A voice. I didn't recognize it."

"What did he say? Exactly."

"Well," I lied, "I didn't take notes." I looked down at the sheets of paper covered with my scratches of sentences.

"What did he say?" Wilson was impatient.

"He said: 'I'm the guy who killed her.' Then he told me to ask about the right rear pocket. He said he'd been reading the stories in the paper. Then he hung up after rambling a bit. I didn't know what to make of it, so I called you guys."

"Will he call again?" Wilson's tone was angry again.

"I don't know," I lied. A small lie, I thought. I didn't really know for sure, even if the killer had promised.

"Christ," Wilson said. "Any ideas . . ."

"No," I replied cutting him off. "No idea who, or where he was calling from. His voice was soft, unpressed. He might have been changing it so that I wouldn't be able to recognize it again. Sorry, I know that doesn't help you guys much."

"What else?" It was Martinez, and I could hear Wilson muttering obscenities.

"I told you, he rambled a bit. I'm still trying to make sense of it. That's all."

"Try harder," Martinez said. "Whatever, anything; it might help us."

"I know that," I said. "I'll try to reconstruct it in my mind and call you back."

"Jesus Christ," Wilson said. I hung up the phone and looked up at the wall clock. I had only a few minutes before the thirty-minute deadline passed and the killer called me back. I jumped from my desk and ran across the newsroom to the city desk. Nolan looked up at me from the sheets of copy paper that he was reading. For a moment I stared at the mass of printed words in front of him, and it was as if I couldn't read.

"Nolan," I said, "the killer called me." The excitement in my voice spilled out swiftly, unchecked. I saw a few other heads, other reporters, editors, look up and stare. I was grinning, and my hands were waving back and forth as if by movement I could hurry the thoughts through my mind and out my mouth. "He's going to call back in just a few minutes. I've got to get a tape recorder, one of those with the tapping attachments that fit onto the earpiece. I've got to get what this guy says down on tape without him knowing about it." I watched as Nolan's face slipped from surprise to excitement. Then he cracked into a smile.

"You certain it's the killer?"

"Yes," I replied. I told him I would explain later—the deadline was approaching. He nodded, and within seconds we had run to the library and were unlocking a recorder from a storage cabinet. We quick-marched back across the newsroom as I assembled the device. I plugged it together and slipped the attachment onto the phone as I tried to answer Nolan's questions. He still wanted to be certain it was the killer who had called me. I told him about the first conversation and showed him the scribbled notes that I'd managed to write down. He looked them over carefully, then raised his eyebrows quizzically. He wanted to know about the rear pocket. I told him what the killer had said, then told him about the shouting match with the two detectives. I kept staring up at the clock nervously, waiting for the minute hand to come to rest on the thirty-minute mark. I heard Nolan mutter more to himself than to me, "Number One," and shake his head.

The minute hand struck the mark.

The second hand swept by. Ten seconds. Twenty seconds.

The phone rang.

I looked at Nolan and he nodded. I pressed down on the recording device and picked up the receiver. "Anderson," I said softly.

"Hello," said the killer. "I suppose you were scared I wouldn't call back."

"I wasn't certain," I said.

He laughed. "Certainty, I have learned, is something that is in short supply in the world."

There was a moment of hesitation.

"Did you talk with the police?" he asked.

"Yes, right rear pocket."

"And?"

"Why don't you tell me what they told me?"

"Ah! Caution," he said. Again I heard the short laugh blow

coldly over the telephone line. It was an awful sound, I thought. "All right," he continued. "I can't say that I blame you for wanting to be sure. What the police found in the rear right-hand side pocket of the young lady's trousers was a folded white sheet of paper. Notepaper, ordinary. On the sheet were written two words. The words were *Number One*. Correct?"

"That's what they said," I replied.

"Convinced now?"

"Yes."

"Good. Now we can continue."

"What is it you want?" I asked.

The voice seemed to catch; I heard a burst of air and breath. Again it seemed as if he were ordering his response. I looked over at Nolan, but he was staring at the recorder and I realized he couldn't hear the killer, anyway.

"I need you," he said. "I need the paper."

"I don't get it," I said.

"People have to understand."

"Understand what?"

"Why there was a number one. Why there will be a number two. Why there will be a number three. Four. Five. Six. You can count for yourself."

I grabbed a piece of notepaper and wrote: *He plans more killings*. I slipped the sheet to Nolan, who looked at it for an instant. Then he took the pencil and wrote *Why*? and underlined it three times.

"Tell me why?" I asked.

He paused again, considering, but after a moment began speaking in a low, even tone.

"When I was a small child we lived in Ohio, in farm country, a land I remember as filled with greens and browns. I can still picture the fields in the springtime, acres upon acres of deep brown earth turned up into furrows by the huge tractors and plows. Sometimes I would stop on my way home from school and watch the farmers astride the machines, driving in endless lines up and down the fields, every so often turning in their chairs, swiveling to see behind them, as if they could read the future in the tracks that they made.

"It was a sensual time then, during the planting; the trees were breaking into leaves, and the wintertime gray and black seemed lost in the growth. The air was warm and I watched, waiting for the planting to be finished. I can recall the distant rumbling sound that the machinery made throughout the day as it crisscrossed the fields.

"We lived in a small house, adjacent to a large farm. The school bus would drop me off a mile or so away from the house and I would walk.

"There were just the three of us, my mother, my father and myself. He was a teacher and he taught in the school where I went, but he taught the older children. There were just two bedrooms in the house, and I can remember at night listening to the sound of the bathwater being drawn and trying to imagine whether it was my mother or my father who was slipping into the wet. He beat me most of the time, punishments for both the real and the imagined. He was a small man, wiry, muscled. He didn't look much like a teacher, though; more like one of the hands on the farms. In the evenings he would sit by the lamp in the living room and read. Almost always great works: Tolstoy, Dostoevski, Dickens, Melville. Occasionally he would stop and read a passage out loud.

"He was always stopping then, searching me out with his eyes, making me repeat the words that I'd heard, testing my memory. When he punished me, it would be in the kitchen. He had a board, an antique paddling board, left over from some earlier time in the school district. My mother would stand aside, often stirring the dinner slowly, watching, saying nothing. He would make me recite my transgression: staying out late, running around with banned friends, mischief, whatever; the stuff of small boys.

"He would always tell me in advance how many times he was going to hit me. I came to recognize what my own tolerances were, what I could attempt, regardless of the capture and punishment. He would lay the blows on evenly, never adding or subtracting from the pressure and the strength that he used. He would have me count out the number as it fell. He was a hard man. His voice still has the same edge of disapproval in it constantly. When the blows fell I would look out the window in the kitchen, and I remember I was able to see up into a tree, through the branches and out into the sky. The punishment seemed to hurt less those times when I could let my imagination run away into the blue, gray, black, whatever color sky there was.

"The punishments were harshest in the summer that I turned thirteen, the number of blows rising, the tone of his voice harder, the force against my backside. I grew that summer, too much for him; I was taller suddenly and wider suddenly, and my voice went deeper like his own. Once he raised his paddle and looked down at me and our eyes met and I said, 'No more,' and he put the paddle down and nodded. I think then that he was afraid of me for the first time. I looked toward my mother then, and she smiled and said, 'Good,' in her small voice.

"I went to bed that night and listened for the sound of the bathwater being drawn, but it didn't come, and I slept fitfully in the night until just before dawn when I awakened, frightened by a nightmare. I remember it to this day: it was of my father paddling me, growing larger with each stroke, stronger and harder. In the dream I felt an absorbing fear, overwhelming, as if I couldn't breathe, that the new blows were knocking all the air from my lungs and that I was being smothered while my mother watched benignly.

"That afternoon I dawdled on the way home from a friend's house and I was late to dinner. My father yelled and swore and complained, but didn't reach for the paddle again. I remember a feeling of loss, as if I'd counted on the punishment, and oddly enough I felt regret then that I wasn't beaten. Over the next few days I tried a few other things, simple maneuvers that would ordinarily prompt his response.

"None succeeded. It was as if I left my childhood behind in those moments. I never slept well after that. Nights would run darkness into nightmare; I would wake up sweating, the sheets wet and cold around me. Sometimes I would lie awake, listening to the night, eyes wide open. Each sound seemed to me like a scream, no matter how small the noise was. Even when we moved to the city the restlessness remained. Sometimes I felt I could hear my body growing at night, and I tried to shut it away. I tried to shut away all the nightmares.

"Later they liked to put me in the perimeter listening post through the darkest time of the night, because the lieutenant knew I could hardly sleep anyway and knew my ears were sensitive to the smallest sound, and so, in a way, it helped to give the others more rest because they knew I would hear anything, sappers, whatever, coming through the wire.

"I would lie, feet out, back to the dirt wall of the hole, head cocked back, listening. My eyes would focus up into the sky most of the time; I remember that it seemed strange then that it looked the same there in that country as it did so many thousands of miles and years away in Ohio. Every so often I would slowly roll over in the foxhole the same way I would in my bed at home and stare out into the darkness of the perimeter. For some, the jungle always seemed to move, alive at night. But to me it was restful. I wasn't afraid. The others all were, but in a way I welcomed it and I would stroke the muzzle on my rifle sometimes while I waited.

"It was peaceful for me then. I suppose that was the essential paradox: that what terrified the others gave me a sense of rest. That's what I feel now. I remember later, during the real horror, that I thought I was part of a play, a dramatic exercise. That the horror my eyes saw wasn't real. I won't talk about that yet. But it was then that I decided something had to be done. You ask why? I'll tell you what this is. It's theater. It's a play. It's a chance for everyone, here in this well-lighted city, to know a little of nighttime emptiness. Of nightmare.

"You want to know who I am? I'll tell you. I am the worst thing in the world."

He stopped then.

His breathing was even, his tone had barely changed. For a moment I tried to think of a reply, a question; then I gave up, listening to the tape machine instead. I could see the capstans moving in slow circles.

"Why did you call?" I asked.

"You," he said, voice still clear, even, harsh, "are the method of expression. My words, your stories. The community's newspaper. Welcome"—he paused—"to the parameters of nightmare."

CHAPTER FIVE

AGAIN, silence dominated the line. I could hear his breathing. Before I could say anything, he started speaking.

"Imagine for a moment what it was like for the first victim; the depth of feelings and emotions she went through during her last hours. We talked, she and I. At one point we cried together. There were moments when I wanted the night never to end.

"At the beginning I suppose she was just scared, but she kept herself together remarkably. She wanted to know where I was taking her, and she gasped when I said to a place where we could be alone. I guessed she thought she would be raped, so I told her that I wasn't going to touch her, that all I wanted to do was talk with her some. That seemed to calm her down and she grew quiet. She wanted me to loosen the bonds on her wrists, but I told her that I couldn't; that it was a matter of trust; later I might. She wanted to know if she was being kidnapped, and I said yes, because it was partially true and I thought she would remain quieter if she had some tangible idea to grasp hold of. I remember driving through the night; I had the windows up, but there was no air conditioning in the car and I could feel the heat at night, a darker kind of heat, seep through the windows. It seemed as if the streetlights were throwing grotesque shapes across the road; I had to fight the temptation to swerve to miss them.

"She asked me when we stopped—a lonely place, not far from the water so that she could smell the sea and it would comfort her—why I was doing this, and I told her that it was just the first act in what would be a longer-running show. She was having trouble understanding me; I suppose I kept speaking abstractly, and it was hard for her to grasp the ideas through the panic. But she remained persistent, asking questions, making me define my terms. My God, she was beautiful, lying against the side of the car, her face bent toward the sound of my voice, trying to hear, trying to feel the ocean.

"I felt a kind of inexorable calm then, and with it came tears. I wondered if all the victims would be so collected, so together. I began to cry, and she joined me, I think trying to comfort me some. I talked about the war, and she told me about her brother who was overseas at about the same time I was. I talked about growing up, and we had a laugh about that because she said that no matter how good your parents are, they still hassle you, and I had to agree. She was a remarkable young woman. For a moment I considered aborting my plan.

"But once started, I couldn't stop."

Again, the voice was quiet, as if he were playing over in his mind the memories of that night. As he talked I thought of all the spots in the county, dark spots near the water, where he could have gone. There were thousands.

"You see, the same feelings that made me want to hold off, to stop myself from killing her, were the same ones that made me realize that she was the perfect selection. I had to shake my head at the thought; I remember I walked down to the edge of the water and ran my hand through it. It was warm, like a midnight bath. I could hear the waves breaking slowly on the shore, a light chop on the bay. The lights of the city and the lights from the sky, the stars and moon, reflected across the water. I went back and sat across from her, watching her in the darkness. I think she couldn't see me in the shadows; she struggled some against the rope.

"I waited until it was close to morning. In Nam that was always the time everyone was scared the most; we were daylight people. A false security, I suppose, but we couldn't wait for the morning. The Aussies—they had some troops there, did you know that? Anyway, they always had a complete alert right before dawn. Everybody up; weapons out, pointed, searching the perimeter. Ready.

"And they never got their asses overrun."

He hesitated, remembering.

"We drove through the last darkness to the golf course. I think that confused her some, because she wanted to know why we were there. I think she had grown scared again about being raped, and I reassured her. When we got into the rough, there where they found her body, I put her down on her knees and turned her toward the east. I said to her then that I wanted her to watch the sun come up; it would be like an explosion of light, I told her. When she was ready, I moved the forty-five into position, so that the shot would deflect up and away; I didn't want to destroy the look on her face. I said to her, 'See, the sun is rising,' and as she craned forward to look, I fired.

"She didn't feel a thing. I'm positive. And she wasn't scared at the end."

He paused. "She might even have forgiven me, if she knew."

There was another silence.

"When I read your story, about the family and who she was, I realized that I'd been extraordinarily lucky; that my first was the perfect choice by luck."

I started to speak. "How did you . . ."

"Easily," he said. "She was walking and I stopped, pretending to ask for directions. It was an easy matter to get into the car, get her tied up."

My mind went blank. The words and images that had risen during the killer's speech disappeared into the silence on the telephone line. Finally, after a few seconds, I said, "I still don't understand."

"It would be difficult for anyone." He thought again. "There was a moment, a series of moments, when I was overseas. A time when reason suddenly was suspended. A time when I participated in a savagery. I can't describe it yet.

"But for years it has been there, festering in my mind, cancerous. One thinks of the ordinary emotions: guilt, anxiety, grief, whatever. None seemed to remove the images. They were like my nightmares as a child, only they were real and they dominated my waking time.

"And then this spring, the sensual time, I watched on the television as the world over there exploded. All I could see were the terrified kicking legs of men and women clutching to the metal runners of the choppers, trying to be dragged to safety. I watched the abandonment of the country. I thought then of all the horrors. I saw on the screen the faces, the fears.

"No one knows, I thought. No one really understands. It's just a television show, a newspaper headline, a grainy gray photograph in the paper.

"And I decided then that I would bring my own horror to them, all the complaisant ones, the ones who sent me there uselessly.

"And that's what this is all about."

He laughed.

"Enough, I'll be in touch after Number Two."

"Wait," I said.

But he had hung up.

I replaced the telephone receiver and shut off the tape recorder. Most of the reporters in the newsroom had turned and were watching me. I pushed back in my chair, my mind a jumble of the killer's words.

Nolan eyed the tape and pointed to a conference room in the rear of the newsroom; no one said anything as we walked to the private office. For an instant my eyes caught the view through the newsroom windows. The sun was filling the city with tropical heat, the light reflecting off the whitewashed downtown buildings, blinding, like so many small explosions. Behind me, the tempo and pace of the office returned, voices, telephones jangling, typewriters clattering.

I was aware of trying to hold my emotions in check. As Nolan listened, I paced in the back of the small office, already writing the words of the next day's story. Nolan let his chin sink down on his chest, scrunching up tighter within himself, drawing himself deeper into the words, letting the killer's voice melt into his memory. Occasionally he took a pencil and wrote a note on a pad in front of him. I was barely aware of the spoken words; they hardly penetrated my growing excitement. I champed, waiting for Nolan to respond. When the tape ended, there was a click, the sound of the telephone being hung up, followed by a humming noise.

"This," said Nolan, unfolding in his chair, "is a hell of a thing."

He stretched, putting his hands behind his head, leaning back, balancing on the hind legs of his chair. He let his breath out slowly, the sound of his exhalation filling the small room. He lit a cigarette, then let the smoke rise, his eyes following the pattern.

"No easy decisions here," he said.

I burst out, "Decision! What decision? Jesus Christ! We've got to get this story into the paper. I mean, you heard that guy. Jesus, what a story he told. This town will rock when it reads what he had to say."

"That's just it," Nolan said.

"Jesus, how can we hold it?"

"I didn't say hold it." An edge of irritation slipped into his voice. "Just try to curb your enthusiasm for an instant."

"I . . ." but I cut myself off.

We waited for an instant. I watched his smoke climb to the ceiling; then I took a deep breath, trying to scour the excitement from my voice. "I just think we ought to go ahead and write the story."

"We're going to write it," Nolan said. "That's not the real issue. It's how."

"Nolan," I said, "it's just a good story."

"Right. A good story. That's going to change things." He paused for another long second to think. Finally he shook his head. "Well, I guess here we go. I wish it were as simple as you seem to think it is."

But before I could reply, the telephone in the office rang. I started, but Nolan swept it out of the cradle and slapped it to the side of his head. He listened for a moment, then turned to me. "Your friends Martinez and Wilson are here. They also have what's-his-name, the chief of detectives with them." Then into the phone he said, "Stall them. Tell them we're in conference and it'll be about ten, fifteen minutes before we can talk with them. Give them coffee, make them comfortable. Assure them we'll be there, but they're just going to have to wait a bit. Be friendly."

Then he turned back to me. "Things are moving fast now. I'm taking the tape in for the higher-ups to hear. You start work on the rough of a story. Type up the notes from the first conversation. I'm going to have a secretary transcribe this so there'll be no debate. My guess is we'll have to give it up."

I had already finished putting the first conversation down on paper when I saw two detectives and another stocky man walk across the back of the newsroom. Martinez gave a little wave; he was third in the line. They disappeared into the managing editor's office. A few seconds later I was summoned by an assistant city editor and told to join them.

The managing editor and Nolan met me outside the office. I could see the detectives sitting uncomfortably on the thick leather couch of the office. "Come on," Nolan said, and we followed the managing editor into an adjacent room. He shut the door. He was a short man, with thick gray hair pushed severely back from his forehead. His glasses rode down on the end of his nose, and when he was excited he peered over the tops, as if to tell you that he was putting you in a totally different perspective. Among the reporters he had a legendary reputation as a hard man on a story and a soft man with his personnel. He usually stopped by and congratulated reporters on stories; brief, almost embarrassing moments that ultimately meant a great deal to the staff.

He looked at me now and smiled. "If I may be permitted a slight cliché," he said, "it seems we have a tiger by the tail." Nolan laughed and I smiled with him. "All right," the managing editor said, "a couple of quick questions: Did you ever promise the killer that you would try to protect his identity; that you wouldn't talk with the police; that your conversation with him was in any way off the record, or confidential in any manner?"

"No," I said.

The editor looked relieved. "There's one hurdle. Did you

ever promise him that you would write the story, or quote him in any particular way?"

"No. I hardly got a word in edgewise. I had the feeling he was making a calculated guess that we wouldn't pass up the exclusive character of the conversation."

"Well," the editor smiled, "he's right on that score."

Nolan spoke. "Do you have any problem working with the police?"

I looked at him. "Yeah," I said. "But it depends on the extent."

Nolan nodded. "So do I," he added.

The managing editor shook his head. "We need more time to make some decisions. But here's one that I'm going to make right now. We will turn over a copy of the tape under the proviso that it is not released in any way to any competitors. As for ourselves, we're going to write the story." He turned to me. "We need these cops, right?"

"They're running the show," I said. "If the killer does go on, we could get frozen out."

"Right," he said. "That's what I thought. All right." He clapped his hands together like a grade-school teacher. It was a mark of excitement. "Let's go do some horse-trading. Don't open your mouth without checking with me first."

I nodded to the two detectives and shook hands with the chief. There was a moment of strained silence, and then the managing editor asked precisely what it was they wanted.

"We want to take a statement from your man here," the chief said. "We also want to see all his notes. We'd like your cooperation; this is a murder investigation, after all, and I don't really see the need for us to go to the state attorney to get a subpoena."

The managing editor stretched and nodded his head. "I don't really see that need, either. But we can't turn over notes. Before you get angry, let me say this. We managed to tape-record a second conversation with the killer. We will provide a copy of that tape for your investigation, but only if you agree to certain conditions."

"What conditions?"

"Just exclusivity," the managing editor said. "No release to other papers or television. Also, the ongoing agreement that we get first crack at developments in the case. After all, the killer may call again."

For a moment the policeman was quiet. "I think I can agree to that," he said. He smiled.

"Good," said the managing editor. He got up.

"We are, after all, members of the same community."

"True enough," said the managing editor.

"So's the killer," said Martinez.

As I walked back to my desk, Wilson stopped me. He placed his hand on my shoulder, and I stared at it until he removed it. "Listen," he said, keeping his voice low, "we still need to know about the first conversation. This is a two-way street, you know."

"All right," I said. "I'll call you when I put my recollections down." I stalled. The act of giving information, *my* information, disturbed me, felt alien. The basic hypocrisy of newspaper work: we collect but don't give.

It was not long before one of the secretaries came up to my desk with a typed transcription of the tape. I looked down at the written words, trying to recall the tone of the voice that spoke them. Again, my mind tried to picture the circumstances of the call: the room, the telephone, probably the gun on the table in front of him.

Nolan walked by. "You keep that thing attached to the telephone at all times. Keep fresh tape in it."

For a moment I wondered how far it would all go, how far I could take the story; then I shook my head, looked down at the notes and the transcription, placed a sheet of paper in the typewriter and started to build the story:

> The killer of 16-year-old Amy Hooks has called the Miami *Journal* and pledged that the southwest section teenager's death is but the first in a series of murders he plans to commit.
>
> "Welcome," the killer said by telephone, "to the parameters of nightmare."

After writing the top, the story flowed easily. I relied mainly on the killer's words, laying out some of his own reasoning.

I held back on the long story of his past he told, referring to it obliquely. I regretted the quotations describing the girl's final moments. I had a fleeting image of the mother and father standing in their living room, surrounded by pictures of their dead child. I wondered how they would react when they saw the story. I closed my eyes for an instant, thinking of this new pain I would bring; then, just as swiftly, the idea left me and I was back working with the killer's phrases and thoughts.

Nolan read carefully through the blocks of prose and quotation. The computer terminal made small electronic noises as he rolled the story on the screen before him. "Jesus," he said.

"What?"

"Look at this, the way he talks. His descriptions, his structure, his thoughts. No broken phrases. No hesitations. You ever know anybody who talked like that?"

"So he's smart," I said. "What does that mean?"

"I don't know," Nolan said, turning to me. "Just be careful, Malcolm, huh?"

"Sure," I said thinking: careful of what?

Nolan turned back to the screen. "I wonder," he said, "how this will all end."

CHAPTER SIX

THE story exploded across the top of the front page the following morning: KILLER PREDICTS "NIGHTMARE"; PROMISES MORE MURDERS.

My telephone rang at 5:30 A.M., just as the main edition of the paper, with the story bannered just under the masthead, slipped from the presses to the delivery trucks. The first call was a reporter from the Miami office of the Associated Press. Christine tried to tell him that I was still asleep, but I rolled from bed and answered his questions groggily. I'd dreamed fitfully that night, a recurring picture of myself chasing after my uncle through the city. The shapes and shadows had been twisted and bizarre, as if seen through a curved mirror, Dali-esque.

As I talked, Christine sat drinking coffee and reading the paper spread out on the table before her, the early-morning light gently filling the room. Every few seconds she turned and looked at me, shaking her head. I fielded questions as best as possible; everyone wanted a copy of the tape. When the AP was finished, I had perhaps two minutes before the phone rang again. It was a reporter from the Miami *Post*, working on their first-edition story. He sounded angry that the killer had contacted me instead of himself. I got rid of him as quickly as I could. Another minute or two passed and the United Press International called. They had the same questions, the same requests. I kept telling them that the story was in the paper; that they could crib whatever they wanted from its pages. They wanted, instead, to interview me. UPI even wanted a photograph. I told them no. Then I took the phone off the hook. For a moment it made a half-beep, half-scream electronic sound; then it settled into quiet. Christine looked up from the paper and said, "You know, this is just the beginning."

I put my hands on her shoulders and kneaded her muscles for a moment, then slipped my hands under her bathrobe and cupped her breasts. I felt the nipples tighten under my touch, but she shrugged and pulled my hands away. "I'm sorry," she said, "but reading this stuff just turns me off. I don't see how you can take it. I think I would have wanted to scream." Then she thought for a moment. "Did you ask the guy to give himself up?"

"No." The thought took me by surprise. "It didn't occur to me. His voice seemed too steady; he seemed too prepared, too involved in what he was doing and saying. He didn't sound like a man ready to give himself up."

"Other times people have. To reporters, I mean. They surrender to the reporters because they think the police will hurt them. Or like at Attica, where they wanted observers."

"Didn't do them any good, did it?"

"No," she said, "but you know what I mean."

"I wish it had occurred to me. I wonder what his reaction would have been."

"What do you think?"

"I think he would have laughed."

Christine thought for a moment. She stood up then and walked to the window. The light framed her face suddenly, illuminating her cheekbones, making her eyes gleam. I tried to think of something to say to her to break the mood into which she was slipping. She shouldn't feel depressed; this was becoming the biggest story of my life. I was excited; I think that inwardly I didn't want the killer caught or surrendering—not yet, I thought. Her mind must have been on the same channel because she asked, "Do you think he'll do it? I mean, go on with more killings?"

"I don't see why not," I said.

She turned. "Do you want him to?"

I shrugged.

"It's a better story if he does, isn't it?"

"Yes," I answered. No denying that.

"A prizewinner?" she asked.

"Probably."

"Maybe even the biggie, huh? The Pulitzer. Have you thought of that?"

"Oh, come on," I said, "don't get carried away." But I had.

She laughed, but not in humor. I guessed she knew I was lying.

"Doesn't that kind of bother you?"

I shrugged again, but her questions continued, rapid-fire. "Has it occurred to you that this creep may need the attention that he's getting in the newspapers and on the television? That without it he would feel ordinary and forgotten? That the attention he gets spurs him on to bigger and greater things?"

"Yes," I said, "those thoughts have struck me. But what am I supposed to do, ignore it? And who knows, he might continue with the killings regardless of what I write or anybody writes."

"Doesn't it concern you?" she pressed.

"Not yet."

I stopped in the *Journal* parking lot. The sky was a virulent pale blue—it seemed to have no end, no ceiling. Andrew Porter spotted me there and came up quickly. "So they make the celebrities come to work, too," he said, laughing.

"What do you mean?"

"You'll see soon enough."

Outside the main entrance to the plant there were at least a half-dozen television camera crews. "See you later," he said. "Remember, keep smiling." Then he seemed to melt away through the crowd surrounding me. I kept pushing myself toward the doors, the day's heat abruptly doubled by the lights from the cameras. The first of the half-dozen microphones were shoved in front of me and I stopped. The questions came in waves, staccato, choppy. I barely answered one before another shot my way.

"What did he sound like?"

"Did he predict when the killings would begin?"

"Why do you think he called you?"

"Do you think he's crazy?"

"Do you think he'll call again?"

"Why is he doing this?"

Finally I held up my hand. "I'm sorry," I said, "but I put just about everything I know in the story that ran in the *Journal* today. I can't add anything. I have no idea what's going to happen next." And then I excused myself and headed into the building. A few more reporters were waiting by the doors, and they laughed and made the same joke Porter had made. I grinned. "Hey, it's just my way of getting a raise." I felt warm inside from the attention. I realized I had enjoyed the questions, enjoyed the focus of the cameras.

I passed the managing editor on the way to my desk. "Terrific story," he said. "Keep at it." He clapped me on the back.

Nolan smiled at me from across the room. He called out, "Good job. Now you'll probably want a television contract," and the rest of the office laughed with him.

I sat at my desk, glancing over the first edition of the *Post*. The killer's call was the lead story in their paper also, and I saw the byline of the reporter who'd called me earlier. Right after the killer's quotes, lifted from my story, were several quotes of my own. "Anderson, 27, a *Journal* reporter for three years, said he was surprised by the killer's calm and singleness of purpose. 'He seemed to be very confident and forthright,' the reporter said today." I read the story over and over.

The phone rang.

For a moment everything seemed to stop.

I put the paper down, feeling my heart accelerate. I punched the recording device and picked up the receiver. "Anderson. *Journal*."

And just as quickly, the excitement left me. I felt my system slow down and adjust. The call was from the main switchboard operator. “Mr. Anderson,” she said as I shut off the recorder, “what am I do to with all the calls?”

“What calls?”

“I have messages for you from reporters at a dozen newspapers,” she said. “And besides that, people keep calling in on the main switchboard and asking for you. I think they're people who want to talk about the story today.” She had a pinched, tinny voice.

For the next hour I answered questions and fielded irate calls. It was almost noon when the ringing slacked off. Each time I hit the record button, each time I had to erase the tape. I took notes, though. I planned to write a a small story about the callers and their angers.

Nolan wanted a big reaction story. He sent several other reporters out to get man-in-the-street quotes. He put others on the phones, calling prominent Miamians for comment. I was to put the whole thing together; that was a decision, he said, made at the top. The stories were to carry my byline. It was for the killer's benefit, Nolan explained, to keep him thinking that I was the one connected to the story. He was afraid the killer would call the other paper or the wires or, worse yet, the television stations. “We've got to keep this guy wrapped up,” Nolan said.

The day seemed to be streaking by.

I had scheduled an interview that afternoon with the psychiatrist. For a moment I felt uneasy about leaving the office. The thought went through my head that the killer might try to call in and get scared off when I didn't answer. After reflection, I realized there was nothing I could do to prevent it.

I tried to call Martinez and Wilson, but they were in the field.

I looked at the telephone on the desk. It was black, a simple, ordinary telephone. I had taken a ballpoint pen and inked in some of the numbers. It had a crack on one side, residue from an angry conversation with a politician when I'd slammed the phone down and it had tumbled to the floor. It seemed to me to be a live thing, breathing on the desk top, waiting as patiently as myself. I stared at it hard before leaving, as if I could tell it not to ring while I was out.

* * *

The psychiatrist was eating a sandwich when I walked into his office. "You don't mind, do you?" he asked, gesturing. "This is my lunch break." I shook my head and looked around. His office was located in a medical building in the downtown area, a place of skyscrapers and glass that reflected the sun. From his desk I noticed he could see out over the bay toward Miami Beach and the ocean beyond.

It was a small office; a wall filled with diplomas, a portrait in pen and ink of Freud tucked in one corner. Another wall contained a bookshelf and several rows of books. There was a Picasso print, *The Musicians*, from the artist's first experiments with cubism. It hung on the wall above a leather couch. I took a seat across from the doctor's desk. He saw me looking around and asked, "Does it make you nervous?" I laughed and didn't answer. He said, "People have the strangest ideas of what a psychiatrist's office looks like. Oh, they know there will be a couch somewhere, but as to the rest..." His voice trailed off. "I had a feeling you would be coming in," he said. "You want to know about your caller, I suppose?"

"Right," I replied.

"Difficult," he said. "Very difficult." He continued to eat the sandwich. He was a short man with wire-rimmed glasses and wore a dark blue suit which I imagined was very warm when he walked outside. His gray hair, still thick, was pushed back from his forehead, giving his face a childlike look, open and unassuming. We'd met before, usually in the courthouse where he did expert evaluations for several of the judges.

"Would it help to hear the tape?" I asked.

He smiled. "What do you think?"

I produced the tape and a cassette recorder. The doctor slipped a pen from his pocket and placed a fresh sheet of paper in front of him. He nodded, and I started the machine.

"Certainty, I have learned, is something that is in short supply in the world..." the killer's voice said. In the room it sounded small but forceful; my own, I thought, sounded hesitant.

For the next few minutes all I could hear was the killer's voice mingling with the scratching sound the doctor's pen made across the white paper. He took notes throughout the tape, only occasionally lifting his eyes toward me; only once did his eyebrows shoot up in surprise at something the killer said. I turned and watched a big tanker slipping through the transparent blue of the bay; the colors of the Picasso on the wall were much the same as the water's. The tanker was heading toward the port of Miami, riding high in the water, empty. In the background the killer's voice went on, a cold passion attached to his words. When the tape ended, I looked back at the psychiatrist. He expelled air then, as if he'd been holding his breath throughout. It evoked an odd memory of driving with my father and brother in the family car. My father once told me that if you could hold your breath through the length of a tunnel you would get a wish granted. By whom he never specified—I supposed there was some tunnel genie or whatever—but for years, I remember, I automatically took a deep breath as the darkness jumped around the car and held it in, straining in silence as long as possible. Around New York it was particularly difficult; the Lincoln and Holland tunnels proved too long for my small lungs. There was always a moment of defeat with each sudden rush of breath from my body.

"Well," the psychiatrist said hesitantly, "this is a problem."

"How so?"

"Let me say something off the record." I nodded. "I know that two of my colleagues have already been called in by the police to hear the tape. I talked with them late last night, knowing you were coming in today. You know, I have a habit of disagreeing with my peers." He laughed and offered a small smile. "But not on this occasion."

"What's the verdict?" I said. "I mean, what can you tell me about this guy? I don't want to sound overly simplistic, but my gut instincts tell me this man is serious. And he's dangerous."

"Well," the doctor started again, "you're right on both those scores." He looked down at his notes. "I'm afraid I can't come up with an instant label that you can take to your readers. There's really not enough to go on, though the tape is remarkable.

"We often bandy about the terms psychotic, psychopath, sociopath. The last two mean just about the same thing. We talk about sexual deviations, aberrant behavior, paranoia, schizophrenia, all the twenty-five-cent terms with which you and many lay people are familiar. This killer seems to have several dominant features which would lend themselves to a number of psychiatric interpretations. I didn't see much paranoia in an obvious sense, but that doesn't mean it isn't there. In fact, some of the conversation that he relates about the victim would lend itself to that type of label. He is obviously very disturbed, near psychopathia. . . ."

The doctor hesitated again and looked at me, his eyes intense. "Let's try to cut through some of the gobbledygook, OK?"

I nodded.

"The psychiatric profession, as a rule, does not try to predict the relative dangerousness of various disorders. However, my belief is that this killer is highly dangerous. It is also my belief that he will kill again. And again." He looked at his notes.

"'People have to understand . . .'" the doctor read. "Well, it seems that he is expressing the need for recognition; that it is important to be justified in what he recognizes is behavior outside the norm.

"The killer then goes into a long description of growing up under stress on a farm in Ohio. That he is in contact with the history of abuse is unusual; usually, that would be blockaded by the mind. He speaks of the act of being punished irrationally. I suspect that the abuse he suffered was greater than he described and more arbitrarily applied than he lets on. Then there is a crisis: he challenges the father for control, and the crisis is exacerbated by the fact that he is successful. In that one moment his world was turned upside down; whatever feelings he had about guilt, punishment, right and wrong, they would be turned around, the apple cart upset. Note that he recalls the way his father made him call out the number of the blows; we see that repeated now in his numbering of the victim. She is Number One.

"I wonder about the mother, too. She seems to be a nonperson; she just watches throughout. I doubt that was actually the case; I think she probably engaged in some aberrant behavior herself, but it's impossible to really speculate.

"Then there is a long period of restlessness; of lying awake at night. Psychiatrically, that time corresponds to the time of his sexual awakening. But by this point he is so confused—I wonder if he really heard the sounds of the bathwater being drawn, or if it was some other night sound involving his parents? But again, I'm only guessing.

"And then there is this remarkable section. Here, see how I wrote this down: '. . . I tried to shut away all the nightmares. Later they liked to put me in the perimeter listening post . . .' You see, he segues from his childhood into the war. Vietnam. So there's the possibility of a type of battle fatigue. During the fifties, after Korea, I helped with some studies. We discovered psychotic symptoms arising under some types of stress and fatigue. OK. Generally, they were short-lived and dissipated when the subject was removed from the stress situation, but some of my friends who have worked with Vietnam veterans report the same syndrome, only to a greater extent; the symptoms do not reduce as swiftly. There are many theories about why that is, having to do with the nature of the war, the counterinsurgency, the savagery, the lack of defined enemies, the lack of a front, the shapelessness of it all, especially when combined with the contradictions of the war. I mean, here were men out in the field, performing routine tasks of terrible consequences: they feared they would step on a land mine, lose their legs or their genitals; that they would be lost in an alien environment; that they would suddenly find themselves in the midst of a firefight, unable to see or to fight the enemy, surrounded by death. And then, moments later, they would be on some hilltop and a helicopter would land, and everyone would drink a cold Coke or have a Schlitz, just as if they were back home, almost. This is incredibly disorienting. In effect, they did not know where they were.

"And in the midst of all this, our man finds peace. '. . . But to me it was restful . . .' Extraordinary.

"But," the doctor continued—"and this is a big but—something happens. He talks for a second about 'the real horror.' And he sees it as some type of a play, a way of describing what we call a dissociative reaction, as if he were outside looking in at himself. And then he says he won't talk about that yet.

"That, I suppose, is the key. If I were a gambling man, I would put money on the guess that the course of murders he has seemingly embarked on is in some way, in his mind—

which is a tangle, let me tell you—a duplication. He is, in effect, reenacting personal experience. It's like those sniper attacks you read about every once in a while: unconscious duplications of moments of war. The mind becomes confused; peace at home becomes the war. And the soldier reacts.

"I suspect that when you find out what the 'horror' was, then we will have come a big step toward understanding the course of the killer's mind. But a word of caution. His mind can still make adjustments. He still appreciates symbolism. It won't necessarily be a one-to-one trade-off."

The doctor swiveled in his chair and stood up abruptly. He walked to the picture window and looked out over the bay. His hands came up in a reflex motion and he pushed his hair back from his forehead. Still looking out, he began to speak again.

"I remember when I was in the Army, attached to the psychiatric facility outside of Vacaville in California. We must have treated thousands of cases of fatigue induced by battle conditions, residue from the Korean War. My God, it doesn't seem like a quarter century ago. Many of the cases remain fresh in my mind; they were like parts on an assembly line, put together with speed and efficiency, but with some inherent defect within, unseen, so that they couldn't function properly.

"On one ward we had to keep the lights burning throughout the night because the men had grown so afraid of the dark; strong men, who had seen terrible conditions and survived, but they suddenly couldn't control their fears when the lights went out. There was one case I remember particularly well; whether it's apropos of the present situation, I'm not certain. You be the judge.

"He came in shortly after the Chinese invasion, when the Chinese swarmed across the Yalu River and whole divisions were cut off before the command was centralized and the lines reformed. You probably don't remember it, and certainly few people in the States had any real idea of the suddenness and the frightening quality of that attack. Some of the racism that we found in the Vietnam War was prevalent then; the fear derived from propaganda about the yellow peril and the insensitive, animal-like Oriental. Much was left over from the Second World War, the jingoism and the anti-Oriental feeling.

Then to be overrun by the hordes. Well, suffice it to say that it was a difficult time.

"Anyway, the disorientation and the subsequent reassignation of emotions that I see in the killer remind me of one of the cases I had then. He was a young man, blond, high cheekbones, the type of face that we would say then reflected breeding. And he was indeed the product of a good household: the mother was a New York socialite; the father, what one would call a captain of industry. The son had grown up, an only child, in New York; he had known private schools and chauffeurs and piano lessons and the opera. At the age of seventeen he entered Harvard, where he majored in history with a minor in political science. He was destined for the foreign service, at least at first; possibly law school, possibly a career in politics. A golden boy—right?—tremendous potential. He told me at length about the conversation he'd had with his father, discussing the future, and the thought they'd both had that a military experience would be helpful, even imperative; another step along the road to success.

"A short time after his graduation, the young man received a commission in the Army. He volunteered for the Korean action after much the same discussion with his family, the thought of a little combat, perhaps a medal or two, prominent in their minds. The father had done his service during peacetime, between the wars. The danger of the situation that the young man was entering was shrouded from them all. I cannot stress this naiveté enough; it surfaced again and again in our conversations. And so, when the Chinese poured over the Yalu, this young man was commanding a rifle company near the front lines.

"They were cut off, encircled by a superior force and slaughtered. The young man was with a platoon that was literally blown apart by heavy automatic-weapons fire. He was the only one of the group alive when the shooting hit a lull. He realized then that the Chinese were walking through the carnage, systematically checking the bodies.

"He decided, in a split second, that he would have to fake his own death to avoid being captured or shot. He dipped his fingers into the blood of his own men and soaked parts of his tunic with it. He told me that he worked swiftly, single-mindedly, really unaware of what he was doing. Finally, when his wounds appeared authentic, he pulled two bodies over him, so that he was beneath them. His last act was to take a handful of blood and brain matter from one body and smear it across his own forehead and scalp.

"Then he shut his eyes and waited, afraid that the cold air would illuminate his breath, feeling the dead weight of the men above him.

"There was a break in his perceptions, you see; he was limited to what he could hear and smell; he was like a blind man, every sound a note of terror, unfamiliar, frightening. He told me of hearing voices approach and of hearing the shuffling of feet. At one point he heard English spoken and guttural responses in Chinese. Then he heard shots, each one seemingly closer. He could feel the cold from the ground creeping into him like death itself, buried already under the bodies of his soldiers, the men he'd commanded, known just a few short hours earlier. His limbs were frozen with fear, he said, and each instant he expected to be plummeted into darkness more profound than that behind his squeezed eyelids. Finally he heard footsteps close by, and he could feel the weight of the bodies shifting on top of him, as if someone were poking them. Then the footsteps moved away, and he remained stiff and motionless for hours, waiting for another sound. He said it took more courage than he thought he had to open his eyes and look about him. He was alone, save for the dead.

"He was cut off for two days behind the lines. He wandered about, hiding mostly in scrub brush and trees. At night he sheltered himself with branches as best he could against the snow. He didn't eat; he couldn't find anything. On the third day he met up with a group of men who'd also been cut off but who had managed to establish radio contact. In another few hours he was safe back behind our own lines. He made a statement to superiors describing in detail the events, the loss of the men. He was able to name almost all, I believe, by memory. He was examined by a doctor, found to be in good health despite the ordeal and shortly thereafter was sent back to the States. The Army gave him the Distinguished Service Medal.

"His first night home he awoke screaming that he couldn't

breathe, as if some weight were crushing his lungs. He began to shiver uncontrollably, regardless of the amount of heat in the room or how many blankets were piled onto his body. He became terrified of closing his eyes, afraid that he would not be able to open them. And then one moment, a few days after, sitting at the table with his mother and father and a few guests, enjoying a meal, he squeezed his eyes shut for a minute, perhaps two, and when he opened them he could not see. He was blind. Shortly thereafter he was sent to me at Vacaville.

"Hysteric reaction was the official diagnosis. A simple conversion from the event: blindness equals death. And so he brought it upon himself, compensating for surviving that which had killed all his friends.

"We talked. We worked. He did not hide the events, but even when he came to appreciate the psychiatric basis for his loss of vision, it didn't return. I wondered then what deeper punishment he was doling out to himself.

"He was given a leave home, arrived at the New York apartment, kissed his mother, shook hands with his father, said he wanted to change—prophetic words, those—and walked into his bedroom. He put down the cane, found a revolver that he'd owned for years and shot himself. Right in the same spot that he'd smeared himself with gore from his companions."

The doctor looked across at me. Outside, I could see the sun reflecting across the bay, and a flight of gulls swung by. They wheeled over the water.

"So," the doctor continued, "don't underestimate the strength of this kind of combination: battle-induced trauma on top of a more elemental mental illness."

"Prognosis?"

"Very bad. Bad for the victims, bad for the killer. And one other thing . . ."

"What's that?"

"They can't catch him."

"What do you mean?"

"This type of killer is the single most difficult to catch. The police uniformly have the greatest of problems with psychotic murderers. Look at Jack the Ripper. He was never caught. You see, they defy the usual methods of detection because of the essential irrationality of their acts. Their motive lies within their minds, not in greed or anger or any of the usual emotions that policemen are familiar with and which prompt homicides."

I stared at the doctor. He turned and gazed out over the bay. "Unless the killer makes a mistake, the same type that an ordinary criminal might make, he'll be almost impossible to capture. There is the chance that someone will spot him, or that some neighbor will detect his behavior, or that his weapon can be traced. That might lead to an arrest. But don't count on it.

"You see, one of the essential paradoxes of this type of killer and the situation he creates is that while he gains a satisfaction by taunting the police, by daring the community to find him—that's the underlying force behind the phone call to you—at the same time he wants unconsciously to be stopped. However, his conscious mind is one that deals in finite detail. He will think of almost everything to avoid capture. You tell me," the doctor said, "how the police can work with that?"

"I don't know," I said. "Do you suppose he'll slip up on the phone?"

"Maybe. Maybe not." A buzzer went off under the psychiatrist's desk. He bent down, flipped a switch and looked back at me. "A patient," he said. I collected the tape recorder. He walked me to the door. "You know," he said, "I surely hope I'm wrong. And don't assume that everything I've said is gospel. This is a severely disturbed individual; he is capable of almost anything. This may sound terrible, but suicide is a possibility. A person such as the one on the tape has a great deal of self-hatred. 'I am,' he said, 'the worst thing in the world.' We'll just have to see."

"Thanks for your help."

"It was my pleasure," he said. As he shut the door I caught a final glimpse of the blue of the bay through the window.

Late that afternoon I began to put together the reaction story; other reporters dropped notes on my desk, usually typed quotations that came from officials or street people. Many seemed skeptical, almost challenging. It was as if people were going to make the killer put up or shut up, a kind of macabre dare. I blended the views of the psychiatrist into the reactions of the other people.

"This freak doesn't scare me. . . ." a teenager, outside a playground.

"I think it's just some guy trying to get attention. I doubt that he'll do what he says. . . ." a businessman stopped on the street.

"I trust the police will get this man quickly. . . ." a housewife in the suburbs.

"All patrolmen have been briefed and will be on the lookout for unusual behavior. All unnecessary leaves have been canceled. Extra patrols will be added to certain high-risk areas. . . ." a local police chief.

I tried to visualize the faces that went with the words, the expressions of anger or fear. I felt as if I were being squeezed between the words of the killer and the words of the community. I continued to type quickly, pausing only occasionally to grab a quote from the pages of notes. I did not look up until I heard the shouts from the rear of the newsroom. When I turned in the chair I saw a young man, I guessed in his early twenties, trying to free himself from the grip of one of the *Journal* security guards.

Everyone in the office turned to look at the disturbance, and the shouts suddenly became clear, like a picture that has slipped into focus. The young man was yelling: "I want to talk to the guy who wrote this. Now, dammit, leave me alone!" The security guard gripped his arm, trying to hold him back. I knew that it was me he wanted to talk with. Out of the corner of my eye I saw Andrew Porter step from the photo lab to look at the commotion. I managed to catch his attention with my hands, making a motion as if mimicking taking a photo. He nodded and reappeared a moment later with his camera. He swiveled the lens and began to snap off shots as unobtrusively as possible. By this time the young man had calmed somewhat and was arguing with the security guard who still held him by the arm. I stepped across the room, and the two men turned and looked at me. "I believe it's me you want to talk to," I said as softly as possible.

The young man's eyes were rimmed with red. He had blond hair that fell over his ears, shaggy, unkempt. He looked at me for a moment and seemed to collapse, as if a string inside him had been sliced. His arms dropped to his sides and he ceased struggling. The security guard, a muscled Cuban with a thick mustache, looked at me. I nodded and he released the young man. He stayed close by, though, his muscles tensed.

"Are you Anderson?" the young man asked.

I nodded.

"I'm her brother," he said.

"That's what I thought," I replied.

"Why?"

I shrugged. "Let's sit down." The young man bent his head, and I motioned to an empty desk. He slid into the chair like a man exhausted.

"I don't understand," he started. "I've read this over and over, and I still don't understand. What did she do? Why should she have to pay for some—oh, I don't know—for something that happened somewhere else? I mean, why blame her?"

"You must have loved her very much," I said.

He stared at me. "She was very . . ." And then he hesitated. I could see him thinking, looking for words. "I don't know. She was . . . she had a specialness about her. We all loved her. She was the baby in the family." His eyes filled again.

"What can I tell you?" I asked.

"I don't know why I came," he said. "I guess that for a moment I thought you and he were the same. You know, you were the link; he called you, and I guess I thought that I should come down and talk to you as if you were him." He paused. "That doesn't make much sense, does it? I mean, I see now . . ." And he looked about the newsroom at the reporters and editors. "Will he call again?"

"I think so," I replied. "It's hard to tell."

"I wish I could get just five minutes alone with the guy. I don't care how much training he got, in the Army or wherever. I don't care what kind of a killer they turned him into. I promise I'd handle him! I'd just want one chance. Listen." He looked at me. His voice had begun to pick up momentum, excitement. "I'm going to write down my address. You give it to the killer, OK? If he really wants to start a string of murders, well, why doesn't he try to start with me, huh? Then we'll see who comes out on top." The young man grabbed a piece of notepaper from the desk and a pencil and started to write furiously. "Give this to him," he said, handing me the paper.

I looked down at the address. It was the family's home in the southern section of the city. "All right," I said. I was lying.

The young man sat back in his chair, deflating again. "Just five minutes," he said. He looked at me. "You tell me why. You've talked with this guy. You tell me why."

I shook my head. "He's crazy. Crazy people do crazy things. What can I say?" I shrugged my shoulders in an exaggerated fashion. Again, I knew I was lying.

"I don't care if he is sick," the young man said. "I want him dead. Just like he killed my sister."

"I don't blame you."

He wiped his eyes, rubbing his palms into the sockets hard for a long moment. "It just doesn't seem fair. How could God do this? She never hurt anything in her life. She even went to a peace march when she was just ten years old. Can you believe that? She was marching along, skipping to keep up with the marchers, singing, 'Peace now! No more war!' in her little girl's voice. She came home in tears because the policemen were so nasty. Can you believe that? Nasty, that's the word she used. And they were, that's exactly what they were. She wasn't afraid of anything. I bet she wasn't even afraid at the end."

"You're probably right."

The young man looked around. "I'm keeping you from your story," he said. "I suppose there's going to be another story?"

"Yes," I said. "People's reactions. It'll be in the papers tomorrow."

"Well," he said, standing up, "when that bastard calls you, you tell him that Jerry Hooks wants a piece of him. You make it a real challenge; tell him I'm waiting." He made a fist and waved it in the air between us. "I'll kill him with my bare hands."

"I'll tell him," I said. Maybe, I thought, maybe not.

"OK," the young man said. He looked over at the security guard. "I apologize." The guard nodded, stone-faced. "I'm sorry," he said, turning back to me. "To have disturbed you like this, I mean. I guess this whole thing has made me a little crazy." He stuck out his hand and I shook it. "I don't blame you," he said.

And then he left, accompanied by the guard.

Nolan walked up then. "Intense," he said. I agreed. He looked at me. "Write it. Word for word. Make that the lead of the reaction piece."

I nodded my head. "OK."

"Terrific stuff," Nolan said. "Jesus, that poor kid must be really bent out of shape by this. Poor sucker." He looked at me again. "Capture it all: the look on his face, the way he wrote out that address. Get it all down. Phenomenal."

I went back to my desk. But before I started writing I played over and over again the young man's final words. They stared at me from the page of my mind like an accusation.

And then I shook my head hard, as if to shake the image loose, and began to reconstruct the conversation. Minus the last words.

Christine was waiting for me when I arrived home. The evening sky had been a virulent purple-violet. The last light of the day illuminated huge thunderheads rising up to the west of the city above the Everglades. "I saw you on the television," she said. "The national news. Cronkite and Brinkley and Chancellor, too. So did your father. He called just a few minutes ago." She put her arms around my neck. "I'm not sure whether to be proud or scared. I suppose a little of both."

I went to the kitchen and opened a bottle of beer. She poured herself a glass of wine, and we sat and talked. She liked to run her fingers through her hair, pushing it back and up, as if to clear it from her ears. The beer was cold and seemed to spread through me, cooling. I loosened my tie and sat back, raising my glass. "Here's to you," I said. She clicked my glass with her own. "So," I said, "tell me about your day."

"It was an ordinary day. We had a child. No, not a child, a boy in that rough time when his voice won't stay low or high. You remember the time that just as soon as you get a crush on a girl a pimple breaks out in the center of your forehead." She grinned and I laughed.

"And?"

"Oh, it was both sad and happy at the same time. I worry sometimes that I let myself get too affected by all the patients who come into the ward. You know, the administrator wanted to know if I'd shift to the terminal ward, to deal with those cases. Hope is all they have. Sometimes not even that. I refused. At least in my ward, the people have a chance. Slim to mediocre, but a chance."

"The boy?"

"He had a big growth on his ankle. You can't tell, you know, before you get inside what it will be like. I mean, the X rays show you it's there, and they give you an idea of the size and everything, but it's not until you really see it, open to the air, in the theater under those bright lights that you really appreciate it. It has an ugliness, a malevolence all its own.

"Anyway," she continued, "the boy came in, and the tremendous thing about a kid that age is that they have an immortality about them; you can tell them the worst news in the world, tell them that they have days, hours, just minutes to live, and they still think that it's forever. They have this incredible confidence and trust in their own bodies. They aren't old enough to know the kind of betrayal that the body can perform.

"So the kid spends the night, jumping around the ward. The night nurse told me that even sedated, he was up and talking almost all night. She sat with him for a couple of hours. Baseball, she said; he wanted to talk about the Yankees and the Red Sox. I wish you'd been there. You could have told him a lot.

"Well, in the morning he's prepped and ready, and the orderly wheels him into the operating room, and he looks up at the doctor and says, 'I trust you, but don't get carried away,' and then he laughs and we all join him. I was standing behind his head to try and make certain he wasn't nervous, but the kid was cooler than I. He went out like a light when the Pentothal hit him. I remember when the section from the tumor was cut off for the biopsy I waited, praying that it would be negative.

"This job is turning me into a religious fanatic; I have conversations in my mind all the time, saying, 'Look, God, this is a good kid. Give him a break, will ya?' Anyway, this time it worked. The growth was benign. The pathologist had a big smile when he came back into the theater with the news, and everyone grinned. Doctors look funny, smiling behind a mask; it seems to catch just the shape of the smile.

"But the bad news was that to get the whole thing out we had to break his leg. The surgeon worked for an hour to try and get it out before going with the bone cracker. He was swearing and bitching; he has a boy the same age.

"It was really hard for the kid to understand. When he woke up he seemed so disappointed; all he could talk about was his American Legion ball team and missing the season. He had this confused look on his face because he couldn't understand why everyone was so happy. It was because the tumor was benign and he didn't lose the whole damn leg. All he understood was that he had a broken leg, and he didn't even have a stolen base or a long slide home with the winning run to show for it."

She drained off the last of her glass and poured it full again. She looked across the room to me. "Can you remember what it was like to be that age? I can't picture you."

I thought for a moment. Instead of a picture of myself, I saw a gangly youth on a dusty macadam road, walking in and out of the shadows on a late spring afternoon. I couldn't focus on the killer's face, but I could see a small room and a board and hear the gasping breath of the father as he labored to beat the son's backside bloody.

"Did you play ball?" Christine asked.

"Shortstop," I said. "My brother was a catcher." I remembered a bright sun. Summer. I laughed out loud. "Once we were in a close game, and one of the guys on the other team hit a screamer to my right, between me and third base. They had a guy, the tying run, on third. The kid on third broke for the plate. Two outs, you see, run on anything was the rule. I made this great leap, probably not such a great distance but at that age everything seems bigger and speeded up, and came up with the ball. More likely the ball accidentally jumped into my mitt. Anyway, at that age one's baseball instincts are nearly perfect. It only comes later with coaching that you get screwed up. I scrambled to my feet and whipped the ball to home. I couldn't make a more perfect throw today. It was waist high, with plenty on it. It beat the runner by almost ten feet. And my brother dropped it. I didn't talk to him for a week."

I smiled, but Christine frowned. "That seems cruel," she said.

"Growing up is cruel."

But I thought again of the killer. Not that cruel. The phone rang, and I went and picked it up.

"It's probably your father," Christine said. She went into the kitchen and started to make me a sandwich.

"I saw you on the news," my father said. He laughed. "You looked exasperated at having the tables turned."

"Well, I guess at first."

"This must be something; did the killer call again?"

"Not yet," I said, "but I suspect he will."

"It must be exciting. I wonder if there'll be something in the *Times* in the morning?"

"Well, one of their reporters called me."

"So," he asked, "how do you like this sudden notoriety?"

Several answers ran through my mind. I thought of saying I was unaffected, that I remained the same objective reporter regardless of the story and the attention. Or that it was just another story and I didn't really think it would amount to much. That would be a transparent lie, though. So I told him that it was exciting and that I enjoyed being the focus of attention. "It's not unlike what you go through," I said, "when you argue a high-visibility case. Suddenly you're projected into the center of the courtroom, and your words become the object of the exercise. I suppose there's an element of that here; for the first time, really, I can see what I've written having an effect. The killer said a couple of times that he plans to create a theater; I guess I've become more than a bit player."

"Ah," my father said, "you're enjoying it?"

"To be honest," I replied, "yes."

He thought for a moment. "In a way, it reminds me of a time when I was younger and with that big Wall Street firm; you remember, Clay, Michaels, Black. The firm routinely did pro bono work; usually class-action lawsuits and the like. This was back in the early fifties, the time old Joe McCarthy was grabbing all the headlines. Anyway, we were asked to represent a young man accused of murder, and I was assigned the case. He was an unemployed dockworker, a tough guy, a member of the Communist party. I remember him telling me about his older brother who'd died with the Lincoln Brigade in Spain. He was accused of killing another man in a fight. One punch to the jaw. The trouble was, the other man was the brother of a city cop, and there was some pressure on the prosecutors to bring a big conviction. No deals. I was tossed into the fray; the papers were making a lot of it, especially the tabs. We decided to argue self-defense. I remember my feelings in the courtroom. I was only a little older than you are now. The issues, the trial, the defense, all seemed secondary to the spotlight. It was electrifying, exciting. Like the feeling one gets after being with a beautiful woman." He laughed at the memory.

"What happened?"

"Oh, winners and losers. The jury tossed out the murder charge but came back with a manslaughter conviction."

"And?"

"It was sad." My father's voice changed slightly. "The judge bowed to all the pressure and sent the kid up. He was killed in a fight in the yard at Sing Sing about a year later." He was quiet for a moment. "I'll say one thing; I don't envy the prosecutor on the case or the defense attorney if they capture this guy. But then"—he paused—"I don't suppose they'll catch him."

"Why not?"

"He seems too crazy, too clever. A bad combination. You should exercise caution."

Again, he paused for a moment. "The notoriety is meaningless," he said. "I regretted it afterwards. So will you."

"Maybe," I said. But I wasn't sure. I could picture my father at his desk in his office at home. He would have a martini; there would be law books piled in front of him, sheets of paper covered with his notes and musings. He was a man devoted to the intricacies of the law. Like a surgeon who works with living tissue, that was his approach to statutes and regulations. It was a world I knew only obliquely; I would see the books and see his work; once I tried to read a brief of his. I was small, and I thought that if he wrote it, then surely it must be about himself and that I would be able to see a little better through his reserve. I struggled for days past each page, each citation, each footnote, searching the text for my father. In a way, I thought years later, I found him but didn't realize it. He was the reason I'd become a journalist; I'd slipped through school relying on my writing to sleep through courses. Finally, he said, what have you learned? Not much, I said. You can write, he said. True, I replied. Then, he said, do something that requires you to write a good deal. And a week later he came home from his office having stopped off at the local library and checked out a copy of *Editor and Publisher Yearbook*, which had full listings of papers and news executives throughout the nation.

"One other thing," he said now. "I'm not sure I buy all this Vietnam stuff."

"How so?"

"It just seems too damn convenient. It seems everyone wants to blame everything on that damn war. The economy, recession, inflation. All because of Vietnam. Watergate, the damn president. Vietnam, they say. Now this guy thinks he can waltz around killing people and blaming it on the war. I just can't see it. Your uncle went through hard times in the war. Damn hard times. And he didn't come home and start killing people."

"Except himself." The words were out before I could hold them.

He hesitated. "Yes, that may be true."

I asked then after my mother, my brother and sister, and we chatted a few moments. Then he rang off with the advice, "Don't get too dependent on this guy, and watch your step." I understood what he meant in the second part of the message, but not the first.

That night in bed, Christine tried to apologize for not being responsive. She said the killer's proximity worried her and threw her off her rhythm. Then she slipped her hands onto my chest and began to stroke me slowly, expertly. Finally she reached over and pulled me across her and inside her in the same motion, doing all the work of the lovemaking. Afterwards she slept, but I was restless. I played over in my head the conversations with the psychiatrist, the victim's brother, my father. I went to the window and looked out. Past the trees I could see the street empty of traffic. In the distance I heard a siren, the wail drowning out the buzzing and clicking of the night bugs. The streetlights seemed dim, the light from the moon strong, shedding a pale color over everything. I thought of the city, lit up by the moon, wondered if the killer were awake, too.

I saw a man walk down the street slowly. I watched him, his shape an outline of darkness. He seemed to be looking for an address, and he paused near the front of my building. He looked up, but our eyes did not meet. Then he walked off slowly, still looking. I followed him until he turned the corner and disappeared through the wan yellow glow of a streetlight. I thought of the phone on my desk in the office and wondered when it would ring again.

And then I realized that I wanted the killer to call. I envisioned the string of bannered stories and the camera light in my eyes, microphones at my mouth. I laughed out loud at the novelty of it all.

Call, damn you, I thought.

Do what you have to, but call.

But he didn't.

For three days the telephone remained silent. I wrote two stories, one on the expanded police search, profiling Martinez and Wilson, the leaders. Then another reaction story from the street. Nolan came up on the third day and said: "Christ, I think the killer may have felt the heat and taken the proverbial hike." He looked down at the tape recorder still attached to my phone. "We'll see," he said.

The phone rang and I jumped.

For an instant I waited, letting the bell sound once, twice, then seized it in the midst of the third ring. "Anderson, *Journal*."

There was nothing.

I tensed, checking the tape recorder to make certain it was working properly. I drew in a deep breath and repeated myself. I could hear breathing on the other end. My pencil poised over a sheet of paper.

"Who is it?" I demanded.

And then laughter, high-pitched, giggling.

"Christine!"

"Good guess," she said.

"Goddammit, what're you doing!" I punched off the recorder. "What the hell do you mean by this!"

"Oh," she said, "try to relax just a little bit, OK?"

"Goddammit, Christine, this is serious business." I was furious. My fist was clenched on the desk in front of me, punching the top to underscore my words.

"I know, I know," she said. "I'm sorry. It's just, well, you're so wrapped up in this. I just wanted you to—I don't know—not take it so *seriously*."

"It is serious! Dammit, you've been telling me that for days now."

"I know," she said. "But it's not everything, is it?"

"Well, damn close."

"Don't say that," she said. Her voice had grown subdued. "Oh, Malcolm, it isn't the end of the world. It's just another story. You said that yourself."

"Well, then I was wrong."

"Hypocrite." She wasn't angry. It was more a statement of fact.

I could feel the muscles in my neck and back relax. "I am," I said. "You're right."

"I'm sorry," she said. "I shouldn't have called like that. But it never seems to relent, not even for a moment." There was sadness in each word.

"It's all right," I said.

She rang off then, and I returned to my waiting. I found myself sweating, nervous. The phone rang other times. Each time I would reach out, like a drowning man for a rope. I could barely hide the disappointment in my voice. At home that night Christine watched as I fielded a phone call: one instant my body tensed; the next, frustrated, slamming the receiver down. "I'm glad," she said, "no one is dead."

She put some music on the stereo, country and western. She pulled me to my feet and started to step around me: "Do, si, do," she said. "Step to your right, step to your left. Salute your partner. Wheel to the right, wheel to the left." I stood in the center of the room while she seized my hand and spun around me. "Oh, come on," she pleaded, drawing out her words. "Try to relax. Just a little bit." She stopped and wrapped her arms around me. "Stand by your man," she sang, though the words didn't fit the music. I laughed then, unable to hold back. Her face broke into a wide smile.

"See," she said. "People, look! The eighth wonder of the world! Right here in our living room! The great stone-faced reporter, just the facts, ma'am, just the facts, has actually smiled! Medical history made!" And we laughed together.

But that night, in bed with Christine asleep beside me, I could think of nothing but the killer. I tried to send a mental order: Call, dammit, even to say it's over. I reached out and stroked Christine's back, and she made a small noise in her sleep and shifted position. We are both, I thought, spurned lovers.

On the afternoon of the following day, late, while the sky was turning color and the heat was slowly dissipating, the phone rang again. It was the fourth successive call; two from cranks, one from a politician. I reached out, tired, angry. "Anderson," I said, clicking down on the recorder, keeping my finger on the button to shut it off again immediately.

"Tested your faith, didn't I?" came the voice. The words breathed a chill over the line.

"I didn't think you'd call," I said.

"I told you this was just the beginning."

He was silent for an instant.

"I saw you on the television," he continued. "Good. Really good. I decided it's just you and me now."

"What do you mean?"

"Explanations later. Action first. Like the Army. Shoot first, ask questions later."

"I don't get it," I said.

"You will. Here's an address. Twenty-two ninety-five Nautilus Avenue on the Beach."

"What about it?"

"Well," he said, "you don't have to do anything, really. I suppose the neighbors will get suspicious in a day or so. And then they'll walk right up and knock on the door. They'll probably catch the smell then. It's an extraordinary smell; it has a sweetness to it at the same time it reaches through your body and churns your insides. Once you smell it, you can never forget it. And the really odd thing is that when you smell it, you know exactly what it is without seeing; even if you don't know, you know."

Another hesitation.

"We'll talk again soon," he said. "So long."

And then the phone clicked, and I was left with an emptiness on the line.

CHAPTER SEVEN

THE story turned then, with the discovery of the elderly couple's bodies. Their deaths also altered my own perception of the events of that summer. Much of the excitement and pleasure I had experienced in becoming the focus of so much attention—the object of interviews on television, seeing my own words quoted in the opposition newspaper and on the wires—seemed to slip away in the shadows on a quiet street in an older section of Miami Beach. Before, I suppose I had seen the killer as merely sick. Now his cruelty became apparent.

The death of the old couple had a singular effect upon the community, too; I began to see the first signs of stress and panic. I suppose I was like anyone in Miami; I thought that the killer was going to confine his murders to teenage girls, that at the root of the impulse to kill there was some sexual urge, misshapen, inexplicable. The old couple's death sent a shock through the community, not unlike an earth tremor that shakes the foundations and brings on nausea. It was as if everyone had the same sudden thought: My God, it could be me next.

When the phone rang on my desk the newsroom would quiet down inappropriately. I could feel the attention of the editors and the other reporters swinging over toward me, watching my face for a reaction. I felt increasingly isolated, as if I were alone with the killer.

After the call, I jumped up and paced across the newsroom to Nolan sitting at the city desk. He looked up and saw the mark on my face. "Again?"

"On the Beach," I said. "I guess he's killed again. He gave me an address: Twenty-two ninety-five Nautilus Avenue."

Nolan hesitated. "Get Porter and get going. I'll call Homicide." In a few moments he was speaking with Martinez and Wilson. I heard him tell them to meet me on the corner of Twenty-second and Nautilus. He did not tell them why, but I supposed there was little question in anyone's mind. He turned back toward me, waving his hand. "Go, go, go," he said.

Porter and I drove over the Venetian Causeway, cutting across the bay to the Beach. I looked out of the car windows at the water; a breeze was kicking up small whitecaps on the wavelets. In the middle of the causeway fishermen were casting lines out into the shallow water. I saw one old black woman leaning over the edge, twisting the handle on her spinning reel, the tip of the rod bending and jumping as the fish on the other end pulled against the hook. She was cackling and laughing, and her voice carried through the afternoon heat into the car.

We waited a few minutes for the two detectives to arrive. Porter adjusted his equipment; he had slung two cameras around his neck, one with a flash for indoor work, the other with fast film for outdoors. He asked several questions, trying to find out what I knew about where we were going, trying to envision what we would see, what he would be shooting. "I love the moment before something starts," he said, "the short time after the referee blows his whistle but before the kickoff. It's like when I shot that big storm down in the Caribbean. There were no phones, no communications. I had a beat-up Land Rover and I just drove from town to town. The storm had leveled everything. Trees snapped in half, houses collapsed, rooftops gone. There was always a moment coming around the last turn in the road before entering a town when I would feel this apprehension about what I would see; wondering how many bodies would be lying out in the street. They get swollen in the sun. That's how I feel now, as if I've just started to pull around that last corner."

I said nothing and looked down at the paper in my hand. I had written down two names: Mr. Ira Stein, Mrs. Ruth Stein. They had come from a fast look into the city directory. It was a quiet street, typical of the Beach. The houses, mostly built in the 1930's, were white stucco and set back a few yards from the roadway. They were trim homes, Spanish design, with archways and fruit trees. I looked down the street and I could see no one. There were a few cars parked out front of the houses, but mostly there was silence. The wind caused a nearby palm to clatter its leaves together. "There they are," Porter said.

The two detectives got out of an unmarked cruiser. They had put a flashing light on the dashboard but hadn't used a siren. The crime-scene technicians remained in their vehicle.

"So," Martinez said, "what is it?"

"The killer called again. Gave me an address." I pointed down the street. "Down there."

Wilson followed my finger. "OK. Let's take a look." He looked over at Porter. "You can come in," he said, "but I want to know what you're shooting. I don't want to pick up the paper and see some piece of evidence on the front page."

Porter nodded. "No hassle."

We got into our cars and drove slowly down the block. Twenty-two ninety-five was the last house on the left-hand side, and Porter pulled the car in front. I said, "Let's move. I want to see," and we stepped across a small green lawn, past some shrubs and up to the front door.

The killer was right. I could smell it. I paused, waiting for the detectives.

Wilson stood next to me for a moment, then turned to Martinez. "Go call for a medical examiner," he said. Then he waved to the technicians. The door was slightly ajar, and one of them took a penknife and swung it open. "Don't touch anything," Wilson said. "Keep your hands in your pockets. If you have to get sick, make certain that you get outside." He took out a handkerchief. "Got one of these?" he asked. "No? Here, use some Kleenex. Hold it tight over your nostrils, it might help. Ready?" Then he looked at Porter. "Really glamorous stuff, huh?" He didn't wait for a reply.

Inside, the smell was overpowering, like a mask being cupped over my face. I had smelled bodies before, covering other crimes, but this was the worst. All the windows were closed; the air inside stifling and heavy. The killer was right; it was sweet. We walked into the living room.

I could not have been prepared for the sight. Not even in a nightmare.

There was blood streaked everywhere, on the walls, the floor, the couch, the rugs, the rest of the furniture. There was a huge mirror on one wall. On it, smeared in dark brown blood, were the numbers two and three. It looked for a moment like a child's fingerpainting.

The two old people were lying on the floor next to each other. They were naked. Around each of their heads was a pool of dried blood. I saw in a corner a common household sponge, barely recognizable, but the same color. The two bodies were swollen, stiff.

"Jesus," Martinez said. He was standing behind me. I watched Porter bring his camera to his eye once, then let it slip down. He strugged for composure, then raised the camera again. This time the room was filled with the flash. I heard the motor on the camera wind the film, a quick whirring sound. Again the flash went off, then another and a fourth time. Wilson turned angrily. "No more photos, no pictures," he said. "Jesus, look at this place." He turned to me. "Take a long look, then get out and let the technicians get to work. Not much of a game, is it?"

I didn't answer him. I made my mind focus on the details of the deaths. I registered the positions, the streaks of blood. Their hands were tied, just as the teenager's had been. I saw a painting on the wall, a bird caught in flight, a gull just above the waves. I looked at the old furniture, the knickknacks and souvenirs of a lifetime. Then I turned and motioned to Porter. "OK."

Outside, I sucked in the clear air in great gulps, tasting the nearby ocean, shaking my head to lose the smell.

Porter started to bounce around, shooting the policemen as they swung in and out. I saw several old people step from their homes out to the street to watch. In the distance, I could hear sirens, probably the Beach police, ambulances, the medical examiner. Probably, too, the police higher-ups. I walked to the couple's mailbox. A letter was inside, sent from New York City. The names corresponded to the ones I'd found in the city directory.

"It's them," I told Nolan on the car radio. There was some interference for a moment, then his voice came through: "And?"

"Very dead. At least a couple of days. Maybe more. The smell was incredible. They were naked and there was blood everywhere. It was sickening."

"Jesus." I thought for a moment, how odd, everyone seemed to react the same, calling the same name. "Talk to the neighbors; try to get some idea who they were, you know what I mean. We're going to be pushing deadline, so let me know as soon as possible."

The radio went off, and I turned and saw the medical examiner on his way up. He caught my eye and waved. "We've got to stop meeting like this," he said, grinning. He entered the house. I took my notebook and began to interview the neighbors, watching their faces slip from surprise to shock to terror as they grasped what had happened behind the closed door of the house so close to them. I stayed at the scene until they brought the bodies out, the same zippered black bags like the one that the teenager had been slipped into. By then the television stations and the competition and the wires and all the others, free-lancers and photographers, the whole bunch of us had collected outside. Most wanted to know from me if the killer had called. I said yes: he provided the address. A few times I felt the heat from the television lights as they played across the waiting journalists, searching me out. I did not tell anyone that I had been inside; only that I knew two were dead and it was bloody.

While we waited I watched one old woman who stood a bit

to the side. I could see her eyes following the progress of the policemen, occasionally turning to look at the assembled members of the press. She wore a white housedress; it seemed to flow from her neck and shoulders down in great billowing folds. The wind would catch the dress and pull it back, outlining the bones and ridges of her aging body. I could see her lips moving, speaking a prayer. The kaddish, I supposed. She had gray wisps of hair that floated around her forehead in the wind. After the bodies were brought out, I saw her turn and leave slowly, walking down the street alone, her body swaying from side to side with the effort, her steps short, hesitant. I thought of the bodies in the bags; swollen, it had been difficult to estimate their frailty. But I supposed they were weak, no match for the killer's strength and anger. I pictured their bodies lying naked next to each other. I wondered how many times, in how much passion, they had sought comfort and pleasure in each other's nakedness.

The medical examiner had lost his humor when he came out. "Wait for the autopsy," he snapped at the sudden crowd of questioners. He looked at me, shook his head, but said nothing as he returned to his car.

Martinez and Wilson were surrounded just as quickly. I had an image of gulls on the beach, screeching around a piece of refuse. Martinez gave a brief synopsis to the crowd, swiftly describing the interior. He would not elaborate, waving his hand in front of him as if he could sweep the questions out of the air. He slipped into the passenger seat and drove off with Wilson. I watched their car travel down the street, then found Porter and left. He muttered and cursed throughout the whole drive. I watched the waves and the water as we crossed the causeway; it was closing fast onto night, and already city lights reflected on the surface of the bay.

The two detectives were waiting at the newsroom. "We want to hear the tape," Wilson said. "We want to hear it right now." I nodded and they followed me into the office.

Nolan saw us enter, and he jumped from the city desk and met us midway across the newsroom. The other reporters stopped their work and watched. "You want the tape?" Nolan asked. Wilson nodded. "I'll have a copy made," Nolan said, his hand reaching down and extracting the cassette from the recorder.

"We want to cooperate." He handed the tape to a copy boy, turned his back and gave instructions, while the two detectives slid into chairs at vacant desks. It was odd, I thought, how nervous their presence in the newsroom made everyone. We were so used to dealing with them, crime being such a staple of the newspaper, yet their presence on our territory was an intrusion, a small invasion. It was as if we wanted to protect the process of putting out the newspaper from their eyes, keep it mysterious. I watched as Wilson adjusted his sidearm; it was a short-barrelled .357 Magnum; its polished brown stock stuck up on his hip, ugly and foreboding.

Nolan sat down across from them. "You wouldn't be thinking about a wiretap, would you?"

Wilson looked up, surprised. "What for? We're getting the tapes."

"I don't know," Nolan replied. "What about trying to trace the killer's phone calls?"

Both detectives laughed. Martinez sat back, smiling, but Wilson let out another short burst. "You've been watching too much television," he said. "Trace the call, hah!"

"I don't get it," Nolan said.

"Well," Wilson started, his voice even, lecturing, as if he were dealing with a child. I saw Nolan begin to bristle. "There are probably, what do you suppose, a couple of thousand lines into this building? Think of all the phones: circulation, advertising, up here in the newsroom. We would have to be able to find the specific wire that leads to this phone, this desk, the line that the killer calls in on." He was gesturing with his hand. "And then, assuming we could get the right type of tap on it, we would have to have people looking at all the various exchanges around the city, testing to see which one was connected to this line.

"It would be an impossible task. Even assuming the killer were to stay on the line for, say, six to eight hours and that we had a man on duty, it would still take that long to isolate the number, then find out where it was. And we have no indication that he's calling from a private line. We could, hypothetically, if everything went perfectly, trace the sucker to a phone booth. What good would that do us? Listen, even with computers and all the fancy electronics equipment developed in the war, it would still be better, we would stand a better chance of interrupting calls at random around the city to see if we happened to stumble upon the killer. So you don't really have to worry about being bugged. Except by the killer."

The copy boy returned with the tape and Wilson pocketed it. They stood up to leave and I asked, "Why were they naked?"

Martinez shrugged and turned away. Wilson looked at me and said, "I think he's just a sadist. No sex, but he probably wanted to humiliate them. Just a guess, though." I nodded.

The story came slowly. Nolan hovered about the typewriter for a few moments, gauging the progress, then went back to the city desk. I toyed with the lead, typing over and over again the same combination of words: elderly couple, bloody scene, execution murders, telephone call. All I could hear was the killer's voice as he gave me the address. All I could see were the two bodies lying on the floor.

I wondered about the victims, Mr. and Mrs. Ira Stein. He was a haberdasher from Long Island and she was a housewife. They had two children, the son a doctor in New York City. They'd retired to the Beach a dozen years before, when the northeastern winter first blew ice into their bones. I thought about how ordinary they were, how frighteningly typical.

Andrew Porter emerged from the photo studio and walked to my desk. His face was set, frowning, an edge of anger in the eyes. He stood for a moment on the far side of my desk, looking down at the words that were resting in my typewriter. "Here," he said, "these will help you set the scene." He dropped a handful of prints onto my desk. Nolan came up, and within a few seconds the desk was surrounded by other reporters and editors. I looked at the photos; they were the ones that had been snapped inside. Black and white, which heightened their impact; had the photos been in color they would have been somehow surrealistic, unreal, but the unforgiving tones of gray that shaded the prints carried the horror.

There were a few exclamations, muffled obscenities, whistles of appreciation as the shots were passed around. There was a picture of the two bodies, a picture of the streaks of blood on the walls, another shot of the wounds in the back of the skulls of the old couple and one, taken at an angle to minimize the flash's explosion, of the numbers written in blood on the large mirror. Nolan held it up. "We'll run this one," he said. He looked at Porter. "I assume you're developing some others, some shots we can put in the paper?" Porter nodded. "All right," Nolan said, "we're beginning to push deadline." He looked at me. "Let's go."

I turned back to the machine and slipped a clean sheet of paper into the roller. The crowd around my desk dissipated quickly, and for a moment I felt adrift, the words running through my head. Then it seemed as if they jumped into focus, and I began to race my hands across the keyboard, the words leaping onto the sheet of paper. I fought off thoughts of the couple's last minutes and replaced them with short bursts of sentences. It was as if by describing what I'd seen, what I'd smelled, what I'd heard, it became less real for me, placed inside the box of the news story; packaged for the frightened consumption of the hundreds of thousands of readers waiting in the growing nighttime darkness.

Writing again. Safe.

That night, before going home, I went to the bar with Nolan, Porter and some of the other staff. We commandeered a pair of tables in the corner, away from where a jukebox blurted country and western. A few of the pressmen and circulation drivers were sitting at the bar. I watched them throw curious glances in our direction, then return to the cans of beer in front of them, their eyes staring off into the darkness and the sound of music. The bar girl brought drinks to the table and shook off one editor's comment on her legs with a short smile and upturned eyebrows. There was laughter, and I leaned back in my chair, holding the beer bottle to my forehead, sensing the cool penetrate the skin. The liquid seemed to race down my throat, and the first gulp made me feel strangely high, released.

"Do you think that we're encouraging this guy?" I heard Nolan ask. "That the more publicity we give him, the greater the incentive there is for him to kill?" Several voices answered at the same time. I closed my eyes, listening to the words, balancing in the chair.

"Of course not," a voice said. "We're just covering the story the way it should be covered."

And another voice: "I don't know. Are we covering it, or are we participating in it?"

"I'll say one thing"—it was Porter speaking—"judging from the scene today, I'd have to say that this guy is just getting warmed up."

"But what are you saying?" one of the voices complained. "That we should ignore this thing to try to remove the incentive? Hell, I don't care if he murders a thousand people, we still have to respond as a newspaper. We're not the police, for Christ's sake."

"But"—it was Nolan speaking—"on a kidnapping, say, we always cooperate. We keep the facts from the paper until the drop has been made, or the person saved; or killed, for that matter. But we do work with them to make certain the situation isn't in jeopardy. Suppose we just stopped printing the story—continued all the research, all the interviews, but stopped putting it in the paper. Then, when the guy gets caught, write the whole thing up. What would be wrong with that?"

Several voices spoke at once. "The competition, the television, the wires, everybody would be all over it. We would be alone."

"I don't know," Nolan said.

"And then the killer would probably call somewhere else," someone said. "And we'd be shut out."

There was a quiet then, and I heard the sounds of music and the bar noise of clinking glasses. That, I thought, made sense to everyone. I opened my eyes. "Lip service," I said.

Nolan turned toward me. "What?"

"Knee jerk, lip service, whatever cliché you want to find. None of them really matters. The bottom line—there's a good cliché—the final analysis will always be the same. No matter how many people this guy kills, no matter how sickening the crimes are, no matter how closely connected we are to the acts themselves, the paper will always pursue the story. We can't do anything else. We're not equipped to react like a responsible organization, like a bureaucracy or the police. Things happen, we write stories. For us, there will always be another story, bigger, more powerful, one that has the people in the street talking louder and more stridently. It may not happen for a month or a year, but it will happen. And then we'll all turn to that story, forgetting that this story ever took place. A year ago the *Post* in Washington broke the President's back, but now everyone is going around saying, 'What have they done lately?' That's the nature of this business: what have you done lately? We're just lucky that crazy people like this killer come along every so often to help us do our job."

I finished my speech and poured the last of the beer into my glass. I watched the suds boil up for an instant, then recede, leaving a white ring around the top of the glass. The voices of the others picked up, mostly in agreement. Nolan looked at me, though, over the edge of his own glass.

We walked out later, alone. "Are you such a cynic?" he asked.

"Am I?"

"It seems that way. And you're a liar, too."

"How so?" I said. I laughed. He didn't.

"I saw you this evening, staring at the pages. I knew what was in your mind. You were looking for the ladder, the gangway. When a cop goes to the scene of a murder, he jokes, laughs, makes sarcastic remarks—his way of creating an arbitrary mental barrier between himself and the scene, of saying, 'I don't belong in that world.' For us, it's easier. We do it with words. I remember once, when I worked for the *L.A. Times*, we had this old guy—you know the type, cigarette burns on his trousers, crumbs on his shirt—who worked rewrite. He used to say he didn't have to see the accident or the murder or the drowning, whatever, to describe it; that his mind created the right setting and pictures. He'd talk to a few people on the phone and then turn to his typewriter, and the most careful, accurate prose would emerge. He was totally removed, went from his small apartment downtown to the paper and returned every day, five days a week, year in, year out, and he wrote the best, most vivid prose in the paper. I think we all want to be that guy. That separate and distinct."

He paused, thinking. The moon had risen early, and the pale light seemed to fuse with the fluorescence of the parking-lot lamps, turning the world a purplish blue.

"You're right, we'd never drop the story, never hide it, even if that killer calls you tomorrow and says the only thing keeping him at it is the publicity. I suppose that's the essential dilemma, the basic joke of this whole existence. Catch-Twenty-two.

"But I wonder, where are we when we start to justify our complicity by shrugging and saying, 'That's the news biz'? And don't protest. I think we are accomplices. After all, it was us he sent to the scene, not the police, not the fire department, no one else.

"No matter what happens, though, it's still a hell of a story."

We were silent for a minute or two. I watched the lights on the thruway cut through the evening. Nolan said, "See you tomorrow. He'll probably call," and wandered off to get his car. I waited, feeling the darkness, turning my face trying to catch some breeze. But there was none; all I could feel was the residue of daytime warmth floating up from the sidewalk, closing in on me like a wave.

Christine was in the living room in front of the television when I came in. "Hurry," she said, "the news just came on." I slumped into a chair and watched the television anchorman introduce the story. Christine was in her underwear, her white nurse's outfit tossed carelessly aside. I looked at her legs as the anchorman's voice droned. "There you are," she said excitedly.

I looked at the screen. I saw myself surrounded by microphones, bathed in the light of the cameras. The wind was blowing across my face, and I watched as I raised a hand and held my hair back. I watched myself tell about the latest phone call, and then the screen shifted suddenly to a shot of the two bodies being carried from the house. Again, the scene shifted, and there was a picture of Martinez making his way through the crowd of reporters toward the police cruiser. The television reporter on the scene ended with a stand-up, facing the camera, intoning the details of the latest murders and finishing with the cryptic statement, "No one knows when it will stop." I grunted and got up to turn the show off. Christine lifted her arms above her head and stretched. I looked at her body carefully, inspecting, my eyes playing over the legs, the stomach, the shoulders.

"God, it's hot tonight," she said. "I thought you looked good. Was it really terrible?"

"The television didn't really explain what went on inside," I said.

"Well, they were shot like the girl, right?"

"Yes and no. Their hands were tied behind like the girl, they were shot in the back of the head like the girl, but the resemblance between the crimes stops there."

"Why?"

"Blood, I suppose."

Christine put her hand to her mouth. "What happened?"

"The place was a mess. He'd streaked blood from the two victims everywhere. It looked like a slaughterhouse. And the two were naked. It looked like he went crazy after the killings. I'm surprised no one in the neighborhood heard anything."

Christine had turned pale. "Why?" she asked.

"That's what everyone wants to know."

"But you should know. You've talked with him. What do you think?"

I snapped back, "He talks, I listen! What else? He doesn't bother to fill me in on all the subtle details. How should I know? I'm no expert."

"Maybe he will," she said.

"I hope so, dammit, I hope so." It was out before I really knew what I was saying.

"And?"

"And what?"

"And what will you do if he does tell you? Will you try to stop him?"

"That's not my job," I said.

"That's disgusting."

I grabbed her by the arm and she gave a little shriek as I shook her. "What do you mean by that?"

She snatched her arm back, seized one of the pillows and put it on her lap, as if to cover part of her nakedness. "I mean, this man is going around killing people. Killing, for God's sake. And you're the one person he's seen fit to contact about the whole thing. And your idea of community pride, of helping out, is to take notes and write stories which probably have the singular purpose of encouraging the madman to go out and do it again. What the hell's wrong with you?"

"There's nothing wrong with me." My own voice was raised, near a shout. "That's my job. I'm not a cop, I'm not a doctor. I can't do anything to make everyone well again. All I do is report on what I hear and see."

"A robot."

"No, dammit, people rely on me as much as they rely on you. They need information, knowledge. How else can they protect themselves?"

"Ah," she said, "you're the savior of the vigilantes?"

"You know, you don't make sense," I said. She turned and picked a glass of wine off a side table. I had not noticed she was drinking. She took a long sip, then leaned her head back against the couch. I looked at her long throat, the muscles and shape of her gorge outlined. I felt suddenly passionate, sexual. I sat next to her. "I'm sorry," I said. "I don't know what else to tell you."

She looked at me and put her hand on my arm.

"What I don't understand," she said, "is why you think being a . . . watcher makes you immune."

I thought about it. There really wasn't an answer. "I think everyone in the business feels that it provides a kind of cloak. No one likes to think about the other. We hide from it. During the war a number of correspondents were killed. Some just took off one day and were never seen again. The actor's son, Sean Flynn. He was in Cambodia, a photographer. Heard there was some action a little way down the road and jumped on a motorbike. Another fellow accompanied him. They were never seen again. There's an old reporter at the *Journal* who covered the Dominican action; you remember, when the Marines were sent in? He got shot up pretty badly. The paper had a ceremony, but then, I think, they preferred to ship him out to pasture. The business doesn't like to have its damaged warriors around inhibiting the survivors on their next assignment. We all think the act of collecting and disseminating the news is a kind of protection. That because we're supposed to be objective, we don't have a vested interest in the outcome. So the bullets will just ignore us and seek out one of the real participants."

"You're talking about wars," she said. "I'm talking about a madman."

"But that's what he's doing," I said, "he's trying to make us all think we're at war."

She was silent for a moment.

"Well," she finally said, "I think he's succeeding. I'm scared. I'm scared for you, I'm scared for me. I feel as if we're more vulnerable."

"Why?"

"Because of you. How do you know he's only going to be satisfied by calling you up? He seems to want you to be involved in this thing. What makes you so certain he's not going to end this whole thing by coming for you? And suppose you write something he doesn't like? What do you think he'll do then?"

"I can't think about that. I couldn't write if I did."

"Ah," she said, "your friend the psychiatrist would call that denial."

"It's the nature of the business," I replied.

"Some business," she said. Then she laughed. "Pour me some more wine." But instead of handing me her glass, she wrapped her arms around me and put her head on my chest. I tried to look down at her, but all I could see was the light catching her hair, bringing out its color. I could feel her breathing as she held close to me. Then she pulled back, handed me her glass and dropped the pillow to the floor.

But the lovemaking seemed jerky, uncoordinated, as if our bodies were out of synchronization. She lay back afterwards, looking out of the bedroom window. I sat on the side of the bed looking at her. She said nothing, but after a moment turned on her side and flicked off the lamp. I went and sat in a chair by the window, letting the night shapes grow around me. I thought about Mr. and Mrs. Ira Stein and my hesitation at the typewriter. I tried to picture them alive, walking the few blocks between their home and the beach, pausing every so often with that distinctive elderly abruptness, turning their faces up toward the sun. My mind kept picturing the two on the floor of their home. I wondered who'd been shot first, and what had gone through the mind of the survivor, during their final moments. Did they welcome the noise and shock and darkness of the explosion behind their heads? Or did they cling to the last seconds of life, even with their partner ripped away so terribly beside them? I thought, I will ask the killer when he calls. And then I pictured the bodies again, but this time I could see their hands flung out in front, reaching, as if for each other. Lovers.

CHAPTER EIGHT

THE headline was a two-decker, 48-point Roman bold, strung across the six columns of the front page: "NUMBERS" KILLER STRIKES AGAIN; ELDERLY BEACH COUPLE MURDERED. Underneath the headline was my name in bold print and a four-column photo, the shot of the mirror and the two numbers he'd inscribed in gore. Below that was another photo of the rescue personnel rushing from the front of the home with the body bags, heading toward the ambulances and the morgue.

The sidebar started out front, too: the story I'd written containing all the quotes from the neighbors, the same shock and disbelief that had accompanied the death of the teenager. The words were different, though; the language was the talk of the elderly, filled with the vulnerability of age. They were more afraid, I thought. Death was closer to them; they felt it more strongly. It was as if stealing life was that much greater from those with so little time left.

Both stories jumped inside, and more words and pictures filled a whole page inside the paper.

Christine was dressed in her whites. "No surgery today," she said. "Thank God. After reading all this, I don't think I could handle it." She drank coffee and looked over the paper.

I turned to the sports section and lost myself in the box scores. The Red Sox seemed to be getting stronger and had taken a 1-0 decision from Jim Palmer in Baltimore. He'd given up just three hits, but one of them was a long home run to Lynn, the Boston center fielder. Lynn was a rookie that year and was leading the league in everything, it seemed. I'd watched him play once in spring practice, before anyone had known who he was. He'd moved easily for the ball in center field, reaching up at the last second to pluck the dying shots from the air, like a magician, only in reverse. He'd always seemed to move at the same speed, regardless of the urgency of the play; had always arrived a split second before the ball, a note in the rhythm of the game.

"Oh," Christine said, "this is just horrible."

For the first time that day, I could feel the pervasiveness of the killer's presence throughout the city. It filled the air like the wind before a late-afternoon thunderstorm suddenly blowing up and around, as if out of control, directionless. I did not spend much time in the office that day; Nolan took me aside early and said that I had to get outside to find out what people were thinking, how they were feeling. We both turned and looked down at the telephone on my desk, wondering if the killer would call, but Nolan said we couldn't wait on him. He tugged at the tie that hung loosely around his neck. He did that whenever he was anxious; by the time the paper went through its final deadline the tie would be more like a noose. He suggested that we take my phone off the hook so the killer, if he did call, would think it busy, not ignored. I nodded but felt a kind of quickened guilt when I lifted the receiver from the hook. The phone made a beeping sound for a few seconds, then went silent, sitting dismembered on my desk. Porter joined me then, and we walked from the building.

The day was filled with voices; the faces, the shapes of the people blended together, melding with the heat and the sun.

We rode a Metro bus, and the driver, a black man with

curls of gray hair just above his ear, turned to me and said, "Why should I fear that man? There's no reason, but I do. I look at the faces of the people who get on my bus and I wonder, are they next? Am I? And I think about the people who ride the bus, the strangers who board, dropping their money in the box. I look at the young men and think, maybe he's the one." The driver had large, heavily muscled arms, and he spun the bus through the congested downtown streets easily, as if driving in a trance. He would turn the bus using just the palm of his right hand, the other resting on the edge of the wheel, his elbow out the window. "The people," he said, "all the riders seem more nervous. You see the whole world on a city bus, just driving the route over the course of one day. People won't sit down next to each other. I noticed that, you know. People seem to want to keep to themselves."

We walked through Little Havana, looking at the faces of the old men, their hair slicked back, the pockets of their Guayabara shirts filled with the elongated shapes of rolled cigars. The men stared out at us with the usual mixture of Latin distrust and curiosity. Some hesitated over their small glasses of thick black Cuban coffee. They had a way of peering over the edge of the glass as if drinking in the smell and the steam as it mingled with the heat of the day, at the same time assessing Porter and me.

We walked down Street Eight, the primary Cuban thoroughfare, reading the signs in Spanish, talking with the old men in the small restaurants playing dominoes in the shade. "Death," said one old man in his hesitant English, "comes to everyone sooner or later. Why worry?" He lifted the edge of his shirt to display a reddish scar underneath his ribs. "Playa Giron," he said, "La Brigada." He spit onto the sidwalk, his spittle a dark mark on the white cement. "I wish we could have this man go to Havana and do some of his work there." Some other men laughed. The old man looked away, out across the buildings, his eyes up to the sky. "It is not in us to be scared of such a man," he said. "But some of the children and the women are. They ask, 'Will he come here?' As he did on the Beach with the old ones there. I say, 'How can we say what such a man will do?' And many are worried, but they think that this man will stick to his own kind for whatever it is that he is seeking.

Myself, I do not know, but I think that he will be killed soon, or that his grief will be too much for him and he will kill himself." The old man shrugged his shoulders and stared back down at the table filled with dominoes in front of him. He took one from the pile and placed it on its end, balanced for an instant. Then the old man flicked it with his finger and it fell over. He moved it into place on the board, and the game went on.

We drove south that afternoon to a shopping center a few miles away from where the first victim's family lived. I had almost stopped thinking about them. For a moment I wondered what they felt now, if they realized they were caught up in something larger than the death of their child. But then I thought, what could be larger for them?

We went into a gun store, a shop called The Great Equalizer. There were a half-dozen people waiting to see the clerk, and he gestured over his shoulder toward the rear of the building when I asked for the manager. I found him in the back, at a table filled with rags and the pungent smell of cleaning fluid. A small-caliber automatic was disassembled on the table. He grinned when I introduced myself and explained my reason for visiting.

"This is the suburbs," he said. "And whenever there is something unexplained out there, the people get nervous. And whenever people get nervous, they go out and buy a gun. So to answer your question, since the news came out this morning I've been doing a steady business. I expect by tonight it will pick up even more. And tomorrow it will get even better. And if this guy goes out and kills someone else, well . . ." The manager paused and grinned. "I know this sounds terrible, but I'll be doing land-office business." He was a thin man, with a pair of muttonchop sideburns, hair that was combed sharply back, a refugee from the 1950s. "Almost everyone complains about the three-day rule; you know, you buy your gun on a Monday, you got to wait until Wednesday to pick it up. A lot of people say, 'But supposing that guy comes by tonight,' and I tell 'em, 'No, that isn't the way he works. You'll be OK.' It seems to relieve them for the most part, reassure them, I guess, though why anyone would think that I know anything about it is beyond me."

The gun dealer paused and looked out at the line of people. There was a steady clicking sound of metallic parts meeting as customers inspected the action on the weapons. He picked up the automatic from the tabletop and began to wipe the sides carefully with a streaked cloth. "I saw a lot of strange things when I did my hitch, let me tell you. And I met a lot of guys who were on the verge; you know, just one step away from the funny farm. There was one guy, I remember, during basic, up at Fort Dix in Jersey. Damn, it was cold. All the damn time, I thought I'd never get warm again.

"Anyway, right at the start the drill sergeant starts shouting at us, 'Call out! Call out! I want to hear your voice loud and clear!' And there was this one kid, about seventeen or eighteen, skinny, never been outdoors, I guess. And for the first week the sergeant just laid it on him. So the kid starts to raise his voice. Everything is shouted now, 'Yes sir! Yes sir!' and louder and louder. And he starts it in the barracks, too. I mean, you can't talk to the kid; everything he says he says at the top of his lungs. Finally, after a couple of days, the drill sergeant caught on. By then the kid was marching around, eyes in front of him, but I don't think he could see a thing, calling out the cadence at the top of his voice. They took him away and I never did see him again. But I got to thinking about the kid the other day; you know, after the first murder. I thought, well, if you send a kid like that over to a place like Nam—you know, my younger brother, he went, said it was terrible—well, you don't know what's gonna happen, do you?"

The gun dealer paused, listening to the sound of weapons. "So everyone wants to be protected. I'm just one way. I bet if you went to the pound you'd find that they've sold every big mean dog they got. Call up the Wackenhunts, those people. I'll bet they say the same thing. A gun isn't so bad. And let me tell you, the one that this guy's got is a helluva piece of work. Probably your standard Army-issue forty-five-caliber automatic. You know why that gun was invented? It was back in the early 1900s when we sent the Marines into the Philippines to deal with the native uprising there. Well, the soldiers used to carry rifles and bayonets, and when some wild man would leap from the bushes the guy could handle it OK; you know, jab and fire.

"But the officers all carried thirty-eights, the old Colts like the cowboys wore. Well, hell, half of them were getting killed because some native carrying a sword would jump out of the bushes and they'd put about three slugs in the guy's chest and the guy would be dead, see, but he wouldn't be stopped, and his momentum and that sword would just slice the officer up like cold cuts. So they had to develop real quick a handgun that would just stop a guy cold; you know, right in his tracks. And that was the Colt forty-five automatic. And damn, they still use that gun today in the Army. Never figured out anything better. Now a Magnum, a three fifty-seven or a forty-four, will do the same damn thing today, which is why you see the cops using them, but that automatic, it's something else. The cops will never trace that gun or that ammo. There must be thousands of those guns floating around. Hell, half the World War Two vets in the city probably have one sitting in some forgotten drawer."

He looked at me and the words filling my notebook. "You ever shot one?" I shook my head. "Well," he said grinning, "here's your chance." He took us through the back door to an adjacent shed. There was a sandbagged target there, and the walls had been soundproofed. He opened a locked chest. "Here you go," he said, handing me a pair of ear protectors. "And here's the object of so much attention."

He held up the automatic. For a second the fluorescent lights in the shed caught the dull sides of the weapon; then it turned back, black, ugly. He handed it to me and put his hands on my shoulders, positioning me in front of the target. It was a blacked-out profile of a human being, like some I'd seen policemen practice with. The gun felt extraordinarily heavy in my hand, and for a moment I wasn't sure that I could lift it. The gun dealer showed me how to stand, with both hands on the weapon. I practiced once, sighting down the short barrel. It seemed that my focus of vision narrowed then, tunneled into a single field: the target and myself. The dealer handed me the clip of bullets and grinned. I slid the clip in, feeling the weight grow, sensing the satisfying click as the clip was grabbed by the handle. "All right," I heard his voice at my elbow. "Let fly. Just one gentle squeeze, OK?" I steadied myself and fired.

The noise of the report filled the room and the smell of cordite surrounded me. My hand felt as if someone had struck it with a hammer, the fingers tingling, electric. I dropped the gun to my side and peeled the ear protectors off.

"Not a bad shot for a beginner," the gun dealer said. He took the weapon from my hand and slipped the clip from the handle. He replaced the weapon in the box and then gestured at the target. "How about that?"

My shot had blown away the top of the target's head. I stared at it momentarily, then turned and followed the dealer back into the store. "See what I mean?" he said. "That's a serious weapon. Not like some of these little women's guns, like a twenty-five automatic or some cheap Saturday Night Special. A forty-five is good for one thing. Killing people very quickly and efficiently."

The gun dealer escorted us partway out of his shop. He paused at the cash register to talk with a man in a business suit who was turning and hefting a large handgun. "Now that, sir, is your Cadillac of handguns," the shop manager said. "A Colt Python, three fifty-seven Magnum, long-barrel. It is the height of accuracy, control and packs a wallop a lot stronger than a heavyweight's punch. Most of the policemen who come in here buy that gun, in the shorter-barrel version. Equip it with magnum load or with regular thirty-eight-caliber ammunition for target practice. I assume, sir, this gun is for yourself?"

The businessman shook his head. "No," he said. "I was really looking for something for my wife." He looked up at the dealer who had turned a cold glance onto the assistant behind the register.

"Well, then, sir, you need something that the little lady can handle. I assume that she is not particularly large?"

"That's right," the man said, "she's more petite. She's afraid, and I want her to have something that will make her feel more confident." The businessman turned toward me and some of the other people waiting for assistance. "I think she's worried about this fellow who's doing the killings."

"She should be," said a woman standing close by.

"All of us are," said a man in a sport shirt.

"But it's not just this killer," said the woman again. "It seems there's so *much* lawlessness. And the police don't seem to be able to do anything about it. They just come and take a statement. That's what happened when I had my home burglarized." She looked at me scribbling notes. "You a reporter?"

"That's right."

"Well, you can quote me, but I don't want my name in the paper."

The businessman joined the conversation again. "What worries me is that every punk who drifts down here looking for the sun and the easy life will see the stories in the paper and figure that here they get a free shot. I mean, what's to stop them from pulling some job and then trying to blame it on this killer? The police won't know what the hell to think."

There was a chorus of agreement. The man in the sport shirt lifted up a snub-nosed .38 special. "Well," he said, "this might prove to be some deterrent. And I plan to keep it that way. You remember the Constitution. The right to keep and bear arms. Well, dammit, I'm not going to let some whacko murder my family without a fight."

There was more agreement. The store manager interrupted to regain the businessman's attention. "Perhaps, sir, I can show you something in a lightweight automatic?"

The businessman looked back at him. "Yes, all right. But I'll take this Python thing, too. And some ammunition for it. And where can I go and practice with the thing? I haven't shot a gun since I was in the service."

"Fine, sir." The manager looked across at me. "We have a range, and you can try it out there. I'll arrange for some time on a practice gallery also, if you like. Now"—and he reached inside of the locked glass showcase—"here is something for your wife." It was a nickelplated .9 millimeter. "This is a bit heavier than I ordinarily recommend," the manager said, maintaining his even, helpful tone. "But then, these are special times. Perhaps you'd like to compare it with this?" And he held out a small .25-caliber automatic with a black finish, polished, gleaming.

"Good," said the businessman. Then he turned back to the woman waiting in the line. "Perhaps you could help me," he said; "my wife is just a bit smaller than you."

"Glad to," she said, stepping up and picking up the weapons.

* * *

I suppose the reactions in the gun shop were predictable. So, too, was the scene outside Morningside Park, near the swings where the children played. Their voices seemed to be swept up into the sky, carried by the breeze that filtered through the big banyan trees from the bay. There was a group of women there, just outside the sandboxes, sitting on benches. They seemed perched, ready, apprehensive. "Children must play," said one of them, peering past me at the group on the swings. "They don't understand danger the same way we do. You can't keep them inside; it would only foster nightmares. You can't explain, because the killings are inexplicable, especially for a child. So," she said, pausing and turning to the other women whose heads were nodding in agreement, "we come here the same as on any summer day and watch the children play as if there were nothing wrong. But there is, and I can feel it."

Another woman joined us, tugging at the sleeve of her shirt as if impatient, the words pressing hard on her imagination. "What do you do if you've got older children? Eleven-, twelve-year-olds or teenagers. How do you keep them in? How do you protect them?" She brushed a strand of graying hair from her temple and looked for a moment out across the water, past the thick brown trunks of the trees and the dark shadows they cast on the lawn. "I worry so much. I tell my boys they can't go anywhere alone. I tell them they have to be in before dark. I tell them if they're in doubt, to stop, to call home or the neighbors and if they see anything suspicious to call the police or for help or to do *something*. But you know all the advice and the orders and the protection in the world can't keep a child that age safe. They just don't know fear. My God, that poor girl getting into that man's car, walking alone at night. How do you teach them to be afraid?"

The first woman added, "It's like it's a sickness. Like . . . all the wrongs that were wrapped up in the past ten years have suddenly come here to roost. And Miami, of all places. You would think Washington or Chicago or New York or San Francisco maybe—but Miami seems like such an innocent place." She stared up into the sun.

"What makes a man do these things," she said, "and how many more will he do?"

Porter looked up from his cameras and lenses. "Why should he stop?"

"I beg your pardon?" the first woman said.

He shook his head. "He wants us all to be scared. He wants everyone to have nightmares. That's why he's doing it. As long as you and I and everyone else in this town react like normal people, with fear and apprehension, with . . . oh, damn, just scared, you know? That's what he's getting off on."

Porter looked at me. "And, boy, do we help him."

In the car on the way back, I asked him what had changed his attitude. "I thought this was just a story to you. What gives?"

"I'm becoming cynical," he said. "More than even I thought I could."

"That's what Nolan called me," I said. "A cynic."

"He's right. We all are. I just don't have to enjoy it."

"You'll go mad," I said.

He gripped the wheel and moved the car swiftly to the right, past another car, then accelerated and shifted back to the left-hand lane. We were running down Biscayne Boulevard, past the offices and trees of some of the exclusive housing developments. It was an area of contrasts; a block of busy offices with well-groomed men and women wearing designer clothes would give way to a block of motels advertising water beds and X-rated closed-circuit movies. I watched a black prostitute on one corner, the hair of her wig piled high on top of her head, but loosened, too, so that it cascaded like darkness around her shoulders. She wore a pink halter top that strained to hold in her breasts and red shorts that showed the flesh of her buttocks. She saw me looking at her as the light changed and smiled, a flash of white teeth, and lifted her finger in a beckoning motion. I shook my head and she pouted. Porter put his foot down heavily on the gas pedal, and we shot forward across the intersection.

"I suppose I will," he said. "Sometimes I can hardly stand the contrasts." He hesitated, then looked quickly at me. "You know what I was doing before your call came in to the photo lab and we went off to the Beach? I was developing my previous assignment. I shot a layout for the Living section; fashions for the hot summer days, I believe they called it. I was in one of the parks with the fashion writer and three models and a couple of PR types. The girls were dressed in bathing suits and wraparounds, flimsy, see-through stuff, and we were trying to pose them in a way that would be provocative yet not offensive for our 'family newspaper.'" He said the last two words sarcastically. "It made me laugh later to think that we were so careful about a bunch of beautiful young women, trying to make certain they weren't too sexy, and then I run off to the most disgusting murder scene I've seen. And that's OK; that's front-page stuff. I feel like a hypocrite. It made me feel dirty, shooting that old couple lying there on the floor. It made me feel as if I were the madman, focusing my camera, centering it on their bodies, robbing them of what little dignity they must have had. Sometimes I think I'm a parasite. We all are."

"Listen," I said slowly, "if you want off this story I can talk to Nolan. He'll talk with the photo editor."

"No." His voice was suddenly free, easy. "See, that's the really crazy thing. I wouldn't want to be off it. I couldn't stand not knowing, not being there." He laughed. "We're all going crazy. A story like this, it just does it to you. To everyone. You know, that guy buying the guns today? He'll probably end up shooting it out some night with his wife after a drunken argument. At least they'll be well armed. My God! Do you suppose the killer realizes all this?"

"Yes."

"Yes," Porter agreed. "I bet he does." And then he added, "You see? No one has any real conscience."

He swung the big car easily into the *Journal's* parking lot.

I watched Porter pack up his equipment and slam the car trunk shut. I could just see past the corner of the building, out over the bay waters. I thought of the sensation of being out on a boat, riding past the Beach through Government Cut, the channel where the big porpoises play, their gray backs rolling through the water. They like to jump in the wake of the sportfishermen, the huge Chris Craft and Bertrams that go out after big-game fish. The porpoises roll up and suddenly shoot through the wake, twisting their sleek forms and landing with great splashes, then turning and dashing back through the wake to race again. The waters sometimes seem alive, rising up against the blue of the morning sky.

The last time I'd gone out was in late spring, the weekend Saigon fell, thousands of miles across the world. Nolan was there and a few others. We got into a school of big dolphin in the morning, a few minutes after we'd crossed the deep blue demarcation line that seems to course through the water, the mark of the Gulf Stream. We were sitting in the fighting chairs, talking about baseball and the war, drinking beer despite the early hour. The sun already hung above us, and the salt air seemed to stick to my skin, mingling with the sweat and the feel of the cold beer can.

The lines ran through two riggers and each made a pinging sound as it ripped free, a sound that rose above the constant churning of the twin diesels at trolling speed. The dolphin had come up and just smacked into the bait, and by the time the lines had come taut the fish were beginning their dance across the waves. They were beautiful fish, their stubby heads and long bodies, silver blue and green as they cut just below the waves and exploded from the surface in a burst of water and sunlight. We boated those two, and three others, before we lost the school; they were good-sized, fifteen to twenty pounds each, and we slapped each other on the back and drank more beer and picked up the conversation where it had been dropped. It was later when the big blue marlin hit the bait.

Nolan had finished holding forth on the coverage of Saigon's fall; it was an emotional discussion of photographs, a retelling of the powerful images of those few days. We'd run a front-page shot of people hanging from the runners of a helicopter as it surged from the roof of the American Embassy. One figure was holding on by just one arm, his legs kicking as if he were trying to swim through the air, the other arm waving to try to keep his grip. It seemed obvious the man would fall, but the moment for his decision to let go was upon him and one could sense the panic in the body twisting in the air. The picture had upset people; the phones had rung most of the day with readers wanting to complain or protest and some who had just wanted to talk.

I was listening to Nolan's voice as it mingled with the engine noise and watching the ballyhoo bait as it skipped on the surface, a small wake rising behind it, the silver sides catching the sun as it bounced and turned. It was hypnotic to watch the bait like that, feeling the beer grow heavy in my head. I did not at first realize what the shape behind the bait was; it just rose up darker and deeper than the water. I saw the long sword protrude from the surface, and then the captain up on a fighting tower began to shout, "Billfish, billfish, Jesus Christ, a big marlin! Right rigger, right rigger, look alive!" The line snapped out of the rigger, and the voices continued. I began to freespool the line. "That's it, drop it back, drop it back!" the captain continued to shout. "Let him get it!" I flipped the reel to strike and put my finger on the line. I could feel the fish hit the bait again with the bill, and then the water exploded and the fish suddenly shot from the blue up against the sky, its belly gleaming. "Good fish!" the captain shouted, and I rocked back hard, setting the hook. The marlin continued to jump, twisting, the sun reflecting off the water as it streamed from its sides.

And then, just as quickly, it sounded, went down.

The captain yelled to the mate, "Where's it hooked?" and the mate turned to the bridge, shading his eyes, his voice sad. "I couldn't see the feather. I think it's belly hooked," and the captain said, "Oh, shit," in a voice that dropped the excitement and turned to the edge of anger.

"Oh, no," I said, "I hope not." I could feel the fish on the end of the line, throwing his weight against the pressure of the boat, the yards of thin filament that held him. He pulled, twisting his head; I could feel the shakes through the rod. Five minutes went by, then another five. I saw the line begin to flatten out.

"He's coming up," the mate said. "Much too early. Damn."

Nolan said, "What do you mean, belly hooked?" and the mate explained quickly. "It means that the fish managed to swallow the bait whole, and when he was struck the hooks ripped into his stomach, not into the flesh of his mouth. It means that even if he were to pull free he would bleed to death. And it means that the pain is too much; he's coming up, and there's still a lot of fight in a big fish. Damn."

I continued to pump and reel the line in, and within seconds I could see the blue shape in the water. He must have measured over six feet, probably more than a hundred pounds.

"Shit," the mate said, leaning over the transom, staring at the fish in the water. He walked to the side and grabbed a gaff.

He looked up at the captain who shouted, "Everybody move back! He's going to come in pretty lively!"

I pumped the fish in a little closer, and the boat swung around as the captain positioned the mate for the gaff. He was a thin man, with brown skin, shoulder-length blond hair and long muscles on his arms. "When he comes over the side," the mate said to me, "get out of the chair fast."

There was a second pause, and I said, "Here comes the leader." I could see the wire leader, just inches below the tip of the rod.

The mate grabbed the gaff handle, turning the sharp hook so that it caught the light. He reached out for the leader and said, "Here goes nothing," and swung the gaff suddenly, violently through the air toward the fish. There was a shower of water and the sound of the marlin's tail hitting the side of the boat. A huge splash shot over the side of the boat, drenching the deck and the mate. "Shit! Shit! Shit!" he screamed. And as his voice raced across the swells, I jumped from the fighting chair and peered down into the green and blue of the Gulf Stream. I could just make out the sight of the marlin, streaming blood, descending into the coldness and dark. The mate held the broken leader in his hand. "He'll go down there and die," the mate said. "A bad end for a beautiful fish. The sharks will feed on him, all the fish will." Then he turned to the captain. "He moved just at the last minute. I hit the leader with the gaff." The captain nodded. "Sorry," the mate said to me. I shrugged.

It seemed unfair, not to me but to the fish. Hooked in the mouth, he'd have pulled, then twisted and leaped, shaking his head, and the odds would have been with him. A kink in the line, a slip on the reel, a little slack, and he would have been free, slipping back to the cool safety of the deep waters. I wondered if the fish knew that he was going to die, or if he sought the familiar darkness instinctively. I could see him there, in my mind, cutting through the waters, his bill pointed straight ahead, his small fish brain clouding with death.

The killer did not call that day or the next.

Christine had none of her previous optimism, though. She said he would call, that he was toying with us, that he liked to see the stories grow thin in the paper and then inject a new element to force them back to the front. She said the patients on the ward talked constantly about the killer; they felt safe because they knew he couldn't penetrate the white walls and clean corridors of the hospital. In surgery the doctors, too, talked about the killer. The younger ones described gunshot wounds they had seen during tours with the Army in Vietnam, or during alternate service in the ghetto hospitals of the North. She said she had discovered a new type of fear, not the clenching, sudden panic when a car swerves toward you, but a dull apprehensiveness that made every small action throughout the day, even just washing her hands, seem larger and more important. Every breath she took seemed heavy with substance, the effort to draw in air a conscious choice. It was as if she were marking time, awaiting the moment when the drama took another step forward and the curtain rose on a new scene.

I had no more routine. When the telephone rang, I stiffened. When it did not ring, I sat tense. Sometimes I took the phone off the hook and walked through the city, a notebook in my pocket. When Porter accompanied me we did man-in-the-street interviews, the voices all rising into the vivid blue sky.

The city was a beast awakening from hibernation, its dulled senses slowly coming into focus, becoming alert.

We were talking about my family; about my father, his books, his laws. I said, "There is no law anymore, not with a killer like this. One cannot write a statute that covers the situation." And Christine agreed. I watched her stretch her arms wide, her fingers pointed out tautly. She threw her head back and asked, "I wonder, do people draw closer together or pull farther apart in this kind of situation?" I got up from my chair and crossed the living room to her. She put her head down in my lap as I sat beside her. I stroked the length of her back, and for a moment she was silent.

And then the telephone rang.

"Don't answer it," she said. "This is our home."

It rang again, the bell seeming to grow louder in my ears.

"Please," she said. "Leave it."

But I stood up and crossed to the phone. I hesitated for a

second, feeling the ring beneath my fingers. Then I picked it up. "Hello?"

It was silent.

"Who's there?" I asked.

But I guessed.

"It's time again," the killer said.

And I knew nothing had changed.

CHAPTER NINE

"I READ your story, the one on the people's reactions," he said. "I particularly liked the sequence in the gun shop. I wonder how many of those people will manage to shoot themselves while trying to learn to handle a weapon? That was something I saw when I was overseas; sometimes the fear was so strong it overcame the natural aversion to self-inflicted pain. It would happen at a base camp, one of those dusty, hot, unpleasant places where we sat around waiting for the next trip into the jungle, a worse place by far. The camps were filled with slow time; it always seemed to take twice as long to do anything, the heat was so intense. Sweat just poured down the underside of my arms.

"Anyway, there was always a kind of military quiet about the camps; the noises were ordinary, choppers swinging in and out, voices raised in complaint. Periodically there would be a sound, sharper, more distinct, more familiar: A single shot from an M-sixteen. Then shouts for a medic with probably a few screams of pain mingled in. You always found the wounded grunt with a bullet hole in his left foot, or a toe blown off. He would be on his bunk, the area around him filled with clothes and smelling of cleaning fluid. His first words would be, 'I was cleaning the fucking thing and it went off,' and then the medevac would come and he'd be lifted out of there. Everyone knew, really, what had happened. No one really cared that much. At least, I didn't. I would shut my eyes and listen to the base sounds, the shouts and all, and sleep. I was never afraid like that."

As he talked I motioned frantically to Christine to bring me paper and pen so I could take notes. I gestured wildly with my hands, making writing motions in the air. She nodded, her face set. In a second she returned to my side with a dozen sheets of white typing paper and a ballpoint pen. I wrote at the top of the first page:

THE KILLER

and then I underlined it three times and handed it to her. She put her hand to her mouth in a quick, reflexive motion, and I saw her eyes fill with tears. She sat down at the dining table, across from me, and watched me throughout the whole of the conversation, she told me later, because my attention had shifted to the telephone and to the pages of empty paper in front of me. I started to fill them as he continued to talk.

"Anyway, as I said, I read your story with interest. All those people thinking and worrying. Think of all the intellectual energy being expended over simple fear of the unknown, of the unmanageable. I suppose all the amateur shrinks and crime buffs think that it gives me a sense of power. Well," he laughed, "they're right. It does. I love it." His voice gathered an edge of anger. "They disgust me, all those people. Those smug suburban types buying the weapons—as if they would know how to use one, anyway—the people on the street with whom you talked, all their clichés of fear, their terror that their secure little lives are threatened. I wish I had a way to get to them all, to kill all of them. . . ." He hesitated. "Well, just have to make do with what I can, right? But I want all of those safe people to feel it right in their stomachs, the worst kind of fear, the type that you know you can't do anything about. The perfect fear. I want them to think of me as a cancer in the gut of society, eating away at their lives."

He took a deep breath.

"I hate them all. I can't even find the words to tell you."

I could hear his breathing, like a runner's near the middle of a race, labored yet steady.

"You're the writer. You tell them."

"And what if we stop?" I asked. "What if the paper were to stop writing the stories, if I were to stop taking down what you say?"

Again he paused.

"Well," he said, "I'm certain that the television stations would love to put my voice over the air." He laughed. "I prefer to have more substance, to see one's thoughts and sayings down on paper in black and white. The daily paper just sits there all day staring out at you. Not like some television show that happens and is suddenly gone. So I prefer to have your co-operation. But it's not essential.

"And," he said, "I doubt that your paper or any paper could possibly voluntarily ignore a story like this, regardless of their complicity in the whole matter. Regardless of how much they were used."

I was aware of the darkness outside the kitchen window. The telephone was a wall model with a long cord. I walked to the sink, away from the paper and notes for a moment, trying to collect my thoughts. I could see the pale moon through the branches; the tree seemed to be filled with wan light.

The killer continued.

"I had another thought, an odd one, while I was reading your latest stories. I found myself thinking back to my own childhood, especially when you described those women and the children on their swings. When I was young my mother would take me to a playground; we lived in a small town then, and I remember the children took turns on the swings, moving their little legs back and forth as fast as possible. I was with them, pumping, and in my memory I could see myself, the parabola of the arc of my swing growing as I forced more and more momentum into my motion. I could see my hands, the fingers turning white, as I gripped the chains. When I reached the apogee of the arc I would thrust my head back, staring for one moment up into the sky, as if I were in flight; then as the swing began its downward flight I would tumble back to earth, my eyes shut. Almost like being weightless, or what I suppose weightlessness is like. I get that feeling sometimes with the forty-five, when it is pointing at the back of a person's head. I felt it first in Nam. Now here at home. The same sensation from childhood exactly, the delightful dizziness of being detached from the earth. Have you ever experienced anything similar?"

I was at a loss and said the first thing that leaped into my head.

"Perhaps with a woman, sometimes . . ."

He laughed, a burst of raucous noise.

"And why not?" he said. "With a woman, yes. The feeling of letting go, of flying free. Not bad, not bad at all. Do you know, Anderson" and his voice switched from a kind of jocularity to a deeper, more pressing anger—"that I had my first woman when I was in the Army? Not until I was nineteen years old and a soldier, a trained killer, did I experience a woman. When I was young and we lived on the farm, I watched the animals mating with a kind of fascination, an envy at their lack of shame, the mere following of instinct. When I was very small there was a girl who lived next door to me, and often, you know, before one really knows one is doing wrong, she and I would play in the woods beside the houses. Not really woods, just a stand of trees and bushes that had grown up haphazardly, shielding the homes from the side.

"There wasn't much space in there; the underbrush was overgrown and pitched together like an obstacle course. It was a perfect place for kids; we could slide under and around the bushes and trees, unseen, private, hidden away from the eyes of our parents.

"She was an adopted child, I remember. She wore the circles under her eyes like makeup, and I thought that I loved her and that she and I would someday run away together. I was six, she was seven, and we played together in that stand of trees. At first we played simple child's games, hide-and-seek, whatever. Then she brought out her dolls; she had two homemade, floppy cloth dolls that she would cuddle. She said that they were our family and that we were in our home there. It became a make-believe house. In the summer we lay under the trees, hidden away, and talked about how we would run away together when we got just a little bit older.

"We didn't wear any clothes. I remember every inch of her body, her skin tanned and brown on her arms and legs, but a soft pink where her dress covered her from the sun. We lay together, sometimes embracing, and I remember the sensation of her body next to mine, comforting, warm, covered by the shade of the trees and bushes. I couldn't get enough of looking at her, all the secret places of her body. I would reach out my fingers and stroke her softly, not daring to push or pull or upset her in any way. It was like touching light, and I remember how I would shake, tremble really, with excitement, looking at her eyes closed. . . ."

He stopped and the line was silent.

"What happened?" I asked.

"We were discovered by my mother. I remember it like the stop-action frames of photographs. Sitting up suddenly at an unfamiliar sound in the bushes. Scrambling to grab my clothes. My mother shrieking with anger, her voice like a gunshot. The girl crying. I dove into the brambles, and when I returned home that night my mother made me strip off my clothes to show my father how I'd been scratched and cut trying to escape her."

"And?"

"I was beaten." His voice sounded like a shrug. "She was beaten. The two families got together and cleared out the underbrush, cut down some of the trees. 'Make good firewood,' I can remember my father saying as he lifted the axe over his head and swung it at the base of a birch. They, the other family, moved away soon after. Why, I never could guess. Another job, another empty opportunity. Who knows?"

"You never found out?"

"I loved her," he said. "No, I never found out."

There was silence then, and my mind raced ahead. I thought of the shifts that the killer manifested, the swings in his mood from a kind of joking friendliness to a darker evil, a virulent hatred. But when he talked of his family, of growing up, his voice seemed to slip into a hazy, soft-spoken tone. It was as if talking about the memories calmed his angers.

"You know, there was a time after that, soon after the girl and her family left, that my mother choked. It was a hot day, like the days we are having now, where the heat seems to blot out everything else, the sun smashing down like a round of high explosive. My father was out; at the schoolhouse probably. He usually took his lunch with him and didn't return until late in the afternoon, even during the summer session, which was mostly remedial lessons for the children who weren't going to be passed on to the next grade.

"So my mother and I were alone in the house, stifling in the heat. The windows were wide open, but there was no air. Nowhere. It was lunchtime, and I watched my mother get up from the divan where she had been resting. She was wearing one of those old-fashioned housecoats, the type that button up the front. It was a floral print with flowers on her chest.

"She had been lying on the divan, complaining about the heat, a glass of water at her side and a kerchief which she dipped into the glass spread over her eyes. In the distance I could hear the noon whistles from a train station a few miles away. The sound hung in the air, echoing. My mother had unbuttoned the front of the housedress. Her skin was red, with a rash, I suppose. She had pulled the housecoat back so that it just rested on the tops of her breasts. I watched her bosom as it swelled and fell with the effort to breathe the still air. I could see droplets of sweat that formed in the area between the breasts, running down her stomach. When she heard the noon whistle she swung her legs from the couch and sat for a second on the side, swaying slightly as if she were dizzy. She took the cloth and dipped it in the glass of water and then squeezed it out over herself, the water mingling with her own moisture, running down her front toward her lap.

"And then she got up, looked at me oddly and complained, 'My God. I wish we lived someplace that the breeze would blow in. Like near a lake or in the mountains. I swear I'll never be cool again!' She tossed her head back a short way as if looking for some sign of the wind. I stayed in my chair and watched. Have you been a good boy? She wanted to know. And then, keeping up the same banter, a kind of childlike talk though she knew I was too old for that, she moved slowly into the kitchen. I'll fix us some lunch, she said, and I followed her in.

"It was just as warm there, and she sat down heavily at the kitchen table. 'Come here,' she said, 'rub your mother's forehead.' She closed her eyes and leaned her head back, and I began to stroke her forehead. She murmured and I saw her face crease into a smile. I watched her body relax. After a moment she opened her eyes and looked at me. 'You are going to become a better boy,' she said, 'and then you will be mine forever.' Forever. What a meaningless word.

"She rose and went to the small icebox. There was beef, left over from dinner the night before. She cut off two slices, one for herself and the other for me, and served it up cold on a plate. She cut off large chunks and slipped them into her mouth rapidly, jaws moving quickly.

"There was a moment, a pause in her eating, and I remember the change coming over her face; a sudden look of astonishment, surprise. She made a high-pitched sound, a half-gurgle, half-scream, and her face turned a whiteness that I'd never seen. Her breath came in short wheezing gasps, and I realized one of the pieces of meat had stuck in her throat. She bent her arms back like bird's wings, trying to pound on her back to dislodge the meat. She gestured for me to help her, trying to thrust her own hands down her throat. I sat rooted to my chair.

"Then, as I watched, she leaped up from the chair and tried to throw herself against the wall, frantic, choking. It was not until she fell to the floor that I got up and moved to her side. I aimed a blow with my fist at the center of her back, waited a second, then let fly. Her breath came shorter, and I hit her again. Then another time, and I kept it up until I realized she was gasping for air and the meat was unstuck. My eyes were closed. She rolled over on the floor, her housecoat undone, falling to her waist.

"I knelt by her, my eyes on her face but fighting not to look at her exposed body. She breathed in slowly, deeply. We stayed that way for a few moments. Then she opened her eyes and reached up and stroked my cheek. 'Thank you,' she said. I suppose she thought my pounding had worked, though I guess now that it hadn't. Who knows? She slipped her arms around me and pulled me very close in an enveloping embrace. I felt then as if it was suddenly I who was choking, who couldn't breathe. I could feel the sweat on her body, taste it against my lips. It was like being in a room in which the lights are turned off before you are ready for darkness. I closed my eyes and listened to her heartbeat. Sometimes when the artillery fired their defensive targets at night and it came whistling high overhead and exploded a thousand yards off, the earth gave great heaving shakes. The sound reminded me of my mother's heartbeat."

I realized I was sweating, the telephone receiver sticking unpleasantly to my ear. "Where are you calling from?" I asked.

He paused, then laughed. "Just a phone," he said. "Do you know how many telephone booths there are in this city? Hundreds. Probably thousands. There are dozens of quiet places from which to call. Of course, I could be lying. I could be sitting in my own room, lying on my bed staring up at the familiar marks on the ceiling as I talk to you. See," he said, pausing, "how silent it is? No way for you to know."

"Why did you call me here?"

"I just had the urge," he said. "I wanted you to know that I know where you are. That I was thinking about you. That these urges come over me at the oddest times."

"What urges?"

"The two that concern you," he said. "The urge to kill and the urge to talk."

I did not know what to say. I had the sensation that the words were not flowing over the phone but were being whispered hot into my ear.

"I was nineteen," he said, "when I had my first woman and I killed my first man. The woman was a prostitute; no, I think whore is a better word. The man was hardly a man, more a boy and probably no older than myself. She worked the strip, a section of bars and motels and sex flicks outside of Fort Bragg in whatever the name of that small North Carolina town was. That was where I did my basic, you see, and it wasn't until the very end that we were allowed to go into the town and partake of the pleasures there. Like everything in the Army, it was done in a defined manner; we were herded onto buses, excited like teenagers, which we were.

"There was a marvelous symbolism attached to the leave.

I doubt the idiots in charge had any real idea, but what you had to do before they would grant you a pass was qualify with the M-sixteen on the rifle range. Learn to shoot one way before you got the chance to shoot another."

I could sense his grin on the other end of the line.

"I remember the faces of those who were having trouble with their weapons; bearing down, cheek to the muzzle, eyes locked on the target, aiming down the long barrel, praying they would hit something. It wasn't a problem for me. When I was young and we lived on the farm, my father taught me to shoot. He had an old twenty-two, a Remington with a single-shot bolt action. On Saturdays we went next door and set up a target and spent an hour or two blasting away. Crouching on that firing range, waiting for the duty officer's command to start firing, I saw myself back on that farm, the target tacked to an old board, hanging against the horizon on the field. I have gray eyes. You know, they say that people with gray eyes are the best shots. Daniel Boone, I think. Sergeant Alvin York."

I wrote that down quickly: gray eyes. For the police, I thought.

"It was odd: I saw the same thing on the qualifying range, and the same memory months later, in the country, when I sighted down the barrel at my first victim. He was running, perhaps thirty yards off, on the edge of a paddy, his black shirt outlined against the tree line. He must have been young, untrained; a real soldier wouldn't expose himself like that. I thought of the farm and the afternoons with my father, his voice harsh, demanding. 'Squeeze! Dammit! Don't pull!' And so I squeezed the round off, one shot, and when I looked I saw the figure stumble and then fall, and all around me the rest of the patrol was shouting and yelling and hooting. I had no problem qualifying on the rifle range. They gave me a marksman's medal before I left the camp. So on a Friday night, just as it was gaining darkness, all of us dressed in laundered and pressed shirts and slacks, our hats pulled down in a jaunty fashion on our foreheads, we were loaded into olive green buses and launched into the town.

"There was a bar, the Friendly Spot, it was called. A Miller High Life sign in the window blinked in invitation, and there was a jukebox against the wall and a pool table in the back that had a long scar down the center where the felt had been ripped. There was only a cue ball on the table and I couldn't see any sticks. The juke played country music, with some rock and roll mixed in. Willie Nelson and the Rolling Stones. It was playing 'Sympathy for the Devil' when I walked in. I had to blink because it was dark, and it took a few minutes for my eyes to adjust. There was a bartender, a big guy, the type who kept his pack of cigarettes rolled up in the sleeve of his T-shirt. He wore a beard. Didn't say much. The noise of the cash register was his language. The girls were sitting at the bar, and when we walked through the door they slipped from their seats and met us, taking us by the arms, leading us to the bar stools or to a few booths in the back. There were five of us, and we started to drink and laugh and joke. She was blond, I remember, and I looked for a long time at the way her skin seemed to rest in folds on her neck. Her breasts seemed worn, as if they had been pummeled by too many hands. She seemed old."

Again he paused.

"And?"

He laughed. "What do you think?" But his tone had shifted again, restored to an edge of anger.

"I don't know," I said.

"Use your imagination."

Silence again on the line.

"Why do you tell me these things?" I asked.

"I want you to know."

"Why?"

"I want everyone to know what they're dealing with."

"Aren't you afraid you'll say something and the police will trace you?"

"No."

"No?"

"What's truth, what's fiction?" he said. "How can anyone tell?"

"Suppose they catch you . . ."

"They won't."

"Why not?"

"Because they're not smart enough."

"Perhaps you underestimate them?"

"I doubt it. But if I do, then I suppose the joke's on me, isn't it?"

"Doesn't that worry you?"

"No."

"Why not?"

"Because I'm already dead," he said.

I scribbled that down verbatim on the page in front of me. I looked up and saw Christine staring at me, at the telephone. I pushed the page across for her to read. Her eyes widened.

"How is that?" I asked.

"I feel like a wraith, a disease without substance. My insides are cold, blackened like from fire. There's no life left inside of me. Only hate. That's like death."

"I don't get it," I said.

"I don't expect you to," he replied. "At least, not yet. Maybe you'll come to understand later."

I was exasperated. "Listen, dammit, you keep toying with me, filling me in on memories of your past, talking of incidents in the war. What's the point? What are you trying to prove? Why do you do this?"

"I remember," he said, his voice turning hard, "a moment in the jungle. I was on a patrol, a few miles from camp with my platoon, a half-dozen of us, struggling through the underbrush. I was walking the point; I liked that, you know; everyone else hated it. That's because you were the first to attract fire from snipers—and you were the first to trip mines. Everyone was scared of the mines, more than any enemy. The earth beneath your feet couldn't be trusted. You never knew when the next step might be the one. The VC had one mine that just exploded when you touched it, blew off your foot. That wasn't so bad, but the one we really hated went off with a little pop! and then a roar. The mine, you see, had two charges; the first, when you triggered it, shot the main device out of the earth up to waist height. Then it would explode. Knees, thighs, balls, prick, stomach. All the truly horrible places to hurt a man. Sometimes it just cut the guy in two and he would be dead before we could reach him, but sometimes it just mangled the grunt, chopped him into hamburger, and you'd see him sitting on the jungle floor, staring down in disbelief at his crotch, watching the blood flow from where his genitals had been a moment earlier.

"But I liked to walk the point. Out there in front, testing the water. Living closer to the line. I knew I was safe the day I walked right over the trip wire, didn't even glance down and see it, just blundered right on past, my eyes looking up through the trees to the gray sky. The next guy wasn't so lucky, and I heard the pop! ka-boom! and even without turning I knew what it was.

"He was a young guy; he'd been in-country a week or two. Hardly long enough to lose the shine on his fatigues. He gave a little scream and then sat down, or was blown down. He looked like someone who'd spilled a plate of spaghetti with tomato sauce in his lap. The medic jumped up next to him and the radio man started to call for the dust-off, shouting into the radio we needed a jungle penetrator, the whole nine yards. The kid looked up, right at me, and said, 'I'm hurt,' and I nodded. Then he said, 'I'm gonna die,' and I nodded again. Then he screamed, and the medic cracked a needle and slipped morphine into him. I remember the sergeant shouting obscenities, over and over. The noise of the explosion made all the jungle birds rise up and tear away through the forest. I just sat and watched and waited, what, ten minutes? Maybe less. You could see the life slip from the kid. The more frantic the medic got, the worse the kid was, their motions in reverse proportion. After a while the kid died, just as the beating sound from the chopper's blades filled the air. The sounds of the jungle birds in flight and the chopper were not much different. The medic was screaming, too, pounding on the kid's chest, trying to revive the heart. It was an ordinary day, that day, just one of three hundred and sixty-five."

He stopped. After a second, he continued.

"Let me tell you about the old couple. I suppose you want to know about them?"

"Yes," I said.

"All right," he said. "It was a strange time."

"Why them? What had they done to you?"

"You misunderstand," he said, irritation in his voice. "The point is that none of the victims have *done* anything to me.

They are innocent. Is that what you want to hear? I know they're guiltless! That's the point."

"Why the blood? It was everywhere."

"To increase the horror."

I took that down. "Well," I said, "if they are symbolic, why don't you explain what they're symbolic of? I just don't catch the meaning."

"You will," he said. "A teenage girl. An elderly couple. You should look at who the victims are. I told you, it's a duplication. There was a moment overseas, an incident. And that is what we're replaying here. You remember during the spring of 1971 when the Weathermen had their demonstrations in Washington? They ran through the streets throwing trash cans and litter, screaming imprecations, trying to disrupt the flow of society. They thought the American people were too complacent about the war, that they didn't understand what was happening over there. How could they identify with the disruption of Vietnamese society if they didn't know what it was like to experience it? The theme of the demonstrations was to 'bring the war home,' to heighten everyone's awareness through symbolic duplication. I was back from Vietnam, and I walked the streets with them, watching and listening. I saw it made no difference really. People saw it as a nuisance, not as a symbol. Well, the Weathermen lacked my resolve. People can't ignore what I'm doing."

"But the war is over," I said. "Finished. Kaput. A mess that's ended. Everyone agrees on that."

"It'll never be over for me." His voice was slow and very deliberate. "I see it every night during my sleep, every morning when I wake. Sometimes I look up into the sun and I think I'm back there, not here. It'll never be over for me."

Another silence. "And those old people?" I asked.

"You mean Mama-san and Papa-san?" He laughed.

"Listen," I said, my eyes fastening on Christine's as she watched the conversation. "You need help. There are programs, facilities for men damaged by the war. I can help you. . . ."

It was feeble, and I expected his reaction.

"Shit! Shit! Shit! It's all shit! Have you seen any of those facilities, sat in on any of those programs? I doubt it. You know what a VA hospital looks like from the inside? I'll tell you. It is wall after wall of cold, pale green. Sometimes I thought I could see scars on the walls where the screams of all the men who'd passed down the hallway had left their mark. Row after row of beds and bedstands, cluttered with cigarettes and ashes and refuse and people discarded so easily. I was there; I know. And I won't ever go back. You think I'm crazy. I know you do. I read the story quoting the psychiatrists. They're real understanding. Sick, they say, disturbed. Reaching out. All the mindless words of their impotent profession. Well, I may be sick, I may be diseased, but I'm a damn sight more alive than any of them." He drew in his breath in a long wheezing pull. "And before I'm finished, a lot of people will wish they were safe from me. I'm not crazy. Goddammit! The whole world is crazy! People walk around acting like nothing is happening. They can't see beyond their own little world. Well, I did! I think I'm the only sane man left in the world," he said, his voice slowly winding down. "The only person who understands that for every action there is an opposite reaction. Well, society sent me there to be a killer, and now I'm back, the reaction, doing what I was taught best."

Again he stopped to gather his breath. "What about you?" he asked.

"What do you mean?"

"Did you go? We seem to be about the same age. So I know you had the same question. Did you go?"

"No," I said. "I didn't go."

"Why not?"

I thought of a number of responses, of conversations with my father and with college students. I remembered growing my hair long and wearing jeans and peace signs and marching and singing. It all seemed so long ago. I thought, tell him about your student deferment; then tell him about the immorality of the war, that you were opposed, that you'd have fled to Canada instead. That's what he expects to hear.

But I said, "Because I was afraid."

"Of what?"

"I'm not sure," I said. "Of killing. Of being killed."

"It was our war." His voice was even.

"I know." I thought of the portrait of my grandfather, dressed in his olive drab, tight military collar clasped at his neck. From the photograph he looked out quietly and at peace, a member of the American Expeditionary Force. He was a lieutenant, barely twenty-two, with the 77th Liberty Battalion. He saw action at Château-Thierry and then in the Argonne Forest. I could see him through small boy's eyes. He talked little about the war, and when he returned he went on to law school and then to become a judge of other men's failings from a seat on the bench. When I was eight years old he called me into his study. It was early fall, and he said the weather reminded him in a gray way of the overcast days of the Argonne. The sky before dawn would be a half-light, he said, as if a storm were breaking, and then the cannons would start, great booming sounds that shattered the night's exit. The sky would warm with dawn and the flashes of high explosives as they ripped across the no-man's-land toward the German lines. The whole earth would shake and heave with the movement of the guns. They created their own heat and wind, as if they were stronger than the weather. He looked across his desk at me and then handed me a present. It was his old steel helmet, so heavy I could barely hold it. He set it on my head and stood back and saluted. "The war to end all wars, that's what we called it then," he said. The helmet made my hair dirty, and I took it off and shook my head. "That's French dirt," he said. "Been there for forty-odd years."

There was another picture, too, in the house where I grew up; it occupied a spot on the shelf next to my grandfather's portrait. It was a grainy, slightly out-of-focus shot of a group of men kneeling on the tarmac surface of a runway. Behind them was the nose of a medium bomber, a Mitchell B-25. The men were slumped in relaxed poses; each had written his name in white ink underneath. Third from the left, right under the drawing of a scantily clad woman with a thunderbolt in each hand that adorned the nose of the plane, was my father. He was wearing a heavy sheepskin flight jacket and had his hat tilted back on his head. One arm was gently around the shoulders of another man wearing the same khaki and leather. Around my father's waist was a belt and pistol. It was probably the same .45 the killer was using.

"World War One, World War Two, even Korea, everything

was clear-cut," the killer said. "But when they handed us our war, it wasn't that simple."

"How could we know?" I said.

"You're right. How could any of us have guessed? I went. My old man went. His father before him went. It was just an accepted thing, I guess. God! How wrong they were."

"Your father and your grandfather?" I asked, surprised.

"Yes," he said. "It wasn't that they were an Army family. It was just accepted. It was my turn."

I pictured my father. He was speaking, pacing the room, trying to maintain his composure. "Canada? Are you certain? Dammit, I know the war is wrong, but what will you be tossing away?"

"It was the same for me," I said.

"But you didn't go?"

"No."

"Did you demonstrate?"

"Yes. Everyone did. It was easy."

"I suppose so," he said.

We were silent for a moment. Then he added, "You see, I bet we have more in common than you think."

The flatness in his voice stopped my thoughts. I saw the old man and woman again.

"Tell me about the killings," I said.

"It was easy," he replied, mocking my own words. He laughed. "They liked to take a walk in the evening, a constitutional. I watched them for a few days; they walked the same route at the same pace. Stopping at the same spots to pause for breath. They walked arm-in-arm. I liked that. Many people don't show their affection for each other the way they used to."

"I don't understand . . ." But he cut me off.

"I simply followed them home that night. They didn't see me until I was right upon them, right in the doorway. There was no one else on the street, and they were too shocked and too scared to even call out. I said something cryptic and frightening, like, 'One sound and you're dead,' and I clapped my hand over the woman's mouth and kind of shoved the pair of them into their living room, slamming the front door shut behind me. It was that simple. Suddenly it was cool and quiet, as if the door slamming had cut the day away like a knife stroke and it was just me and them.

"I waved the gun under their noses for an instant. The old man was terrified. He stepped in front of his wife and said, 'You take what you want, young man, but stop trying to scare us!' And then he thrust out what little was left of his chest. 'I've seen tougher than you,' he said. And I smiled at him and motioned them to the couch in the living room. There was another chair, which I plopped down in, and, holding the gun on them, I said, 'Oh, yes? Where?' And the old guy gave a little shiver. 'Auschwitz,' he said, and he held up his arm and the sleeve dropped away from his scrawny wrist to reveal a tattooed number.

"I was, to put it mildly, nonplussed. I couldn't believe my luck. 'Tell me about it,' I said, and the old guy put his wife's hand in his—she hadn't said anything up to this point, just stared straight ahead, eyes glazed over—and he said, 'So what is there to tell? You've seen the pictures?' It was a question and I nodded my head. 'We all went in. Some came out. Not many. What's to say? Who likes to remember these things? But you cannot scare me, young man, not even with your big gun.' I loved him then. Who wouldn't? After a minute he said, 'So you going to rob us? Or what? You think we're rich? Not living here.' I shook my head. 'No robbery,' he said. 'What else is left? Murder? For what? Rape? We're too old. What's left?'

"But I didn't answer him. He was a proud old man; he sat with his back straight, his eyes right on me throughout. He kept one arm around his wife, the way a bird covers its young with a wing. He held her hand. I saw his eyes focus on the gun. Then he smiled. 'A forty-five, perhaps?' he said and I nodded. 'It makes some sense now,' he said.

"Then he turned to his wife, and his voice was so soft I could barely hear him. 'Ruth,' he said, 'you know that I have loved you all these years. Now it's going to end. This man is the man in the papers, the one who murdered that pretty young girl. He means to kill us, too.' When he said that, she stiffened suddenly, and her eyes went wide and scared. She reminded me a little bit of animals, you know, a dog or a rabbit. But he swiftly shushed her and said, 'We're old. What do we care?

Is this something we should be afraid of?' His voice was marvelous—soft, reassuring, almost hypnotic. I watched the effect it had on his wife. She seemed to slow perceptibly and move even closer to him. She shut her eyes and nodded, and he turned back to me. 'So,' he said. 'Do your worst.'

"Tell me about your lives, I asked him. But he shrugged and said, 'What's to say? We were born. We met, we loved. We survived. We lived. Now we are going to die.' I shook my head. 'Please,' I said, 'I want to know.' His wife opened her eyes then. She gave him a small nudge in the ribs. 'You tell him,' she said. 'I would like to hear it, too.' So the old man looked at her with a kind of smile and started to tell me their life story. We must have sat for—oh, I don't know—an hour, two hours, three. You hear something like that, time just passes.

"Did you know that after the Second World War ended, the survivors of the death camps were kept in new concentration camps run by the British and the Americans? Relocation camps, they called them. That the United States—that's right, us, you and I, our fathers—had a quota, wouldn't allow many of the displaced people to enter the country? I heard all about that. The old man talked of coming here, one of the few allowed in. It was because he had a cousin already here, a man he hadn't seen since they were small children. The cousin sponsored him. He said he came into New York Harbor on a brutally cold day; there were icicles hanging from the docks. But he said he took off his coat and breathed in the air. He said he could taste it; it made him feel dizzy.

"I think they had a good life. Nothing exceptional. His sons did better than he, which gave him great pleasure. He had seen his grandchildren grow up, if not into adulthood, at least past adolescence. He said he'd worked hard and enjoyed most every minute of it. Making and selling clothing, an honorable profession. Clothing the people, he called it. Good clothes, he said, sturdy, utilitarian designs of good quality. When people bought a suit from him, they knew it was a garment that would last. Then he turned to his wife and said, 'Like us. We've lasted.' She just tucked her head down onto his shoulder and smiled, closing her eyes. You know, I could tell they were still in love, probably as much that moment as any during their decades together. 'How did the two of you meet?' I asked him, but the woman looked up. 'The old-fashioned way,' she said, 'through a matchmaker.' She talked awhile, telling about their courtship, their marriage. They were separated in the camps, but afterward they found each other. It took six months, but she found him. She said she knew all the time he hadn't died, that there was too much life in the two of them. She was smiling throughout her story, every so often leaning over and touching her husband. And then she looked at me and said, 'You must be a very sad young man to be doing these terrible things.' You know something—I agreed with her. I nodded my head and I could feel tears in my eyes. 'It hurts,' I told them, and the two of them nodded sagely. They wanted to know about my mother, my father, and I told them about growing up. Just a little, you know, to keep them interested. I talked about the farm, and then the city and the differences.

"Isn't it remarkable? Each second, each minute that passed, brought them closer to death, and in the same time we grew closer as people, moving from meeting to acquaintanceship to friendship. It was the same with the girl. I feel I can only know people, really know them, in death. All the masks, all the bullshit, just drops away. It's a pure thing, pristine. Perfect.

"The three of us had a little cry then. I finally wiped my eyes and thanked them for the memories that they had shared with me. I saw the fear enter the old woman's face. She had white hair pulled back from her face, and a strand had come free. She shook her head to get it out of her eyes. 'Are you still . . .' she asked and I shushed her. 'Nothing changes,' I said. 'Don't be afraid.' I saw her give a little shiver and shrink closer to her husband. He looked at me. 'Are you going to tie us? Or what?' And I produced the rope from my pocket."

I interrupted him: "How did they get naked?"

"Simple," he replied. "I simply told them it was going to be like going to sleep. And I told them to get ready for bed.

"She had to help the old man off with his shirt. She turned to me and said, 'Arthritis,' and grimaced. He dropped his pants to the floor, then his underwear, and stood naked.

"He made no attempt to cover himself. I have to admit the old man moved with grace throughout. He helped the old woman off with her shirt, then her skirt. She hesitated for an instant in her slip, then pulled it slowly over her head. Stockings, lace underwear; everything lay in a heap on the floor. She looked down at the piles of clothes for a minute; then she reached over and picked them up and arranged them neatly on the couch. I suppose old habits die hard. The old man watched her with a half-smile on his face. I'd never seen two elderly people naked before. I stared at them. The old man's penis had shrunk, shriveled. His hair was gray. So was hers and her breasts deflated, the nipples a dark brown. Her chest and his were both sunken. Yet he filled his with air and stared at me. 'Would you hurry now?' he said. I motioned them to the center of the room, and in a second they were kneeling, side by side.

"I tied their hands swiftly; I doubt that I needed to, but I was concerned that one might panic in the seconds between the shots. They were composed, though I could see the old woman's shoulders start to shake, palsied. 'I'll go first,' the old man said, 'but send us together.' I felt as if I were in the midst of a dream; they were cooperating, their voices so calm. It was as if I were merely an instrument and this was their suicide. 'All right,' I said, 'say what you will to each other.' They put their heads together, kissed lightly on the lips and smiled. 'We have no more words,' the old man said.

"I saw them close their eyes. I grabbed a pillow from an armchair. It was as if I were outside myself, watching myself perform the act of execution. I placed the pillow against the old man's head and looked for a moment at the forty-five. I could see my finger squeezing the trigger. Each minute space, each micrometer of the pull, took seconds, minutes. Then there was a roar and the familiar jolt running from my palm up through my arm. I could feel my fingers tingling, numb. The old man pitched forward. I saw the old woman grit her teeth. She was saying a prayer, I suppose; her lips moved. I was behind her almost before the old man had finished twitching on the floor. This time the movements seemed speeded up, like a movie picture being run at the wrong speed. The pillow was on her neck, the gun barrel poised, and then the shock of the explosion and she spilled forward, too.

"I think I went berserk then, playing in the blood. I went to the kitchen and found a sponge which I dipped in the mess on the floor and used to write the numbers. I do not know how long I was there. Five minutes. Maybe an hour. I danced around the bodies until darkness filled the room and I could barely see. Then I left the house, door ajar. I walked down the street toward my car, the streaks of blood on my clothes gleaming. I was invisible. No one walked from their house, no one was on the street, no car drove by. I carried the forty-five in my hand, and the night stood still as I made my escape."

He hesitated.

"They were perfect innocents," he said.

I felt a complete exhaustion and let the silence on the line grow until it filled the room. My eyes refused to focus on the pages of notes and quotations that I'd hastily scribbled. My own handwriting was unfamiliar, alien.

"I feel," the killer said, "like a thirsty man after the first long taste of cold water. I'll call again soon. Maybe here, maybe at your office. Depends. It just depends."

And then he hung up the phone.

CHAPTER TEN

CHRISTINE started to dance then.

She said it was her method of dealing with the release of energy created by her fear. I would find her in the mornings on the floor of the living room, curled around a pillow, sleeping. On the stereo turntable was soft jazz; she preferred Miles Davis and Keith Jarrett. Sometimes, however, she used classical string quartets, the volume turned down so low that only the barest of rhythms could be discerned. She danced naked, dropping her bathrobe to the wood floor, arching her body back in salute to the sound. I think she felt the music mingle with the nighttime sounds of cicadas and distant traffic. She would dance until exhaustion brought her to the floor, and then curl up and sleep soundly until morning.

Her eyes showed no sign of the nocturnal activities, her voice was clear in the mornings. Her work at the hospital continued unchanged, too: three days a week in surgery, her hands seizing the instruments and dealing them to the doctors with the confidence of a Las Vegas blackjack dealer; two days on the ward, checking the progress of the diseases, all the varieties of cancer that peeked out from under the coverlets at her as she swept past, resplendent in her white uniform. She passed cancers of the blood, cancers of the organs, cancers in retreat and cancers charging unchecked. She talked often of the diseases that lived on the ward, the stages they went through, the prognosis for this one, the projection for that. Of the killer she said little but to point out that if he knew our phone number, then he knew where we lived. When the police came to install the recording device on my home phone, she watched with a kind of detached fear, her face registering the same look of concern I suspected she adopted when she walked past the bed of a patient on her ward and in the morning light saw the appearance of some new manifestation of the disease.

As for myself, I began to stare at people in the street.

I divided each passerby into one of two categories: a potential victim or the potential killer. I began to wonder about everyone I passed, who are you? What are you thinking? Are you the next? Are you him? Often I stopped people randomly, slipping my notebook from my pocket as I introduced myself and began to interview them. Most people refused to give their names, as if afraid the killer would single them out and punish them for expressing their fears. They averted their faces when Porter was with me, and he would drop the camera to his waist in frustration. The comments and quotes that I collected all began to sound alike, variations of the same themes of fear, anger and bewilderment. More and more, people criticized the police for not catching the killer. There was a new wariness in voices, and I discovered that people turned away from my stare rapidly.

At night, I took to driving through the city after dark, trying to determine what was different and what was the same. In the suburbs and the residential enclaves of the city, there was a hesitancy: houses seemed to gather the darkness around them in retreat. There were fewer children in the summertime streets; as we entered the dog days of August, the sounds of laughter and play were seldom heard. There was a shutting up, a closing down; people talked of staying inside.

There were exceptions, of course. The winos and bums who proliferate in Miami's downtown were still on the streets, guarding their few possessions, scraping together their pennies toward their next drink. I talked to a few who seemed unaware, or unconcerned. One old man, whiskered and streaked with dirt, looked up at me and said, "Why should he kill one of us? What the hell would that prove? We're all dying, anyway." The other men around him, seeing me scribble the words in my notebook, called out and wheezed congratulations. I wrote a story that night about the derelicts and the lack of fear they felt. Porter had taken fine art and Nolan loved the story. "Terrific, terrific," he said. "More like it."

The next day I found a teenage couple in a McDonald's, eating hamburgers and drinking milk shakes; it caused Porter to laugh and say, "Cliché, cliché. Can you believe that?" The couple, after gentle prodding, told me that the previous Saturday night they'd gone to a "numbers killer party." There'd been booze and dancing, and they'd all played a game; one of the partygoers was designated the killer, and he had a list of all the kids and numbers assigned to them. Over the course of the party he symbolically killed them all, catching them alone and taking a red pen and marking their foreheads. The teenagers warmed to the story, telling how two of their number were designated the police and had to try to figure out who was the killer. It had been fun, they said, because the killer had managed to dispense with about a dozen of the guests before he was uncovered amidst much laughter and more liquor. "I just hope we weren't being prophetic," the girl said. I wrote that story, too, describing the party and talking to the teen who'd played the killer. "It was easy," he told me. "No one suspected me because I shouted the loudest that we had to find the killer. It was fun." I asked him if he was scared, but he said no. Later, his father called me, begging me not to print the kid's name. I talked it over with Nolan, and we agreed to use just his initials. Nolan loved that story, too.

I had not been able to get the story of the killer's latest phone call into the next day's paper; when he'd hung up and I'd looked across the table at Christine, it had been close to one A.M., too late for that day's editions. The main run was already winding off the presses, bundles of newsprint tied together heading on metal runners toward the loading docks in the basement of the *Journal* building. By the time I was able to get through to Nolan, awakening him at his house, the press run was in top gear, huge Goss Metro printing machines spitting papers out at a rate of close to one a second. When the presses were running it could be felt throughout the whole building. The floor of the newsroom trembled and shook, and my ears could just pick out a distant rumble.

Sometimes, when I was in the building late at night working on a story, I got up from my desk and went to watch the start of the press run. The huge, cavernous room would be filled with blue-shirted pressmen wearing the traditional paper hats to protect their heads from flying ink. There was a lot less of that now with the new high-speed printing machines, computerized and sophisticated, but the pressmen clung tenaciously to the forms of their jobs and wore the small skullcaps with élan. There were clocks on all the walls, and an insistent clanging bell signaled the start of the run.

I would stand to the side as the men fed the huge rolls of paper into the machines, switched on the presses and stood back. A great whirring and shaking began then, gathering momentum until finally the machines were at full speed and the papers rolled from the presses in great streams, like water. A few stories had stopped the presses; it was still an extraordinary moment. The bell clanged three short bursts followed by a loud long peal; the pressmen, glancing at each other for a second, stepped to the machines, and the room slowly came to a halt, suspended, as if arrested by some giant hand. It was like the moment in an operating theater when the patient's heart stops—a second of nightmare—then starts up again, renewed, reinvigorated.

"We'll sit on the story," Nolan said, his voice clearing quickly from sleep. "We'll hold it for tomorrow's paper, so we can do it right, OK?" I agreed. "Now, the important thing is that the wires and the *Post* and the television stations don't catch wind of this." He hesitated. "We have to go to the cops. That was our part of the bargain. But you make certain that they understand their half. No leaks. This is our story." Then he paused for a moment. "Did you get extensive notes?" I described the pages of paper filled with scrawled quotes. "Good," Nolan said. "Don't turn those notes over. You allow them to question you, take a statement, whatever. But keep the notes. What did the guy say, anyway?"

"He said he gets the urge to kill and he gets the urge to talk."

"Unbelievable. That sounds like the lead to me. What else?"

"There was a lot about his life, anecdotes really. I'm not sure why he tells me. And then he described how he killed the old couple."

"In detail?"

"In great detail."

"My God," Nolan said. "What a story."

Christine wanted to come with me to Police Headquarters. She said she could not stand to be alone, that she had the sensation the killer was somehow close by. I told her she would just be bored and that she had to work in the morning. I waited as she prepared herself for bed, watching as she slipped out of her clothes and left them on the floor. I thought of her nakedness, and for an instant the picture of the old couple slipped into my mind. Then, just as quickly I dismissed it and put my hands on her breasts, pulling back the thin sheet under which we slept. She closed her eyes and rolled onto her side, facing me. I rubbed her neck, then reached over and switched off the light. "I wish you could come to bed," she said, "and just hold me. I don't know if I'll be able to sleep."

"Don't be foolish," I replied in the darkness. I would bolt the door securely and see her in the morning. In the weak light filtering in from the street through the window I could see the outline of her body. I wondered why I was not more aroused and then let the thought pass as I stepped from the bedroom back into the living room, closing the door gently behind me. My eyes swept the room, looking for my notes.

Martinez was waiting in the lobby of the headquarters building that night. He was wearing a suit but no tie, and his shirt was opened, exposing the hair on his chest. He grinned at me when I entered. "A stewardess," he said.

"What?" I replied, shaking his hand.

"Blond. National Airlines. About twenty-three years old. She was teaching me how to fly." He grinned again.

"Sorry," I said.

He shrugged. "Business before pleasure. Anyway, I should never have given her number to Wilson. I bet he's glad to crawl out of bed in the middle of the night."

We got on the elevator with a pair of uniformed officers. They stared at me for a moment, then turned away. I listened to them talk about a fight they'd broken up earlier in the evening; one man was complaining that he'd pulled a back muscle. The other wasn't sympathetic. "This way," Martinez said when the doors opened to the third floor. For an instant the lights filled my eyes and I blinked back the glare. The homicide office was a large room divided into dozens of smaller areas by partitions that did not reach to the ceiling. Inside each was a pair of desks, back to back, chairs and telephones. The desks were old, gray metal and scarred by cigarettes.

The detectives watched Martinez and me walk through the aisles as they stood in the doorways, their suits and ties somehow incongruous in the bleak world around them. I saw a black man, his hands cuffed behind his back, sitting in one of the small offices. He was leaning back in a chair, listening to a detective speak. The black man's face was set in a sneer, and periodically he shook his head. I turned away and looked at the walls. They were institutional green and reflected the fluorescent lights. There were photographs on the walls, mug shots and wanted posters, a duty roster and a large handwritten sign that said: Those Assigned to Numbers Killer Squad *Must* Check Daily with Sgt. Wilson or Duty Officer. I continued to follow Martinez through the room, pausing once to glance in at a desk.

There were dozens of glossy color photographs strewn about the tabletop, and as I passed by I realized the shots were of a murder scene. I could see a body, covered in blood, twisted into the rear of an automobile trunk. Martinez stopped when he saw me looking. He stepped into the room and pulled a photo off the desk. "Ever seen what a twelve-gauge shotgun does to someone at close range? Not too pretty huh? This is a gangland thing. Barely made the local section of the *Journal*.

You see, crime doesn't stop when there's a psycho loose. We still have to get the rest of it done."

I looked at the photo. The victim's face, streaked with blood, was frozen in shock, mouth open, eyes rolled back. His chest had absorbed the blast; it was a mess of entrails and blood. I closed my eyes and handed it back. I was dizzy for a second. "Did you make an arrest?" I asked.

"Just a matter of time. We've got a guy in a holding cell now who is making his mind up to talk. Drove the getaway car. I don't think he's too anxious to take the fall for the triggermen."

We continued toward the rear of the room amid the hum of voices and the ringing of telephones. A dozen conversations were going on at once; the noise seemed a backdrop to the activity, like in the newsroom. Detectives swept in and out of the room, some carrying sheaves of paper, others strapping on their weapons. I could hear sirens outside, penetrating through the walls, and the hum of the air conditioning.

We passed by an office with a closed door but a small window. Martinez peered in. "Ah," he said, "confession time." I looked in the window and saw another black man, smoking a cigarette. Two detectives were in the room, one with paper and pencil taking notes. In the corner sat a man at a stenographic machine. His fingers moved above the keyboard, taking down words. "Killed his wife," Martinez said. "She'd been chipping on him. They got into it at their home, and he decided to show her who was boss. Beat her to a pulp." We walked further, and I saw Wilson waiting outside an office.

"Thanks for calling," he said. "You ever been up here before?"

"No."

"Not too fancy, is it?"

I shook my head.

"Listen, what I'd like is for you to go over what the killer said with us, and then, when the steno's finished down the hall, we'll bring him in and you can run through it again. Sometimes you remember something the second time around. Did you take notes?"

I hesitated. "Yes. But I need them for my story."

Wilson looked at me. "How about a copy?"

I shrugged. "Why not? It's the same as a tape." I envisioned Christine and what she had been saying. I was a citizen, too. And I hadn't promised the killer that I wouldn't cooperate with the police. "But you've got to remember the agreement," I said. "No leaks to anybody. I don't want to have to start fielding phone calls from the rest of the media before I get the story into my own paper."

"Agreed," Wilson said. "I understand." He looked angry. "Everyone's got to get their money's worth out of this."

"What do you expect?" I replied.

He turned away. "Who cares?" We walked into the office and sat in silence. My eyes drifted around the room to a blackboard with names on it. Wilson followed my glance. "You know how many guys are working this full-time now? Thirty detectives. More than a third of the staff." He got up and walked to the board. "You haven't seen this," he said. "It comes out, it's my ass." Martinez got up and shut the door. "I don't know why I'm helping you," Wilson said. He rubbed a hand through his cropped hair.

There were four lists of names on the board, detectives divided into four squads: ARMY-VIETNAM, MENTAL HOSPITALS, SEX DETAIL, STREET. There was another listing in a different part of the blackboard with more names under the headings: BALLISTICS, HANDWRITING, VOICE. On the wall above the blackboard were blown-up photos of the bullet fragments taken from the bodies. Points of comparison were listed by numbers in red pencil.

"You see," Wilson said. "We're checking into all this stuff. Each team, around-the-clock coverage, works on a specific section. For example, we're running down all the mental cases in hospitals in Ohio, Chicago and Florida. We figure that the city the killer moved to was Chicago; it's just a guess. We're going through draft records, schools, you name it, trying to get a handle."

"Are you getting anywhere?"

Wilson turned away. "It's an either-or thing. We know the weapon; we're checking all the dealers for ammunition, that kind of thing. We compile lists, ideas, you name it. But nothing really amounts to anything until we get a good subject. And we don't have anybody yet. No name, no identity."

I looked at my own notes. "He says he has gray eyes."

Wilson's face changed quickly. It gathered a kind of intensity, and he peered across the room at me. Martinez slipped a notebook from his pocket. "He told you that?" Wilson asked.

"He said he was a good shot. Gray eyes. Like Daniel Boone."

Wilson nodded. "That's helpful. Especially with army records."

I looked across my pages again. "He said he was out of the army by 1971. He said he'd been in a VA hospital."

"He told you that?" Wilson repeated excitedly. "All right, all right."

"This helps," Martinez said, grinning the same smile as when he had mentioned the stewardess.

I handed him the sheaf of papers. "Run those off and we'll go through it line by line. We'll see how much I remember. The guy was talking fast; we'll just have to see."

Wilson put his hand on my shoulder. "Don't worry," he said. "You have my word there won't be any leaks to the other papers."

I thought of the killer's voice; his memories, his arrogance. I felt I was shifting the balance between him and the police, somehow lending weight to their side.

I should have felt exhilarated. Instead, I felt queasy. I wasn't sure why.

The story, of course, dominated the next day's paper.

It was morning when I left Police Headquarters. Martinez walked me out. "You keep this sucker talking," he said, "maybe we'll have a chance." He shook my hand. I looked up into the front of the building; the windows stared down at me like the vacant eyes in the photo of the murdered man. Martinez turned and waved as I walked down the street toward my car. I felt a light-headedness, which I attributed to the night without sleep. The morning sun was beginning to gather momentum, and I could feel the first of the day's heat around me.

I closed my eyes when I slid into my chair at my own desk. It was a sensual familiarity, like slipping into bed next to a familiar body; the curves, the pressures on my own flesh, were all safe, known. I fingered the keyboard of the typewriter, not pressing down but just touching the letters.

Nolan walked up to me. "How did it go with the cops?"

"They say I'm a big help," I replied. "He said several things which might contribute to his identification."

"How do you feel?"

"OK, I guess," I said. "I feel as if I'm doing something that I shouldn't, though."

"Why?" Nolan persisted. "We trade information with the cops all the time. And what makes us different from the rest of the citizens of this town? If you or I witnessed a crime, wouldn't we be just as obligated to bring the criminal to justice? What makes us any different?"

"I don't know," I said. "It just makes me feel strange."

Nolan laughed. "You're just like any reporter," he said. "Can't stand to part with information except in a news story." He reached over and picked up my notes. "He must have talked for some time." I nodded. "OK," Nolan said, "write it up, and then go home and get some sleep. If there are any problems I'll call you this evening."

It was not difficult to write the story. For the most part I used the killer's voice. At the top I used the most sensational parts, quoting him on his urges and his description of the murders of the old couple. I said his voice was steady, even enthusiastic throughout the conversation, but I did not describe the mood swings, the sudden anger, and I excised most of his personal history, paraphrasing and condensing it into a narrative instead of using his own words. It crossed my mind that I was somehow protecting his memories, trying not to lay them raw on the page, as if they should remain private.

Nolan looked over the pages I handed to him. The story was long, but I knew it would be all right. I watched his red pen flick through the sentences, adjusting a phrase here, editing a word there. "OK," Nolan said, "this ought to open the eyes of some of the people out there. Talk to me after you get some sleep."

But later we had little to say. The story was dummied, edited and set in type. Once again the headline ran all six columns, stretched across the front page, bannered just below the masthead: "NUMBERS" KILLER CALLS AGAIN: "I GET URGES," HE SAYS.

I looked at my name underneath the headline, and then at the words:

> The man dubbed the "Numbers" killer by local police has once again telephoned this *Journal* reporter to recount the grisly details of the recent murders of an elderly Miami Beach couple.
>
> Ira and Ruth Stein, the killer said in a voice devoid of emotion, "were perfect innocents." And once again the killer pledged to continue his string of murders, a reenactment, he said, of an as-yet unspecified act of violence in Vietnam during the conflict there.
>
> Police, meanwhile, have renewed their efforts to identify and apprehend the killer.

My eyes glazed over the rest of the text; the words seemed to melt into a great gray mass on the page in front of me. I was aware of a pleasurable warmth, the satisfaction of seeing the story so prominently in print. Just him and me, I thought. That's what he said. Together, putting the story out slowly but surely. I wondered if I was starting to need him as much as he needed me.

In the days following the phone call and the subsequent story, I returned to the psychiatrist to see if he had any advice. He seemed glad to see me, held out his hand and shook my own warmly. He gestured for me to take the chair across from his desk and then took a moment to light a pipe, swinging back in his own chair, balancing behind his desk as on a high wire. It was late afternoon and the sunlight filtered through the window. "I read all the stories with great interest," he said. "Let me compliment you. I think they are very well done."

I nodded thanks.

"So," he continued, "what brings you back? Oh, you don't have to answer, I know. More instant insight needed." He laughed.

"I just wanted to ask you your impressions," I said. "Perhaps something has occurred to you. Maybe you can think of something that I can ask the killer, something that will trigger more information about himself."

"Well," the doctor said, smoke slipping from between his lips, "I don't think that there is any single question you could ask that would cause him to explode. That's the stuff of fiction, really. The great sudden breakthrough. The revelation. Honesty suddenly plucked from a world of lies." He shook his head. "I wish things worked like that. Hollywood. We should all move to Hollywood, perhaps. No"—and he dragged in deeply on his pipe again—"even when there are revelations, sudden catharsis, they're usually accompanied by setbacks, denial, and the mind compensating for the admission it has made. It's always a slow process. There are victories, don't get me wrong, and days of great progress, but it isn't quite so quick as one would like." He paused again. "Anyway, from reading the stories, particularly the one the other day where he described the second murders, it seems you're getting more information about this fellow than you can use."

"I don't get it," I said. "He ricochets back and forth between some incident during the war, his family, growing up. It comes across as a jumble."

"You would prefer someone totally calm, rational and explicitly helpful? People like that seldom commit series of random murders. And they certainly don't sit on the telephone giving clues to the press, the police and the public at large."

"All right," I said, laughing. The doctor smiled with me. "You add it up for me."

The doctor thought for a moment, swiveling in his chair, then stopped abruptly and turned toward me. "I don't think the situation has changed much from the first time we talked. The killer sees himself as invulnerable, yet at the same time he gives up clues to his identity. A part of him wants to be caught; a part of him loves the act of toying with the whole world. He mingles the two courses of his life in the conversations with you because they're confused in his mind. The reasons he enjoys killing today are for the most part rooted in his childhood. A seductive mother, perhaps worse; a father who alternated between demands and beatings. A sense of isolation, alienation. He grows up, his anger unchecked. Then he goes to the Army—or says he does—and learns to kill. He says, I'm already a good shot, or, translated, I'm already a killer. I wonder, though: this is an intelligent man. Did he really go to Vietnam? Or is he using the collective national guilt to obscure the feelings he already had, the course he was already set upon?"

I interrupted. "His descriptions are explicit. His knowledge seems very real, very familiar. . . ."

"Almost too much so, I would think," the doctor remarked.

"I don't buy that."

"Just a theory, mind you. Just a possibility. As much evidence that I'm wrong as that I'm right. So much of this is guesswork, really. Psychiatry is not designed to anticipate, to predict."

"What is past is prologue," I said.

The doctor laughed. "Touché." He thought for an instant. "Let's assume that he's telling the truth, there was an overseas incident—and I caution you, be wary, because what is truth for a psychotic is not necessarily truth for a journalist. This incident overseas, I would suspect, would tie in with some experiences that he had here, as a child." He waved his hand. "I know, I know, journalism doesn't want to hear about latency and anal phases and all the preadolescent stuff that is the cornerstone of my profession. But you look for it, and it will help."

Again he paused, swiveling to look out the window.

"It's all a game to him, I think. I still don't think he'll be caught, no matter how much information he imparts."

"Still pessimistic," I said.

He laughed. "It still goes with the territory."

I asked him about the reactions I'd observed on the street: the concern, fear, even challenges.

"I think people will continue to fear this man. Whether we see any hysterical symptoms . . . who knows? A colleague of mine told me he has a patient who can talk of nothing else, hour after hour. That, I suspect, is the exception rather than the rule. And don't underestimate the ability of people to ignore that which stares them in the face. You've read Poe?"

I nodded.

"'The Masque of the Red Death.' Very appropriate, dancing as death enters the ballroom." He got up and walked to the window. "Miami is a city that is spared so much," he said. "We have the sun, the water, boating, tennis, outdoors, the beach. It's a community that thrives on escape. There are no winters here. When was the last really big storm? Nineteen thirty-seven or thereabouts. No one even remembers. It's harder here to feel those old people's deaths, to believe that underneath the sun and in the warm air there is something inherently evil stalking us. Oh, don't get me wrong, you'll see fear everywhere you go. You take out your notebook and you remind people. But can we really understand what's out there? I don't know."

His voice trailed off. He turned and looked at me.

"I must be getting old. I ramble on. I spend so much time listening that when I get the chance to talk it just pours out. Forgive me." We shook hands a second time. "I find it all very interesting," he said. "Anytime I can be of assistance."

I did not hear from the killer for nearly two weeks.

The time seemed to pass interminably from second to second. I'd had the impression so firmly that he would act again swiftly that each moment seemed elongated unnaturally. Miami crept through August, the pace of the city dictated by the heat; slow, irritating. A man was shot during an argument over a fender bender, the assailant standing in tears by the dented automobiles, waiting for the police while the victim choked in his own blood. There was a series of convenience-store robberies, two of which ended in the shotgunning of the teenage bandits by a police stakeout squad. There was a scandal in the local government; an accountant uncovered a significant loss of money from a petty-cash fund, and the prosecutor's office subpoenaed records from the mayor and two commissioners. I worked on none of the stories; Nolan kept me in the office most of the time.

I wrote one long piece detailing the police activities, describing how one team was working with army records at Fort Bragg in North Carolina and the Pentagon in Washington.

There were other items as well. One night I rode in a police cruiser through the section where the first murder had taken place and talked with a pair of officers about their beat. They told me it had changed in subtle ways; first there had been fewer people out in the evenings, then fewer teenagers. The neighborhoods were a lot quieter. The officers spoke angrily about the killer, vicious talk about getting him alone for a few minutes, about the chance to shoot it out. They were both young men and had served in Vietnam. Sure, one of them said, it was bad over there, but we're home now and it's over. He repeated himself, saying "over" again and again. His partner agreed, grunting as he swung the patrol car down darkened streets, past homes that seemed closed, shut away.

During those two weeks I spoke with Wilson and Martinez every day, sometimes twice a day, trying to develop stories out of their leads. They were both open and circumspect in their dealings with me; they showed me some areas of investigation, the ballistic exams, the canvassing of ammunition dealers trying to find who had purchased .45-caliber bullets in recent months. About the probes into Army records, they were more reluctant. I suspected that they had developed some ideas, perhaps even gained a few names, but wouldn't tell me. I went to Nolan with my thoughts and he put pressure on his source, the homicide lieutenant, to find out, but the source related only that there had been some progress but nothing concrete. My suspicions remained.

Nolan decided then that we shouldn't rely on the police as much and put me to working up a profile of the killer based on the tapes and the notes of the conversations. Near the end of the second week, as I was completing the profile, the managing editor called me in to ask if I thought perhaps the killer had departed. He stood up from his desk and walked to the window in his office that overlooked the newsroom, his eyes scanning the activity in the huge room.

He was worried, he said, that the paper might be prolonging the atmosphere of fear by daily stories about the killer and the progress of the police. Let's hold off, he told me, until we're sure this guy is out there. He spoke his words into the window, and I had to strain to catch them. He was a dapper man who wore well-tailored suits. His sleeves were forever rolled up, though, and his hands were often darkened with the stains of newsprint.

Nolan was there listening to him speak, and I saw his head nod in agreement. The trouble is, I heard Nolan say, that he was torn. One could argue that perhaps we were preventing more murders by continuing the stories; that the killer seemed to respond to the lack of news more violently than to the constant flow of stories. Every time the flow slackened, he acted, or that's what he said. The managing editor agreed that this put the paper in a difficult situation, but that we couldn't let our decisions be made by a madman. All right, Nolan said, let's see what happens.

As for myself, I didn't think the killer had disappeared. I could sense him just outside my reach.

The profile was in the form of notes, not intended for publication; only, as Nolan said, something for us to measure him by. I wrote:

Only child.
Beaten.
Humiliated.
Seduced?

I went to the library just off the newsroom and took out an almanac and an encyclopedia. I looked up the state of Ohio. It stared out at me from the pages of thick books, square, solid, like a Midwesterner's unwavering gaze. My eyes tracked the roads that crisscrossed the state, stopping at the small dots that corresponded to the small towns. I saw the serpentine shape of the Ohio River, and I tried to imagine flat fields stretching from its banks inland, crops reaching up under the August sky to the sun.

Porter happened by and stopped to peer over my shoulder at the map. "Ever been there?" he asked. I shook my head. "Cold in the winter. Hot in the summer. Conservative. I was at Kent State when the guardsmen shot the students. It was a clear day, sun out, bright. I remember the whole thing seemed more like an exercise; the crowd swept over the hill, slogans, shouts, the usual. There was this one wretched moment after the volley was fired; I didn't know what had taken place, but I was stunned nonetheless. It was as if the knowledge that they'd fired into the crowd was inside my head, fighting to get into my conscious thought, like the last few minutes of sleep in the morning. There was a scream, more like a wail—it reminded me of the Arab women in *The Battle of Algiers*—and I knew then, without seeing what had occurred. Of course, I ran. Everyone did. I ran right past one of the bodies. I still remember the blood against the black macadam of the pathway. You know, there's a sculpture in the center of the campus, a sharply defined piece filled with angles and lines. It's made from a kind of steel that looks bronze. There's a bullet hole through it, right through one of the corners, a small round circle. You know, the type that you simply have to put your finger through and feel? Perfectly round."

I returned to my desk and wrote:

The City.
The Army.
The War.
The Incident.

What was the incident? In the office of my college newspaper, we had framed the famous photo from Mylai 4. It was an oversized poster, a great mass of yellow and green and in the center a tangle of bodies streaked with the red of their own blood. I thought of other photos, too: the girl running naked toward the camera from the explosions of napalm, her mouth open in a great terrified circle; the blank look of death on the face of the VC in the microsecond his head began to blow apart from the force of the police chief's bullet. What was the incident? What had the killer done?

I wrote:

Age: twenty-five to thirty.
Time in VA Hospital.
Gray eyes.

I wondered if he was telling the truth. What's fact, what's fiction. Those were his last words.

The telephone rang as I was stepping from the shower. I heard Christine answer it, and I hurriedly grabbed at a towel and began to dry my body. There was a knock on the bathroom door, a small sound that seemed to hide in the steam. She pushed the door open and her eyes were wide. "It's him," she said. "I'm sure of it. He hesitated a moment when I picked up the telephone, then asked for you by name. He's waiting."

I slipped a bathrobe around my shoulders and sponged my head swiftly. I could still feel the moisture on my back when I picked up the receiver.

"That must be your girl friend," the voice said. "She sounds very nice."

"Where have you been? It's been nearly two weeks."

"Here and there," he said. "Uptown, downtown, all around the town." I waited for something else, but he had stopped. After a pause he started again. "Tell the police to keep checking those records, they're sure to come up with something. They've got the gray eyes, what else? Oh, marksmanship. I got a medal. Tell them to check into that, it should narrow the field some. Diligence has its rewards; you tell them that."

And then he hesitated again.

"But it won't do them any good."

A pause.

"They'll never catch me. No matter how much help I give them."

Another silence.

"You must be anxious to get to work," the killer said. "Well, here's something to work on: Number Four."

"Where?"

"Out to the west, off Krome Avenue, where it cuts close in to the start of the Everglades. That's a marvelous area, quiet, deserted. A person can really think out there, no sounds except for the animals and an occasional jet passing overhead. Go three miles down Krome from where you get on after the expressway. You'll see a dirt road to the left. Take it for six-tenths of a mile. Stop and walk about a hundred yards through the underbrush. There'll be a clearing. Better hurry, because there's a surprise."

And then he hung up.

It was barely eight in the morning. I heard a chair scrape behind me and knew Christine had sat down at the kitchen table. "He's killed again," I said. She made no reply. "You were right, it was him." I looked back at the telephone. I had better hurry, that's what the killer had said.

Wilson took little time in reaching the phone. I pictured him on the other end, his face already beginning to twist with anger, reddening up toward the roots of his salt-and-pepper crew cut. "Again?" he asked, prescient, as he picked up the telephone.

"Out Krome Avenue, toward the Glades," I said. "He said there was a surprise. As well as Number Four."

"What do you mean, surprise?"

"How the hell do I know? He plays with me as much as he plays with you."

"That's a big area," Wilson started, but I interrupted him.

"Here, listen for yourself." I took the recorder the police had placed on my phone and rewound it. Then, holding the receiver down to the speaker, I played the conversation to Wilson. The killer's words filled the room, and I turned to Christine. She sat shaking her head.

It was over in what seemed a second. I stopped the tape and put the phone back to my ear. "Did you get that?" I asked Wilson.

"Son of a bitch," he replied.

I waited.

"Fucking son of a bitch. I'm going to get him. I'm going to get him myself." His voice changed. "Thanks for calling. I'll see you out there."

After I hung up the telephone I walked over behind Christine, put my hand on her shoulder and squeezed, trying to convey a sense of support. She reached up and touched my hand with her fingers but said nothing, just continued to shake her head. But my mind was already back to the conversation, and I was trying to imagine what it was that was waiting out on Krome Avenue. I went to the bedroom and began to dress.

It was several minutes before I realized that I had neglected to call Nolan and tell the city desk. The thought came over me suddenly, and I felt a type of panic, like a child in a classroom who's been caught by a question from the teacher when he hasn't been paying attention.

And so, tucking in my shirt, I dialed the city desk. As I waited for Nolan to come on the line, the image filled my mind of the pressroom chief, hesitating for a last second, his eyes scanning the big room and the waiting presses, and then hitting the button that started the machines rolling and filling the air with noise.

CHAPTER ELEVEN

THE killer's "surprise" was an act of transcendent cruelty.

It stirred an almost universal rage throughout the city at the same time it increased the tenor of the fear that had become so commonplace. For the first time people began to meet in groups, civic organizations held rallies, community patrols were initiated. The publicity redoubled, also: *Time* and *Newsweek* devoted considerable space to the killer and his series of murders and telephone calls. My photo ran in each magazine, and I was quoted in both. I was also interviewed by television newsmen, but that had become almost routine. The *New York Times* and the *Washington Post* sent stringers over to talk with me and then ran lengthy pieces. The *Chicago Tribune* sent a feature writer down to Miami. She stayed at one of the hotels on the Beach, and I took her around to the spots where the bodies had been discovered. They ran the story stripped across the bottom of their front page; she sent me a copy a few days later. I began to clip the stories myself—my own and the ones that I saw in the national press—and kept them on my desk in a file which thickened daily.

I had dodged through the city traffic as quickly as I could, heading toward the expressway. The morning rush hour was in the other direction, downtown toward the bay and the center of Miami, and so I pushed the car past the speed limit easily, the window down and hot air sucking through the car. The sun glistened off the road, and I held one hand on the wheel as the other slipped my sunglasses from their case. Within a few seconds I saw a car come up fast behind me; it was Porter, far above the speed limit, swinging the big sedan from lane to lane, oblivious to obstacles. He waved as he went past and I accelerated to keep pace.

We were both doing close to ninety. The Krome Avenue exit came up fast, and as we swung down onto the two-lane road I saw a green and white police car roar past us. It was then that I caught the first sound of sirens and knew that we were part of a wave of vehicles descending onto the Everglades. As I swung the car onto the road, I saw a flight of white herons swing out of the swamp up into the sky, a half-dozen birds, their feathers reflecting the sun, wheeling against the blue sky and disappearing. A rescue-squad ambulance came up behind us, its lights blinking red and yellow, its siren filling the air with harsh urgency. We slowed to let it pass, then accelerated to keep up. I knew it was not far away, and within seconds I saw a dozen cars and unmarked cruisers pulled haphazardly to the side of the road, lights flashing in an uncoordinated symphony of sight. The ambulance pushed as far through the mass as it could, then stopped, tires throwing off gravel and dirt. Three yellow-jump-suited rescue personnel leaped from the ambulance, pushing a stretcher. One carried a black doctor's bag and had a stethoscope hanging from his neck. I stopped and followed, watching the uniformed officers as they guided the rescue squad through the swamp. Porter shouted at me, "Let's go, let's go!" as he turned and rushed through the scrub brush and sickle weeds, down a path that had already been trampled by thc hurrying policemen. As I followed him, two television trucks and a car from the *Post* pulled in.

The ground underfoot was marshy and soft, and we slid as

we ran. The brush seemed to reach out and trip us as we swept past. On either side of the small pathway leading from the road was dense swamp; we were running on the only hump of dry land. I saw a small island ahead, a patch of solid ground covered with saw grass and weeds. It was there the policemen were gathered. And it was from that scene that I heard the first cry.

It was a high-pitched, wordless sound of despair and loneliness. I did not recognize it for what it was; I think Porter did, for he turned momentarily and stared back at me. We scrambled up a small embankment, and several of the uniformed officers saw us and halted us from going any closer. Porter was already snapping pictures through a long lens, the camera whirring and clicking. "There," he said, pointing the camera. I followed the lens and saw a body pitched forward, obscured by the foliage. A single officer stood over it, as if guarding it. But the policeman's eyes were locked on the crowd of rescue personnel and other officers a few feet away. I could make out a rough, makeshift lean-to that seemed to be propped up in the midst of the crowd. And then I heard the cry again, wailing, piercing the morning heat. "My God," Porter said, putting down the long lens for an instant, "it's a kid."

As I watched, the policemen seemed to pull back, and I saw them slapping each other on the back and two uniformed officers' hands being pumped. The three rescue-squad personnel turned and, half-jogging, headed toward the pathway crowded with reporters and cameramen as the policemen cleared a trail.

The man in front had the child in his arms, wrapped in a rough blue blanket pressed tightly against his yellow jump suit. He was smiling and talking to the child as he went past, shielding the baby from the cameras and lights. "How old?" I asked as he swept past.

"A year, maybe," he answered, "eighteen months."

"Is he hurt?" I called.

"It's a she, and nothing except a little exposure, I think." He continued down the gauntlet of press toward the ambulance, speaking in a soft voice to the child.

"Jesus Christ," I heard Porter say. "Can you believe that?"

The police would not let us out into the scene of the fourth murder for close to two hours. By that time the sun was high overhead and the morning had dissolved under the probing heat. As usual I was questioned by the other reporters, and I confirmed that the killer had called and provided directions to the location. After about an hour, word came in over a television-truck shortwave that the baby girl seemed to be fine and was in the pediatric-care ward of a big downtown hospital. I told the other reporters that the killer had promised a "surprise," and it was my guess the child was what he had had in mind. The questioning dropped away and we waited. I sat by the side of the path on the damp ground, watching the crime-laboratory personnel combing the area and the assistant medical examiner attending to the body. Porter complained about the lack of shots and jumped to his feet when the body was brought out; I remember thinking it was the fourth black bag I'd seen that summer and wondered if it was one of the same bags that had been used to carry any of the other victims.

Wilson and Martinez finally came and briefed the press, myself included. They said that it appeared the child and the victim—a white woman in her late twenties—and the killer had stayed in the clearing for a day or so. There was debris, they said, indicating they'd had several meals. They would not give us the woman's name. Martinez nodded when asked about the cause of death and the style; the same hands bound behind and wound to the back of the head. Wilson said the same knots that had been used to bind the hands had been used in the construction of the little lean-to. It was obviously shelter from the sun for the child. He said there would be no further comment. I caught his eye for an instant, but his return glance told me nothing.

Single-file, the reporters and cameramen were led through the scene. We were told not to touch anything, and for the most part the tour was conducted in silence. I could see the bloodstains on the saw grass where the woman had lain. A pile of items was being tagged and registered by a technician; I could see empty hamburger boxes from a fast-food chain, several disposable bottles, some diapers, and a few crumpled packs of cigarettes. I paused by the little lean-to. The walls were constructed of scrap wood and boards, and the top was a thatch of grass and palms. A few strands of rope held it together, and I had the impression a strong breeze would blow it apart.

En masse the press interviewed the two officers—patrolmen riding their regular shift out in the countryside—who had found the scene and the child. They had been told to secure the area for the detectives, but one of them had heard what he thought was a cry, and they had blundered through the brush toward the lean-to and the child. There was a combination of pride and anger in their faces; they were pleased with saving the child, but confused and angry over the circumstances. "What kind of guy," one of them said, a young man, blond-haired with a thick mustache, "would leave a little child behind like that after murdering her mother?"

And that, of course, was the question everyone had.

My father called after the articles in the newsweeklies appeared. I answered the telephone hesitantly, with a tentativeness brought about by my lack of contact with the killer. I had adjusted, but only in part, to my dependence upon the telephone. When it rang I still felt a rush of excitement, thinking it could be him, and, when it proved otherwise, disappointment mingled with relief. I had not realized up to then how often the telephone rang or how closely it had become entwined with my life. "I saw your picture," he said. "This seems to be turning you into a celebrity." I made no reply, and he added, "It seems a terrible way to become known. Do you suppose the police are any closer to capturing this guy?"

I told him I didn't know. The killer seemed to be toying with the police, with his partial descriptions of himself, but no one was certain he was telling the truth.

We continued to talk, small talk about my brother's law practice, my sister still in college, my mother. She had taken up social work at a local hospital, my father said, a psychiatric ward, interesting stuff. He said she was worried about me, in particular the closeness that had come to exist between the killer and myself.

"What closeness?" I asked. "I'm on the end of his rope. He tugs, I respond. He calls, I write. The distance remains infinite."

"No," my father said, and I realized suddenly that the fear was as much his own as my mother's. "You're wrong. In each call, each conversation, he brings you closer. The distance, I think, diminishes."

"I'm not afraid."

"You should be."

Distance, I thought, has always been important in my family.

His mind must have been working on the same thought. He continued, after a moment: "When you were young and growing, you were always the silent one. Your brother, your sister, both threw themselves into things more readily. You always hesitated. I suppose I always thought you would become a journalist. You spent so much time watching."

"I'll be all right," I said, but my voice was like an echo in a canyon.

The story dominated all other thoughts.

For days the woman and child remained unidentified. All the reporters in Miami working the story chafed under the mystery, unable to give the murdered woman a past, a sense of being. As each day passed, speculation grew. We wondered where she came from, whether she had some special connection to the killer, what her role was in the symbolic drama. A lover, some thought; a woman who knew his identity; a sister, perhaps. We struggled with the possibilities, making her death larger than her life.

I wrote, over and over again, every particle of the story that I could discover. The meeting with the managing editor and Nolan was forgotten; the story gained its own momentum. The headlines developed a manic sense; the words "Massive Manhunt" and "Unrelenting Around-the-Clock Investigation" crept into the prose. All the clichés of a big-city crime were there. We shifted, calling him sometimes the "Numbers Killer" and sometimes the "Telephone Killer." Regardless, everyone knew who we were talking about.

A local movie house brought in a double feature: *Dial M For Murder* and *Wait Until Dark*. It played to packed houses, and I spent an evening talking with the people lined up outside the theater waiting for the next show. "It's incredible," one girl told me. She had blond hair, and she clutched her boyfriend's arm in mock fear. "It seems so Hollywood, and yet it's really happening, isn't it?"

I used her quote to lead a story.

There were many others. I spent another night riding through the southern section of the city, row upon row of trim, single-story, white-washed middle-income homes. This time I was not with the police but with a group of neighborhood home-owners. They had formed an "association," and part of the association's duties was to patrol the area. They had foiled a burglary on their first night, the driver said. The other man in the car, a big man with thick arms and sideburns that curled down the side of his head, turned to me then and whispered, "The cops say we shouldn't carry weapons, but . . ." and pulled up the corner of his sweat shirt to display the pearl handle of a short-barreled Colt .32 stuck in his pants. He laughed, his voice filling the inside of the car and spilling through the windows into the dark outside.

He, too, became a story.

I went to a civic-group meeting and listened to speaker after speaker rise to question the police efforts at finding the killer. The meeting was held in a high school gymnasium, and I looked up through the lights to the ceiling where a huge banner, a championship season, hung. The words all seemed the same that night, the same as those of the people on the street, of the men in the car, the same as the words heard everywhere. A woman rose and looked over the crowd. I could see her face twist as she struggled with her thoughts. Finally she opened her mouth. "What can we do?" she asked, and I thought: nothing. Nothing can be done. I scribbled her words into my notebook and kept my pessimism out of the story.

The local politicians, too, had their say. There was an almost endless series of press conferences and publicity stunts; they rode with the police, they wore weapons to meetings at City Hall. They, too, became part of the canvas.

And then there was my own role.

At a similar meeting there was another woman; small, barely five feet, but with a high-pitched voice that projected far beyond her size. Her face was pinched, and the wrinkles on her forehead seemed like lines drawn with a pen. She stared at me, open-mouthed, when I asked her a question, as she sorted through her memory. Finally, she said, "You've talked with him!" and I nodded, and she continued, "You're the one he calls!" and I nodded again. Her voice rose against the auditorium noise; a crowd swiftly gathered, and I felt a sudden rush of heat as the bodies pressed around me. Porter was close by; I could hear the sound of his camera. "Why don't you tell him to stop!" the woman went on. "Why don't you make him stop!" Her voice had become a shriek, but one that bore the sympathy of the others gathered around her.

"I've tried," I said.

"Try again!" she screamed. "Keep trying!"

"How?" I asked.

But she had turned her head, shaking in anger and tears.

A man, thickset, shook his fist. "Tell him we're waiting for him! Tell him we're not afraid!"

I thought how simple it all was. Fear engenders such basic reactions: the man threatened responds aggressively, posturing; the woman, realistic in her way, responds in anguish.

Porter punctuated my thoughts. "Just once," he said, smiling, "I'd like to see some guy standing around wringing his hands, tears running down his face, shouting, 'What can I do, what can I do?' and have his wife walk up and gruffly shake her fist in our faces and say, 'Dammit, I'm ready for the sucker. Let him show.'" He laughed and continued to take shots of the meeting.

That night I sat at the typewriter thinking of the woman's words. Try again, keep trying. But how do I do that? I put it out of my head and began to write the next day's story.

Wilson called one night just as I was preparing to leave the office. "I've got something you probably want to see," he said. I walked out into the Miami evening. The black seemed to gleam, alive with small breaths of wind. I felt I could reach out and touch the night, grasp huge handfuls out of the air. I drove through the downtown, the headlights mingling with the lights on the street, cutting a brightness out of the dark sky. Wilson met me at the entrance to Police Headquarters. "Come on," he said. "Have your horizons broadened." He laughed at his cliché and led me through the entrance. The high-intensity fluorescent lights hurt my eyes for a moment, and I blinked as we walked to an elevator. The eyes of the policemen followed me across the lobby.

We got off on the homicide department's floor, but instead of entering the main workroom, Wilson took me down a side corridor. The walls were painted white and there were no signs, no posters, nothing to say where it led. I followed the detective's back, keeping pace as he marched down the center of the hallway, leaving not enough room for me to walk beside him. Finally he paused outside of an unmarked brown door. "All right," he said. "Don't say anything until it's over. Don't make any fast movements, don't light any cigarettes. Just watch, got it? Listen and learn." He swung the door open quickly, and the two of us entered a small darkened room. There was only one light, and that was shaded severely so that only the shadows of the men in the room could be made out. I saw a table with a flat reel-to-reel tape recorder. A man sat behind it, watching the reels turn, but my attention went quickest to the window. It was about two feet by four feet, and through it I could see into an adjacent room, one where the lights were turned high. "One-way glass," Wilson muttered. I stood next to him, peering into the second room.

A young man sat at a table. He had long brown, nearly red hair and a meager beard. His eyes were rimmed and dark, and he kept wiping at his nose throughout the conversation. He used the back of his hand, drawing it in a slow, unthinking motion across his face. His head jerked about as he spoke, trying to follow the glance of the two detectives in the room. One of them was Martinez, his tie loosened and the top button of his shirt undone. His vest was open, and I could see his empty holster. The other detective, also in his shirt-sleeves, sat on a chair, leaning back, arms folded, looking skeptical and angry.

"All right," Martinez said, "run through it again for us, will ya, Joey?" He paced about the room, walking behind the man and pausing, then moving on, varying his speed, moving his eyes to the ceiling, to the floor, then suddenly boring in on the man at the table.

"What is it you guys want?" the man said. "I did it. Each one. What more do you need?" His voice was choppy, anxious and sounded tinny through the speaker built into the ceiling.

"First the girl, then the old couple, now the woman and the kid. I'm tired of it now."

"That's why you turned yourself in?" Martinez asked.

"Yeah."

"Where's the gun?"

"I threw it into a canal."

"Which canal?"

"I don't know. How should I remember?"

"When?"

"Before I came here."

"And you don't remember? Come on, Joey."

"I tell you I just don't remember."

"How'd you get here?"

"I walked."

"What route?"

"From uptown."

"No canals there."

"Yes, there was." The voice was whining, pleading.

"OK, Joey, tell me about the girl."

"What's to say? I killed her."

"Got to do better than that."

"OK," the man said, after a moment. "I raped her, too."

Martinez shook his head. "Why did you call the paper, Joey?"

"I wanted to tell them about it. I wanted everyone to know."

"Why?"

"So they would know I was important."

"Killing makes you feel important, Joey?"

"That's right."

"You feel important now?"

The man hesitated, wiping his nose vigorously. "You bet," he said. He smiled at the detectives. I saw Martinez nod at the other detective. He uncoiled explosively, his arm suddenly up above his head, then his open palm smashing down on the table a few inches from the confessor's own hands. The noise resounded in the small room.

"Liar!" the detective shouted. "Fucking jerk-off liar! Wasting our time!"

The man recoiled, throwing himself back in the chair, his hands springing up to shield his face.

"No!" he shouted. "The truth. I swear."

"Liar!" the detective repeated. Martinez had slipped to the rear of the room and was leaning against the wall lighting a cigarette, as if oblivious to what was going on. The other detective jumped to his feet and circled around, standing over the confessor. He bent over and I saw the man shrink in fear. "You come in and tell us this bullshit! That's what it is! Bullshit!" The detective raised his hand. "I ought to knock you . . ." Then he paused. There was silence in the room, save for the worried scratching of the confessor. The detective moved behind him, and the confessor kept shifting in his seat, trying to keep him in sight. Suddenly the detective leaned forward, his mouth only inches from the confessor's ear. "Fucking liar!" he screamed. The man quivered, as if hit. The detective grabbed the back of the seat and shook it hard for a moment, and the man almost tumbled to the floor. I saw Martinez take a long drag of his cigarette and give a small hand signal to the other detective. The detective nodded, leaned down once again, shouted, "Fucking liar!" into the confessor's ear, then backed off, out of the man's sight.

"Now, Joey," Martinez said slowly, "why don't we try again?"

The man started to cry, and Martinez waited patiently for the sniffling to stop.

"I'm sorry," the confessor said. "I didn't mean nothing."

Martinez stood up, stretching. He took out another cigarette, lit it and passed it to the man.

"Can I still spend the night in jail?" the confessor asked, puffing gratefully on the smoke. Martinez started to laugh, and after a second the other detective joined in. Finally the confessor did, too, but his laugh was hesitant, and he kept turning nervously, looking for the detective.

Wilson touched my sleeve. "Let's go."

We met Martinez in the hallway. "Quite a show," I said. He grinned.

"Easy. No challenge left. But getting to be a real pain in the ass. That's the fifth off the street this week. People come in saying they're the man, wanting to unburden themselves. Sometimes it takes an hour, two, three, before we get the guy to change, and all the time we know he isn't the guy. They just don't have the right information, the right personality. And mainly, they don't have the evidence. Like no gun."

The detectives walked me outside. After the confines of the small room it was a relief to look up into the dark sky. I asked them how the records check was going. "No computers," Martinez said. "They have to check by hand, each file. A big slow pain."

Wilson looked at me. "Hasn't called again?"

"Not yet," I said. "How much more do you need?"

"How about the dates of service, the rank he reached? It would be a big help."

"I'll try," I said. I seemed to be promising that a lot. The two detectives walked back into the building, and I went back to the office. My description of the phony confession became yet another story. Nolan liked it, as did the news desk. It ran in a corner of the front page.

Christine would only make love with the telephone off the hook. She said she could not stand the thought that the killer might call while we were, as she put it, engaged. I shrugged and went along with her wishes, but afterward I would rise from the bed and replace the receiver, wondering if I had missed any moment of contact in the interim. "Is it all you can think of?" she asked.

"You don't understand," I replied. "A story like this is everything. It won't stop now—it can't stop. It's not just me. Any reporter would be the same."

She shook her head. "I don't believe that," she said.

I walked to a window and stared out. An image rose in my mind: myself at age eleven, staring from the second-story window of my home. I could see the others, my father, mother, brother and sister in the yard, sitting close to a picnic table. I saw my brother and father get up and begin to toss a ball back and forth while my sister moved closer on the bench to my mother. One instant I was staring through the glass, and then things moved in stages. My hand tightened as I balled it into a fist; I heard the noise, a splintering crack, like an alarm. Blood was streaming down the back of my hand, and shattered pieces of glass lay on the window frame. I turned, with a small boy's cry, and ran to the bathroom where I immersed my hand in water, watching the rim of the sink turn pink, then red with blood. After a moment the pain seemed to diminish, and I wrapped my hand in a towel. In another few moments the bleeding subsided, and I looked down at a ragged cut across my knuckles and a deeper cut in my index finger. I kept the towel wrapped tightly and returned to my room. I did not look out to see if they had heard the sound of the window breaking, nor did I look up an hour later when my father poked his head through the door, glanced at the window and then sat on the side of my bed. I remembered the sensation of his hand resting on my forehead, cooling, like an ice pack.

Christine saw my expression, rose from the bed and slipped her arms around me. She rested her head on my shoulder, and I could feel her hand reaching up for the back of my neck in caress, almost as if I were that small child again.

It was early evening, a week after the fourth murder, that Wilson called me. I could hear voices in the background and the sound of a cash register. "This is Wilson," he announced. "We know who she is."

"Who?" I reached for note pad and pencil.

"You want to know, meet me here. Otherwise, wait for the general press release later tonight."

He was in a bar called The Alibi in a hotel across from the county's large criminal courthouse. It was a place I'd been inside before, dark like most bars, little decoration save for the liquor bottles stacked up behind a fake mahogany counter. There were booths where conversations could be held quietly, served by women in short skirts and black mesh stockings. It was frequented by detectives, defense attorneys and prosecutors, a place where the rules of court did not apply, where deals were struck and insults traded. It was always full and always loud.

I discovered Wilson in a booth in a corner. Martinez was with him, his head stretched back and feet out, relaxed. "What are you drinking?" he asked. I ordered a beer. I looked at the two detectives, waiting.

"Shit," Martinez said, straightening himself in the chair. "Here you go." I saw Wilson's eyes follow the younger detective's hand as he reached inside his jacket pocket and pulled out a sheet of white paper. He handed it across the table to me, and then the two men's eyes fixed on me as I read the words.

At the top of the page were the words "PRESS RELEASE" and the county seal. In the center were the words:

> The fourth victim in the "Numbers Killer" case has been identified as: Susan Kemp, 29, a resident of Building 6, number 110, in the Fontainebleau Park apartment complex. The child has been identified as her daughter Jennifer, age 21 months. The child remains in stable condition at Jackson Memorial Hospital. The investigation continues.

"It doesn't tell me much," I said. "Like how you made the identification and how she was selected and picked up."

"We were hoping," Martinez said slowly, "that by now you would have provided that information."

"Why won't the fucker call?" Wilson said. He took a long drink from his glass.

I shrugged. Martinez glanced over at Wilson, then continued. "We don't know why she was selected, or how. Obviously they used a car to get out to the Glades. And obviously, from the debris that remained behind, they were there for some time, possibly overnight. But motive; Christ, who knows?"

"How did you identify her?"

Again Martinez looked over at Wilson. He nodded and took another drink. "She had no ID on her, no name tag, driver's license, nothing. Neither did the kid. This morning, though, this woman calls up the office. Says she lives out in the development. Says her next-door neighbor fits the description of the woman in the papers; she hasn't seen her for days, and she's worried. We went out to check it; routine, you've got to do that sort of thing. The manager lets us into the apartment; seems he was kind of worried, too. We walk through the door, and there on the wall is a nice photo of the woman and kid. Probably taken about a month ago. No doubt about it."

"Who is she?"

Martinez leaned back, holding his glass against his forehead. "No one special," he said. "Just divorced. A schoolteacher taking the summer off before returning to class. She taught the fourth grade."

"Husband?"

"Businessman from Tampa. Flew in this afternoon, ID'ed the body. Gonna take the kid, too, when he gets over the shock."

"Where is he?"

Wilson put out his hand and Martinez cut off his reply in midbreath, before he could get started. "Give us a break," the detective said. He shook his head. "Don't you think the guy has had enough of a rough time for one day?"

"Maybe he wants to say something," I said. "Usually, they do."

Wilson put his head against the back of the booth and closed his eyes. "Tell you what," he said, "I'll ask him. Give him your number. Leave it up to him."

I agreed. He was probably upstairs in the hotel, anyway. It would be no problem to check.

"Still no idea how the killer managed to pick her?"

"None," Martinez said. "No one in the apartment complex saw or noticed anything unusual. No strangers hanging about street corners. No nothing."

"How about the records check? The Army?"

"We've taken the years 1963 to 1973. At a minimum we're talking about several thousand names—and those who have to be cross-checked for unusual eye color. And then we have to come up with addresses. It's gonna take forever." His voice was flat, depressed. "We stand a better chance of somebody seeing something here. Unless we get more out of the guy."

"The psychiatrist I talked with thinks he'll continue to give information out. Teasing, just daring you to catch him."

Wilson closed his eyes. "That's what really fucks me up," he said. His eyes blinked open and he stared across the table at me, through the bar darkness. "You know, today I decided to send my wife and kids away to visit their grandparents. In fucking Minnesota, for Christ's sake. Maybe that's far enough away." He laughed, a short snorting sound. "Martinez doesn't have to worry. All those girl friends, hell, he wouldn't even miss one or two."

Martinez smiled but did not laugh.

Wilson continued talking, pausing only to wave for another drink. "We go out, you know, cruising the streets, talking with informants. Anybody who might have a line. I've twisted more arms in the last three weeks than I have in years. Nobody knows nothing. Hell, the junkies in Liberty City are just as scared as the mothers in Kendall."

Martinez spoke. "We get calls, you know, every day, sometimes every hour, especially after the first edition of the *Journal* comes out. This guy wants to report on his neighbor, acting suspicious. Another guy thinks he saw a forty-five-caliber pistol in his brother-in-law's house. We take the information and then out we go, check it out. We check everything out. Every little detail, every little tip, no matter. And we're no fucking closer now than we were at the start."

"Something will break," I said.

"Yeah," Martinez said. "Like maybe the fuck will dump the next body off on our doorstep. At least then we'd know about it before the rest of the world."

Wilson looked up, across the room. His eyes fixed on a man carrying a drink, heading in our direction. "Oh, shit," he said.

The man approached and seemed to hover for an instant on the edge of the darkness. He stared at the two policemen, ignoring me. I watched as he slowly raised his glass to his lips and, eyes still focused on the policemen, drained off the glass. His voice, when he spoke, was unsteady. "So," he said. "Off duty, huh? No need to hunt murderers when you can have a drink, huh?"

Martinez stood up and, reaching over to an adjacent table, seized a chair. "Mr. Kemp," he said, "please sit down."

I pulled out my notebook again.

"I don't want to sit with you," he said, but he slid into the chair.

"Mr. Kemp," Martinez said, "this is Malcolm Anderson. He's a reporter with the *Journal*." Martinez motioned at me. I nodded.

"You're the one who talks to this guy, right?"

"That's right. It was your wife?"

"That's right." He was wearing a conservative blue suit,

but it seemed to hang from his body, as if he had shrunk in size over the course of the day.

"I'm sorry," I said.

He looked at me. "No, you're not. They aren't, either. . . ." I started to protest, but he moved his hand up in a half-drunken wave. "Don't let it bother you," he said. "I mean, why should you care? Why should anyone care?" I saw tears forming at the corners of his eyes. "You know, the stupid thing is, two months ago, when we were going through the divorce, we were yelling at each other all the time. Real bitter over the baby, the home, the car, all the little things. I must have wished her dead a dozen times, a hundred times. And now she is."

He looked at me for an instant, his eyes watery; then he slowly shifted his gaze to the two policemen. "Just another dead body. I bet you see hundreds of them, huh?"

"Mr. Kemp," Martinez started in, but the same hand motion cut him off. "Oh, don't let my attitude make you angry," the man said, shaking his head uncoordinatedly. "She was nothing special. Nothing to get upset about. Just another murder. Hey, you get some free time, maybe you'll find this guy. I know you've got better things to do." He stood up sharply, and the chair behind him turned over with a crash that quieted the bar and turned all eyes our way. "No, don't get up!" he shouted as Martinez started to stand. "Don't put yourselves out. Do your little investigations, write your little stories. . . ." He looked at me. "It doesn't mean anything. Nothing means anything." And he turned sharply, unsteadily, and looked across at the men in the room staring at him. "Fuck you all, every one of you." No one moved. His words hung in the air for a second. He balled his hand into a fist and made punching motions in front of him. Then he stopped, suddenly looked about him, and with his head abruptly sinking into his hands, he ran from the room.

In the darkness, I hurried to scribble the words and the motions, to capture it all in my notebook. Wilson watched me. "Get it all?" he asked, sarcastic.

I looked at him and paused before answering. "That's what it's all about," I said.

I got up to leave and Wilson's eyes followed me. For a moment our glance locked, and I watched as he seemed to be turning something over in his mind. Finally he spoke: "Set him up," he said.

Martinez also stared at me. "Do it," he said; "set him up."

"I'll think about it," I replied. I turned and left them in the bar. I walked out into the beginning of the night, a blue-black sky naked of clouds. I breathed in deeply, the leftover daytime heat filling my lungs, replacing the stale air-conditioned air of the bar. I felt a sudden dizziness as I replayed the detectives' words in my mind. They mingled with my father's and Christine's. I saw the murdered woman's husband, lurching in grief, striking out at the emptiness in the bar, confusing that for the helplessness in his mind.

CHAPTER TWELVE

I RETURNED late that night to the office. I could feel the vibration from the presses coursing up through the floor as I walked into the newsroom, the early-edition run streaming through the catacomb network of sorting and assembling machines. It was as if the steady shaking rose through my legs and into my body, that as I sat at the typewriter to write I was a part of a huge machine.

Earlier, Porter had met me at the murdered woman's apartment. We started in, knocking on doors, talking with the neighbors. They seemed resigned, a glumness marking their faces and voices; they had seen the police officers earlier in the day; they had talked with the detectives who'd probed them with many of the same questions I asked. They knew the woman was the killer's victim, and they were trying to ignore the fear that had stepped up so close to them.

A sweet, gentle woman, they said. She managed a smile throughout the day, always quick with a greeting. A woman, though, who kept mostly to herself and her child; she had no close friends that I could find in the complex. Visitors, I asked? None, said the next-door neighbor, a middle-aged woman, hair pulled sharply back from her head in a red bandanna. Her husband leaned over her shoulder, the two of them crowded into the doorway, unwilling to step into the hall as if refusing to be lured out from sanctuary. She was quiet, the man said; kept to herself mostly.

I took down his words, knowing they would find their way to the top of the story. I felt as if I were taking part in an ornate dance, an Elizabethan set piece filled with dips, bows and flourishes. I knocked on the doors, took down the words. I knew what the neighbors would say; I could have guessed the quotations beforehand. Yet it was an intrinsic part of the ritual of newspaper death. Reporters always ask the neighbors, and the neighbors always say the victims were quiet and kept to themselves. And then the reporters put that in their stories.

Behind me Porter snapped pictures, cursing the light, his flash a sudden burst behind me, another entry in the dance. It did not take us long to find the apartment building's resident manager. An older man, he walked slowly, deliberately, running his hand across his head, brushing gray hair away from his eyes. He told me the woman had paid her rent on time, rarely complained; he'd fixed a stopped toilet once inside her place and she had shown him pictures of her family, away on the west coast. He, too, had never seen any boyfriends or men hanging around.

At first he refused to let us into the apartment—private property, he said—but I persisted, cajoling and finally discovering that a twenty-dollar bill would turn the trick. "For five minutes, only. At the most," he said, slipping the money into the pocket of a work shirt. "Just to take a quick look, that's all. And don't touch nothing."

He opened the door after looking to be sure all the neighbors had cleared the hallway. We were like thieves, seeking to steal a few details, some substance, so the woman would come alive in the columns of newsprint in the morning. We were barely inside before I heard the click of Porter's camera. On one wall was a row of photos; the woman and her child, posed professionally, standing on a green lawn underneath a tree. There were others, smaller: candid shots of the child, naked, crawling on all fours; the mother rocking the baby in her arms. There was a family shot; I recognized the husband and what I assumed were relatives. They all stared out at the camera, smiling. I turned away and surveyed the apartment. There were two small bedrooms, each immaculate, frilly with lace and colors. A woman's place, I thought.

A mobile of small plastic animals, smiling lions and elephants, hung over the child's crib. A paperback bestseller, a book on self-improvement, lay cracked open beside the woman's bed. I wrote down the title, picked up the book and read the admonition: Treat every day as if it were a new challenge. I took that down, too.

The old man was getting nervous and anxious to close up. I wandered into the kitchen. Baby food and frozen dinners, cottage cheese in the refrigerator. A diet schedule had been posted on the door of the refrigerator. In the living room there was a stereo, tapes and records. I looked them over quickly; they dated to the late sixties. California sound, rock and roll. Everything was trim, in its place. The furniture was modern but not striking, the type one buys at discount warehouses, knockoffs of designs. There were two posters on the walls, framed in steel: a Sister Corita that carried the message, Do Unto Others; and the famous Ben Shahn of Sacco and Vanzetti. I wondered if she knew who they were.

The manager was standing by the doorway, gesturing with his hand, trying to wave us out of the apartment. I nodded at him and stepped back outside.

Porter was right behind him. "Hard to shoot," he said. "But I got pictures of the wall of pictures and the kid's room and hers, too. Should be OK." The manager asked us if there was anything else. He seemed angry. I told him his night was just beginning, that the press release would soon be issued and the place would probably be crawling with television people trying to beat their 11 P.M. deadline to get something on the late news. As I spoke I saw the first of the television trucks rolling into the parking lot.

We left. Before we got our cars, though, Porter turned to me, shaking his head. "Do you notice," he said, "that all the victims are so ordinary, so . . . unexceptional? Except for those who know them, I guess." He bent his head and slipped behind the wheel. The car door slammed shut, cutting off his thought like a knife.

I knew then why the killer had waited so long to call. It was a test. He was waiting to see how long it took for the police to identify the woman.

When I returned to the office that night it was close to deadline; there was no time to polish words. I put sheet after sheet of empty paper in the typewriter and tore the filled pages out. Nolan was still there, waiting on the story, treating each segment as it slipped from the roller into the computers. He said little, other than exhortations to hurry:

> The most recent victim of the man called the "Numbers Killer" has been identified by police as a 29-year-old divorcee who lived in a western-section apartment complex.
>
> Friends and neighbors of Susan Kemp described her as a friendly, outgoing young woman who kept mostly to herself at the apartment complex. She was, they said, devoted to the upbringing of her 21-month-old child, Jennifer.
>
> The victim's ex-husband, Tampa businessman Martin Kemp, arrived in Miami yesterday to take custody of the child and to identify the mother's body.
>
> Police are still searching for the means the killer used to snatch Mrs. Kemp and whatever motive may lie behind the crime. The killer has, as yet, failed to telephone with his explanation as he has done on each previous murder.

The story went on, racing into a description of the apartment, the photos on the wall. There were jumbled-together quotes from the neighbors and the husband. His anguish was described in one or two paragraphs in the middle of the story. The police efforts and their frustration were recounted. I quoted Wilson, but not by name, removing the expletives from his feelings.

As the kicker to the story, the final paragraph, I described the posters on the wall of the murdered woman's apartment, the flash of color flowing against the white background of the Sister Corita, and the hard, black-ink eyes of the two martyred workmen staring blankly out from the Ben Shahn. I let that description flow into the message from the book open by her bedside.

I saw Nolan's eyes as he scanned the final take, the last page that had raced through the typewriter. I knew he was on the final words and I saw his head move slowly, a nod, an approval. I watched his fingers slide to the keyboard, make a simple adjustment, then punch the keys that would send the story electronically to the copy desk for layout and headline. He held up his hand, made a small saluting motion and smiled. I followed his eyes to the wall clock. "We make most of the run," he said. "Maybe all the Final and all of the Home. The Street has gone already, but—" And he shrugged.

Nolan walked me over to my desk and put his hand on my shoulder. "Why don't you go home, get some rest?" he said.

I thought of my father, when I was young, no more than ten or eleven. He would sometimes come out and play tennis with me. I was learning; he was an expert. His thick legs hid remarkable speed; his hands were quick. He would rally effortlessly, racing me back and forth across the court until I made an inevitable error. He would call, teasing, "Need a breather?"

I looked up at Nolan. I shook my head. "He'll call now. Tomorrow probably. Maybe the next day. After he sees the story."

"Here or at your house?"

"I don't know. What's the difference?"

"None, really," Nolan said. "Still, you should get some rest."

We walked out together, but we did not speak again that night.

I was wrong. It did make a difference.

I did not know then that Martinez and Wilson had gone before a friendly judge, a one-time police officer himself, and obtained a wiretap for my home telephone line; nor did I know that the phone company had developed a slow yet accurate capacity to trace the incoming calls through a computer system at their central switchboard. These facts were explained to me afterwards by Martinez, when he told me of some of the events that had taken place outside of my presence. I had foolishly assumed when the detectives told me they couldn't trace calls coming in on my office line that the same was automatically true for my home telephone. I didn't see the detective, dressed in work clothes, khaki pants and denim work shirt, who slipped into the door of the apartment building behind me and walked down to the cellar where the telephone terminals were located. I met him later, a bookish man, a technician with glasses. He was the listener, two wires wrapped onto the terminal for my phone, another that connected him with Police Headquarters. Another man was waiting at Southern Bell's offices; he was the computer man who would start feeding possible exchanges into the system until he arrived at the right one. Then it was merely a matter of making the computer system race through all the open lines in the given exchange until the right connection was found. At a trial run, Martinez told me, it took slightly under ten minutes.

Christine would no longer answer the telephone when we were home together during the night. She did not want the killer to know she was there, she told me; she did not want him to know anything. It was all she could do to tolerate the telephone at all; on several occasions I found she had taken it off the hook.

On the night after the latest story appeared, the killer called. I did not even look at Christine who sat as before at the kitchen table watching and listening to my half of the conversation, filling in my long silences with her imagination. It was close to midnight when the telephone rang, the insistence of the bell seeming to signal the identity of the caller. I flipped on the tape recorder, then picked the telephone from the hook. "Be careful," Christine said, as I lifted the receiver.

"Yes?" I said.

"It's me," he said. "I suppose you've been waiting?"

"I knew you would call."

"Yes." His voice seemed distant, hazy for an instant, as if he were thinking as he spoke. "I guess you did. So, she was divorced. She told me that her husband was coming home soon, that she had to be there to meet him. She was hysterical much of the time, and it was only when the child started crying that she regained her senses."

In the basement the detective stiffened. For a moment he felt a rush of heat. He listened just a few seconds before dialing the headquarters' number. He was a young man, excitable. He misdialed and cursed, then dialed again on the small hand-held telephone-tapping device. He reported later he could feel the basement darkness harder than the night. At the second ring a headquarters' detective answered. "It's him," the man in the basement whispered, "calling now!" And he listened as the killer gathered himself and continued to speak.

"She was the hardest to snatch, you know." His voice was calm and deliberate. There was none of his usual teasing and jocularity this time. I wrote notes as quickly as possible.

"I had to watch her for several days to understand her routine. She seemed a person of habits, of cleanliness, neat; the type that would walk the same route every day. In the mid-afternoon she would take the child for a walk. They would exit the apartment and turn to the right, heading toward the tennis courts. That's where I was waiting. I pretended to be working on my car, just off the walkway. I had the hood up and the trunk open. I remember it was so bright, I thought the sun was like a spotlight on a stage, tracking me, illuminating everything, every small little movement. She approached. I looked around and saw no one. I readied the automatic. She stepped closer. I could feel the tension in my mouth, my breath catching fear with every second. I had never really worked in broad daylight, you see. She was next to me then, looking over, smiling a little, friendly."

He hesitated, but I did not fill the silence with a question.

At the telephone exchange the detective supervised the computer check of exchanges. He fed in the first three numerals of all the different areas of Miami. He, too, was sweating, watching as the system digested, then rejected each three numbers and he typed in a new series. Wilson and Martinez waited, too, in the parking lot of Police Headquarters. The engine in the cruiser was turning over silently, and they had the air conditioner on full blast. They were waiting for the radio to speak to them, to give them an address.

"She did not cry out when she saw the automatic. She put her hand to her mouth as if to cover a scream, but she remained calm. I said for her to take the baby and get into the car. She seemed to be dazed and I had to repeat myself. But I did not have to touch her, that was the oddest thing. In a second she began to cooperate, lifting the child from the stroller and slipping into the car. I folded the stroller and threw it into the back seat with the supplies I'd gathered. I kept the automatic in my hand where she could see it, and then the three of us just drove away as easy as could be."

Another pause. "Why her?" I asked.

"A mother and child," he said. "I wanted a mother and child."

He waited another long moment, and I closed my eyes.

"There was a famous photograph," he continued. "Taken at the start of the Second World War. In Hong Kong, I think. No, it was Shanghai. When the Japanese bombed the city. In the center of the photo there is a baby, covered with dirt, its mouth open wide in tears and fear and screaming for its mother. In the background all you can see is burning refuse, debris; the upheaval caused by bombs. I remember looking at the photo and wondering, where was the mother? And wondering what would happen to the child. I suppose they both died. I suppose the children always die.

"You see, this woman, Mrs. Kemp—you know, I didn't even know her name?—wasn't the first mother that I killed. There was another, carrying a small child the same way; protective, frightened. In Vietnam. I told you, there was this incident, and she was a big part of it."

He sucked in his breath then, a quick, harsh noise.

At the telephone station the detective was swearing to himself. It was taking longer than the trial run. "Where are we?" he shouted to a technician sitting at a bank of television screens filled with electronic numbers of computers.

"Key Biscayne," the technician replied. "Seven sixty-five exchanges." His fingers were typing in numbers. Then suddenly he leaned back in his chair and turned to the detective. "Got it!" he said. "He's out on the key."

The detective turned to the telephone and spoke to headquarters.

"We did not talk," the killer said. "She was too upset. She kept asking, 'What are you going to do to us? Are you going to kill us?' I think she thought I would rape her. I tried to tell her, but she wouldn't listen, and finally the sun went down. I made her eat then, and feed the child and change its diapers. I had built the little shelter for the child, and after a while it went to sleep. But the woman just stared at me through the night. The moonlight caught her face, seemed to make it swell with fear. After a long time I gave up trying to talk with her. It made no difference. Her hands were tied, she could go nowhere. I told her she should try to sleep and made her move away from the child, out to the spot where you found her. She was restless, but fear exhausts most people and finally, toward morning, she fell asleep. I waited until I knew she could feel nothing. You know, the shot didn't even awaken the child. She slept right through. The birds around, though, rose up suddenly, crying and shrieking. They were egrets mostly and gulls; I could see their white feathers."

He paused. "That's all," he said. "I'm tired."

"Don't go!" I raised my voice.

"What?" he said. "I'll call again. Later."

"I want to meet," I said. "Face to face."

Silence. I heard Christine's sudden intake of breath and heard her whisper, "No!"

"Don't be ridiculous," the killer said. He laughed briefly and hung up. I turned to Christine, but she was already crying and turned away. I wanted to explain, to tell her this was the only chance. But I could not find the words, so I simply sat across from her at the table feeling the distance between us grow.

In the basement the detective glanced at his watch. "Shit!" he said. "Eight minutes."

Martinez and Wilson were driving fast through the darkness. They cut through downtown, running the red lights. Martinez was behind the wheel; later he told me how excited he was. This was where it was all going to end, he thought. Wilson checked the action on his revolver as they drove, the older detective barely aware of the centrifugal force as the cruiser bent around corners. The engine sound grew as they headed through the toll booth and over the causeway. The moonlight reflected off the bay waters on either side, and behind them the lights from the tall apartment buildings on the shoreline were like beacons. Martinez pushed the car up to eighty, then ninety, the wheels screaming as they flew over the bridge past the empty beaches.

At the telephone station the detective wiped sweat from his face. "He's off," he said. "Where was he?"

The technician bent over the screen, watching the computer make its final sortings. He made a small sound of exultation and clenched his fist. "Got it!" he shouted. He punched the numbers into the keyboard and watched as the computer screen blinked, then typed an address. "The pay phone at the tourist booth!"

The detective shouted the address into the open telephone line, then slumped back into his chair. "They got him," he said.

The radio voice was thin, disembodied. It repeated the location to the two detectives and then put out an all-cars call for the whole key. Martinez swore and slammed the car into a 360-degree turn, tires squealing, the steering wheel shimmying in his hand. "Damn!" Wilson said, "we passed it." The detectives raced back, heading in the wrong direction on the four-lane roadway.

The tourist booth is a small building, one room with a window for a person to ask directions. It is open only during the winter season. Behind it is a pay phone, set off the road some thirty yards, surrounded by palms and ferns. It is a lonely place.

By this time there were sirens wailing all over the area. The two detectives arrived first, skidding in, their cruiser turning sideways under the braking pressure. Martinez said that his weapon was already out when he slipped from the door, crouching in the darkness. Wilson was running, weapon extended, for the booth.

It was empty.

"Dammit, the bridge," Wilson shouted. He ran to the car, to the radio, and told the dispatcher to have the span raised, trapping cars on the key. By now there were a half-dozen police cars at the booth, their lights throwing shadows over the brush and palms, cutting red and blue streaks into the darkness.

The policemen returned to their vehicles and headed in a convoy toward the bridge, some three miles away. Martinez could see the raised span when they emerged from beneath the trees, back out into the wan moonlight. Four cars were stopped by the barrier, waiting. He and Wilson stepped from their car, weapons out, and began to walk the line slowly, peering through the darkness at the people inside the cars.

There was a family inside the first, a station wagon, a man, a woman and two sleeping children in the back seat beneath a blanket. The man rolled down his window. "What's wrong?" he asked. "We've been to visit friends." But neither detective replied, continuing to walk toward the front, Martinez on the driver's side, Wilson on the passenger side.

There were two teenagers in the next car, a Volkswagen. They stared out at the policemen's weapons silently, frightened. Martinez heard the sound of doors opening and shutting behind him as the other officers removed the people from the vehicles. He was peripherally aware of Wilson's presence moving as if in step, in time.

The third car contained a pair of older people, and the detectives swept past, ignoring them. The woman in the car gasped when she saw the weapons. Martinez told me afterwards the adrenaline in his ears was like the ocean, constant, pulsating. He felt heat under his collar, a moment of almost shattering excitement.

There was only one head in the final car in line, behind the driver's wheel. It looked straight forward. Martinez felt the muscles in his hand tighten, knotting almost in a cramp on the handle of his service revolver. He thought wildly about the small automatic that he kept as a backup fastened to his calf under his pants leg. He wondered if he had taken the safety off. He could not remember. He and Wilson continued forward, moving slowly, deliberately, still in tandem, each step unsteady as if moving on ice. A few feet from the door he stopped. "You!" he shouted. "In the car! Police! Step out! Hands out front!"

There was a moment then when Martinez held his breath. He watched as the figure began to move slowly from the car; the detective could feel the pressure of his partner's weapon tracking the back of the driver's head. Martinez watched, his own weapon up, pointing, as the door opened and first a leg, then a torso, emerged. His eyes strained against the moonlight and the city lights across the bay. Sweat ran into his eyes, and he blinked furiously to clear them. He clutched a flashlight in his left hand, and when the figure turned toward him, the detective shouted, "Freeze!" and switched it on, the powerful beam cutting the darkness between them, smashing into the driver's face like a blow. He saw the driver's hand come up to his eyes. Then he heard Wilson's voice, hard and angry. "Fucked. Fucked. Fucked. Dammit!"

The driver was a woman, the light from the beam shining off her blond hair. Martinez turned away, hearing Wilson's voice begin the explanation, and walked to the side of the bridge. He told me later that he'd looked out over the water, dizzy, still queasy from the tension, listening to the sound of the light bay-water chop as it tapped against the pilings. The noise was like laughter, he said, the cackling of the escaped killer, adrift, free in the city night.

CHAPTER THIRTEEN

NOLAN listened to the latest tape intently. He was bent over slightly from the waist, his elbows on the table. He tracked the turning spindles on the recorder; twice he scratched notes in pencil on a plain sheet of copy paper. When the tape finished, he straightened and looked across the room at me, holding my gaze for a moment before speaking: "Well, you tried."

"I guess." I shrugged. "Perhaps."

"I'm concerned about the tone," Nolan said. "The changes in this past conversation. He seems hurried, different. He didn't take his time. He didn't mix his feelings with descriptions like he has in the past. Why was he so uptight about this murder? I'd like to know."

He rewound the tape, and for a second time the killer's voice filled the small room. "Listen," Nolan said, "he sounds nervous. Where's his confidence?"

". . . I had to watch her for several days . . ."

"He stalked her," Nolan said. "This wasn't spontaneous."

". . . I thought the sun was like a spotlight on a stage . . ."

"So, he was afraid. Afraid he would be seen."

". . . In the center of the photo there is a baby . . ."

"Right there," Nolan said. "He connects with one memory."

". . . this incident, and she was a big part of it."

"See, he remembers the photo and then his own memory."

". . . Don't be ridiculous." The phone clicked off.

Nolan walked about the room impatiently, rubbing his hand against his head. Occasionally he paused and looked up at the copies of the stories I had written on the killer that were pinned to the wall. "I think he's undergoing a change," Nolan said. "Nothing positive, it's just a feeling. He may have had enough killing. Suppose we're dealing with some kind of split personality? Perhaps one of the other characters is beginning to take over. Did you ask your psychiatrist friend about that?"

I shook my head. "I don't think he saw any evidence of a split in the tapes that I played for him. But how would he know? I mean, as long as the personality he heard was consistent. Psychopathic, he said. Born killer." Nolan looked at me, an editor's look. "All right," I said. "I'll call him and ask him."

That afternoon I played the tape over the telephone for the psychiatrist. As always, he paused to think before he spoke. "Interesting," he said. "Imagine the conflict that must be functioning in the killer's mind; killing the woman, leaving the baby. I wonder if he was symbolically killing his own mother."

"Nolan says he thinks the killer is a split personality and that another personality is beginning to infringe on the one that kills people. What do you think?" Again, the doctor hesitated. I imagined the smoke from his pipe curling up around his head.

"Not impossible," he said. "We don't know much about that particular illness."

"Probable?" I asked.

"No. But not improbable, either. Actually, it's not a bad idea. But there would be no way to tell unless the killer began to demonstrate different personalities under a clinically controlled situation. I suppose it is conceivable. I do not offhand remember a case in the literature of one personality being homicidal while another was not, but it could happen. One personality psychopathic, another suicidal, another homicidal and yet another, oh, say a librarian. All struggling together. One would think it would cause an explosion . . . but these things are remarkably complicated. Tell your editor that it's a good theory but as of this time impossible to prove."

"What about the tape?" I asked. "Doesn't he seem different?"

"No, no different. Perhaps a bit disappointed. The killing was less of a success than the others. His selection seems to have been less propitious; there seems to have been less interaction between him and the victim. That must have been a disappointment to him."

"Predictions?"

He laughed. "Out of what, my crystal ball?" His voice turned serious. "Well, you know one thing. That this incident in the war, the one he says he's recreating, contained a mother and child. Those are potent psychological bombs. And another thing . . . I would be very careful suggesting any meeting."

"You think he would hurt me?"

"Why not?"

But I didn't believe him.

I went to the hospital one day, to go up to the pediatric ward and see the child. I was tempted to stop and see Christine first but realized she was probably in surgery. I had never visited her in the hospital and thought it best I didn't: let her tell me of her impressions rather than forming my own. The nurse at the station was reluctant at first, but she recognized my name from my press card and decided it would do no harm to look through the glass window into the ward. I followed her down a white corridor, listening to the proper clicking of her heels against the polished tile floor. The world inside the hospital seemed blank, bright, like the moment the sun glints off the water and fills your eyes. The nurse took me up to a window and pointed. "There, second bed in." I peered through the glass at a room filled with cribs. "She's off critical. Should be ready to leave in a day or so." I watched the child for an instant. She was sleeping on her side, tucked over, sucking on a pacifier. I did not know what I was searching for or what I expected to see. Perhaps some look of fear, some memory of the sun, the swamp and the afternoon heat. I turned away, thanking the nurse.

"Not much to see," she said. "You look at her and you can't tell anything. She looks just like the other children, cries the same, everything. I wonder, how will she be different?" She paused and then asked as we walked back, "Why? I mean, what possible reason could there be?"

I shook my head. "Outrage, I think. Vulnerability. Heartlessness. I don't know, either." She was a young woman, dark hair pulled back unfairly from her face by the nurse's cap. She smiled at me as I left, the elevator door closing on the ward with an abrupt metallic sound.

I thought about what I'd said. Trying to find a rationale for the murders was absurd. They existed in a different plane, a different time; they were senseless, that was the point. They were savage, that was the point. They were inconceivable, that was the point.

I wondered, too, why it was I could not bring myself to hate the killer, like so many of the people that I'd seen and interviewed, whose words had ridden my fingers into the columns of the newspaper.

In the afternoon Porter stopped by my desk. He was holding the body of a camera in one hand and fitting it with an assortment of lenses from a strap around his neck. After he fixed each one to the body, he lifted the camera and peered through it, sighting across the expanse of the newsroom. "You know what I did yesterday night?" he started in, barely pausing for the shake of my head. "I went to the scene of what the cops like to call 'a domestic.' It was up in Carol City, in the working-class section; you know, mostly black, guys who bring home a weekly paycheck from the county for working on a garbage crew. When I got there, oh, there must have been four or five cop cars parked on the lawn and the street.

"It seems that some guy stopped off at the pool hall after work, managed to lose a good deal of his paycheck. Rent's due at the end of the month; utility bills, grocery bills, no more credit at the supermarket, that sort of thing. So, as you might expect, they get to shouting at each other, man and wife, loud enough so the neighbors can hear just about everything. After a while the woman hauls off and slaps the old man hard on the side of the face. He doesn't like this too much, so he lets her have it, too, right in the chops.

"He likes it, you know, and so he decides to let her have it again. Takes another swing at her. She starts to back up, finds herself up against the kitchen sink.

"The old guy's coming hard for her now, going to really lay one on her. So she grabs the first thing that hits her hand. Turns out to be a big carving knife, and she slashes out with it. Catches the husband on the side of the neck, severs the jugular. He goes right down in a pile at her feet.

"She stands there crying and screaming until the neighbors come and call the police. The guy must have bled to death in a couple of seconds. Anyway, the cops come, take pictures, take her confession right there and charge her with murder. And off she goes to the Women's Detention Center. I got a good shot of the police leading the woman away from her house; she has this confused and crushed look on her face. As they put her in the back of the patrol car, she called out for help. You know who she called for? Her husband, the man she just killed."

He looked across the desk at me, took out a corner of his shirt and wiped one of the lenses, then twisted and peered through it. After a second he continued, "I asked one of the policemen how many murders they'd had lately, not counting, of course, our boy. He looked at me and said, 'Oh, same as usual. Somebody usually gets killed every night. No end of business for us.' And the thought hit me: it makes no difference. No difference at all. They don't have to catch the killer."

He stopped and I said, "I don't follow."

"Suppose," he replied, "that we just ignored the killer. Let him continue doing what he's doing. It wouldn't change the totals at the end of the year, you know. I mean, there'll be just as many murders in the city regardless of what the killer does. In reality, he's just another statistic. Another angry act amidst hundreds of the same. That woman's husband is just as dead as any of the killer's victims. So was the guy who got killed the night before, so will the people who get killed tonight. He's no different from anyone else; he's just more consistent."

Porter straightened up and laughed. "You see," he said, "how jaded we become."

But I didn't join in his humor.

His story did give me an idea, though. I rode that night with a homicide team to the location of another killing, a murder in a bar in the downtown ghetto. The dead man was sprawled on his back, the blade of a flick knife deep in his chest. The blinking lights from a beer sign in the window reflected off the blood smearing the barroom floor. In the back I heard the sound of a pool cue striking a ball; two patrons oblivious to the routine of death before them.

In another corner I took in the look of compressed rage on the face of a prostitute as she watched the detectives and the medical examiner work swiftly, efficiently around the corpse. The suspect was already in cuffs in the rear of a cruiser, staring from the window at the half-interested crowd that had gathered.

I wrote all that and numbered the murders that had occurred in the city since the first of the killer's slayings. It ran front page under the headline: THE ROUTINE OF VIOLENCE: "ORDINARY" KILLINGS CONTINUE. It was a slow news day and I was allowed plenty of space, three legs of copy running outside, then the rest jumping to a display page inside the paper.

I saw Porter after the story appeared. He smiled across the room at me and held his thumb up in the universal salute. The managing editor sent me a note through the interoffice mail: Good story, puts it all in perspective, it said.

I wondered, though, had it been the killer who'd stepped into the bar and shot the man dead with his .45 whether the pool game would have stopped in fear.

Porter found the photo that the killer had described. I sat at my desk staring at it through the course of one afternoon, my imagination running wildly, as if I could hear and feel the explosions from the bombs. I thought, too, of my father; I wondered how many children had wailed in the wake of his own raids. I could see my father hunched over in the nose of the B-25, peering down through the bombsight at—what? A city? A railroad? A factory? They would be shapes without substance, like drawings upon a sheet of paper. He would read the coordinates off from an attack plan, sight down through the nose of the plane and at the proper moment, or as close to it as he could, release the load. The plane would be buffeted by flak exploding close by and would surge forward, lightened by the release of the racks of bombs, accelerating away from the fury and smoke, up into sky and clouds.

He flew most of his missions out of North Africa, from a strip cut from dirt and dusty hills, out across the Mediterranean toward Italy and Sicily. I imagined he felt suspended between the blue of the sea and the ceilingless blue of the air. I supposed there were moments of terror, too, when it seemed as if the earth were reaching up angrily for him, shaking the space with explosions. He never talked much about the war itself. He talked instead of the return, the cheers and parades, the flush of victory before the return to routine. It was a heady time, he said once, a time of spirited drunkenness and excitement. He marveled in the mere knowledge that he was intact, that his organs and extremities all seemed to function. It was as if he could feel the blood in his body traversing the network of veins. He went then to visit his brother, still in the medical facility, adjusting to the loss of his eye.

At my desk I raised my hand and held it over my right eye. I looked about the newsroom, surveying the activity. I twisted my head to take it all in: reporters working the telephones, editors at the banks of computer terminals. I thought of the way my uncle must have turned his head at the sound of the hospital-room door swinging open, rotating in his bed toward my father.

For an instant the noise of telephones and voices faded away, and I tried to imagine the two men staring across the room at each other.

What did they say? One intact, one damaged. Going different directions.

When I was young, caught in age between my brother and sister, my father would settle our disputes in mock court. Each would get a moment or two to explain his side; my brother speaking quickly, excitedly, amassing facts, impressions and desires in a linear way, the words thrusting out from his mouth, falling quickly and persuasively. Or my sister, halting, her tears overcoming her voice, finally relying on the most persuasive argument of all, tumbling across the room in a run to be swept up in my father's arms. And myself: anger flooding my brain, standing in the way of the words I wanted, blocking all the reasons, the arguments. I stuttered and stumbled—and I lost. My father, leaning back at his desk, a pencil in his right hand, thumping on a pad of paper unconsciously, would issue his decisions, render his opinions. He was not a harsh man, nor unfair. He was a man of codes and rules. To me it seemed as if his decisions came down from on high, inviolable, precise—as explosive as the bombs he had unleashed from the bombardier's position in the nose of the plane, suspended above the horror in a thin plexiglass booth.

My own voice such a failure, I took to writing other people's voices. . . .

And then the telephone rang.

The newsroom noises seemed to increase, like the volume on a radio, then to settle back into the constant familiar hum. I reached across the desk and punched on the recording device, my hand functioning independently as if it belonged to someone else. I felt the cool plastic of the receiver under my palm, and I slowly lifted the telephone to my ear. I waited for the voice.

He spoke coldly, unhurried. He began with no note of familiarity or introduction. One moment there was silence on the line, and the next he was speaking in a flat, expressionless tone.

"I've been thinking about you," he said.

"And?"

He said nothing, instead letting the silence hang on the line.

"When I was overseas, I remember a moment. I used to volunteer for what the Army called LURPS, which was an acronym for Long-Range Reconnaissance Patrols. There'd be myself, a radioman and another rifleman, alone in the jungle, moving through the bush at that infuriatingly slow pace that the jungle demands. The humidity would be so thick, so high, that I'd feel as if the air were creating friction against the skin of my arms as I swung a machete at the vines and weeds that were everywhere. It was as if I could feel the heat steaming around me; we would be soaked by our sweat. Almost like it had rained.

"I loved the sensation of being alone—almost alone. The

radio was really the only link back to safety, and it was, of course, unreliable. I think there's nothing as exhilarating, as sensual, as walking abroad in an alien and dangerous land. I could feel the fear and excitement right through my body. I would think, 'I'll die out here, and no one will ever find me. It will be as if I'd disappeared, simply faded away from life,' but that never happened. Close, though, many times.

"There was once . . . we were cutting our way through the growth, moving so slowly sometimes I thought the jungle would have the time to grow behind us. A VC patrol must have been cutting through from the other direction, their minds the same as ours, concentrating on the weeds and vines and just trying to free themselves for another step forward. The two groups bumped directly into each other.

"I was out on the point and suddenly became aware of the sounds of hacking and pushing coming toward us. I stopped at precisely the same instant that the VC point man must have hesitated. There was a long second, and then I lifted up my rifle and let loose on full automatic in their direction. The radioman and the other rifleman joined with me. At the same moment precisely the jungle around us started to rip apart with the fire from their automatics, AK-47's, I remember, because of the distinctive sound, like a sheet of paper ripping. Everyone must have panicked simultaneously; one instant there was silence, the next the jungle was being ripped apart by fire.

"And then there was this remarkable instant. Everything stopped. Sudden, total silence.

"Everyone's weapon had been on full auto, and in the same instant all the ammunition was expended. Then out of the silence came this perverse clicking. I looked down and realized it was coming from me as well as the others. Everyone was changing the clips in their rifles as quickly as possible. Click, click, out came a clip. Click, click, in went a new clip. I started to laugh at it all. So much fear exhausted in one swift second, so much murderous intent. My voice rose above the silence through the jungle. The other two looked at me, and I made a hand motion. We slipped back down the path we'd cut, moving away, disengaging. I suppose the VC did the same, the social inappropriateness of our meeting hitting them, too. I had to laugh.

"I feel much is the same now. It would be a cliché to tell you that the city is the same as the jungle to me, but it is. I think of myself cutting a swath through the city as I did the jungle: out on patrol, searching, destroying, abroad in a dangerous, strange land. I walk the streets the same as you, staring at the people, locking onto their eyes, watching their glance turn.

"One night I went to a neighborhood meeting. You know the type; you've been to some yourself, I've read the stories. I've read every word you've written. Anyway, I went one early evening to a school auditorium—the type of place that all these meetings are held. There is something about the fluorescent lights, the bright school colors, pennants and plaques that is reassuring and familiar. A stream of people headed inside, mostly in groups of two or four. I simply followed them into the building and sat in the midst of the crowd, another concerned face, worried and frightened.

"There was a man sitting next to me, alongside his wife. She was plump and flushed with the exertion of squeezing into a seat designed for a child. He was angry, a frown set on his face, staring up at the podium. I watched his hands clench into fists and then retreat, relax for an instant, then tighten again. He turned to me at one point: 'Dammit,' he said, 'this has just about gone on too long. What the hell's the matter with the police?' I nodded sagely and replied, 'I just don't think they're doing everything they should.' And the fellow's head went up and down sharply in assent. 'Damn right,' he said. 'You're damn right,' and he mumbled that several times more.

"The auditorium was nearly filled by then, and as I watched, a man got up on the stage. He blinked in the lights for an instant and then introduced himself. A politician. He thanked everyone for turning out and made a few remarks about the police. He trusted them. He was sure they were doing all they could. Then he introduced an officer in uniform, the type of ranking officer I knew in the Army, who is privy to information yet doesn't understand a word of it.

"He stood at the podium, rocking back and forth slightly, eyes surveying the crowd. He made a small speech, outlining all the man hours and detectives they have working on the case—just the stuff that's been in your stories. My neighbor kept saying over and over, 'Bullshit. Bullshit. Get to the point.' But the cop never did. He just stopped, saying, 'I know it's hard to be reassured, but the police are following up every lead, no matter how small. Every piece of evidence is being scrutinized. We have teams going through Army records at the Pentagon.'

"He offered to answer questions from the floor, though he cautioned that he wouldn't be able to go into specifics. I watched as people shifted in their seats for an instant or two. And then, one after another, the people got up and started to ask questions. Did they expect to make an arrest? How far through the records were the investigators? Why was it that the police seemed helpless to act until I had already found a victim? I think you would have been pleased; the questions were good ones, tough. The cop squirmed under the lights, shading his eyes so as to be able to see the questioners.

"He had few answers, and the less he was able to say, the angrier people got. It was infectious, the spirit of outrage amidst all those secure, middle-class mothers and fathers, husbands and wives. As the cop continued to dodge their verbal bullets, they grew more and more unruly. Questioners started to shout from their seats, no longer standing up and speaking politely. A few obscenities rolled through the auditorium. They exploded among the crowd like grenades, increasing the fervor.

"I saw my neighbor's face contorting, and he, too, shouted out, 'Why aren't there extra patrols out at night?' And when the cop started to talk about manpower shortages, they shouted him down. I finally couldn't hold back anymore, I had to join in. It was as if I heard my own voice speaking from some other place, a recording, perhaps. 'What we want to know,' I yelled above the crowd, 'is one thing. How is it that one man can hold an entire city, in effect, hostage? And the police, for all our hundreds of thousands of tax dollars, can't do a damn thing?'

"Everyone grew quiet. My neighbor clapped me on the knee and said, 'That's damn right. That's the whole ball of wax.' He grinned at me and I smiled back at him. On the stage, the policeman turned my way. 'All I can say,' he said, 'is that we're doing our best job.' The rest of his response was lost in angry shouts and cries.

"The meeting broke up then, and we all stood and filed out. I lost track of my neighbor. I remember how different it seemed outside; it was no cooler than the auditorium, but the air seemed less oppressive. I felt a breeze as if the darkness were cleansing me of the crowd and I was alone again. I was walking toward my car when I spotted the two policemen. They were standing next to their cruiser, watching the crowd filter out and away through the parking lot. For a moment I thought of running in the other direction as fast as I could, but it was as if I were outside of myself, watching my actions from apart. It was like walking the point in Vietnam; I had the sensation of being ahead, exposed, vulnerable. And so I walked past. Their eyes were elsewhere. I don't suppose they even noticed me. I knew then that I was free. Invisible."

A hesitation; then he continued.

"When I got into my car, I could hardly contain myself. I laughed and laughed. I rolled the windows tightly shut so they couldn't hear me. There were tears coming down my cheeks, and after a few moments I was gasping for breath."

Again he paused.

"They'll never catch me," he said. "Not unless I want them to."

I interrupted. "How long do you intend to keep this up?"

"The killings? Oh, a bit longer."

"How long is that?"

"Not too long. Don't be so impatient."

"And what then?"

He thought for an instant. "Perhaps another city. Another identity. A new life. Or maybe," he said, pausing between the words to add emphasis, "a continuation of the same."

"Murders."

"You can call it that," he said. "Or reminders. Memory lessons from the past."

"They'll catch you," I said.

"No. And if they do, what of it? What a trial that would be. That would be best for you, I suppose." Again his voice slipped away, and he seemed to be thinking. "But I doubt that will come to pass. I think instead that I'll just fade away in confusion. I will become like those men declared missing in action; a body decomposing somewhere out of sight, out of smell. But not out of mind."

He laughed. "Gone but not forgotten."

I sucked in my breath, listening to his joyless laughter as it strained over the telephone wires. "Why do we have to talk this way?" I asked. "Why don't we meet face to face?"

Abruptly the laughter ceased.

"What for?" he asked. "So you can lead the police to me?"

"No, I wouldn't," I lied. "It would be just the two of us."

"No, it wouldn't," he said. "It couldn't."

We were both silent. After a moment he continued, again in the same singular tone.

"What makes you think we haven't met already?"

I coughed. I couldn't answer.

"On the street, perhaps. In a crowd somewhere? On an elevator. Haven't you ever stopped and looked at the person next to you and wondered, 'Is that him?' Haven't you ever been at a stoplight in your car and swiveled in your seat when you felt the sensation of being watched and discovered the eyes of the driver next to you peering at you? A moment of contact, almost physical. Then the light changes, and the two of you head off intact, alone. Think about it. One of those times, it might have been me. Think of all the little signals that I might have made, the look in my eyes, the nod of my head, the wave of my hand. Anything small, private, between the two of us, something so that you would know: it's him. And yet you never knew. We are so close, you and I, and yet you cannot recognize me. You are blind, stumbling, your hands outstretched seeking the wall. And I'm there beside you."

He breathed in, hissing.

"I don't believe you," I said.

I could hear his shrug over the line.

"Believe what you will. Remember: truth and lies are often the same . . . fact and fiction divided by such a thin line."

Another quiet. I was aware of the sounds of the newsroom around me taking precedence, as if the killer's voice was fading out and the world around me coming back to life.

"I am most ordinary-looking," the killer said. "Just under six feet tall, about one hundred and sixty-five pounds. Brown hair. Like yours. Tell that to the police. Perhaps it will help them."

"What makes you think I tell the police?"

"Don't lie to me," he replied. "They tap the phone. They get the recordings that you make. They follow you. You talk with them and then they talk with you. It's a partnership of sorts. You should be more independent." He stopped and inhaled before continuing. "You see how much I know. I could be anywhere. I could be anyone. So don't lie to me."

"Why are you doing this?" I asked. They were the only words I could think of. He didn't respond.

"Good-bye, Anderson. We'll talk again soon."

And the phone clicked off.

CHAPTER *FOURTEEN*

THERE were big storms throughout the Caribbean during late August of that year, blowing in on the islands haphazardly, spending themselves in great ripping gusts of wind and rain. The city, though, seemed immune, protected; the storms that threatened the mainland spun off into the Atlantic to die out of sight in the reaches of the ocean. In the city the heat was like a mask, covering every feature.

The killer's latest conversation spawned renewed anger; the thought that he walked abroad so easily seemed to cause the city dwellers to withdraw further. Eyes on the street met and turned away; distances were maintained; to be aloof became routine. There was a jumpiness, too, as if contact were somehow dangerous. I saw a woman accidentally brush up against a young man while they waited for the streetlight to change. At the same instant they sprang apart, scowling, staring at each other for an instant in fury. Then they each set out across the street, on the same path but ignoring each other.

There was no end of stories to write. I wrote that the police had come up with a list of 250 possible names from Army records and that they were slogging through the list, trying to find the killer among them. Martinez laughed when he told me about it. "As if he'd be here under his own name," he said. "He's not a fool."

The evening paper, the *Post*, actually brought in a famous psychic from New York to try to find the killer. He went to the locations of the murders, poked around meaningfully, sniffed the air and pronounced the vibrations to be very strong. He then predicted that the killer would never be found but would die in a bizarre accident. This, I suspected, was not what the *Post* wanted. Nolan ripped the story out and put it on the office bulletin board. He scribbled a note on it: "Why can't we have more enterprise reporting?" The office got a great kick out of it. There were many kidding suggestions: divining rod, seances and the like. Christine found none of it amusing. She reminded me instead that the killer was between killings and that his pattern was now to kill again.

"What will you do next?" she asked.

"I don't know," I said. "Just wait, like everybody."

She frowned. "I hate the waiting."

"That's what it's like. It's the nature of the business."

"I still hate it," she said. "And I think the killer means to change all that."

I made a negative sound, a snorted denial. We did not talk about it again, but, of course, she turned out to be right.

Martinez called one evening, and Nolan and I walked from the newspaper to a downtown bar to have a talk with him. He was sitting at the counter, an empty glass in front of him. He gave a little wave toward the seats on either side and motioned to the bartender, rubbed his eyes hard for a moment, then pushed his fingers back through his black hair. His voice was tired and low, mingling with the sounds of glasses, liquid and the other soft voices in the room. I wondered where Wilson was. "We've got to get more out of this guy," he said. "We need something else to work on." He drained off part of a scotch the bartender had set down in front of him. "I think we're no better off than when we started."

Nolan looked at him, his editor's eyes cautious over the rim of a glass of beer. "What about the list of names from the Army?" he asked.

"He won't be on it," the detective replied. "He enjoys the game too much, this guy. He feeds information that probably misleads us, not helps us."

"But the doctor said . . ." I interjected.

Martinez cut me off. "They don't know everything. In fact, sometimes they know very little. Listen, he's just guessing, the same as everyone. Let me give you an example. We've spent weeks going through army records, at the Pentagon, Fort Bragg. We've even sent people through the Ohio draft board records, trying to come up with something. And all along I've thought it was bullshit. You know why? Because of the weapon. This guy really knows how to handle that forty-five. I mean, he knows how bullets can deflect, how to control the shot so it doesn't blow his victim's head off. So I figure he's been trained with it. That means he was an officer in the Army or, more likely, a military policeman, because they got training in handguns. The regular grunt got a rifle. But on the other hand, the forty-five was standard issue to Marines. And they learned how to work one, had to qualify. You see what I'm getting at? If he saw the combat he described, and at the same time gained access to and learned how to use that forty-five, well, then he was probably in a different branch of the service than the one we've been looking at. Just a theory, mind you. But it makes me think. It's all lies, half-truths and made-up stuff. Maybe a little true experience mixed in."

Nolan interrupted. "So what you're saying is that you're really nowhere with this thing."

"Right," Martinez replied. "My opinion." He hesitated for a moment, then continued. "Look, I didn't call you up expecting to see a story tomorrow about how we're a bunch of screw-ups. I just wanted you guys to know the whole picture."

"All right," Nolan said. "For now."

"It's fucking depressing," Martinez said. He finished his drink and motioned to the bartender for another. "Tomorrow I'm going to Ohio with Wilson, just for the day. Gonna check out some names. Be back tomorrow night—empty-handed."

"What does Wilson think?" I asked.

Martinez smiled, looking down into his drink. "Now, he's a piece of work, isn't he? You know, when I first started to work with him, I figured we'd last together, oh, maybe forty-eight hours at best. It's been close to six months now. He's crazy, you know. They always say that a cop isn't supposed to take his work home with him. That's a crock. You never forget. Hell, they don't let you. Always supposed to have a gun on you, anyway. How can you forget with a gun strapped to your leg? Wilson, let me tell you, he's dying, he wants this guy so bad. First off, the first victim was just like his daughter. Second, he can't stand the way the guy calls you. Being a cop is being in the know. I mean, that's why I went into homicide, the same as Wilson. Because you like to find things out, like to put things together.

"And here we're always waiting for this guy to call you. Nothing much we can do about it, but it gnaws away at us. Wilson especially. Did you know he lost his nephew in the war? Kid was nineteen. Wanted to be a cop like his uncle. Wilson's brother died a long time ago—heart, I think—and Wilson was the kid's father, kind of. Kid gets drafted coming out of high school, gets blown away overseas. By a mine, I think he said. Just walking around. I don't know, but it makes him a little crazy sometimes. I think he's going to kill this sucker if we get the chance. He hardly leaves the office now. Just catches a few hours on a cot in the corner. Showers, shaves over at the jail. Not me. Sometimes I just got to get out, go back to the apartment, listen to some music. Forget it for a while. Wilson never forgets."

"So what do you think will happen?" Nolan asked.

Martinez laughed. "Maybe we get lucky. Maybe he decides to quit. One or the other. Like the way he snatched Mrs. Kemp—anybody could have been looking from their apartment, noticed a plate number or the car. Something like that."

"We had this conversation weeks ago," I said. "You said the same thing."

"See," Martinez said. "That should tell you how close we are to catching the guy."

We stepped from the bar into the night. Nolan and I walked together a few steps, leaving the smell, the sound of glasses clinking and the detective behind us. After a minute, Nolan stopped and asked me what I thought.

I shrugged. "Who knows what to believe now?"

He nodded and we walked on a few more steps. "Should we write the story?" I asked.

"Which?" he queried.

"Martinez," I said. "That they're really no closer to a solution than when they started. It's a helluva piece."

"I know," he said, but he waited before answering. We walked a half-block in silence. "No, let's hold off."

"Why?"

"What do you think the effect would be on the people in the city?"

"Bad," I conceded. "More vigilante patrols. More homeowners buying guns. More of the craziness."

"That's what I think. Let's hold off until they've gone through this list of names, at least. And let's try to find some way of softening the blow when it happens, some extra perspective."

We walked again in quiet.

And then he added: "You've got to remember. We're the ones who count. No one gives a damn what the television stations say; or the *Post*, for that matter. The killer calls us. He calls you. We're the ones with our heads in the middle of this thing, so what we say is a hundred times more important. If we say that the cops are fuckups, everyone will believe it. If we say they're doing the best they can, well, everyone will believe that. We are—God, it sounds funny—the paper of record for this murderer. If we tell everyone to panic, then, dammit, that's what they'll do. You know that Circulation reports subscriptions have increased by ten percent, and we thought we were already at saturation level? And on days when you have a story above the fold on page one, the street sales go up some fifteen thousand copies? They did a survey; most of the people buying the Street already get the paper delivered. They just can't wait until the morning to read the next story." He grinned. "Sometimes I think the killer is someone down in the circulation department. They're going crazy. They love this guy.

"So we've got to watch what we say. Everyone is looking at us—at you. Circulation did another study. You know, nobody reads bylines? Well, they started asking subscribers who you were. A helluva lot of people recognized your name and associated it with the stories. Fame may be fleeting, but at the moment, you've got it."

He hesitated for another instant while we walked. I heard a siren in the background, and I stared up at the massive *Journal* building, standing square on the bay, the lights in the offices still bright.

"So you see the situation. We've got to be damn sure of what we write. Oh, I know, we're always careful. But people are counting on us. More than I think you or I realize."

We stopped in the parking lot. "Helluva way to become famous," I said.

He smiled. "You love it," he said. "We all love it. A story is like a live thing, isn't it? Slippery, beating with life, hard to catch, hard to hold. But we love it."

And the two of us shook hands in agreement.

The following morning I received the letter.

It was typed haphazardly through a bare ribbon, the letters making a faded imprint on the single sheet of white paper. I fingered the cheap dime-store envelope for a moment before opening it; it had arrived in the morning delivery at the office with the usual press releases and political statements. There was no return address; only my name, the *Journal*'s address and a stamp. I opened it and read:

> DEAR MR. ANDERSON:
>
> I have followed your many stories concerning the recent wave of killings in Miami with great interest.
>
> But it was only after the latest murder that I realized that the pattern the killer professes to be following duplicates an incident that I witnessed while serving in the U.S. Army in Vietnam. The killing of the mother and the abandoning of the child was what convinced me that I saw the incident that the killer has said he wishes to recreate.
>
> I am willing to talk with you only. No police, no cameras, nobody else. If I see anyone else, I will deny everything.

I will be at my apartment at 671 NW 13th Avenue at 1 P.M. on the date you received this letter. Apartment Number 5.

The letter was not signed.

I drove through the downtown ghetto, a system of decrepit woodframe houses and battered two-story apartment buildings constructed from cinder block. On the sidewalks was a mix of the displaced and the disadvantaged: tired black men, the lines in their faces like scars of age; drifters and hoboes, Miami's regulars, grizzled with time and tattered clothing. They leaned against the whitewashed brick of the buildings, eyes vacant. The sun sliced down through the heat of the day; the sky was the same rich, living pale blue that hung above the luxury yachts and speedboats moving across the bay. It was a stark world, illuminated by the unforgiving light. I sensed the stares from the sidewalk following me as I passed. In the background I heard the deep muffled sound of construction work. It mingled with the noise of children who skipped among the derelicts and the sidewalk domino games, oblivious.

A sign hung outside the address I was hunting: Furnished Rooms. Daily, Weekly, Monthly. Inquire Within. It was a typical downtown building, but painted a faded red in contrast with the ubiquitous white of the other buildings. It rose up three stories, just higher than the others on the block. A single outside stairway, black steel, steeply pitched, led to the upper floors. There were two apartments on each floor and a small cement courtyard crisscrossed with clotheslines flapping a few sheets and shirts in the light breeze. I hesitated at the bottom of the steps, catching my breath against the heat, struggling against the gazes of the neighbors who had stepped out onto the street to watch me. I suppose they thought I was a bill collector or a detective. None of them made a sound. I climbed the stairs slowly.

I found Apartment Five at the top of the stairway. There was no nameplate, no mailbox, just a painted number on an old wooden door. The door showed signs of abuse, a deep gouge near the lock; probably the result of a failed break-in. I knocked once, then four more times. The sharp sounds hung in the hot air around me, reverberating.

The door opened a crack. I could not see inside, but I could feel the occupant's eyes moving over me, checking, inspecting. A muffled voice asked, "Alone?" and I replied that I was.

It was a moment before I could inspect the premises, my eyes blinded from the transition from light to dark. I blinked hurriedly, trying to hasten the adjustment. "I'm glad you came," the person said. "I'm not certain what I would have done if you hadn't come." I looked down and saw the voice was coming from a man in a wheelchair.

I nodded, and he turned sharply in the chair, spinning in place for a moment, then heading deeper into the apartment. The dim light filtering through one small window threw shadows across the room and glinted on the spokes of the wheels and the polished steel of the frame. "Come on," he said, motioning with one hand and pointing toward a seat at a kitchen table. There was little furniture in the apartment: a lumpy couch, a plastic-coated table next to a stove and small refrigerator, a few odd chairs spread about. On all the flat surfaces there were cigarette butts in ashtrays. A few magazines—*Time*, *Newsweek*, *Playboy*—were tossed about. There was also a stack of newspapers on the floor. My latest story was on top. I could see huge red circles drawn around different paragraphs. I sat down and pulled out my notebook and tape recorder. The man in the wheelchair looked at them.

He wore large, aviator-style glasses, tinted yellow, and his blond-streaked hair was brushed severely back from his forehead and hung down over his ears. He seemed halfway between a shave and a beard, the hair on his face seeming to be darker beneath the yellow of the glasses. His arms were long, with bunched muscles. He wore a gray T-shirt and jeans but kept a white sheet over his legs. The side of his face seemed swollen; he saw my eyes on his cheek and said, "Don't worry. Just an abscessed tooth. Go down to the VA hospital tomorrow, get it out. They take care of me pretty good." His eyes returned to the tape recorder. "You gonna use that thing?" His voice was thick from the swelling.

"If you let me," I replied.

He shrugged. "Hell, why not?" He grew quiet. After a moment he said, "You know, I spent so much time wondering whether you would show up, now I don't know what to say."

"Why don't we start with your name?" I said, pushing the record button.

"I don't know about that quite yet," he said. "You gotta promise not to use it."

"Why?"

"'Cause I know this guy, the killer, and I don't think he'd wait one instant before coming over and wasting me." He laughed. "I'm half-wasted already," he said, pointing to his legs. "I got to try to hang on to what little I got left."

I thought for a moment. What harm? I'd get the story first, then the name. "OK. I'll give you anonymity, but I know the cops'll want to talk with you."

"Let me think about it," he said. "First let me tell you what I know." He hesitated again. "I don't suppose there's any money in this; you know, for expenses, maybe?" I shook my head. "Didn't think so. Just thought I'd try, you know. The payments from Uncle only go so far, you see. It's not like this is a real fine place to live, you know."

I nodded again. "What happened?" I asked. "I mean, if you don't mind."

He shook his head vigorously. "Don't bother me much now." He put his hand to his face and rubbed at his beard. I could hear the crackling sound under his fingers.

And then he spoke, his words at first exaggerated, thrust toward the tape recorder. "My name is Mike Hilson. Former Spec-Four in the U.S. Army. I caught a piece of shrapnel from a mortar round in January 1971 near some little dink village I don't even remember the name of. Batangan Peninsula. A real shithole. You know the real bummer? I was really short at the time. Done nine months in-country and was just about ready to pack it in, get a transfer out of a combat platoon, go back to Saigon or Da Nang or someplace and file shit for a while, work regular hours, you know. Anyway, all of a sudden this one night there's all sorts of shit coming down, and I wake up and all I can hear is everybody yelling, 'Incoming! Incoming!' and the whump! sound the mortars make, and everybody is scrambling for cover. Except me.

"I'm lying there flat on my stomach, wondering why I can't move and whatever the hell is this numbness in my back, you know. And then it all gets kind of dizzy and goes around and around, the way you get when maybe you've had too much to drink and that last second before you wipe out. And that's it. They took a hunk of metal out at the base hospital and then shipped me back home to the States. Only hassle was I couldn't use my legs no more. Couldn't get it up, either. I did about three years in the VA hospital, and then I had to get out." He looked around the room, his eyes glazing over empty, pocked walls and unraveling furniture. "Not much of a home, huh? Let me tell you, it's a damn sight better than the para wards. I got a nurse, comes here in the afternoons, helps me out some. I get about, you know; the hospital ain't too far away. I get over there just about every other day. Groceries, the works, you name it."

His hand swept around the room in a broad gesture.

"Do you come from here?"

"Folks did. Died a year ago. Car accident up north. Wiped 'em both right out. I've got a sister, lives in Orlando. That's it."

"So tell me," I said. "Tell me about the killer."

He laughed. "I don't know his real name. That was one of the things about the war. Everybody seemed to have a nickname. They called me Slick because I wore my hair in a ducktail like, you know, from high school. In the platoon everybody had a different name. It was almost like you didn't want to make the name you was born with dirty, you know, over there in the war, killing."

He reached down and drummed his fingers against the wheel of his chair. He started to speak about the war, about the platoon. When he grew excited he rapped his fingers against the chair to underscore the strength of his memories. Sometimes he rocked back in the chair, raising the wheels in front from the ground, spinning them underneath his legs, as if to rearrange his thoughts.

"I mean, there was a nigger from Arkansas we called Big Black and another kid from the Bronx in New York we called Streets. Another guy, drafted out of some fancy school in Boston, he became College. You see what I mean. In the Army they make you wear this little name thing on your shirt, even your fatigues. Hilson, mine said. I don't think anybody 'cept maybe some of the officers ever called me by that name. And if some dude didn't know enough to call me Slick, then he would find some cuss word and shout it at me, and that would work just about as well."

He lit a cigarette from an open pack in front of him.

"I mean, you gotta understand this was a very strange place in 1970. I still ain't got most of it figured out, and that's what I do most of the time. Sit and think. The Army helped me with that." He waved his hand at the chair. "You bet your ass."

He blew smoke rings, and I followed the circles through the still air of the apartment.

"Did you do any time there?" he asked.

My mind filled with images of those years: high school, college, graduate school. I had a fleeting memory of the conversation between my father and myself. To run or not to run, that had been the question. I recalled the letter from the draft board requesting I show up for a physical examination. I had been reclassified 1-A. My father had been angry, his face a deep red, complaining. I had neglected to fill out the proper forms at the college, forms that would guarantee the continuation of my student deferment. "Damn," he'd said, "how could you forget?" I hadn't answered. I hadn't forgotten. I'd remembered the forms; all I'd had to do was write in my name, classification number, course load, address and that was it. Drop it in the mail to the registrar's office; they took care of the rest. But the forms had stayed on my desk for months. Occasionally I'd picked them up and looked at them in wonderment, trying to figure out why I would not fill them out. It was as if I were daring the real world outside of the college: come and get me. And they tried.

I took care of it easily enough, though. The local draft-counseling service, which had offices on campus, got me out; I transferred my physical from location to location throughout the course of the dangerous semester. Once, when scheduled to go, I simply slept through the meeting time. Eventually my deferment was restored. It was that simple.

Sitting in that small apartment, I thought of all the aspects of the war that had filled my life. I read the latest on the front page every day; I stared at the grainy black and white photos of the faceless men in helmets and flak jackets walking through the strange country. I marched; I handed out leaflets; I raised my voice at dozens of protests, my fist in salute to a hundred different speakers. But I really did not know what I was doing.

My last year in college my next-door neighbor in the dormitory was a returned vet, a tall man with black curly hair that grew wildly from the top of his head and fell in great folds over his ears and neck. He walked with a limp and a cane, the reminder of a foot wound. On the wall of his room he kept a photo of himself, taken by a *Life* magazine photographer; full color. He was set back in the center of the shot, his face contorted, his hands reaching down toward the ground and a mass of blood welling from his shoe. The photographer had captured the scene as a still life: a medic vaulting over some sandbags, another reaching out his hand. There was an explosion in the rear of the photo, kicking dirt and mud up in the air. Everyone seemed streaked with the same filth and terror.

My neighbor did not go to marches, nor did he attend the rallies or speeches. He refused to talk about the war and slammed the door to his room in the face of the campus activists who sought to enlist him. "You don't understand," he would say, then shut the door. I asked him why once, but he simply shook his head.

One morning, not long after graduation, I spied his picture in the paper. There had been a march on Congress by a veterans' group; a ragged line of soldiers in their old fatigues, marching out of step down the boulevards of the Capitol toward the Hill. They were returning their medals. The photo, transmitted by the AP, showed my neighbor standing at a fence, flinging his award onto the steps of Congress. The caption said he was giving back a Silver Star, the nation's second highest medal for bravery. I wondered what he had done to deserve the honor. It was as if for him, and for the others, there were two lives: home, normalcy, cheeseburgers and fast cars; then the war. I never saw my neighbor again but read in the college alumni magazine that he had graduated from medical school.

"No," I said, "I missed it."

"Student, huh? Got a deferment, I bet," the man in the wheelchair said.

"That's right."

He laughed, his voice ending in a cough, and grinned at

me. "Ah, you should have been there. I mean, it was really something."

"I know."

He shook his head. "No. No you don't. You had to be there. That's the problem. Nobody understands unless they were there."

"You tell me about it," I said. The phrase I live by.

He coughed again. "OK," he said. "Sit back and relax. Have I got a war story for you."

I heard voices from the hallway outside, footsteps against the cement of the landing. The man in the wheelchair turned sharply toward the sound, his hands grasping the armrests, his knuckles turning white with sudden effort. A voice called out, "In yo' face, mother!" and there was the sound of running feet. The man in the wheelchair relaxed, visibly relieved. He stroked the sheet over his legs smooth. "Sometimes the neighborhood kids try to break in. Little fuckers. I ought to get a gun and shoot one or two. Maybe then they'd stop. This may not be the best neighborhood, but it suits me OK."

His eyes followed my pen scratching on the pad, then shifted to the tape recorder. "OK," he said, "like I told you, we knew everybody by nicknames, and the guy I think is doing these murders was called Night Eyes, because, man, the dude never seemed to want to sleep at night. You'd be out on the perimeter catching your shift, trying to keep your eyes open, so fucking scared of the dark—and this guy would come sliding along, eyes wide awake, looking out over the wire into the jungle as if he could see plain as day. He'd catch a few hours in the evening, waiting for the sun to go down, then in the morning when it started to get light, he'd crawl into his hole, pull his poncho liner around him and sleep. He just seemed to need less than everybody else.

"Anyway, he was there the same time I was. Longer, in fact, though I heard he got flaky—I mean flakier—after I caught the shrapnel. I heard they shipped him off Section Eight to a psycho ward somewhere. I believe it, man; look what he's doing now. I don't think I ever saw the dude stoned, or drunk, or anything. All he did was play soldier. He liked to kill, you could see that. Never talked much to anybody. Liked to walk point, so's to be away from everybody else. I mean, he was one very quiet, very strange guy. I don't think the platoon would have put up with him too long if it hadn't been that everybody was a bit spaced out over there. There was a lot of weird heads."

"You didn't know his real name?"

"No, I told you that already."

"Well, what was the outfit? The commanding officer?"

"The CO was a lieutenant named O'Shaughnessy. First name, Peter. I couldn't forget a name like that one. Red hair, just like you'd expect. Able company three hundred fifty-second field infantry, American Division."

"And where—"

"I told you that, man. Batangan Peninsula."

"That's right," I said. "Just trying to keep everything straight."

He smiled and started to drum his fingers against the steel again. "That's cool," he said. "I want everything to be right."

"Do you remember any other names from the outfit?"

"No. Like I said, just the nicknames. Strange, huh?"

I shrugged. "Where'd this guy learn how to use a handgun?"

He exhaled sharply. "Man, I don't know. But I remember he had one over there. A big mother forty-five just like he's using over here. Probably got it in Saigon on the black market. You see, we were doing what they liked to call Search and Destroy. Everybody was always looking for an edge, you know, something that might help them out of a tough spot. This guy carried a forty-five. I knew a couple other guys that did, too. Sometimes in the afternoon he sat on the edge of the perimeter, you know, when we weren't out in the fucking swamp or jungle, and he plunked away with that thing. Shot at coconuts, birds, anything."

"Anybody ask him about it?"

"No, like I said, he was strange. Wigged out. Everyone, even the CO, left him alone. Why not? Wasn't doing any harm. And the dude would volunteer for all sorts of shit, like lurps out into the country. Not me, man. I wanted to keep what little ass I had left intact. So as long as he did that, and as long as he took the dog shift at night, man, everybody just left him alone. And let him think whatever was in his head."

"And you don't know what happened to him?"

"Just rumors. Flipped out, screaming and shooting. Somebody said he shot some peasants and just started laughing and laughing until they came for him. Hushed up, I guess. You know, the Army didn't mind publicizing heros like me who get their ass shot off while they're asleep, but the guys who went over the deep end, well, mostly they just got shipped home and shipped out, if you catch my drift."

I nodded. The man in the wheelchair was shaking his head, repeating under his breath, "Weird, man, very strange."

"So," I said, "tell me about the incident."

Another long exhale as he thought.

"It was so damn hot; that I remember as clear as anything. Like right now, you know, the heat just hangs around. No air at all. As I said, we were doing Search and Destroy, which was the pits, man, the absolute worst." He laughed. "Number ten. That's what the grunts used to say. We'd get picked up by the choppers in the morning and flown into the target area for sweeps. You should get the chance to ride in one of those things sometime. The pilots were just as scared as we were; one second you're hanging up in the air a couple of thousand feet, the next second the slick's screaming down into the landing zone. The engine's wailing and the door gunner's shouting and swearing and firing off the fifty-caliber as fast as he can, chopping up the jungle. You know one of the really strange things about Vietnam? We was always shooting at things that weren't really there. I mean, when we went into a landing zone, everybody was emptying their weapons at an imaginary enemy hiding in the bush. At night the artillery would fire over our heads, to get the coordinates right in case we was attacked during the dark. And there was never anybody there. Well, hardly ever.

"On this one day we were put into a cold LZ; there was no return fire, which made the chopper jockeys happy and they split right quick. We were supposed to make two separate sweeping actions, meeting up at some village that was on the map. There we were supposed to move through some paddies and chase anything we came up with toward another company that was heading toward us, in a block. It was the kind of damn-fool idea that looked real good on the paper back at the division HQ but which didn't work worth a shit once we got into the field. Anyway, I remember the CO, O'Shaughnessy.

Christ, he was as big a mick as you could find. And big, man, the dude was at least six feet five and about two hundred and forty pounds. I mean, when he said to do something, it got done. Big, bad temper, too. I was always surprised nobody ever blew him away in a firefight. As far as I know, nobody did. And got to give the guy credit: when I got hit he was screaming at that chopper jock and told him he'd shoot him hisself if he didn't pick my ass out of there. So I guess I got no complaints, really.

"So like I was saying, we was all tossed into the middle of this paddy, collected around O'Shaughnessy, and the choppers were tailing away into the sun. I remember the feeling of being alone; even though you were surrounded by other men and weapons and you had the radio to call in help, I never could shake the sensation of being abandoned, just like I was adrift at sea; you know, like some Robinson Crusoe. It was so damn hot; in just a few seconds we were all dripping wet. The sweat used to run down between my eyes under my helmet. I couldn't stand it, you know; I wanted to scream. But there's no way to wipe it out when you've got your weapon and maybe you need to steady yourself with your other hand. I saw guys go crazy in the heat, start yelling, refuse to move, up to their ass in mud and water and leeches in the paddies. The sun was as bad as anything the VC did sometimes.

"He split us into two squads. He took one, and the first sergeant took the other. We were supposed to maintain a common distance, like a quarter mile or so between us, but, hell, that never worked over there. I mean, one squad would get bogged down in some shit, and the other would get ahead, then slow down, then speed up. I think it was all crazy, man, every bit of it. Being out in the field was no different. So we took off, about a dozen of us. And pretty soon we're slogging through the shit, just like always. I remember that morning like it was a blur, you know. It was just like so many other fucking mornings in Nam. It wasn't until we got close to the village that things started in different."

He paused, taking the moment to light another cigarette. His eyes, behind the glasses, followed the smoke as it rose from the ashtray.

"We got there first, a good ways ahead of the other squad.

We camped down on the edge and started to wait. It wasn't so bad; I mean, we all needed a blow. Well, the dude I was telling you about, the guy doing these killings, he was out on the point as usual. And when we halted, he was off sitting a little ways away, just as usual. And while we're sitting there, he's staring through the brush into the village. Then suddenly he stands up and turns to the rest of the squad.

"'I saw something,' he says. 'Looked like a chick with an a-kay.' Well, everybody grabs their weapons and straightens out real fast. You got to remember, this guy had eyes that could pick a shape out of the middle of the night, so we always trusted him. And I remember what he said, because he was standing right there, with his back to the sun, and I remember having to shade my eyes so I could see his face.

"Well, there was a lot of discussion as to what to do. Most everybody wanted to wait for the lieutenant and the other squad to show, but the sergeant, he was a lifer, and I guess he was looking for some kind of promotion or medal or some such shit, because he says, 'No way,' and the next thing I know we're all spread out and humping very carefully into the village. Moving from hut to hut, just like in the movies. Only scared, man, truly scared.

"There must be, oh, I guess maybe five, six pathetic little huts in this whole town. I mean, it hardly qualified as a village at all. Just a little bump on the ass of the world. So it doesn't take us long to move through it, even if we are being real careful 'cause of what the guy said he saw."

Hilson rubbed his hand through his hair and pulled at the cigarette. Then he started drumming his fingers again against the side of the chair, as if to increase the tempo of the words as they flowed out into the still of the apartment.

"I never told nobody this story," he said. "I'm not looking to get put on trial like that dude Calley."

I nodded at him. "I understand. This is confidential."

"You got it." Then he started in again.

"At the end of the village we stop and collect ourselves. The sergeant puts men out on the perimeter and sends a couple of guys back to wait for the other squad. I was jumpy, man; we all were. Something about the heat, you know. And we'd been told the VC were real strong in the sector. We were told we'd probably have contact, that anyone we saw was probably VC. So I guess it was to be expected.

"I mean, that's what *they* told us! Trust nobody! Not even the oldest, dumbest dink in the world. He'll blow your ass off as soon as you turn your back. Cut your balls off if you smile at him. Or her. We just had no way of knowing, man! No way. Not even when they sent those VC deserters or ARVN guys with us. They'd just as soon tell you to kill somebody as question them. They were no fucking help at all. And we didn't even have one of them with us on that day.

"So we lined up all the people in the village. There were nine of them. Old men and women, kids. No young men. There was this one old guy, spoke some American. He was the one that got questioned. I remember he just sat there bobbing his head up and down. 'No VC here,' he says. 'No VC.' And the sergeant is yelling, 'Bullshit! Bullshit' and the dude, Night Eyes is saying, I know what I saw. He's standing there, fingering the forty-five. He used to wear it in a breakaway holster in his armpit, up under his flak jacket. But he had the fucking thing out, and he was clicking the safety on and off, fiddling with it.

"So the sergeant yells at the rest of us to start checking inside the hooches, and pretty soon we're tearing the places apart, pretty angry 'cause it's hot and we're scared. And sure as shit, one of the guys finds a rifle stashed up in the rafters, in the brush alongside the ceiling. And then we are really scared and pissed.

"The sergeant is still yelling at the old guy, but he just keeps saying, 'No VC here,' even when we shake the a-kay under his nose. The rest of the people are looking very frightened. There are a couple of small kids crying and a baby wailing. I remember turning to the guy and saying, 'I guess you was right,' and he just nodded, kind of, and grinned. The sergeant was just about to give up when the guy says, "I'll take care of it, sergeant,' and the sergeant just shrugs and says, 'Do what you like.'

"So the guy walks over to a teenage chick, who's sitting on the ground just about ready to piss in her pants, and he grabs her real hard by the arm and pulls her over in front of the old guy. He clicks back the hammer on his forty-five and says, 'Where VC?' And when the old guy shakes his head, the guy pulls the trigger.

"Damn! I can still remember the click as the hammer came down on the empty chamber and the second click as the automatic thrust up. I mean, no one knew whether he'd emptied it purposely or not. And he just smiled at the old guy and said, 'Where VC?' And the old guy just shook his head.

"And the next thing I remember is the explosion from that big fucking forty-five. It was loaded, after all. And the kid just pitched forward, half her head gone, landing at the feet of the head man. I remember it like it was a picture. He got some of the blood and brains spattered on him. I saw his face just twist then; all sorts of things must have been going through his head—fear, I guess, mostly—but he just stayed right there shaking his head, repeating over and over, like some fucking record that gets stuck, 'No VC. No VC here.' The first sergeant is looking at Night Eyes like he's crazy, which I guess is right. But the dude hasn't barely budged, and his face is still set, cold and looking the old guy dead in the eyes. He walks nice and slow over to the group of people and pulls an old couple out. He looks over at the head man. The head man says, 'No VC,' and then that fucking forty-five explodes, Boom! Boom! and the old couple are in a pile on the ground. I remember the blood mixing with the dust. And everybody else is just standing around. I mean, we were just frozen, watching what was going on. I don't think I ever thought of trying to stop the dude. He seemed to be the only person who was *doing* anything. It was like it was all happening in some weird nightmare, man.

"Hey! I ain't proud of it. Shit, no. But you got to understand, we was all a little crazy that day. The sun, maybe. The fucking jungle, the fucking paddies. I don't know. I remember the sun most when I think about Nam. We were all off the end for that little bit.

"So I guess that's why no one stopped him."

There was a moment of silence. I watched the eyes behind the yellow glasses. They were raised now, looking up at the white ceiling.

"The next person he grabbed was some mama-san with her kid. Nobody moved. Boom! went the forty-five. And then I heard the dude laugh a little. Like he wasn't getting mad at the head man at all. He just wanted it all to keep going. Like it was some game. 'Where VC?' he asked, and he laughed again.

"But the guy didn't answer, because we found out.

"Suddenly out on the perimeter there was that sound. Man, once you hear the sound of small-arms fire, you never forget. And behind us there was a whump! and an explosion as a mortar round disintegrated one of the hooches behind us. I remember the guy just laughed. He picked up his M-sixteen and everybody was yelling to take cover. We were all running back towards the direction we knew the lieutenant was coming. Shit! There were mortars coming in all over the place, and the air was full of shit and shooting. I was cutting loose, too, to the front, I don't know at what. I do remember one thing, though. When I turned around I saw the whole pile of villagers in a heap, all of them gunned down. Except the little kid, the mama-san's baby. The kid was bawling and screaming. I could hear it for a minute, maybe just a second. And then there was too much noise.

"We all collected back at the rear of the clearing. I remember the radioman screaming for the lieutenant. And the lieutenant coming on and telling us to withdraw towards him. Then he said he was calling in an air strike. It was all simple, you see. That's how we did things over there. The bunch of us, still firing a bit, you know, at nothing except fear, headed away from the village. And in a few minutes I heard that sound, you know, the real high-pitched sound of a Phantom when the jock cuts it down to a couple of hundred feet and he comes winding in. There were four of them in the flight. I could see them come through the sun. It reflected off the wings, just like they were lights. They dropped those canisters and just blew the hell out of that village and whoever was anywhere near it.

"And if there was any evidence of what that dude did, then it went up in smoke, man, because that place was scorched."

He took another long pause, thinking, I imagined, of what he had seen.

"We made a report. O'Shaughnessy called all of us in, asked us what we'd seen, what we'd done. Even called in the dude. You know the really weird thing, man? Nobody lied. Nobody told the CO anything different than what happened. And you know who he told? That's right. Nobody. I remember he came out and I overheard him tell the sergeant, 'Fuck it. Who cares?' And the sergeant nodded. And a week later he got his transfer back to Saigon. And I got my ass in this sling. And that was all there was to it."

We were quiet for an instant.

"No investigation?" I asked.

He shook his head.

"No records?"

Again he shook his head.

"And the CO?"

"Killed, I heard. Fragged, I bet. Who knows?"

My imagination raced with the details: The girl. The old couple. The woman with the child. They were all there.

"Let me get this straight," I said. "When you turned around, the whole group of villagers, they were all dead, right?"

He nodded, his eyes fastened on my own.

"How did they die?"

"What d'you mean?"

"Well, did this guy mow them down, or were they caught in the cross fire, or were they killed by the mortars?"

"Is it important? I mean, man, they were dead."

"Yes," I replied. "Oh, yes, it is very important." My mind jumped ahead, dizzy with the possibilities. If Hilson were right, either the killer was finished—or he was just beginning. And I was the only one who'd know. I could feel the excitement rising up in me.

He hesitated, his hand rubbing his beard.

"I just don't know, man. I think I see what you're asking. I mean, what's this dude going to pull next, huh? I don't think I can help. All I remember is hitting the deck when the first explosions came in, and then getting up and hightailing it out of there. You know, you don't do a lot of sightseeing under those circumstances."

He paused again.

"Still, I remember the bodies, all in the same general area. Just like somebody'd opened up on them with an automatic. But I couldn't say for certain who did it, 'cause, shit, there was firing all over. You know what I mean? Anything could have happened."

Disappointment flooded me, but still, I thought, he'd given me many answers. If the major question remained, it was still a great deal closer to an end. I tried to picture the cluster of villagers, streaked with dirt, blood and their own gore, but I couldn't. At least not the way this man had seen it.

"So," he said, "you gonna figure it out from here?" He grinned, showing a row of even white teeth. "It's good, huh?"

"Yeah," I replied. I peered down through the smoky off-light of the room at my notes. Here it is, I thought, in a way the beginning and the end. I was getting closer to the edge of the killings. My imagination started in, blocking out the paragraphs. I pictured the headline, the front-page play. I sucked in a deep breath and stood to leave.

The man in the wheelchair led me to the door. We shook hands; his was slick with sweat. I stood in the doorway, looking out at the late afternoon. I paused, turning back to him. He was fiddling with the dead-bolt lock on the door, nervously sliding it closed, then open. "I've been a big help, huh?"

"Yes," I said. "No doubt."

"That's good."

I raised my hand, then remembered the key question, one I'd foolishly let slip past. "Listen, just one more thing. I need to know who can confirm the story."

He shrugged. "Maybe God. But I think He didn't care much what went on in Nam."

Then he shut the door, and I heard the dead-bolt lock slide into place.

CHAPTER FIFTEEN

IT was, of course, the lead story.

They'd stripped the morning headlines across the top of the front page beneath the *Journal* masthead, the same position where so many of the stories had run: EYEWITNESS RECALLS KILLER'S "INCIDENT." I lingered in my bathrobe at the kitchen table, drinking coffee, racing my eyes over the page of newsprint, feeling a quickening excitement as I read. I felt I had managed to shake a tree, and now I merely had to wait for the vibration to work its way up the trunk and out through the branches before the fruit came tumbling down from the sky.

I was alone; Christine had left early, sliding naked from the bed in the half-light of the summertime dawn. She had early-morning surgery scheduled. She had placed the paper, still folded in the newsboy's delivery fashion, unread on the table. She had been waiting up the night before when I came in after deadline.

I had paced through the apartment describing it all to her,

while she sat, hands clasped, listening patiently. She said little; instead I paused, asked myself questions, interrupted myself with comments. It was as if I were acting in her stead, trying to anticipate the questions she might have forming in her own mind.

I told her, too, about the struggle in the newsroom to get the story into the paper. Nolan had listened to the first few minutes of the tape recording, then to my reconstruction of the conversation from my notes. He, too, had been excited, but he'd stumbled on the issue of confirmation. I hurriedly placed a late-afternoon call to the office of public information at the Pentagon, but it was too late to confirm if either Hilson or O'Shaughnessy had been overseas at the relevant time.

Nolan had hesitated. "What happens if we hold off for a day? What do we lose?"

I had shaken my head. "An edge. This guy could go to the cops, could go to the television stations. Or he could disappear. I want to go with it."

Nolan had nodded and we'd struck a compromise: I would withhold the informant's identity, describe the unit that was involved in the operation and include the commanding officer's name. I would also omit anything that indicated the officer knew about the incident, so as to leave the question of an army cover-up untouched.

"But keep at it," Nolan had said. "We'll break that later."

I'd sat at the typewriter, convinced the story would flush the killer from his camouflage in the city. The story would break the rhythm of the murders; we would move ahead of the killer. He'd want to know from *us*, not the other way around.

Christine had shaken her head, though. "It'll just speed him up, make him realize his time is limited," she'd said. When we went to bed later she was hesitant, unresponsive, but I exploded inside her and then slipped from her body. Within seconds I was asleep as she turned on her side away from me.

It was mid-morning when Martinez called. "We're coming over," he said. "Right away." It was a call I'd been expecting.

I expected to hear from the killer, too. The morning had passed quickly as I accepted congratulations from the other reporters and the editors at the paper. I placed a call to the

Pentagon's public-information office, and they promised a quick response to the two names and the unit number. It was mostly a matter of waiting.

Nolan came over, expecting the detectives at the receptionist's desk. The night before he had raised his hands and shaken his head when I'd started to talk about the man in the wheelchair. "I don't want to know," he'd said. "The cops may have a subpoena, and I don't want to be put in that position. He's your source, and you're going to protect him. The paper stands behind you. It is that simple. I hope." We'd laughed.

A copy of the paper lay on my desk now, and he picked it up. He read out loud: "On a blisteringly hot day some five years ago, nine men, women and children in a Viet Cong-controlled village in South Vietnam were executed by U.S. troops in the 'incident' that has prompted the recent wave of murders in Miami, according to a now-disabled veteran who was an eyewitness."

"Eyewitness," he said. "God, what a great word to have in the beginning of a news story. It's as if the veracity of what follows is no longer in question."

He skipped over several paragraphs and then started to read again. "'I'm scared,' the witness said, as he started his description of the atrocity that he believes is the basis for the recent Miami killings. The witness, whose name is being withheld by the *Journal*, was able to recount the incident in extraordinary detail. 'Hell, I'm not proud of what we did,' he said." Nolan stopped and looked at me. "I bet the cops just about croaked when they saw this." I nodded. "Well," he said, "they should be here soon." He left me for a moment to answer the telephones at the city desk.

I had little doubt about what would happen with the man in the wheelchair. Now that the story was out, I would go back to him, and he would agree to be interviewed by the police. It always worked that way. Once the story was told it could be repeated a hundred times, a thousand times. It was as if it had become safe, no longer a memory banging angrily in the interior of the imagination.

From Hilson's memory would come the names and addresses of the men in the unit. For the first time I felt as if the story had almost run its course. It was only the proverbial matter of time. The man's memory would squeeze the killer from his hiding place, out into the sunlight. And, I thought, I had done it. I felt as if I were shaking my fist at all the fears of my life: my family, Christine. I could not help breaking into a smile.

Nolan's voice interrupted my reverie. "They're here."

We stepped away from the desk, and the telephone rang.

I looked at it for a moment, wondering, then looked at Nolan, and he shrugged. "I'll go ahead," he said. So I reached out and picked up the receiver, clicking on the recorder simultaneously. I watched Nolan step away as I brought the receiver to my ear.

I think back. I try to remember, but my recollection is more a blur than an etching. I wonder when it was that I lost what little control I had, and I suppose it was then, at that first call, that I began to realize the walls of the room that held me, to sense the suction at the bottom of the pool grasping at my legs, pulling me under the surface.

The call was from the public-information officer at the Pentagon. He spoke in a clipped, military manner, his voice filled with the jargon of the Army. "Sir!" he said. "I have personally checked those records you requested."

"And?"

"Negative, sir."

"What do you mean?" I felt a sudden heat on my forehead.

"Well, we keep all records of men and units. I have determined that the outfit you cited was in fact performing search-and-destroy missions in that sector of the combat theater. But I was unable to find any record of any PFC Hilson or any Lieutenant Peter O'Shaughnessy operating with that unit."

"Not with that unit?"

"That is correct. I further checked the list of men wounded in action during that time period. Again, negative on those names."

I stumbled. "Perhaps at a different time?"

"Possibly, sir. But I checked thoroughly for surrounding months, also. It is possible, if the year is incorrect, that I may be mistaken. But in a different year I doubt that you'll find that unit operating in that area. Units were shifted about with some frequency, sir, as you will recall."

"All right," I said. My mind was fighting with the information. I could think of nothing further to ask.

"May I ask a question?" the officer said.

"Go ahead."

"Does this have anything to do with the murders down there?"

"Yes," I said. "It has a good deal to do with the murders."

"Well," he continued, "I wish I could be more help. If you want other dates and names checked, just call me, sir. I'm afraid we haven't been much help. Especially to the police. But it is not difficult to check specific references such as you provided."

"Thank you," I said.

"Anytime," he replied, hanging up the phone.

I looked at the newspaper on my desk. A lie, I thought, it was all a lie. I took a deep breath, fighting a sensation of nausea. I got up from the desk and looked back to the conference room. Through the glass windows I could see the detectives waiting for me.

I sat next to Nolan, slipping him the note: "Pentagon says negative on Hilson, O'Shaughnessy." I underlined "negative" three times. Nolan's eyes widened, and he looked at me as he comprehended the sudden shift. But he had no time to make a response, to get us out of the room, before Wilson thwacked the table with his open palm. "We've played fair with you!" he was shouting. "And now you get a break, a huge break, and you shut us out! I ought to arrest the two of you for obstructing justice."

"Listen," I said, "there's a problem—"

"You bet there's a problem! There's a fucking murderer out there, and you guys have the key to finding his ass, and you won't even give us the courtesy of a fucking telephone call! Christ! What a bunch of fucking hypocrites!" He slammed back in his chair. "I want to know," he said. "I want to know everything! Don't hold back anything! Goddammit, we can get this guy now! Today! You tell me where this 'disabled veteran' is. I want to talk to his ass! Now!"

Martinez broke in, his voice also strained but under more control. "We feel this guy is a material witness. If we have to, we can come back in about thirty minutes with a subpoena. But we shouldn't have to do that. We've been up front with you," he said, looking first at me, then fixing his eyes on Nolan. "And I think it's your turn to be up front with us."

"There's a problem," Nolan said.

"What fucking problem?" said Wilson, leaning toward me. Nolan looked at me, too. "Tell them."

I hesitated, looking for words. "We checked the Pentagon this morning. They have no record of the informant's name. They also don't have any record of the man whom he said was the company commander."

Wilson slumped back in his chair. "Christ!" he spat.

"Explain," Martinez said.

"The guy gave me a phony name. A couple of phony names. I don't know what else was phony in the story he told."

Martinez nodded. "You mean you didn't bother to check beforehand?"

"I tried."

"Good try."

For a moment there was silence in the room.

Nolan broke it after a few seconds. "That means his confidentiality no longer has to be protected. I mean, if he lied, we don't have to protect him." He nodded at me.

"Tell us," Martinez said, pulling a pad out. Wilson leaned forward on the table, staring at me.

I began to retell the story from the beginning. I described driving across the city into the downtown ghetto. Then I described climbing to meet the man in the apartment.

"Stop there!" Wilson said. I held in mid-sentence. Martinez turned and looked at his partner, as if wondering what he was thinking.

Wilson spoke. "The man was in a wheelchair, right? Spinal cord severed, right?"

I nodded.

"How many flights up?"

"Three."

"And he says he gets out every day to the hospital?"

"He said that, yes," I replied.

And then things happened very swiftly.

Wilson slumped back in his chair for an instant, his eyes locked onto mine, and put his hands to his face. Then suddenly, without warning, he shot his body out of the chair, stretching it across the table, his hands seizing me by the shirt. I could feel the strength in his arms, and he jolted me out from the chair, pulling me across the table to meet his face, contorting with rage. "You dumb fuck!" he screamed. "You stupid, stupid idiot fuck!" I could feel the spittle in my face. "You damn fool!"

"Let me go!" I shouted. Both Martinez and Nolan had pushed out of their chairs and were trying to separate us. For a second all four of us were twisted in the middle.

And then, as swiftly, Wilson dropped his hands. I fell back into my chair as he slid into his. His eyes seemed glazed over. He was simply repeating, "Fuck, fuck," over and over again.

Martinez started to shake him, and Nolan turned to me. "OK?" His face was concerned. I reached up, straightened my tie and shirt. I nodded. We both looked at the detective.

"Don't you see?" Wilson asked. His voice was empty.

And then we did see.

Nolan let out his breath and sat down hard in the chair.

Martinez put his hand to his eyes and shook his head.

I felt ill, as if I were going to be sick to my stomach.

It was him, I thought. A meeting, just as I had requested.

Andrew Porter swung the big car hard through the lunchtime congestion. At the intersection in front of us the stoplight changed from green to yellow. He put his foot down hard on the accelerator and we shot through, people on the sidewalk stepping back quickly. I heard Nolan muffle an obscenity from the back seat. Porter glanced into the rearview mirror. "Stayed right with us," he said. I turned and saw that Martinez and Wilson in their unmarked cruiser were only a few feet back. Porter slid the car around a corner, and suddenly we were leaving the boulevard behind and cutting through the tall downtown buildings. I saw the sun gleam off the white roof of a city police car as it braked at a side street and then swung into line behind the two detectives.

"Coming out in force," Porter said. "But for what?" He

laughed. "I don't know, but I tend to doubt he'll be waiting for us. It would be too much like Jimmy Cagney in *White Heat*. 'Come and get me, coppers!' No, I don't see it."

Nolan swore.

A block from the apartment we stopped, pulling sharply to the curb. I could hear the tires complain as the police cars came to rest next to us. Wilson was out of the car before it quit quivering. "Let's go," he said. We headed down the block. Halfway there, he turned to Nolan. "Stay back." He motioned at Porter. "You, too." I could see the other police taking positions around the perimeter of the building, out of sight of the landing. I watched the men working their way into locations, weapons out. I saw shotguns and pistols gleaming in the noon sun. It was like a battlefield, and any second the order to attack would sweep me along, out of control. "Come on," Wilson said. "It's just you, me and Martinez." We started across the courtyard. I felt the heat rebounding from the cement floor, curling like smoke around my feet and ankles. I couldn't see any of the people who'd populated the courtyard before; they had sensed trouble and faded into the shadows, invisible.

We climbed the stairs slowly, each step taking more effort.

"Now, you're really in it," Wilson whispered. "How does it feel?"

I didn't reply. Martinez looked at me carefully. "You certain you want to do this?" he asked. I nodded, despite myself. The two detectives paused at the landing, checking their weapons.

"All right," Wilson said. "It's time."

I tried to keep in mind what they had told me. I stepped out onto the landing and walked the few feet to the doorway. I saw the same deep gouge as before. Standing to the side, I knocked on the door loudly.

There was no sound.

I knocked again.

Still no response.

I glanced back at the detectives. Martinez made a motion with his left hand, turning his wrist as if opening the door. I put my hand on the handle and tried it.

It opened easily.

I pushed the door open fully. I could see the sunlight cutting into the darkness of the cavernlike apartment. For a moment I thought I saw movement inside and jumped back against the wall, my mouth dry. But there was no sound.

I called out.

No reply.

Slowly I peered around the corner, moving my head as carefully as possible, so slowly I thought each micrometer took seconds, minutes.

And then I saw the sunlight glint off an object in the center of the room. It took a moment to realize what it was, but when I knew, I turned back and pressed myself against the wall again, breathing in and out heavily, feeling the hot air fill my lungs, like a drowning man suddenly brought to the surface.

It was the wheelchair. Empty.

The two detectives pushed by me, swinging themselves, weapons extended, into the apartment. I knew they would find no one. I had seen the message left behind. I heard Wilson muttering obscenities. He came to the door. "Is that it?" he asked, and I nodded my head. "Well," the detective said, "that's all he left behind."

But he was wrong.

Martinez called out suddenly. I followed the detectives inside. "See that?" he said. He was pointing to the center of the wheelchair. There was a small cassette tape in the middle of the seat.

Wilson looked at it for a minute. "Have you got your machine?"

I pulled the portable recorder from my jacket pocket.

"All right," Wilson said, "let's see what the fucker has to say." Using the end of a pencil, he picked the tape off the seat and, without touching it, slipped it into the machine. I pushed the play button, and for a moment all we heard was hissing.

And then laughter.

It continued unabated, growing in volume for perhaps thirty seconds, a minute, then ended abruptly, leaving the room suddenly empty. The tape spun quietly and I stopped the machine. I stepped out onto the landing and looked up into the sky, picking out the white trail of a high-flying military jet against the light blue. Around me the landing filled with policemen and technicians. I heard Nolan's voice and Porter's camera as he stood by the doorway taking pictures of the abandoned wheelchair. But around me the sounds of voices faded, and all I could hear was hypnotic laughter.

Nolan sat at the computer screen, his hands playing on the keyboard, his face twisted into a frown as he surveyed the words blinking white against the gray background. "Damn," he said. He rearranged a sentence, words disappearing when he pushed buttons, other words jumping into their places. "Damn," he repeated. He pushed himself back from the screen. "I just don't have any fucking idea how we're going to say this." His eyes swept across the newsroom to the managing editor's office. Again he frowned and turned back to the screen.

I had written a description of the police raid and what they had discovered. In clipped, proper journalese, I had written that the man in the wheelchair had, in all likelihood, been the killer himself. We had hedged on that point, trying to write around the obvious, trying to obscure my own foolishness. It was that section with which Nolan was struggling. "The problem is, we just don't know how much of it was the truth. I mean, how can we write that he told a whole series of lies, when we don't know that? Suppose the only lies were the names? Like O'Shaughnessy, for example. Suppose he merely changed it slightly; the real commander was an O'Hara or a Malone or some other Irish name. It wouldn't be past him. Shit." He looked back at the screen, changed a few other words around.

"They're still waiting," I said. Martinez and Wilson were in the back of the newsroom, sitting at a vacant desk, their eyes fixed on us. The detectives had arrived after finishing with the management of the apartment building and canvassing the neighbors. No one, it seemed, knew much. A man came in. Paid cash for a week. Wasn't seen again. Wore a hat, dark sunglasses. Didn't say much. It was the type of apartment building where few questions were asked, especially with cash up front.

"I know," Nolan said. "You might as well go with them. And bring the sketch back, so we can run it with the story. I'll work on this while you're gone."

I nodded and watched as he continued to play with the story. I felt a kind of loss, watching him maneuver my words. It was the first story since the first murder that had undergone such severe editing. I could feel the story slipping away from me. I started to speak as I watched a change made but turned away. I motioned to the two detectives and reached for my jacket, draped over the chair at my desk.

And the phone rang.

My first thought was, "Not again." The continued ringing was a summons, a seduction. I looked back at the two detectives. They stared at me. I punched the recorder and picked up the receiver. "Hello," I said softly.

All I could hear was laughter.

"You!" I said. It was loud enough so that motion seemed to stop in the room. Martinez and Wilson started toward me; Nolan, at the city desk, stopped his work.

"So," the killer said, the laughter ceasing abruptly. "You wanted to meet. You wanted a war story. You got one."

"Why?" I asked.

He did not answer my question.

"You see," he continued, "you're not immune, are you?"

"Dammit, why?" I shouted. "What are you doing?"

"No one is safe," he said. "You thought you were. In school. Studying. Marching. Drinking beer, getting laid. And now it turns out there are no deferments."

"What do you mean?" I was furious.

His voice went soft, very cold and calm.

"I study, too," he said. "Habits, routines, schedules. It is surprising how organized, how regular our lives really are."

"What are you talking about?" I asked, slowing my voice.

"One merely has to wear a white jacket. Perhaps a stethoscope folded and hanging from a pocket. One becomes invisible, capable of checking any schedule, especially one posted so prominently."

Christine, I thought suddenly.

"So, imagine one wants to meet a particular person, a nurse, say. He would know when she leaves the hospital, when she walks through the big parking lot to the assigned spaces. And suppose her car wouldn't start. How would she know that the battery cable had been sliced? And, you think about it, would she turn down the offer for help from a young man, so obviously an intern, or maybe a resident, who happens by at that moment?

An offer of a ride to a service station? An offer that turns out to be something altogether different."

"Leave her alone!" I yelled. "She's done nothing!"

"Look at the time," the killer said. "It's already done."

Abruptly he hung up. The line was dead.

I turned toward the clock on the wall. It was five minutes before four P.M. The time she would be leaving the hospital.

"Well? What did he say?" It was Nolan. Wilson was next to him, rewinding the tape.

I grabbed the telephone, dialing the number of the nurses' station. I misdialed and, cursing, dialed again. "Christine!" I shouted at the voice that answered.

"I think she's gone for the day," came the reply.

"No!"

"I'm sorry," went the voice on the other end. "She's gone."

"No! Goddammit, stop her!"

"Who is this?" Suddenly suspicious.

"Have her paged!" I screamed. "She's in danger!"

"I'm sorry," continued the voice, cool, the collected tone of a nurse not swayed by demands. "I must know who this is."

"For Christ's sake, it's Anderson! Her boyfriend. Now stop her, please!"

"Oh, Mr. Anderson, I didn't recognize your voice. Hold on while I page her."

I held the telephone in my hand, squeezing it. I was fighting the pictures in my mind: the parking lot, her car disabled, the sudden offer of assistance. Around me I could hear Wilson, Martinez and Nolan trying to ask me what was going on. Then the nurse came back on the line.

"I'm sorry, Mr. Anderson, but she doesn't answer. She's probably out of the building."

I slammed the phone down.

I could think of nothing except speed.

The afternoon traffic seemed to reach out and stop me. I twisted the car through the streets, running the lights, leaning mercilessly on the horn, ignoring the shouts and curses from pedestrians and other drivers. I swerved to avoid one collision and forced another car to careen into the curb, but I was barely aware of them. They were like slides in a show. I knew the two detectives were following behind me, but I paid no attention to their progress. I remember the afternoon sun filling the windshield, blinding me, and I held my hand up against it, as if I could block out all the terror within me.

The car pitched wildly as I slammed into the hospital parking lot. Another car jolted to a halt, tires squealing, blocking my path. The man inside shook his fist at me, but I ignored him, jumping from the car, running across the lot. I could hear the soles of my shoes slapping against the black macadam, like an angry drummer's beat. The heat seemed to surround me, pushing me down. I pumped my arms, running as hard as I could, sprinting toward the rear where I knew she parked her car. I heard the caterwauling sound of sirens as the police began to descend on the lot; the noise filled my ears and mind, adding to my fears. I could hear other feet behind me running; the detectives, I guessed, but I pressed on without turning.

And then nothing.

I stopped sharply, stumbling, steadying myself against a car. I looked through the lot, my eyes racing as madly as my feet had just a second earlier.

No sign of her.

No sign of the car.

"Christine!" I yelled. My cry flew up and away, useless.

"Where?" went a voice beside me. It was Martinez, breathing hard.

"Here," I said.

His weapon was out. His eyes followed the same path as my own.

"She's not here," I said. My voice wavered.

Martinez turned to Wilson. The older man was gasping for breath, leaning up against a car. "She's not here. She's gone. No car?" He turned to me.

"No car," I said. I inhaled sharply. Another thought formed slowly, then burst forth explosively. "Oh, my God!" I said. "He was lying. About the parking lot. He's waiting at home!"

For a moment Martinez looked wildly at me, his eyes blinking wide. "Shit!" he said. Wilson seized a portable radio from a jacket pocket and began talking into it.

I raced back to the lot entrance for my car, but it was blocked by a police cruiser. "Move it! Move it!" I screamed. "Move the fucking thing!" A policeman looked oddly at me, then saw

Martinez behind me, waving his arms wildly. He jumped into the seat next to me, and I floored the accelerator and the car shot backward. The gears complained loudly as I shifted, and we shot forward, fishtailing, barely under control, heading down the street.

We sped through the expressway toll booth without pausing. I headed through the traffic, cutting back and forth, leaving a braking, swearing mass behind me. Martinez had gripped hold of the door but was urging me on. "Hit it! Hit it!" he kept saying. I aimed the car between two others and shot through. "The shoulder," he yelled above the noise of the air pouring madly through the windows. I slid the car onto the roadway shoulder, and we raced up past the traffic. "Lean on the horn!" he shouted, and I complied, the sound rising and trailing off behind us like a boat's wake.

We cut through quiet suburban streets, through stoplights and stop signs. I was no longer aware of what was taking place behind me, my mind centered on what was waiting. "Hurry!" the detective urged. "Keep it up!" The car swerved wildly as I turned toward the small apartment building where I lived. It was on a quiet street, and the noise of the tires broke the air around us. I stopped the car and thrust myself out, stumbling, catching myself and then running hard, my mind filling with noise and fear. I could hear Martinez laboring a few steps behind me. "There!" I shouted.

It was her car.

"Oh, no!" I said, stopping suddenly, staring ahead.

The hood was up.

"Christine!" I shouted. My stomach was clenched tight with tension. "We're too late," I said. "He's taken her." Martinez pulled up beside me. He, too, was staring at the car.

"Shit," he said. "You sure?"

But another thought cut through me, and I jumped for the door to the apartment. My mind filled with a picture of her body, twisted, misshapen in death, on the floor of our home. "Upstairs," I cried, my voice passing back over my shoulder. I took the stairs two, three at a time, my feet crashing against the wooden steps, the stairwell echoing with noise. I threw myself against the apartment door, my shoulder meeting the wood with a crash just as I twisted the doorknob with my hand.

I felt myself slipping, falling into the living room, my balance suddenly evaporated. The floor rose up to meet me, and I held out my hands to brace my fall. Martinez was behind me, leaping through the open door, sweeping inside, half-crouched, gun extended in both hands, his voice near a scream. "Freeze!" he shouted, before knowing whether anyone was inside or not.

And then we both stopped as if our frame was indeed frozen.

She was standing in the center of the room. I saw her face contort in abrupt fear and confusion. A magazine fell to the floor, pages fluttering. Outside, the sound of sirens filled the superheated air, growing in tempo and volume as they approached.

She gasped, choking, and put her hand to her mouth.

"Oh, my God!" she cried. "What is it?"

For a long moment I felt suspended, unable to respond. Martinez turned, his face marked with the struggle to comprehend. He shook his head slowly, in disbelief; his hand fell limply to his side, quivering slightly, the gun pointing downward. I rolled over onto my back listening to the sounds increase: footsteps on the stairs, car doors being slammed, sirens winding down, voices raised in mistaken urgency. I heard Christine's voice, too, struggling against thickening tears, trying to ask her question again. I breathed in great draughts of air, trying to contain my racing heart, and then all the other noises slipped away into the background, and all I could hear repeated over and over again were the killer's words:

There are no deferments.

CHAPTER SIXTEEN

CHRISTINE left the following morning.

I watched her from the bed as she packed her things into a large plaid suitcase. Her hands moved swiftly, seizing items from her bureau and the closet. I envisioned her in the operating theater moving with the same studied efficiency, the same quick, steady motions. She said little, except to wonder out loud where she might have misplaced an article. Throughout the packing she averted her eyes from mine. When she finished, she squeezed the lid of the suitcase down hard, leaning her body's weight against it. It snapped shut with two resounding clicks that filled the space between us. Then she straightened, lifted the case from the corner of the bed and set it down firmly on the floor. "It's heavy," she said, finally looking toward me. She managed a small smile just at the corners of her mouth, a slight turn and shape upward. She shook her head, as if to loosen the smile. "I've got to go," she said. "I just can't stay now. Even the detectives said that."

I nodded but said nothing.

She looked at her watch. "Will you drive me to the airport?"

"Of course," I replied. I kept my voice flat.

In my memory, the time seems to melt together. It was as if a starter's gun had fired at the first stroke of the killer's phone call and extended through a long race, first to the hospital, then to the apartment, through the rest of the night, into the dawn, directly to the moment I waved as she stepped through the gate to her waiting plane.

It had all been confusion in the apartment as the room jammed with policemen and detectives. Christine's exterior calm had shattered, and within minutes, even before she knew what had happened, she was sobbing, repeating to herself, to me, "I knew something would happen. I just knew it." It was minutes before I was able to explain. I sat next to her, my arm wrapped around her shoulders, trying to help her pull her emotions under control. She touched hysteria for an instant, turning to me savagely and saying, "I told you! I told you! I knew what would happen." I recoiled at her sudden anger, but within a moment she had slipped her head back onto my shoulder. I wondered why I was not able to comfort her better. Each minute retrieved some of her reserve, however, some of her control; and finally she relaxed and said, "Explain carefully for me so that I know what's happened. So I understand what I'm up against."

"What we're up against," I corrected.

But she shook her head.

I told her about the killer's phone call and the seeming kidnap plot he'd outlined to me, then about the race across town and the second sprint to the apartment. She made me go back over the conversation, particularly the description he'd given of himself in the guise of a doctor by her disabled car.

"But he was there!" she said abruptly.

Martinez and Wilson, standing to the side, turned their heads sharply. At the same time she turned from me to the two detectives. "I saw him. Just like he said."

Martinez sat down next to her, notepad out. "Carefully," he said, "try to remember what you saw."

Christine took a deep breath, nodding her head. She smiled

at me for an instant, then shuddered. "My car was disabled out in the parking lot. I left work a little early, maybe a quarter to four. When I got behind the wheel, it wouldn't start. It was just dead."

"Like he said," I interrupted.

The detective glared at me, and Christine continued. "I was sitting behind the wheel, swearing, cranking the engine over, pleading, the way, you know, I talk to my car when I want it to go. Then all of a sudden there was this shape by the window, and a face bent over, peering in."

"Do you recall what he looked like?" Martinez asked. Wilson was close by, too.

She hesitated. "Not precisely."

"Just describe what you remember, as many details as you can recall."

"He seemed tall, perhaps a little over six feet. Brown hair, a little long, like over the collar. But he was wearing those big mirror sunglasses, with really large lenses. He was standing with his back to the sun, too. I remember I had to hold my hand up to shield my eyes from the glare. It seemed to flow right over his shoulders. And when I could see, all I could see was myself in the reflection of the glasses."

"What did he say?"

"He just asked me what the trouble was. He was dressed just like he told you he would be. White coat, dark slacks, a stethoscope. I thought he was someone on the staff."

"Go on."

For a moment she gathered her thoughts. I felt suddenly excluded. I wanted to interrupt, interject a comment, something.

"I popped the hood and started to get out of the car, but he said for me to stay behind the wheel. Then he said, 'I can see the problem.' I could just make out that he was fiddling with something, and then he shouted, 'Try it now.' I turned the ignition key and the engine started. I remember he slammed down the hood and stepped to the side all in one motion."

"What did he say?" I blurted. The detective nodded at Christine.

"He said, 'All fixed. Nice seeing you.' And that was it." She paused. "No, he said one thing. He said, 'Life is filled with mystery, isn't it?' And then he just faded away behind me."

"Did you see a car, or where he was heading?"

"No," she said, tossing her head back and forth. "He just seemed to disappear into the sunlight."

Martinez scratched a few more notes. I listened to the sound of his pencil moving against the page, irritating, like a screech of chalk against a blackboard.

"What had he done?" she asked.

"Probably the battery cable, just like he said," the detective replied. Christine shuddered again, a long, involuntary motion up in her shoulder blades. She reached out and squeezed my hand. I wondered why the killer had passed her up. The phone call. It had been five of four when I'd looked up at the clock, listening to his voice. It's already done, he had said. He was right.

"But why was the hood of the car up when we arrived here?" the detective asked.

She looked back at him. "It overheated in traffic. It's been doing that lately." She turned to me. "Remember, I asked you to fix it the other day?"

But I had not remembered.

I telephoned Nolan from Police Headquarters to fill him in on what had occurred. He was already revamping the story, incorporating the latest tape and the threats to Christine. "It's a mess," he said, "and we're getting behind." I told him what had actually taken place. "Jesus," he said, "that was close."

"I don't know," I said.

"I don't get it."

"Was it close? Who knows? I mean, what was he trying? Did he mean to take her and stop, or did he see something which caused him to give up, or did he just mean to scare me? He's succeeded, let me tell you."

"I know," Nolan said. "How's Christine?"

"Home to the folks."

"Where's that?"

"Madison, Wisconsin. Far enough away, I guess."

"I hope so," he said.

I could hear the clicking noise of the computer as Nolan

took down the notes I dictated. I felt odd, a sense of violation, as I quoted Christine, knowing her words would be in the story. He kept asking for description. I was reluctant, and he had to push me before I gave in and fully detailed what I had seen.

"All right," he said finally. "I'll get it all in. It'll be a hodgepodge, but it's the best we can do. I'll see you in the morning. And take your phone off the hook when you get home." Before I hung up he added, "Oh, the byline will be yours. As usual."

I shook my head but said nothing. I could not bring myself to say that I didn't want it, that I wanted to be divorced from the story and the killer. I didn't say it because I couldn't. It wouldn't have been true.

The police artist finally completed his sketch late that night. The two detectives sat by quietly as Christine and I talked with the artist and he put together his composite of the killer. She kept shaking her head, saying, "It's just not quite right," but as the shape of the cheeks, the eyebrows and the chin took form on the sketch pad, I felt the likeness was growing close. The artist drew in thick aviator glasses, which helped the effect. Christine shrugged. "I didn't really see him. I can't really tell."

Martinez looked over at me. I nodded.

"It's a start," the detective said. Wilson stared at the composite for a minute before moving his hand in a fist and shaking it at the blank eyes staring out from the white sheet of paper.

I took a copy of the sketch to the office that night, late. Nolan was gone, but the night city editor was there. He looked over at Christine for an instant, admiring and studying her at the same time; then he took the sketch and went to the copy desk. They pulled a photo from the final edition and ran the picture adjacent to the story with the cutline in bold, thick, black type: HAVE YOU SEEN THIS MAN? There was an earlier edition in the newsroom, and I could see my name beneath another striking headline, but my eyes glazed over the words. They were no longer mine.

We drove home together silently. The streets had emptied of most people by now and been taken over by Miami's derelict population: drifters, old men, young men, some in on buses, some hitchhiking, others who simply materialized on the streets.

Many lived underneath the thruway ramps, making huts out of discarded cardboard boxes, scraping together a few filthy possessions. They were older men covered with sores who moved silently through the darkness, looking, for the most part, toward their next drink and their next drunk. They mingled freely with the younger men, the runaways who moved south down Interstate 95, that great wide roadway that ended in the middle of Miami, all the way from Maine.

At night the two groups came out on the street. We waited at a stoplight and watched a pair of teenagers tease an old man; they had stolen a baseball hat from his head and were tossing it back and forth, just beyond his outstretched fingers, making the old man twist and pirouette trying to capture his property. "Why do they do that?" Christine asked. I did not know. As we watched, the old man finally stumbled and fell to the ground. I could see his chest moving up and down, heaving with the exertion and probably with emphysema. The two young men looked down for a moment, then tossed the hat back to him. He did not reach out for it but remained in a heap on the sidewalk.

I saw a car stop and a window roll down. The two young men went up to it, and, after a few words, one went to the other side and disappeared through an open door. The remaining teenager stared after the disappearing lights, then wandered off into his own darkness. Our stoplight changed, and I accelerated up a ramp to the freeway.

"What was that?" Christine asked.

"A pickup," I said. "A chicken hawk; that's what the cops call them. An elderly homosexual picking up his date for the night." She made a sound of distaste, and then we were silent.

At the airport they announced her flight over the loudspeaker, and she raised her hand and stroked her fingers across my cheek. "You must be tired," she said. "I'm sorry it has to be like this."

I shrugged.

"We haven't touched very much, you know," she said.

I nodded.

"Will you call?" I asked.

"Of course."

"Will you come back?"

She hesitated. "I don't know." There was a moment of quiet between us. "Suppose he tries for you?" she said. "Are you scared?"

"I don't think so," I replied.

She frowned. "No. That's the trouble. You see everything. And yet you're totally blind to what's really happening." Tears formed at the corners of her eyes. "I'm so sorry," she said. She turned, seized her pocketbook, a parcel of magazines and a paperback copy of Hemingway's short stories, and firmly, quickly, walked across the gateway to the entrance to the plane. I waved, a short lift of my hand, but then thought better and stopped. She didn't turn back, anyway.

And then my thoughts returned to the killer.

At my desk that afternoon I took out all the sheets of notes I'd kept on the killer. I went through them, culling a list of traits, clues, all the efforts to try to sort out the identity of the man. I made a separate list of all those items and then stared at it.

Only Child was at the top.

Youth in Ohio. Adolescence in city.

Father, vindictive, weak. Mother, seductive, strong.

Army.

Cruelty. Others followed, through the most recent conversation. I wrote at the bottom: No Deferments.

Then, one after the other, I drew lines through each entry. All the stories, all the words and sentences that had filled the columns of the newspaper, meant nothing. No more existence, no more substance. I looked down and saw I had drawn a large question mark on the page. I smiled. Appropriate, I said, but quietly so that none of the other reporters would hear me. Out of all that had happened, all that had been said, I really knew nothing. I stared at the police artist's sketch and thought back through the conversations with the killer. I remembered something he'd said early on in the killings: it was just him and me, he'd said. I understood that now.

The manager of the gun shop looked up as I walked through the door. The store was empty except for a pair of men looking at shotguns displayed in a locked glass case. The manager smiled, and I saw he was reading the *Journal*. He held out his hand. "You know, I was just reading your latest story. I kinda had the feeling we'd see you in here. Got to be ready if he tries again, huh?"

"Right," I said.

He rubbed his hands together. "Don't get too many young types like you in here," he went on. "I mean, we get plenty of young guys, but they're not like you. Educated, is what I'm saying, whitecollar jobs. No, most of the customers your age, they're mainly construction workers, cops, an occasional fireman who likes to do some shooting. Duck hunting or maybe deer, out in the Glades. Of course, since this killer hit town, we get all types. But not like you."

I said nothing in reply, so he continued. "I think it's got something to do with the war, you know what I'm saying. They don't go in much for weapons. Handguns, rifles, hell, not even a good slingshot. Just a theory, mind you, an observation. You see a lot of life from a gun shop.

"So," he said. "No story this time, huh? Not looking for quotes, I guess. What'll it be? How about a Magnum three fifty-seven. I think I showed you one of those before, didn't I? No? Well, should be what you're looking for."

I shook my head.

"How about one of these?" he said, slipping an automatic from a display shelf. "Nine-millimeter automatic. Takes a thirteen-shot clip, ejects the cartridges. This is a particularly smooth model. Never jams, or so they tell me."

Again I shook my head. "I want what he's got," I said.

The gun dealer smiled. "I should have guessed. Fight fire with fire. Make things equal, huh? Figure then, little bit of brains, little bit of luck, you can gain an edge. Good thinking." He stooped down and pulled out a gray metal .45 from the case. "Here it is. The basic model. This ought to stop that sucker at the door. Nothing fancy, no frills at all, just the essential weapon. Why go with something more than you need, huh? I mean, this weapon has a limited and specific purpose, right?"

"Right," I said.

"A judge of human nature, that's what I am. You get that

way when you sell guns. Got to be able to anticipate the customer's needs. What he's got in his mind. A gun is like that, you see. An extension."

"I'll take it."

"Whoa," he said. "You know about the seventy-two hours. The cooling-off time?"

"Come again?"

"You're a reporter, you ought to know. Not supposed to let anyone just buy a handgun and walk out with it. County ordinance. Show your license, pay your money and come back in seventy-two hours to get the gun. Designed to prevent you having an argument with your next-door neighbor or your wife or your brother-in-law and coming down here and buying something to blow them away. Legislature figures that in a couple of days you'll figure out another way."

"That's a problem," I said.

He looked across the counter, his eyes locked onto my own. "That's what I'm thinking, too." He leaned across and brought his head close to mine. "Tell you what I'll do. You give me your word it never leaves here, and I'll back-date the sales slip. And you can have the weapon. I never done it before, but I figure one time I won't get caught. And I'd sure feel guilty to find out that sucker came and wasted you during the cooling-off time. Call it sympathy, huh?"

"You've got my word." I didn't recognize my own voice.

As he rang up the sale I hefted the automatic in my hand. It seemed to fill my fist, covering every pore in the skin. It was a satisfying weight, shape, cool to the touch. I looked down at it, feeling a sense of excitement sweep out of my hand, up my arm and into my body. The killer, too, must have felt much the same thing at some time.

"We are responsible people," Nolan said.

I watched as his eyes tracked across the pages and headlines, boring in on the photographs. He was sitting at a desk, looking up at our coverage of the slayings pinned to the wall of a small office.

"I simply can't see it," he said. He leaned back in his chair, rubbing his eyes with his fingers. "We've handled ourselves in a completely ethical fashion. Look at the stories—no screaming frontpage editorials calling for vengeance, no hate mongering, no panic inspiring. I'm trying to think where we've gone wrong. How have we instructed this guy? How have we encouraged him? Hell, the *Journal*'s been careful. Aggressive, sure, but *careful,* right up to the last stories. Would the *Times* or the *Washington Post* have handled it any differently? I don't think so. Oh, they might have made the decision to gang-bang it, sure, with a half-dozen reporters on the story, but I'd still defend the decision to stay with you alone. It kept a focus, a center. And hell, he was calling you, not the whole staff."

He paused, thinking. "I suppose if we'd been a Hearst paper it might have been different . . . or one of the British papers, a Fleet Street type. We could have brought in psychics and written open letters to the killer. We could have shouted *Murder*! in the headlines every day, built it up into some journalistic frenzy, like promoting a holy war. We could have run the goriest photos in full color.

"But we didn't do any of that. We remained calm—aggressive, like I said, but circumspect. We acted with all the respectability and . . . *responsibility* one would expect from this city's paper of record. No one can accuse us of leading this guy on."

Again Nolan rubbed his eyes with his fingers. He was less talking to me than to the stories on the wall.

"You know, I even had the library pull all the paper's editorials on the Vietnam War. Just to check, to see where we were. Moderate, from the start. Initial support that faded in the late sixties to a call to bring all the troops home immediately in 1971. Also to end support of the puppet regimes. I guess we weren't first, but we sure as hell weren't last, either."

He let out a long sigh. "I'm getting old," he said. "I think this has all started to get to me." He looked at me. "You know, I sent my wife and kids off to visit my brother and sister-in-law, all the way to California. Two weeks ago."

"Why?"

He frowned. "Are you kidding? Because I was afraid. I'm in the phone book. He could decide to go after me just as easily as after Christine or anyone else.

"I suppose," he said after a momentary pause, "we are all vulnerable."

And so I began to wait.

At home and at the office I stared at the telephone, willing it to ring, trying to bring the killer into grasp. I don't think I was scared; not like Wilson or Nolan, who'd sent their families away; not like Martinez, who needed to lose himself in a drink or a different girl to wrestle his thoughts away from the killer. I concentrated, trying to focus my thoughts. I fantasized a meeting, alone, some lonely place. I could see the two identical weapons jump into our hands and hear the twin explosions. In my imagination, he was always that small second slower. I saw him twist, fall, shatter under the impact. Sometimes I thought of myself as bait, bouncing along the surface of the water, hook hidden deep inside but deadly. Already dead myself.

And as the wait lengthened, I took to playing the tapes of the killer's calls, filling the air with the sound of his cold voice. Just him and me, alone.

There were no stories to write. Simply a wait.

Then the call came from O'Shaughnessy.

The ringing, as always, was like a church bell's sudden peal, and as always, I thought first of the killer, snapped on the recorder and lifted the phone with the thought: here it is; now is when it begins to end. It was as if I had only to remove him to restore myself to the world. I said nothing until I heard the voice on the other end of the phone.

"Hello? Hello?" it said. My hands loosened their grip.

"Yes," I said. "This is Anderson."

"Mr. Anderson," said the voice. "My name is Peter O'Shaughnessy. Formerly a lieutenant in the U.S. Army."

For a second I was unable to speak. I had assumed, after talking with the Pentagon, that the names were all lies.

"My God," I said, "you exist."

He laughed. "I should hope so. I did this morning when I woke up, and I assume I still do."

"But I don't understand. The Pentagon told me there was no O'Shaughnessy."

He interrupted. "Oh, I'm not sure I'm the man you want.

But the similarity in names, well, I figured I just had to call you to find out."

"Where are you?"

"Memphis, Tennessee. I'm a lawyer. A friend of mine who lives down in Miami sent me a copy of your story, the one with my name in it. I've been sitting around for a couple of days trying to figure out whether to give you a call or not. Curious, I guess. The coincidence was just too great, and anyway, I'm not too certain there were any other O'Shaughnessys in the service when I was. It really isn't that common a name."

"Where did you see combat?" I asked.

"Well," he said, "that's the really odd thing. I never did see any real shooting. Not like what this fellow describes. You see, I was in control of a section of clerks, back on the air base near Da Nang. The only combat I ever saw was an occasional rocket or mortar round that came into the compound. Sometimes you'd see the type of stuff the VC pulled on the roads—land mines, mostly—but combat, the way some of the grunts saw it? No way. I pushed paper, forms, all the stuff the Army always needs in triplicate."

"Clerks?" I said.

"You got it. Oh, I don't know how many, probably fifty to a hundred different guys during the eighteen months I was there. All different sorts, but everybody had one thing in common."

"Which was?"

"They were there because they wanted to avoid getting their ass shot off."

"I don't get it," I said.

"Well," he replied, "the Army would offer you a deal right before you were shipped off to some fire base in-country. Re-up—that's re-enlist for an extra year or two—and they'd send you back to division and a job with a typewriter and a filing cabinet and clean uniforms."

"So—"

"So we were all the cowards, I guess. Scared and safe."

He and I talked for almost an hour. His physical description, he conceded, matched the one the killer had provided. He talked about the military, about life within the barbed-wire limits of the compounds, where every so often you stared out at the streams of refugees as if the wire were a barrier that stopped your feelings just as surely as it stopped sappers. He said he never could tell whether the soldiers were trapped inside or the civilians were trapped out. I took notes rapidly, for the first time in days. His voice seemed to rejuvenate me. I felt a malevolent glee, and the thought kept going through my brain: now I've got you.

O'Shaughnessy spoke, too, of riding into the city and walking the crowded streets, shoulder to shoulder with other Americans towering over the locals. He talked of dark bars, where the sun outside was shut away and red light reflecting off the naked skin of a nameless nude dancer was the only glow in the room. There were many stories there, he said, stories of killings, atrocities, murders, all wrapped in the guise of war; thick voices, clouded by beer or cheap scotch, speaking horrors in the gloom. "We all heard them, you couldn't avoid it. The soldiers from the field used to drink to forget, but it's a slow process, you know? Moves in stages. And there's one point where these nightmares loosen up and tumble out, you know, like a confession. Like telling it would make it go away."

I could see the killer there, listening to other voices, the words flitting in and taking hold in his imagination.

"You know what the damndest thing was?" O'Shaughnessy asked.

"Tell me."

"You heard so much, and yet we were so divorced. It was so unreal. Kind of like when you wake up and you can remember the dream you just had. It's real, but then, it's not. Sometimes now I'll be sitting around, and someone will say something—a word, a tone of voice, perhaps—and some remembered conversation will come back. It's almost like feeling a ghost inside of yourself." I could sense he was shaking his head on the other end of the line, trying to free his thoughts from his memories.

"Why do you think it affected you so much?" I asked.

He paused. "I didn't tell you what my section of clerks was in charge of."

"Well?"

"We processed our own dead. Names. Identifications. Making certain that the right effects accompanied the right casket. Our offices were just off a morgue, you see. Bodies on slabs, some recognizable; others, well, just all chewed up. That's why there was so much turnover in the section. It was just too macabre, too bizarre, working all day right next to all the stiffs. It was air-conditioned, you know, but I still wake up sometimes smelling death. Get sick to my stomach. Not much I can do about it; the doctors say it's all in my head, anyway. You know, that was the trouble with the war. It was always in our heads too much."

I couldn't think of anything to say. I pictured the killer at a desk breathing in and out, slowly, all day. Getting the stench in his nostrils with every living breath.

"Have I helped?" O'Shaughnessy asked.

"More than you know," I said.

CHAPTER SEVENTEEN

Now I've got you, you bastard.

I didn't tell anyone at first about my conversation with the Tennessee lawyer. Instead, I let my imagination whirl and dance. Visions of capture formed in my head; I felt I had suddenly jumped the huge gap between the killer and myself, that his lies would all evaporate now. I stayed at my desk, rocking back and forth in my chair. Who's the hunter now, I thought, and who's the game? I clenched my fists in exultation. Nolan saw it and wandered over from his seat at the city desk. "Something new?" he asked. "Something good for a change?"

I nodded and he grimaced slightly, then faded it into a smile. "Please, for my sake, not something like the meeting fiasco. And not something dangerous."

I shook my head. "We've got him," I said.

Nolan smiled and held up his hand. "Please, not the conclusion, just the evidence."

So I played him the conversation. He listened silently, his

hand to his chin, rocking slightly forward. Then he leaned back in his chair. "You may be right," he said. Then he laughed, a great burst that filled the small conference room. "Damn! This could be it."

"It's almost over," I said.

"Right. Call the Pentagon."

"They'll have the names. . . ."

"And we'll have the killer." We looked at each other. "Maybe. Suppose he's using an alias?"

"You think so?" I replied. "You think that's his style?"

Nolan shook his head. "No. No, it isn't."

We stared across the table at each other, the tape recorder between us. On the walls the stories stared down, marking our days, our lives, the highs and lows.

"Let's get the son of a bitch," he said. "You get him, goddammit. You get him."

The public-information officer at the Pentagon snapped his responses like so many salutes. "Yes, sir. A list of names, sir. Can do." I heard his pencil scratching as he took down the information. I let my voice trail off. "Yes, sir," he said again. "That will be sufficient. Let me just get this straight, now. You want an accounting of the names and possible addresses of the clerks who did part of their tour of duty in Da Nang."

"That's right." I gave him the section and unit numbers again, just as O'Shaughnessy had provided them. I also asked the public-information officer to check out O'Shaughnessy for me.

"Roger," he replied. "When will you be needing this information, sir?"

"As soon as possible."

"Take about twenty-four hours," he said. "But I will see to it personally, then get back to you."

"Fine," I said. Suddenly I felt relaxed, as if I had all the time I needed. I'm after you now, I thought, closing in. I wanted the killer to call me so I could tell him, obliquely, make him sweat. Closing in.

In the afternoon I went to see Martinez and Wilson in the homicide offices. I followed them through the maze of desks and cubicles unchanged from previous visits. It seemed as if the same interviews were going on, the same tired voices replaying the same information. Sunlight penetrated the room awkwardly, throwing shadows into the corners and across the floor. The voices rose up through the smoky air, mingling with the strained humming of the air-conditioning system. We talked in the room set aside for the investigation of the killer. Now, in addition to the list of names, places and dates, the walls were littered with copies of the police sketch.

"Has he called you?" Wilson asked.

"Not yet," I replied.

"He will," Martinez said. "He always has. Once a killer establishes a pattern like this, it's very difficult for him to break it. It's true of the worst psycho—like this guy—or the coolest contract killer. They get accustomed real fast to the system they create, their own way of doing things. They've got to stick with it, or they get no satisfaction. It's like a signature, you know; sometimes it wavers just a bit, seems a little different, but the whole thing stays pretty much the same. And this guy's pattern is to call you."

"You don't think that last call may have been his last?"

"No. Just a guess, but I think he's beginning to wind down. Maybe one of the detectives out working the street got close, you know, just asking around; maybe he's scared. But I don't think he will be able to resist talking with you again. Or killing, for that matter. He's made it too important for himself. I don't think he can go on without it; too much ego. That's why we'll catch him."

I thought of telling them about my conversation with O'Shaughnessy. Wait, I told myself.

"You think I'm in danger?" I asked.

"Hard to say," said Wilson. "He may have done what he wants to do to you, what with the scare and everything. On the other hand, it could be just the start. We have to assume you're in danger."

"That's not logical," I said.

"Logic. Who gives a flying fuck? Certainly not this guy." Wilson turned away and looked at the walls.

"He could have killed me a hundred times," I said.

"Sure," said Martinez. "That doesn't mean there won't be a hundred-and-first."

I shook my head. He's not after me now, I thought. I'm after him.

"You got to realize," Martinez continued, "that he likes to establish a personal relationship with his victims. That's why he was so frustrated by the woman and the kid, out in the Glades. She wouldn't talk. But of all the people, he's developed most of a relationship with you. Why wouldn't he kill you? And think of the headlines that murder would get."

"I still think he needs me, that he won't try for me. Just a gut feeling."

Wilson swore. "A feeling that could kill you. Don't be so dumb. And don't think you can shoot it out with this freak. This isn't the Old West. That guy knows his weapons and he knows that gun."

"Don't try to fuck with him," Martinez cautioned. "He'll drop you certain."

"What makes you think . . ."

"Oh, shit," Wilson interrupted. "You must think we're really stupid."

"We know about the forty-five you purchased the other day," Martinez said. "Get rid of it before you shoot yourself or blow your damned foot off."

I said nothing.

"Don't even think about it," Martinez said.

"What's next for you guys?" I asked, deflecting the subject. "Where do you go from here?"

"Back to the streets," Martinez said. "With the sketches and the flyers. Something will turn up soon. A suspicious neighbor, a bartender who stares at faces, someone will recognize the picture. And then we'll start to move in. It'll happen. Take a few days, but it'll happen. Just a matter of waiting."

"That's it?"

"That's all we're saying."

I envisioned the final story. I could see the words materialize before me. First the hard news: the killer's identity, the capture, perhaps the shoot-out. That would segue into the path taken to the killer's door, the information provided by the Pentagon and by O'Shaughnessy. Then it would return to the active, to a description of the final confrontation, the cornering, the running to ground.

I thought of T. S. Eliot. No whimper here, I thought. A bang all the way.

The last story. No more lies, no more half-truths, no more misstatements or misleading information. The real truth: names, places, facts, identities.

It will set everything right, I thought.

The truth.

I called Christine at her parents' home in Madison. Her mother answered the telephone, pausing when I identified myself. "She may not be ready to speak to you," she said, "but I'll ask her."

I heard voices in the background, noises, no discernible language. In another moment Christine came on the line.

"How are you?" she said.

"Good," I replied. "Will you come back?"

Silence. I could hear her breathing.

"Why?"

"It can be the same again."

"And the killer?"

"It's almost over."

"How do you know?"

"I have a lead. I know this is it."

"And if it is, what makes you think that things will be different?"

"Christine, this is the end. I feel it."

"Maybe for this story," she said. "But there'll be others."

"Why, yes, sure, of course there will be. I mean, it's what I do—"

"It's all you do," she said. "They squeeze everything else out of your life. There's no room for anything else. Especially me."

"I want you. I'll make room."

She gasped, and I could hear her lose control, tears creeping into her voice.

"It's just not true," she said. "Malcolm, you know it's not.

Let me ask you this: would you rather have me or break the story on the killer?"

"That's not fair."

"Nothing is fair," she said. "Would you take a plane tomorrow to come get me?"

"Of course."

"Then why don't you do it?"

"I—" I was silent.

"See."

"I *will*," I broke in. "I just can't believe you'd ask me."

I sensed her shaking her head. "No, don't. I'm not asking. I don't know if it would do any good. You'd just be miserable. You care more for the story than for me. You always did."

"That's not true. You just name what you want. I'll do anything you ask. I just want you back."

She caught her breath and laughed a little. "I wish I could believe you. It sounds so nice."

"Try me," I said. I was praying she wouldn't ask.

There was a second of tension. I could feel the plastic of the telephone wet with sweat under my palm.

"No," she said finally. "Call me again. When it ends."

"All right," I said. "When it ends."

"If it ever does," she added. Then she hung up.

It was late the next day when the officer at the Pentagon called back. "Sir! I have compiled the list you requested."

I felt an instant rush of excitement. "How long?"

"Approximately one hundred and seventy-five names, sir. That's one-seven-five."

"Addresses?"

"Yes, sir. But I cannot guarantee their complete accuracy. The addresses were gathered at the time of the men's service. Many factors could have altered their situation since that time. Veterans move about and often fail to notify the VA. So I cannot guarantee their authenticity, sir."

"But the names . . ."

"Oh, that's different, sir. We kept very good records of those particular clerking sections. Had to. Didn't want any foul-ups there, if you follow my meaning, sir. Everyone who worked those details is on the list."

"And O'Shaughnessy?"

"Lieutenant Peter O'Shaughnessy, serial number DR one-seven-one-four-three-oh-seven. His records correspond with the dates and times you gave me. Honorable discharge, 1972, March. Present address, Memphis, Tennessee."

I felt suddenly drained. It is over, I thought. This time it really is over.

"Thank you," I said.

"Our pleasure, sir. The list will be sent down by overnight courier."

The list arrived in the morning. It came inside a thick manila envelope; I could see it protruding from my mail slot from several feet away. I hefted it in my hand, feeling the bulk, feeling the excitement. He's here, I thought, in the palm of my hand. I knew he hadn't bothered to change his name, that he had laughed at the idea of taking that rudimentary precaution. Why choose a new identity when he had so carefully obscured the old? And yet, left doors open. I remembered what the psychiatrist had said: he wants to be caught. Well, so be it. He set his own rules, he played by them—as I, too, had done. I tore the envelope open and without looking inside walked toward Nolan at the city desk.

He stared up from his computer terminal, frowning. For a moment his eyes met mine, questioning; then he saw the yellow envelope in my hand. He smiled.

"That's it?"

"This is it."

I went to my desk and stared at the names on the page. At the top was Adams, Andrew S., serial number AD2985734, hometown, Lexington, Kentucky. I flipped over the sheets of paper to the last page. Zywicki, Richard, serial number CH1596483, hometown, Chester, Pennsylvania. I looked over at the corner of my desk, at the large telephone book resting there. It can't be that simple, I thought, reaching out for it.

But it was.

I stared at the name in front of me, my finger resting, trembling slightly on a page in the Miami phone book.

It was name number forty-seven.

Dolour, Alan, serial number MB1269854, hometown, Hardwick, Ohio.

And there on the phone-book page: A. Dolour. Two Twenty-four NE Seventy-eighth Street.

It's him, I thought. No doubt about it. I waved at Nolan, and he walked swiftly to my desk. Without saying anything, I pointed at the two names. His eyes went wide for a moment, and then he nodded. No smiles now, I thought, serious.

And the phone rang.

I knew it would be him. The coincidence of timing was too great for it not to be. There was something new in his voice, a tone of urgency, as if his breath were short, his chest tightened and his lungs laboring.

I punched down on the recorder and nodded at Nolan. I frantically pointed at the phone number next to the name in the telephone book. Nolan nodded and stepped to an adjacent phone.

"It's me," he said. "I suppose you've been waiting for my call."

"That's right," I said.

"What have you learned?" he asked suddenly. I thought for an instant he was talking about the list before me. "Have you begun to understand?" he said, and I realized he was still back in the war he'd created.

"What should I have learned?"

He did not answer. I looked over at Nolan. He was staring down at the receiver in his hand. While I watched he pulled a sheet of paper from the desk and hurriedly scrawled a note: *busy*.

"We were all caught up," the killer said. "We were all guilty. You. Me. Everyone."

"And what's left?" I asked.

"Nothing. Just darkness. Evil. Death. Destruction."

"You're going on?"

He ignored me. "We're all sick. Diseased."

"Are you going to kill again?" I shouted into the phone.

"I will never stop," he said.

I gambled. "I know who you are."

He stopped, and I heard his breath sweep in suddenly.

"Good-bye, Anderson. Good-bye for good."

"I know!" I said. "Dammit, I know!"

He laughed again.

"Missing In Action. Gone, but not accounted for."

I started to say his name, but the line went dead.

I stared at the receiver, holding it just away in front of me as if uncomprehending. Then everything happened around me all at once. Nolan was talking to Martinez and Wilson on the phone, explaining quickly, efficiently. Andrew Porter was running from the photo studio, throwing cameras over his neck, his musette bag of film and lenses swinging wildly in his wake. "This is it! This is it!" he shouted. "Let's go, let's go!"

Then I was on my feet, Nolan pushing alongside me, the two of us a step behind Porter, heading for the elevator bank. "Go! Go!" he repeated. He screamed ahead, "Hold the elevator. Goddammit, hold it!" I was swept along, as if caught in the morning riptide off the beach. "I'm not missing this," Nolan said as we piled into the elevator. "Move!" he shouted at the machine, and we were plunging down, descending from our sanctuary.

The heat was like a wall outside. "Come on! Come on!" Nolan and Porter called in unison, and again I was swept along.

The car thrust forward, engine and tires screaming angrily under Porter's abuse. We headed north on the Boulevard, cutting in and out of the afternoon flow, horn blaring.

I heard sirens in the distance.

"Boy! Adrenaline is pumping," Porter said.

I saw the faces on the street staring at us, so many frames per second in the window as we tore northward on the Boulevard. People stopped to see what the commotion was; I saw faces turn in curiosity, in fear, in excitement. And still we raced on. Flashing blue lights appeared in the distance; the police, I thought, moving in.

"There, there!" Nolan shouted.

I saw a modest apartment building, surrounded by police cruisers and unmarked cars. As I watched, the special-weapons-and-tactics truck screeched to a halt on the opposite end of the street, quickly disgorging a squad of flak-jacketed men wearing blue jump suits and baseball caps. I recognized their automatic weapons. They were carrying M-16s, just like the ordinary foot soldier in Vietnam. "Christ," Nolan said. "It looks like they're ready for World War Three."

Porter was already out of the car, running forward, snapping off pictures the way an infantryman snaps off bursts of fire. It was a small building, perhaps four or five apartments spread over two stories. I noticed a crack in one wall and a long streak of dirt running down under the red tile roof. No lawn, just the city street and dirt. A dozen policemen and plainsclothesmen were in the entranceway, weapons out. As I watched, the SWAT team penetrated the door, weapons held ready. Time seemed to wait, holding still underneath the sun.

And then it was over.

I sensed a relaxing. The guns were being holstered, the detectives turning and talking angrily to each other.

I walked forward with Nolan toward the crowd. Martinez was in the center. He waved me over.

"Gone," he said.

"Where?" I asked.

"He's close," the detective said. "We'll get him now."

Wilson came down the stairs and joined us. He turned to Nolan. "Thanks for the call. But what scared him?"

For a moment I was quiet; then I said, "It was me." The two detectives looked at me. "I told him I knew who he was."

Martinez groaned and Wilson turned away.

"We could have had him easy," Martinez said. "You know that?"

I didn't reply.

"Well," he continued, "I suppose you still deserve a look." He turned and led the three of us into the building. It seemed cooler inside, and for a moment I had trouble seeing through the sudden darkness. "Cheap," Martinez said. "Not much different from that place downtown." We went up to the second floor. A SWAT member was smoking a cigarette outside the open door to one of the apartments. Martinez nodded at him and said, "Lab crew will be here in a minute." Then he turned to us. "Same rules. Don't touch. Just look." He looked over at Porter. "Use your judgment," he said, "but don't fuck us up." We stepped inside.

The apartment was small, cramped for space. In one corner

there was a small stove and refrigerator, in another corner a bed with a single dirty sheet. There were clothes strewn about and a musty, unused smell. The telephone had been ripped from the wall and lay on the floor, its wires twisted and exposed. My eyes fastened on the wall.

He'd built himself a montage. In the center was the huge yellow, green and red photo-poster of the massacre at MyLai. Mushrooming out from it were dozens of other images in different sizes and shapes: Jane Fonda, General Westmoreland, Robert MacNamara, the Chicago Seven, LBJ, Daniel Ellsberg, Ho Chi Minh. Pages torn from old *Life* magazines showed soldiers slithering through swamps and paddies under fire; children, their eyes blank with despair, staring from behind barbed wire in a refugee camp. On some he'd done creative surgery: Nixon and Agnew, arms raised in victory, cradled a dead Vietnamese child. Henry Kissinger, in black tie, escorted an evening-gowned figure wearing a forlorn Vietnamese woman's head. From ceiling to floor, the images marched, adding to the eeriness of the apartment.

I turned away and saw a tape recorder left on a small table next to the apartment's only window. Beyond that was a mirror on the wall next to the bathroom. The mirror was shattered, its center a black, gaping hole. Shards of glass were scattered about the floor.

I looked back at the table. A paperback, its spine worn and cracked, lay open next to the recorder. I looked closer. *Man's Fate* by Malraux.

Martinez saw them, too. Gingerly he picked up the paperback, after wrapping his hand with a cloth. He read for an instant, then held it out so I could see. A passage was underlined on a page close to the end.

". . . He had seen much of death . . ." the killer had picked out. ". . . He had always thought that it is fine to die by one's own hand, a death that resembles one's life. And to die is passivity, but to kill oneself is action . . ."

Martinez and I looked at each other. We said nothing.

Wilson came over to where we were standing, and Martinez placed the book back in the space it occupied by the recorder. "Let's see what the sucker has to say," Wilson said. He punched the play button on the tape machine.

At first there was quiet.

Then his usual short laugh.

Then a voice: "Hello, Anderson. Hello, detectives."

Again the same laugh.

"You'll never catch me."

There was a hissing and Wilson moved to shut it off, but another sound interrupted. It was the killer humming. I recognized the tune instantly, a memory from college rallies.

He began to sing in a high-pitched, strained voice:

> . . . And it's one, two, three
> What are we fighting for?
> . . . Don't ask me, I don't give a damn
> Next stop is Vietnam.
> . . . And it's five, six, seven
> Open up those pearly gates.
> . . . Ain't no use to wonder why
> Whoopee, we're all going to . . .

But the last word was drowned by the explosion of the .45 and the shattering of the mirror's glass.

"Jesus," Martinez said. We had all jumped at the sound of the explosion on the tape.

"That's it," said Wilson. "We've got an APB out on Dolour with a description. A neighbor gave us his car. White Plymouth. We should pick him up today, tonight at the latest. Where can he hide?"

I looked down and saw the capstans of the tape recorder turning in circles, continuing to run. Martinez reached out to shut the deck off, but as his hand hovered over the button, the killer's voice, even, hard, almost taunting, returned:

"Anderson . . ." He drew my name out, accenting each syllable. "Just for you, Anderson. One more. Got it? One more."

Martinez looked at me suddenly. "What the hell does that mean?" said Nolan. Porter's camera swung toward me, the lens like the barrel of a pistol, shooting my reaction.

"Now, don't worry." Martinez was calm, reassuring. "He could mean almost anything."

"You think he means me?" I asked.

Martinez shrugged. Wilson replied, "So what? We've got this sucker now. We'll nail him this afternoon. You've got nothing to worry about." Then he looked at me closely, his eyes searching my own. "I love it," he said. "Seems a whole lot more real when it's you on the line, huh?"

"Look, don't worry," Martinez said. "We've got him. No problem."

But he was wrong.

CHAPTER *EIGHTEEN*

THE headline filled two decks in forty-eight-point Roman bold type:

"NUMBERS KILLER" IDENTIFIED;
POLICE MANHUNT UNDERWAY

I led the story with the hard news—the name, the address, the race through the city to the killer's apartment—and went from that to a description of the wall and the apartment. The news desk set the opening paragraphs in fourteen-pica type, spread over two columns, dominating the front page. Above the fold, next to my story, was the police sketch of the killer and a photograph, years old, transmitted by the Associated Press from Washington. The photo had been obtained by the Pentagon. I described the raid on the apartment, the tentacles of the police search, the telephone call from O'Shaughnessy, the list of names from the Pentagon. The main story jumped inside the paper to a display page with more photos: a four-column shot Porter had taken with a wide-angle lens, capturing the whole of the interior of the killer's room. The figures in the killer's mural were distinct in the background, like so many ghosts.

Nolan had paced by the side of the desk, peering over my shoulder, urging me on like a cheerleader at a football game. "Get it all. Get it all. Don't worry about length, just get it all down. More. More."

I did. When I pulled the last page from the typewriter platen, setting the roller spinning, I felt a burst of exultation, almost sexual excitement. My mind raced momentarily to Christine, but I hurriedly pushed the thought away.

Nolan stared at the final take.

"Dammit, there it is," he said. "There it all is . . . except for one thing."

I heard the killer's voice in my head: one more.

"Should I—"

Nolan cut me off. "No, no, we don't know, do we? What's he mean? You're the expert, I guess. What do you think?"

I shrugged.

"That's right," Nolan said. "Why add more fear when we don't know?" He turned away, the final page clutched in his hand.

But my stomach clenched involuntarily, cramping suddenly, as if someone had grabbed hold of the muscles and twisted them violently. I sucked in breath and rocked in my chair, feeling the color flow from my face. Dizzy, I bent over, head between my knees.

I do know, I thought.

It's me.

Nolan walked me to my car after the story had been edited and set in type. The city sounds of traffic blended with the darkness. "You going to be OK?" he asked. "Look, they'll get him tonight. Bet on it."

I drove home, circling my block several times to examine the neighborhood. All seemed quiet, normal, in place. I sat in the car watching, waiting for my eyes to adjust to the nighttime. Night eyes, I thought.

I did not switch on the lights as I entered the apartment; I slipped inside the door, waiting, holding my breath, trying to feel any other presence or shape in the dark rooms. I exhaled suddenly, the small noise filling the apartment, startling me. Still in darkness, I went to the bedroom dresser and pulled the .45 from the top drawer. I slid a clip of bullets into place and snatched back the automatic's action, chambering a round. Then I slowly made my way through the apartment, checking each closet, each closed door; each an adventure, a moment of panic, a wave of relief, then a slow buildup to the next. Finally, satisfied, I turned on a few lights, barely creasing the darkness, and sat facing the front door—waiting.

I jumped when the phone rang.

Heart beating, I stood by the receiver. Once, twice, three times. I let it ring. Five. Seven. Nine. I counted until thirteen. It stopped.

Just you and me, I thought.

I did not sleep that night.

When I went into the office, Nolan was pacing the newsroom, his hands clenching into fists, then relaxing. "Idiots," he said. *"Idiots."* He turned to me. "Nothing. No sign of him. Every cop in town looking. They've got a fucking photo, for Christ's sake, a description, the car, everything. What do they need, an introduction?"

"No sign?"

"Nothing."

I felt sick again.

That morning I called a Mr. and Mrs. Raymond Dolour in Hardwick, Ohio. The first three times I rang the number, the line was busy. On the fourth try a gruff voice answered. I introduced myself carefully: "Mr. Dolour, I'd like to talk with you about your son."

"I have no son," he replied. The phone crashed as he slammed it down.

Nolan was torn; we had to send someone; he wanted to know if I wanted to go knock on their door. "It's your story," he said. "But we haven't written the ending here."

For a moment I thought of going. It would be safe, I thought. No fear there. I felt the tension within me: personal safety versus what? I couldn't put a word to it. "No," I told him, "I'll stay here." Another reporter was dispatched.

I couldn't bring myself to read her story.

That afternoon, the city police chief went on all three local stations to make a plea to the killer to give himself up. The chief said it was only a matter of time before he was spotted. "If you're out there watching," he said, staring into the television camera, unblinking, frowning, "give yourself up. Save yourself. Let's try to avoid any further bloodshed."

Nolan roared with laughter, and I joined him. We had a bank of televisions in the newsroom, and the chief came across like so many mirrored images. "I love a good cliché," Nolan said. "Just like some crime-busters show from the fifties."

Still, there was no sign of the killer.

MANHUNT FOR KILLER CONTINUES; POLICE NOOSE TIGHT AROUND CITY. "Where the hell is he?" Nolan asked. "I can't believe they can't find this guy." He continued to stomp around the newsroom, his attention focused solely on the police search, delegating all responsibility for other stories to subeditors. I waited for him, my own apprehension taking shape.

I rode with Martinez and Wilson, sitting in the rear of their unmarked cruiser, the three of us leaning forward, staring out through the windows at the faces on the street, absorbing them, then rejecting them quickly. I wrote that story; the details of the search, the locations checked and discarded, the suspects interviewed, examined and released.

On the third day a security guard at the University of Miami found the white Plymouth. The plates had been changed; a quick check showed they were stolen. A list of all the reported stolen cars during the three days of the killer's disappearance was circulated to detectives. They staked out the bus station, the airport, the train station. Extra personnel were brought in; overtime mounted. I documented all of it in the following day's story.

The city seemed to fill with rumors: he'd grabbed a private plane or boat and headed out of town undetected. He was spotted in Key West one instant, in Fort Lauderdale the next. Some people thought he'd taken a family hostage and was waiting in suburban quiet for the attention to fade, and then would slip through the city, walk calmly away.

On the fifth day I collected all the rumors into another story. It ran on page one under the headline: WHERE IS HE?

"That's right," Nolan said. "Just where the hell is he?"

In the cruiser one afternoon, Wilson turned to me. "You still got that illegal forty-five?"

I nodded.

"Good," he said.

"Why?" I felt my stomach tighten again.

"I don't know. I got a bad feeling about this."

"Shut the fuck up," Martinez said. "Pay no attention," he said to me, accelerating the car down the street. "He's out there trying to keep his own ass safe. No way he's worrying about yours. It'd be ridiculous to think he was looking for you. No matter what he said." Martinez glared at Wilson, but his partner just snorted and said nothing. Ridiculous, I thought. I remembered when I had heard that word before.

I slept fitfully, if at all, the .45 next to the bed.

More often, I would fall asleep in the living room in a chair facing the door. The night noises seemed to penetrate even my sleep; I would awaken, startled, eyes suddenly wide open, at the smallest sound. I could feel my heart straining, muscles stretched and bursting. I waited.

The detectives grew surly and morose with the failure; their tempers shortened with each passing hour. Nolan, too, took the delay personally, as if it were an affront. I spent as much time as possible with the detectives, watching Wilson idly polish the blue metal of his service revolver as Martinez chauffeured the cruiser down another empty street. "I'm not going to call in the SWAT boys," Wilson said under his breath. "This sucker's mine. I'm going to take him out myself."

Martinez kept quiet. Once, he turned to me: "You shouldn't have told him. It could have been easy."

I shrugged. I kept my own weapon in the car whenever I drove anywhere. When I went home I entered the apartment, gun held out in front of me. Safety off.

On the seventh day after the killer's disappearance, he called.

The phone rang; I followed my routine, snapping on the recorder, seizing pencil and notepaper. Still, I was taken aback when I heard his familiar voice. He was laughing.

"I told you," he said. No introduction.

I fought off the urge to hang up, to hide.

"Where—"

He interrupted. "Not so fast."

"You can't get away," I said. "Why don't you give yourself up?"

He laughed again.

"It's time, Anderson."

I choked out the word: "No!"

His laughter seemed an echo across the line.

"Anderson," he said slowly, "good luck."

"What?" But I was talking to an empty line.

Emotions wrapped around my throat. I did not know what to do. I shut off the tape and peered across the newsroom to Nolan. I thought of the detectives. I pictured: NEWSMAN GETS KILLER'S PHONE CALL. But what had he said? What did it mean? The two of us. Luck? In the back of my mind I realized a panic was trying to break through; I fought to deny it. No, he wasn't going to come for me. And if he did? The two of us. It had to be the two of us. I swallowed hard, took the tape out of the machine and dropped it into the top drawer of my desk.

"Anything new?" Nolan asked later.

I shook my head.

"He's got to be somewhere," he said.

"He's out there," I replied.

That night the heat in the apartment seemed heavy, uncontrollable. I sat in the chair, fingering the gun. The phone rang once; Christine? My hand reached out for the receiver, then pulled back. I couldn't be sure. At midnight I dozed, half-awake. The sound on the steps outside the apartment penetrated through the demi-sleep; for a moment I struggled, trying to pull myself to alertness. The sound increased; a scraping, footsteps. I was awake. My eyes fixed straight ahead.

The sound hesitated outside the apartment.

It's him, I thought.

There was silence. No motion, no noise.

I breathed in quietly. Held it in.

Still no sound.

Get ready, I thought.

I brought the automatic up to eye height. I leveled it at the door. My ears were electric, alive for sound.

I heard a hand close on the door handle.

I fired.

The roar of the .45 seemed immense; the force of the thrust threw me back against the chair. My nostrils filled with cordite and smoke. For a second it was as if I had been knocked out; my reactions seemed slowed, awkward. Then the noise faded, my ears no longer rang. I jumped across the room, my eyes fastened on the black, shattered hole in the door. I seized the handle and swung the door open quickly, crouching at the same time, the .45 ready to fire again.

And nothing.

For an instant I was confused. Where? I thought. Where's the body? Where is he? I saw a bullet hole in the plaster across from the door. But someone was there, I said out loud. I heard him. He was there. I spun and ran down the stairs, out into the night. The street was empty. "I know you're here!" I shouted.

A voice behind me said, "Where?"

I spun, rocketing the .45 up into position. But I did not pull the trigger.

"Jesus Christ, man! Watch what you're doing!" It was one of the neighbors, in pajamas, holding a baseball bat. He stared at me. I was aware of lights clicking on, of other voices coming into my hearing. "Are you OK?" he asked. "Was he there?"

"I'm OK," I said. But I didn't believe it.

CHAPTER NINETEEN

THE letter arrived the next day, the eighth day after the killer disappeared.

It was the same common notepaper, the envelope without a return address. When I picked it up, I knew there was only a single sheet inside. I looked at the postmark, Miami, but the rest was blurred. My name was printed carefully on the outside, in large black letters. I waited until I was back at my desk to open it. Nolan was on the phone, his back to me. I tore it open carefully. The lettering inside was the same.

ANDERSON:

Here's a quote for you.

Sometimes it is as reasonable to represent one kind of imprisonment by another, as it is to represent anything that really exists by that which exists not.

Think about it. And here's a message for you.

Don't believe everything you see.

Got that? And here's the most important thing.
I'm alive.

It was not signed.

I do not know why I did not show the letter to Nolan or to the police; it went into the top drawer of my desk, locked, with the last tape recording. I know it seems odd; I could have built a story around the letter the same as around the tape. It would have underscored, for all to see, the relationship between the killer and me; it would have been another detail, crucial, perhaps, for the readers to note, another brushstroke in the portrait painted over the course of that summer. I sat, thinking there were dozens of reasons to show the letter, to publicize it. But I did not.

I'm alive.

What is it I'm not to believe?

The answer was five days off.

I had fallen back on writing updates on the police search—eight to ten paragraphs reporting that there was nothing new to report. I went out and talked with the psychiatrist again. I tried to call the victims' families, but none would speak to me. I did the man-in-the-street interviews. The reactions were pretty much the same: a quickened tension waiting for an arrest, coupled with relief that the killer had a name, a picture and a past. One woman said, "It's only a matter of time." She smiled at me. "But I think he's gone, long gone. To California, probably." I didn't ask her why that particular state.

Some information began to come in about the killer. His Army record: unexceptional. Attendance at state schools in Illinois and Ohio. He never stood out; his teachers could remember nothing. I tried to find someone who knew him. No success. The same with the neighbors of the apartment house where he'd lived. He kept to himself, they said. I could have guessed their words. But even the lack of information was part of the story—people able to say they didn't know the killer were as quotable as someone who did. The desk liked that story. They stripped it across the bottom of page one, below the fold.

Nolan took the call at the city desk.

He swiveled in his chair, raising his arm above his head, gathering my attention and waving for me to join him.

It was September then, August melting away; more heat, more storms out in the Caribbean blowing up hard and taking wild runs at the islands. The hurricane season still had more than a month to go; some of the newsroom elders talked about the late storms that seemed to bide their time through the oppressive summer and then, as the weather gave signs of shifting, formed and charged across the waters. Still, the heat dominated, the city shuddering under the scorched air. I slept little; since the night I'd heard the hand on my door I'd taken to lying awake until early morning. The gun remained close; I could not make up my mind what I'd heard on the steps outside. Martinez and Wilson had stared at the shattered door and shaken their heads in unison. "It's close," Wilson had said to me. "It's real close in here, isn't it?" I hadn't understood what he was driving at.

I punched Nolan's line on the telephone and picked it up, Nolan gestured frantically: I was to speak. "Yes?" I said.

"This Anderson? The reporter?" The voice was tinged with a southern accent.

"Right."

"I got a letter for you," the man said. "Found it this morning in one of my boats. Right on the seat, mind you, in plain sight. Shit, I'd been looking for that damn boat for nearly three days. Finally catch up wi' it, and there's this damn letter. You want me to open it?"

"Yes." I looked over at Nolan and shrugged. He was bent over the desk, hanging on the words.

"Shit," said the man. "Don't say much."

"What?"

"It says, lemme see, just this: 'I'm out here waiting.' That's it. No signature, nothing else. Seems pretty strange to me."

I stared over at Nolan. His eyes had widened and they locked in on my own. He pushed back in his chair, his face alight with excitement, and shot a hand up in the air, as if in victory. "This is it!" Nolan said, "Goddammit, this is it!"

Nolan's clenched fist waved in the air.

The city slipped behind us in a haze of heat and sunlight.

Porter drove; Nolan sat in the back seat, staring out the window, a small smile on his face. I watched the highway unfold through the scrub brush and weeds toward the west as we cut through the great Everglades expanse of swamp and water. "You know, he could hide out here for months if he wanted to," Porter said. "I used to go bass fishing out here. Got lost once. I remember night was dropping awfully fast and the sky was all purple. I could see gators in the water and some water moccasins. I thought I was going to die; there was nobody. I was so alone, I had this crazy thought that there was no more civilization, that I was abandoned. The rangers found me around midnight. It wasn't cold, but I was shaking. If he's been out here, no wonder no one's found him."

"We still haven't found him," Nolan said. "You think he plans to shoot it out?"

I didn't answer. Porter shrugged. "Maybe," he said. "Look!" He bent down and pointed through the windshield. A police helicopter plowed through the air above us, the rotors filling the car with noise, shaking us. Porter accelerated, pushing the car faster.

An hour out we turned off the expressway and started down a two-lane side road, the big car rocking on the bumps and potholes. The huge cypress trees and palms reached out over the highway; we cut between the mottled colors and shadows. I could see the pale blue of the sky high above the treetops, vanishing, it seemed, in an expanse of white light. My eye caught a hawk circling slowly in the distance. He floated above the earth, turning with the small wind, as if suspended invisibly like a mobile. Then, just before we passed out of sight, the bird rose suddenly, its wings shooting up over its body, and plunged downward toward some sighted prey. I imagined its shriek of murder as it fell from the clear sky into the shadows.

We pushed on.

Up ahead I saw a clearing, a few shacks strung out against the edge of the swamp, adorned with crude hand-painted signs advertising beer, bait and boats for hire. Behind the shacks I could see a few fishing skiffs pulled up on the shore and a pair of airboats idled, high and dry. "That's got to be it!" Nolan said.

On the far edge, closing quickly as Porter mashed down on

the accelerator again, were the familiar flashing blue lights of police cruisers. Another helicopter passed overhead, the pressure from the blades seeming to drive us down into the ground. I ducked involuntarily.

"Christ," Porter exclaimed under his breath, "they've got a fucking army."

Squads of jump-suited SWAT members from two huge blue buses milled about outside. Most of them were checking their weapons and ammunition. Off to the side I saw the medical examiner's truck. They're expecting bodies, I thought. A roadblock had been set up, and the car jammed to a halt outside it. Porter was loading quickly, grabbing his cameras and bag. Nolan leaped out of the car, and I followed quickly behind. The heat wrapped my body like a noose.

Another chopper swept overhead, kicking up dust. I shielded my face and saw Martinez and Wilson down by the boats, talking with a weathered old man. The postman, I thought.

The two detectives waved us through. Martinez thrust a piece of paper at me. I saw the block printing, the same as the other. "Look familiar?" he asked.

"That's it."

"Stay close," the detective said. "It's going to get exciting."

We waited with the old man in one of the shacks. A tired air conditioner stirred the air feebly, making a tortured beating sound. He said he'd discovered one of his boats missing several days back; gone out looking for it, without success. It had turned up a few days later with the letter on the seat in a protective plastic bag. "Damndest thing," he said. "I was certain I'd looked in that spot before. Damn if I can figure it out."

He's gone back to the jungle, I thought. The jungle he was scared to fight in before.

"Can he last in there?" Nolan asked.

"Shit, if he wants to," the man replied. "It ain't nice, though."

I waited. My mind filled with images from the war: mud, sun, blood and death. This is it, I thought. Nolan spoke the same words out loud: "This is what I expected. This is it."

One hour passed. Two. We continued to wait. The policemen went out in teams; I heard their radios crackling with static as they coordinated their positions with the circling and buzzing helicopters.

Another thirty minutes. The old man said, "Shit, they ain't never gonna get this buck."

A sudden shift: I heard a cop yell back at a resting SWAT squad, "It's him!" Men leaped up, slapping at weapons. Porter was swearing hard and fast. "I've got to get out there; damn, I've got to get my shot." Nolan grabbed hold of my arm, not to hold me back but to steady himself.

And then, just as at the killer's apartment, a relaxing.

"What's going on?" Nolan asked. There was no response.

I tried to ask some of the cops, but they shook their heads. Martinez and Wilson were gone. So was the medical examiner. We waited again, by the swamp's edge. Another thirty minutes. Time seemed stretched like leather, cracking, not elastic.

I saw a boat with two uniformed officers head into the shoreline. Their jump suits were blackened with sweat and mud. One of them looked at us and steered the small outboard toward us. "You Anderson?" he shouted from a few feet away.

I nodded.

"Get in. The detectives want you out there. The body is about a half-mile in."

"Body?" Nolan asked.

The policeman didn't respond. He restarted the engine. The three of us crowded into the front; the metal seats were scalding.

"I can't figure it out," the cop said as he turned the boat. "He couldn't have swum from where he put the boat to where he is now." He maneuvered the skiff past a mass of weeds and logs. A flight of egrets rose up to my right. I remembered the killer's description of his fourth victim, the woman at the edge of the Glades. We were much farther in, much more hidden. "You see," the cop continued, "you can't really swim through this shit. Weeds grab you, drown you. Snakes can kill you. Alligators, hey, look there!" I swiveled and caught sight of a six-foot gator sliding through the brush. "How'd you like to tangle with that sucker in the dark, huh? Not likely." Porter snapped off pictures.

We rounded a corner in the small channel, and I saw a humpbacked rise in the water, a slight island of mud and bushes. A few more uniformed policemen stood on the edge, but in the center were Martinez and Wilson bending over alongside the medical examiner. I could not see what they were focused on. "Chopper spotted it," the cop said. "You'd never see anything from the water, not even if you was next to it." The boat grounded itself on the mud. "End of the line." I stepped out and sank down more than an inch into the marsh. Martinez waved us over.

I was unaware of the stench until we were almost on top of the body; a small turn in the breeze brought the smell sweeping over us. For a second I thought I would gag; then the feeling passed, and we were left with the horrid sweet stench of death. I thought for an instant of the house on Miami Beach. Wilson saw the effect of the smell on my face and said something to the medical examiner. The two of them laughed. I did not catch the joke.

Martinez spoke first. "Take a look," he said.

The medical examiner was lighting his pipe, eyes following my movements.

"Look at what?"

"Right here," Wilson said. He pointed down at his feet. "Not pretty."

I stepped over to the three men and stared down at the shape on the ground.

At first it was hard to tell that it had been a man. The flesh had grown pasty, white, like fish left in an oven hours too long. The eyes were open, but the sockets were empty, the eyeballs gone. The skin seemed pulled tight, cracked and ridged, and burned brown at the edges by the sun. The lower half of the man's face was gone; a few jagged white bones protruded where the jaw should have been. The top of the skull had been blown out. I turned away, nauseous.

"Keep looking," Wilson said.

I took a deep breath and looked down again. The body was wearing Army jungle boots of canvas and rubber. His jeans had faded like his life under the hard sun. There were rivulets of dried blood on his chest, streaking a white T-shirt. "What am I supposed to see?" I asked.

Martinez pointed, and I saw the gun. The gray metal .45 caught the sun for an instant, and the light refracted, spinning, into the brown and green undergrowth. The automatic rested a few inches from an outreached hand, as if half-dropped, half-tossed in the moment of death.

"So," Wilson said. "Seen enough?"

I nodded.

"Then," he said, suddenly quiet, "who is it?"

For a moment I was confused. I shook my head. "You know," I said.

"You tell me," Wilson replied.

But I remained silent. I looked down again at the features ravaged by the gunshot and the sun. Who is it? I thought to myself.

Martinez stepped beside me and motioned to Nolan to join us. "We need an identification," he said, "to make it official. To be certain."

Nolan spoke before I had a chance. "What the hell do you mean?" His voice was angry. It carried over the stillness of the Glades. "There's the gun. Hair color. Physical size. It's all right there. Check his fingerprints, for Christ's sake. What about teeth? The Army must have dental records, you know?"

The medical examiner joined the conversation, pulling on his pipe stem, releasing clouds of smoke into the breeze to be carried across the marshes. "No good," he said.

"Explain 'no good' to me," Nolan said.

"All right." His voice was steady, a lecture suited better to a classroom. "Number one: too much decomposition of the skin for fingerprints. Impossible with all the stretching and loss of tissue consistency and integrity to get an accurate print, so that method's out right away. Number two: eye color. It would be a help to check against Army records, but the local birds have taken care of that for us. Let's move on to another method: teeth impressions. Great. Records available from the Army almost instantly. Only trouble is this guy must have been anticipating that, or else he was just lucky. He put the gun against his chin and pulled the trigger. Blew the mouth all to hell but left a bunch of the face intact. Other indentifying marks or scars? That would be the next step sure, but the Army records say the killer had none. So we're down to one last method of identification: personal observation. Oh, the gun will turn out to be the killer's, of course, but that doesn't prove anything. Is it him? He's been out here a number of days. Hard to tell precisely. At least three, more likely five, possibly a week. Wouldn't even count on his mother recognizing him now."

The medical examiner held up his hand to cut off the obvious question.

"Yes, she's been contacted. Refuses. Hasn't seen her boy since the war. But that was in your paper already."

He paused, looking at me. "See the dilemma?"

I thought of the letter in the top drawer of my desk. How close, I wondered?

"So many factors aid in the decomposition of a body," the medical examiner went on. "Sun alternates with rain. Humidity. You know, out here, it can rain like the dickens a half-mile away, but this area stays dry. Just no scientific way to determine absolutely the length of time. There was a body once we knew positively had been dumped out here, not too far away. Contract killing. We got the shooter. By the time we got to the body, it was virtually a skeleton, picked clean. One week. Lots of factors."

I'm alive, I thought. Don't believe everything you see.

Wilson interrupted. "You see, we got to be positive. You got the best look at him, in that apartment. Is this the man you met there, the man in the wheelchair?"

I hesitated. "I don't know."

Wilson exploded. "Look, goddammit! Look! Look at the face! The cheeks, the nose, the ears, the eyebrows! Is it him? We have to know. Not later; right now! Is it him?"

I stared again at the features, breathing in hard and holding it. Nolan grasped my arm, turning me toward him, but I kept my eyes on the torn face. "It's important," he said. "They're right. It's important. Look," he whispered into my ear, "this has been our story from the very start. No one else's. We have to write the end to it. If we don't write that it's him, then no one will ever know, no one will ever be certain. It's not just an identification, it's the whole city, the whole mood. We can't waffle. We can't be unsure. It doesn't matter one damn bit what anyone else says, just what *we* say. We're the only paper anyone will believe on this." I could feel his own eyes marking me, measuring me. "Look again," he said. "We have to be sure. Is it him?"

"Is it him?" That was Wilson. He was standing over the

body, shaking his fist first at me, then down at the inert form slowly melting into the earth and air. "Is it him?"

I looked over at Wilson, then to Martinez and the medical examiner. I saw the ME slip a photo from his pocket and bend over the corpse. He stared hard for a moment, shook his head, shrugged and turned to me. Nolan, too, was watching me. Porter hung to the side, his camera whirring. Then he, too, stopped, waiting for my answer.

"Is it him?" Nolan asked again.

I forced myself to stare into the sightless eye sockets.

The sunlight seemed to spiral down, freezing everyone in a blast of heat and brightness. I felt the warmth on my scalp, boring into my brain. Images jostled and elbowed for space in my mind. I saw the killer's grin as he peered through the smoke and shadows of the darkened apartment, his fingers drumming against his wheelchair prop. I imagined him leaning over the window, staring at Christine. I saw the victims as if in array: the teenage child, the elderly couple, the young woman and her crying child. I searched around me, my eyes sliding over the surrounding marsh and trees. I thought of the war; the morgue by the runway. The killer's words came back again: the two of us, him and me. I thought of the letter in the drawer. Is it him? Don't believe everything you see. But what was I seeing?

My mind produced an instant's scenario: a picture from the night he'd played his charade of murder with Christine. I imagined the young men on Miami's ill-lit downtown streets, aimless, nameless, abandoned. The casual pickup, I thought. How easy it would have been for him to cruise the streets, looking for a surrogate, searching for the proper height, build, the same common brown hair. A stop, a quick hand motion, perhaps the flash of money, and his victim would be seated in a car, unknowing, unafraid. Drive west, deep into the Glades. Steal a boat. Out to the rise. Place the gun against the victim's chin and pull the trigger. Toss it down by his hand; the apparent suicide. I remember the lost boat, the carefully prepared note to summon me, the cop who drove me to the rise. He didn't swim out here, he said. Perhaps two came out and one went back, melting away into the darkness, searching for another city, another identity.

I looked at the corpse on the ground. Was it him? I looked closer. Was it an imposter? Was this another lie, another fiction? Possible. Everything was possible. I looked at the body.

No, I thought, it's him.

I looked again.

No, it isn't. It's someone else.

No. Yes.

Who is it?

Nolan was at my side, his voice soft, yet insistent: "We have to know for certain. No doubts, no maybes. The city has to know, has to be freed once and for all. That means it's up to you. It has been from the start. Is it him?"

Wilson burst out, anger flowing from the air: "Stop jacking around," he yelled. "Come on! Is it him?"

I thought of Christine, of my father, of my uncle and his flag-draped casket. The sun seemed like a pendulum, swinging in the wind, moving inexorably closer to me.

"Is it him?" I heard the voice but did not know who spoke.

And so I lied.

"Yes," I said. "It's him."

CHAPTER TWENTY

My lie expanded, took root and flowered. The morning headline jumped at the city:

"NUMBERS KILLER" A SUICIDE;
CORPSE FOUND IN GLADES.

One of the news-desk editors told me it was the largest type they'd used since the President's resignation and, before that, the walk on the moon.

It was the last story, a rushing forth of all the other stories. I'd worked the telephones the evening before, following the long drive back from the rise in the swamp. This time the victims' families had talked; I'd collected quotes and reactions to blend into a description of their feelings. Nolan had pulled the best quotes out of the story and had them set in a bold, black-lined box which ran in the center of the inside jump page. "It's a relief," one person said, "to know it's over."

But was it?

As I strung all the impressions of the day, all the assembled voices and facts together into the mainbar and sidebars, I came to believe that my doubt was unfounded. As I talked and as I bent over the typewriter keyboard, I searched the ravaged features in my mind, measuring, contrasting, matching the ears, eyebrows, nose and cheeks with the shadowy figure I'd seen in the dirty apartment. In my mind's eye I overlaid the features against the sketch the police artist had drawn, then against the photo provided by the Army. I clenched my teeth; dammit, it's him.

I'm alive.

Don't believe.

When no one was looking, I reached into the top drawer and slipped out the letter. I stared down hard at the words, trying to force them into clarity. A final lie? After so many conversations, so many twists of his imagination, turns of his plot, I still did not know what the truth was. Nolan had been ecstatic, reading the story as it marched through the typewriter. "This is it!" he'd said, waving a sheet of copy covered with words. "This is the story. It's all right here." He'd fed the pages into the computer scanning equipment himself, shaking off the copy aides and assistant editors. He's wrong, I thought. It's never all there. But that thought hadn't stopped me from continuing, from massaging the lie into the story, making it beat like a drum inside every paragraph, sentence, word and phrase. For an instant, as I wrapped the end tight—a final description of the murder weapon catching the sunlight—I imagined the killer reading the story. I could see him smile, then fade into whatever oblivion he had selected for himself: officially declared dead and forgotten on the front page of the *Journal*.

I shook my head to clear the image. No, I thought, the body I saw was the killer.

Nolan was hunched over the video screens, absorbed. For the moment I was ignored. I looked again at the letter.

No. He went out there alone, to die alone, never discovered, a final gesture of mystery and confusion. That would be like him. Enigmatic, especially at the end.

But.

The word hung in my consciousness. I fought the rush of possibilities. I took a page of copy paper and listed the factors:

It's time, he had said. Time for what?

I'm alive. Well, he had been, when he wrote it.

Everything you see. But had he counted on me seeing his body?

The note on the boat. *I'm waiting*. And there he was. Dead.

Or was he? How did the boat get back to shore, away from the body's location? Did he put it there?

I wanted to scream: I just don't know.

And then I shuddered hard.

I would never know.

My eye caught the telephone on the corner of the desk. The wires running to the tape machine were tangled around the receiver. I thought: ring, dammit. Tell me the truth. Whatever it is.

But it remained inert. Suddenly, after so many weeks, silent, dead.

Christine wrote: "I am not coming back to Miami. What we had is lost. It sounds trite and corny, doesn't it? I wish I could express myself better, but if I had been able to, maybe this wouldn't have happened. I'm sorry it has to end this way. Or any way, for that matter. But it has to."

I packed some things she had left behind and sent them to her home in Wisconsin.

Nolan wanted to get drunk after the story had been sent to the composing room. He called back to the photo department to collect Porter and escorted us to a nearby bar. He said we would get pleasantly drunk, then go back and catch the edition as it came off the presses. The voices in the dark bar flooded over me as I walked through the door. Most were from the paper; most were talking about the story. A few turned and nodded, waved or clapped me on the back. They wanted to buy me drinks in celebration. I took a glass of beer from one offered hand, feeling the release in the room. I raised my glass and there were cheers. Nolan swallowed a scotch and added a quick beer. He maneuvered the three of us into a corner booth, waved for more drinks and leaned back against the seat. "What a story," he said. "Jesus H. Christ. What a story. Can you believe it?"

Porter sipped on his drink and lowered his head toward the table. A small smile slid across his face, and he shook his head slowly. "I've been thinking," he said. "What was it, really?"

Nolan looked quizzically at him.

"I mean," Porter continued, "a man kills four people and calls the paper to tell us about it. Is that such a helluva story?"

"I don't follow," Nolan said.

Porter went on. "There've been so many other killers a whole lot worse. Speck in Chicago . . . the guy in the tower in Texas . . . what about Leopold and Loeb? The crime of the century, they called it. And the Lindbergh kidnapping—that was the crime of the century for a while, too." He took a cautious amount from his glass.

"What are you driving at?" Nolan asked.

"It was just a story. There'll be another tomorrow."

Nolan thought for a moment. "That's true, but it's always been that way. It doesn't diminish the moment. That's what journalism is—a celebration of the instant. No past, no future, no history, no vision. Now is what's important." Nolan threw back his head and laughed. Some of the others at the bar turned to look, then turned back to their drinks. He pointed a finger at Porter. "Still, it was a helluva story."

And Porter joined in, laughing long and hard himself.

"I agree," he said, raising his glass in mock toast, "even if it means contradicting myself."

The next day Nolan told me to take a vacation. I deserved it, he said. He told me to fly to Wisconsin and bring Christine back. I shook my head. "Another story," I said, "just another story."

He was slow to respond, his eyes searching my own. "Only if you really want it."

"I really do."

"All right. Up in the Panhandle. There's been a resurgence of Klan activity up there. They've been burning crosses, holding marches, generally making life a pain. How about a piece on the new nightriders, that sort of thing?"

"I'll go Monday," I said.

"Suit yourself," he replied, turning toward the city desk.

I went back to my desk and once again pulled out the letter from the killer.

One more, he'd said.

I'd thought it was me. Was it him?

Missing in Action.

My mind swirled with possibilities again. Then, making certain no one saw me, I tore the letter into small pieces and tossed it into the wastebasket.

At noontime I left the office to walk the streets. Big thunderheads were forming over the west out over the Glades, and I felt a steady breeze hitting the city from that direction. I figured an hour or two at the most before the storm hit the city, sheets of rain riding the air currents. I looked at people's faces, trying to discern some difference, but I was unable to detect any emotion, any memory. All that had seemed so obvious so recently had slipped away. Had I imagined everything? All the fears? What had happened?

That weekend I flew to New Jersey to see my uncle's grave. It was beginning to turn from Indian summer to real fall. The change in seasons showed on the edge of the leaves, rolling up, browning slowly with age. I rolled the window down as my father drove me toward the cemetery and felt the wind in my face. It was cool, unfamiliar, intoxicating.

At the gravesite there were flowers, freshly picked. I wondered where they had come from. My father stood next to me, looking down. After a moment he spoke matter-of-factly. "I tried to tell him, years ago. The war is over, I said to him; let's get on with it. But he never really adjusted. Sometimes events are simply too powerful for the mind to comprehend, sort out and put away. Most of us adjust and grow old with indifference, but for some the memories just won't let go. Some people get choked by their memories. Like your uncle."

He caught my eye. "And you?"

"I should have gone," I said.

"What? To war? To that godforsaken little country to get killed for no reason other than stupidity?" He was angry. "You would have been worse than him. Crippled more than by any bullet."

He was silent for a minute.

"There are two types of wounds," he said, finality tinging his voice. "Some heal. Some never do. You make your own choice which you'll have."

We drove home without speaking.

I have not heard from the killer again.

Sometimes, when things in the newsroom are slow, I go back to the morgue and pull the file marked NUMBERS KILLER, July—September 1975. I spread the mass of words that mark the biggest story of my life on the desk before me, my eyes searching through the columns of newsprint for the clue, the statement, the forgotten phrase that will answer the question that persists in my mind. But it remains a mystery. Nolan likes to point out, after a few drinks, that it was all luck that broke the case; that the hours we spent and the police spent, and all the fears and frustrations of the people of the city, were all useless in cracking the killer's game. I wonder, though, if that wasn't how the killer meant it to play.

Sometimes I see the story of another murderer or of an inexplicable killing in another city or another state, and it causes me to pause and wonder. Sometimes faces leap out at me; I find my imagination comparing the features in front of me with those I saw decomposing under the harsh sun. Often when the telephone on my desk rings, I hesitate before reaching out, wondering whether this will be the time the familiar voice blows cold through the earpiece. I think, too, that it was my lie that set the city free from the same fears, the same doubts.

And for that, I suppose, I take some comfort.

About the Author

John Katzenbach, thirty-one, is the criminal-court reporter for the *Miami Herald*, and formerly of the *Miami News*. His work has appeared in many other newspapers, including the *Boston Globe*, *Washington Post*, *Chicago Daily News* and *Newsday*. Born in Princeton, New Jersey, he is the son of the former Attorney General of the United States Nicholas deB. Katzenbach. He lives in Miami Beach with his wife, journalist Madeleine Blais, and their young son, Nicholas. *In the Heat of the Summer* is his first novel.

About the Author

[illegible]